# The Weather in Berlin

BOOKS BY WARD JUST

NOVELS

A Soldier of the Revolution  *1970*
Stringer  *1974*
Nicholson at Large  *1975*
A Family Trust  *1978*
In the City of Fear  *1982*
The American Blues  *1984*
The American Ambassador  *1987*
Jack Gance  *1989*
The Translator  *1991*
Ambition & Love  *1994*
Echo House  *1997*
A Dangerous Friend  *1999*
The Weather in Berlin  *2002*

SHORT STORIES

The Congressman Who Loved Flaubert  *1973*
Honor, Power, Riches, Fame, and
the Love of Women  *1979*
Twenty-one: Selected Stories  *1990*
(*reissued in 1998 as* The Congressman Who
Loved Flaubert: 21 Stories and Novellas)

NONFICTION

To What End  *1968*
Military Men  *1970*

PLAYS

Lowell Limpett  *2001*

# THE WEATHER IN BERLIN

## WARD JUST

HOUGHTON MIFFLIN COMPANY

BOSTON · NEW YORK

2002

For information about permission to reproduce selections from
this book, write to Permissions, Houghton Mifflin Company,
215 Park Avenue South, New York, New York 10003.

Visit our Web site: www.houghtonmifflinbooks.com.

*Library of Congress Cataloging-in-Publication Data*
Just, Ward S.
The weather in Berlin / Ward Just.
p.  cm.
ISBN 0-618-03668-7
1. Motion picture producers and directors — Fiction.
2. Americans — Germany — Fiction. 3. Berlin
(Germany) — Fiction. 4. Creative ability — Fiction.
I. Title.
PS3560. U75 W43  2002
813'.54—dc21  2001051885

Printed in the United States of America

Book design by Robert Overholtzer

QUM 10 9 8 7 6 5 4 3 2 1

*To Sarah*

## AUTHOR'S NOTE

My Mommsen Institute shares an address with the Hans Arnholt Center of the American Academy in Berlin, where my wife and I spent four highly enjoyable months in the winter of 1999. The resemblance ends there. The Rektor, the chef, the fellows and their spouses — all fictitious, as are the other characters and episodes in *The Weather in Berlin*.

My deep thanks to the American Academy for its Berlin Fellowship and the staff in Wannsee for its matchless hospitality and good humor.

# The Weather in Berlin

# Oral History
# Wannsee, March 1999

ARE YOU QUITE COMFORTABLE, Herr Greenwood? You seem to be in pain.

Comes and goes, Greenwood said. The cushion helps. Let's begin.

You may speak freely, Herr Greenwood. The tape goes into the archive, under seal until the year 2010. If, later on, you want to extend the release date, that's your privilege. Your lawyer has the agreement. Obviously I have made this arrangement in order to encourage complete candor.

Obviously, Greenwood said.

So that students of film and other interested parties can study the creative process, the way you worked, the choices you made, and the choices that were made for you. What you were thinking day by day.

Yes, Greenwood said.

I have told you of my admiration for *Summer, 1921,* a superb American film, remarkable for the time it was made. I'm interested in how it was made, where the idea came from, and how the idea was translated into film. There's been so much written about it and yet, if you will forgive me, your interviews on the subject have not been illuminating. I suspect there's a mystery you want to preserve —

A dirty secret?

Is there one?

No, Greenwood said.

Begin with the title, if you would.

I wanted to call it *German Summer, 1921* but the studio refused. Any film with the word "German" in the title was poison. They had surveys to prove it. They were very insistent. Loved the film, hated the title. Of course they didn't love the film. They thought it was an interesting curiosity that might do well in Berkeley and Cambridge, and with luck some legs that might carry it to New York and Chicago. But "German" was poison. So they promised to increase the promotional budget and we went with *Summer, 1921.* They weren't thrilled with that title, either, but their surveys had nothing against either "summer" or "1921," so they agreed.

So the film began with a compromise, Herr Greenwood.

It certainly did, Herr Blum.

Inauspicious, wouldn't you say?

Not at all, Greenwood said.

Why not? The title —

It was a miracle the film got made at all. This is Hollywood, Herr Blum. And the title isn't the beginning, it's the end. The movie is the movie, no matter what you call it. The audience is there for it or it isn't. The title doesn't mean anything, it's just a title, convenient shorthand. If they'd called *Casablanca Ishtar,* it's the same movie, a classic movie either way. But if they'd called *Ishtar Casablanca* — or *Gone With the Wind* or *The Godfather* — it would have been the same bad movie. No clever title could rescue it.

Well, then. Begin at the beginning.

It has to do with my father, Greenwood said.

Your father?

Harry Greenwood. Not Harrison or Harold, Harry was his given name, like Lady Di's little prince. We were that kind of family, North Shore bourgeoisie, Anglophile to a fault. Harry's father, my grandfather, was a banker. Church deacon, civic leader, married a Gibson Girl from Rye, a union of opposites but apparently happy.

She died young and the old man never recovered. When he died, he left his son a handsome trust fund so he'd never have to work, and he never did.

And you were close?

Only at the end. He and my mother were divorced when I was in school and before that he was often away on his travels. He called them research. Later on, he retired to Los Angeles and I saw a little more of him then. We'd shoot a round of golf and have lunch. He'd tell stories, wonderful stories of the old days, when he was footloose — his word, "footloose."

First memory?

He had a vague recollection of his father in Vienna, a long letter written on Hotel Sacher stationery. It was the year before the war, his father in Europe on unspecified business. His mother read him the letter, an account of a night at the opera, a colorful parade, lunch in a castle in the woods near the city, skiing by moonlight. When she finished, she handed him the letter without comment, and then she left the room. He took the letter to his room and put it in the bureau with the others. The old man was a beautiful skier. Beautiful skier, beautiful horseman, beautiful raconteur, every day a fiesta. Harry Greenwood was a man who knew everyone. That's what your father does, his mother said. He meets people. And they become his friends, so he's never lonely wherever he goes in the wide, wide world.

You want to make *movies*, Dixon?

I know Gary Cooper. I'll call Coop.

Watch out for the West Coast, though.

They're desperadoes.

Have a lawyer with you at all times.

Harry Greenwood's letters came from all over the world, Rome, Rio, Singapore, Cape Town, Bombay, Cairo. They were written on boats, in hotels, on café tables, from country houses and the libraries of men's clubs. They always contained advice along with an instructive anecdote, riding an elephant with the maharajah, shooting pheasant with the ambassador, dining al fresco with a ballerina or a polo player or the governor of New York — or crossing the Atlantic on the *Normandie* and meeting F. Scott Fitzgerald in the saloon bar. Gray-faced Zelda remained in her stateroom, emerging only for meals. Harry told the story many times, playing liar's dice with "Scott," who was then at the height of his fame. The great writer was handsomely turned out in white ducks, a blue blazer with silver buttons, and a yachting cap. This was the summer of 1927 or 1928, Harry a year out of college, unmarried and taking the summer off. He was searching for a good-time girl on the *Normandie* but abandoned the search when he discovered Fitzgerald alone in the bar, morose because his wife was bad company owing to seasickness. She's got her head under the pillow, wouldn' even say good morning to me, told me to clear out and leave her alone . . . Harry was always good at cheering people up and before long he and his new friend were inventing parlor games, guessing the occupations of the men and discussing which of the women were available.

Much later, Harry told his son to listen carefully always to the stories that people told. Listen to the words and the music, too, the cadence. That was the way you came to know people, by the stories they told and the manner of their telling. Really, a good story was a film scenario — not the action but the contours of the action, and something left to the imagination. When you listened hard enough, the stories became yours. A story belonged to whoever could tell it best. Harry said that a great director had told him that a scenario had the same relation to a screenplay as the shadow to the shadow puppet. The angle of the light was salient, the source of the light more salient still. The figures the puppets made were reflections of the skill and compassion of the puppet master, and if they were artfully made — unforgettable.

Dixon knew from the fifth grade that one day he would make films, and that in each film there would be a meeting of strangers, and stories exchanged.

Harry Greenwood was a great mimic and one night at a party many years later he was telling the *Normandie* story, imitating Fitzgerald's Princeton-via-Minneapolis accent, and a woman walked up to him and asked if he would please stop. She had tears in her eyes. She said that when she heard his voice she thought poor Scott had come back from the grave. He was such a lovely man. He wasn't anything like they said he was, you know. People told lies about Scotty. He made it easy for them, too. And he was entirely different from what you've heard or even seen yourself. I knew him well when he was in college. He and my brother were friends. We dated for a while but he was waiting for his Zelda so it never went anywhere. It was only that he had no tolerance for alcohol in any form. He told me stories, wonderful stories, and once he used my name for one of his heroines, except she wasn't much of a heroine. She was a tramp-with-a-heart-of-gold, and when I wrote him about her and asked if that was what he thought of me, he answered right away, apologizing that he had hurt my feelings and explaining that he was only taking a name, not my soul. Writers did that all the time. He said he had always loved my name, April. And if I didn't mind he'd use it again, next time for a woman with a wholesome character.

So please don't mimic him anymore because I can't stand it.

And Harry complied at once. By then, he was complying generally. When Dixon was a boy, his father read him F. Scott Fitzgerald's stories and novels. He assigned special voices to all the characters. Bedtime was a performance, and it was only a condition of their life together that the next morning he would be gone to another continent; but he always remembered the story he had been reading, and the place in the story, so that when he returned he knew where he had left off. Dixon was so young, he thought the characters in the stories were his father's good friends, Anson Hunter, Charlie Wales, and the others, come to life in Harry's ventriloquism. Daddy, is there really a diamond as big as the Ritz? What's the Ritz? Later on, Harry confided that Fitzgerald was his personal beau ideal, a gallant gentleman who was roughly treated by critics and contemporaries. That bastard Hemingway. They appreciated Fitzgerald once he was dead, but isn't that often the case? They wait until you can't do them any harm, because they're still in the race and you're out of it. A man of exceptional charm, Harry said, though not when drinking. Drinking, he turned himself inside out. It's all in the genes, you know. He got handed the drunk gene, along with the talent and the gallantry.

Later still, Harry Greenwood moved to Los Angeles. Dixon was just getting started in the movie business. Harry decided that his traveling days were ended. His friends were dying. F. Scott Fitzgerald was long gone. Coop was dead. Cancer and heart attacks were carrying away his classmates, and twice in the past year he had gone to services for the sons of friends. He had been everywhere and done everything, so what was the point? He let his passport lapse. He withdrew from the world, concerning himself mostly with his golf game and the garden. Harry reminded Dixon of one of those slender film stars from the 1930s, still well turned out, his cheeks pink from professional barbering, but faded like a photograph left in the sunlight, or one of Fitzgerald's prematurely aged characters from whom all emotion had been drained. He and Dixon saw each other once a month but the visits were a trial because Harry wanted to talk about his ex-wife, Dixon's mother. She had remained in the house in the horse country out near Libertyville, married to a property developer.

Never thought she'd choose a developer. Jesus, how boring.

Probably she had had enough excitement.

And a developer would be developing, wouldn't he?

I was gone a lot, Dixon. Probably it wasn't fair.

To her, or to you, either.

But I had a wanderlust. Every so often I'd need to travel, someplace I'd never been or some other place I wanted to go back to. I'd get a call from a friend in the morning and be gone by the afternoon. Your mother got tired of it. I can't blame her and you shouldn't. She wanted to settle down before I did. Your mother, she's a different breed of cat.

Still. What do you talk about with a developer?

Dixon went to Chicago for a shoot and learned there that his father had died of a stroke. He had been dead three days when they found him in the bedroom of his bungalow near the Bel-Air Country Club. The house was in disarray, as if its occupant could no longer be bothered; and Harry was always fastidious. Dixon found four whiskey cartons filled with correspondence, including two postcards from F. Scott Fitzgerald and a friendly letter from Gary Cooper. There were more whiskey cartons full of shipboard menus, old dance cards, and photographs, and an attaché case crowded with wristwatches, expired passports, and billfolds. On his dresser he had a little metal model of the *Normandie,* a child's toy that went with him wherever he traveled. Dixon had taken it from the dresser and given it to a friend who collected ship models; and then he told the friend the story, Harry and F. Scott Fitzgerald playing dice games in the bar, gray-faced Zelda belowdecks owing to seasickness. Dixon tried to tell the story the way his father told it, but he did not have the gift of mimicry and somehow lost the thread, and his friend only smiled mechanically, though he was happy enough to have the model of the *Normandie,* and know its provenance.

He appears to have been an impossible man, Herr Blum said.

Not impossible, Greenwood said. Charming.

To you, perhaps.

Everyone liked Harry. Harry walked into a room and people began to smile. Before the evening was over, they'd entrusted their life stories to him. Probably responsibility was not his long suit. His own father was responsible to a fault, and Harry was reacting to that. His father died having spent his whole life accumulating a fortune, and Harry spent the fortune.

You do not resent him, then?

I resent not having the gift of mimicry. Apparently it's not a gene you can pass on, like gallantry or dipsomania.

Perhaps you could be more precise about *Summer, 1921* and your father's connection to it. When I asked you to begin at the beginning, you began with him.

To explain that would take more time than you've got.

I have time. I have as much time as we'll need.

He was an accidental man. His life, his fate, was an accident. He meets a writer in the saloon bar of a ship. They make a crossing together, and the encounter stays with him his entire life. What did it mean to the writer? One encounter among many, memorable enough so that a few months later he sends a postcard from Antibes. Having wonderful time, wish you were here. Harry saves the postcard, and over the years his shipboard encounter becomes the centerpiece of his repertoire. He's a storyteller after all; it's what he does for a living. He brings people to life! But his table is crowded. Cooper is at it and Paulette Goddard and one of FDR's sons, Eddie Arcaro, Henri Matisse, Byron Nelson, Piggy Warburg, the Duke of Argyle, too many others to list — and, late in his life, April. April who believes she has heard the true voice of F. Scott Fitzgerald, a narrative from the grave, and she can't bear it. Please stop.

These people are his audience, here one day and gone the next. Random encounters, they live inside his brain, in the hall of mirrors called memory. This is the way he lives from year to year, fashioning twice-told tales, and he likes it. He's very good at it. It's footloose. It's crowded, and he's never lonely because there's always another trip to take and a party at the end of the day where there are more stories. It's fun-filled until the night in Winnetka when he meets April. Listens to her rebuke, concludes that he's run dry. On that one occasion his narrative has failed to enchant. On that one occasion his mimicry has been too successful.

Please don't mimic him anymore. I can't stand it. Poor Scotty.

This is cause for reflection. Storytelling is an illusion, and now he begins to doubt the illusion, or his ability to master the illusion. That which he saw as true is false. Like Don Quixote, he slips into melancholy, a fugue state in which the counterpoint spans but a single octave. He's exhausted his repertoire and decides that it's time to ease into retirement. He takes up golf, attracted by its repetitive motion. He takes a father's pride in his son's work, and confesses to having seen *Summer, 1921* a dozen times, finding something fresh each time; the finish, he says, is heartbreaking but not totally bleak. Disconsolate, perhaps. In the spirit of the modern world.

Of course, he adds, his eyes alight with the old mischief, it's not the same as a story told in person. Film is only a reproduction, one step removed from the stage. The lights, the sound, the cameras, the direction. It's not the same as the story itself, ad-libbed pure, in front of your eyes in someone's party room.

At lunch with his son, Harry Greenwood picks over the past and seems filled with regret, an emotion new to him. Almost without his noticing, the curtain has fallen. His audience has vanished — and a little while later he vanishes, too, because, as he says, what's the point? The hall's empty.

Very interesting, Herr Greenwood. But there's something missing, isn't there?

And what would that be?

Forgive me. This is not a question we ask in our country. But it seems worthwhile to ask it of you. What did your father do in the war?

Heart trouble. He didn't come in until the end.

And when he came in, what did he do?

Greenwood paused, thinking that Herr Doktor Professor Blum was not as dumb as he looked, nor as affable as he pretended to be. Greenwood stood, stretching his bad leg, and clumped to the bay window that looked into a narrow courtyard fringed with box hedges. Behind him, he could hear the whir of Blum's tape machine. He stood for several moments looking into the empty courtyard, thinking that it had no cinematic possibilities at all. Herr Blum's courtyard was a dead end.

He said, My father was fluent in German. He had a grasp of German history, as I do. In April 1945 he offered his services as an interrogator and was immediately hired. He knew half the OSS crowd so there were no difficulties. They were delighted to have him. You can imagine the confusion in those days, so many Germans to question, so few Americans or English with the background to question successfully. Or the wish to do so. The chief apologized to Harry, all the big fish were spoken for, Goering, Goebbels, Speer, and the others, the real war criminals — why, they were the crown jewels and reserved for the senior staff. Harry said he wasn't interested in war criminals, he was interested in marginal characters. He was interested in the ones who went along, the ones who made the machine work. Not the drivers, the mechanics. I'd like to debrief the ones who changed the oil and cleaned the spark plugs, got the paperwork from the In box to the Out box. I have no interest in the vultures at the top of the tree, only those farther down.

Harry was rich in metaphor in those days.

So he spent the late spring and summer in 1945 in Berlin, interrogating.

He told me later that he worked twelve-hour days in Berlin, probably the first time he had ever *worked*. He felt guilty that his bad heart had kept him from combat, so he was determined to make up for it. He called his interrogations "auditions" and his witnesses "my mechanicals." And at the end of it he had filled five fat looseleaf notebooks, Q and A and Q and A and Q and A and Q and A. And then he went home.

And that was it? What did his interrogations mean to him? And to you?

He said the Germans were inspired mechanics, fanatical attention to detail, no detail so small that it could be ignored. They had the ability to ignore context. They had the ability to ignore most anything unconnected to their specific job. One did not take responsibility for what one ignored. And one step further: the responsibility was assigned elsewhere. The Bolsheviks were candidates, and naturally the Allies themselves bore some responsibility for the excesses of the regime. Cowardice at Munich, for example. When they talked about Hitler, it was to condemn his deficiency as a military strategist. Of the camps they knew nothing. When asked about the Jews, one of Harry's mechanicals replied casually that he knew no Jews. It was his understanding that there were no Jews in Germany. They had emigrated to America, where they were well cared for. He himself wished to emigrate to Milwaukee, where he had relatives. He wanted no more to do with Germany. Germany was finished.

Harry had a girlfriend in Berlin. She didn't know about the camps, either.

And there were others who knew quite a lot and were voluble about what they knew. And still others who knew more and refused to say one word, kept counsel behind a sullen façade and a smirk that seemed to say, If you knew what I knew, you would not be asking these foolish questions. They were easily dealt with. Taken outside into the yard where the colonel spoke bluntly to them. He gave them a choice. Those who cooperated would be removed to a detention camp in Florida, and those who didn't to a camp in Siberia. Of course it was all bluff, but they didn't know that. In any case, no one chose Siberia.

Harry stayed on in Europe after his interrogations were ended. My mother met him in Paris and he went on to Spain when she returned home. She said he had changed in ways that were not agreeable to her. He was drinking more, and showing it. He was sleepless. He worried that he no longer fit in. The Europe he knew was gone and America was newly triumphant. Harry was not attracted to triumph — "hence," he said, "Spain." He showed up in Libertyville at Christmas and at that time he told me a little of what he had done in Berlin. I was very young and didn't understand much of what he said. But I remember this. He stated that Germany was prodigious. It was subterranean, its soul hidden somewhere in the forests. Its people were disciplined, yet given to savage moments of hilarity and recklessness, and profound sorrow. You never knew which mood would show up.

Yes, Harry concluded. A self-conscious people.

Herr Blum cleared his throat and opened his mouth to speak, then thought better of it.

At last he said, Did your father ever return to Berlin?

No, he never did.

Disgusted with us, I suppose.

He preferred Mediterranean climates, France, Spain.

Benign climates, Herr Blum said.

Except for Spain, Greenwood replied.

But you —

When it came time to film *Summer, 1921,* there was no question in my mind that I would film in Germany.

Herr Blum looked at him with a pained expression. He said, You see, this is what I do not understand. I do not understand why you decided to write a screenplay about Germans. German artists in 1921. And then film the story in Germany. Isn't there material enough in America, such a turbulent society with sorrows of its own. Why Germany?

Greenwood continued to stare into the narrow courtyard. Shadows advanced as the light failed, causing the courtyard to diminish under its rectangle of pale blue sky. The walls were without windows, and he could not see the entrance. Its purpose seemed to be to provide a plot for the hedgerow. He heard Herr Blum stir and wondered how you would live if you saw your fate tied to your nation's. And if for a hundred years that fate had been a deluge of misery, would the weight of this not be intolerable? Yet it must be tolerated. A Christian nation had an obligation to seek forgiveness, but in the circumstances charity and compassion — the virtues of the church — were ill fitting. In America the past was discarded as tiresome, in some settled sense, impractical. He reached down to massage his leg. The courtyard was now entirely in shadow, and the sky a soft gunmetal gray. The little hedge had disappeared, and a bird flitted from wall to wall.

Herr Greenwood?

As for the artists, they were finding their way in the postwar world. Across the ocean, the war was called the war to end wars. The artists were too smart for that. One of them had spent five years on the Western Front, and knew in his bones that nothing good could come from such a prideful struggle, its cost measured in millions of souls. The artist knew that the war was not an end but a beginning. Prelude, he called it.

Greenwood turned from the window and answered the professor's question.

It's where the modern world begins, Herr Blum.

# Los Angeles, October 1998

WEDNESDAY NIGHT was overcast with fog so that the lights of L.A. were gathered within it, and refracted as if the sky were a giant footlit screen. The air was warm but an ocean breeze was stirring, an early warning of the chill to come. The neighborhood was quiet except for the occasional siren. Dixon and Claire Greenwood were sitting outside, complacent over drinks, watching the evening news on their portable TV and straining to hear over the muffled noise of insects, but not paying close attention because the news that day had nothing to do with them. Now and then Claire rattled the ice in her glass and made a sarcastic remark about the boyish demeanor of the anchor and the monotony of the mayhem, traffic accidents, a forest fire, two deaths in South Central, and then, the last item, Ada Hart dead at sixty.

Did he say Ada Hart? That can't be.

My God, Dixon said.

Ada was an old friend, an actress long retired. Dixon moved to increase the volume, and they both rose from their chairs. Ada had been found dead in her bed, a suspected overdose, though the police weren't saying and her agent could not be reached. The obituary had been hastily cobbled together, incoherent even by the standards of the local news. The reporter in the street outside her house suggested that actresses of a certain age were cruelly treated by the Industry and she was but the latest victim, so perhaps it was no surprise that observers hinted that she died of a broken heart. The bulk of the report had to do with the circumstances of her death, but the last thirty seconds were devoted to her Academy Award nomination and the films she was best known for; the boyish anchor mentioned two, not her best, and got one title wrong. The clips they showed were of Ada as a young woman in her familiar tomboy pose, "aggressive" would be somewhere in the director's notes: head turtling forward, hands on hips, mouth worked into a snarl, telling off some hapless thug twice her size. The final one was a photograph of a charity affair the year before, Ada looking every minute of her sixty years but with a wisecracking smile, a glint in her eyes, and a glass in her hand. The glint was especially effective owing to nearsightedness.

God, Claire said. Poor Ada.

She was sixty-two, Dixon said. Not sixty.

And she loved not working. "Died of a broken heart." What gibberish.

She did her best work for me, Dixon said. *Anna's Magic.*

I think she did, Claire said. I'm sure she did. No doubt about it.

But that was twenty years ago.

Twenty-five, Claire said.

Yes, twenty-five. Just after the accident.

A terrible obit. The photograph at the end, she would have hated it.

She didn't give a damn, Dixon said.

Yes, she did give a damn. Ada always gave a damn about her hair.

They watched a commercial in strained silence. Dixon was not shocked at Ada Hart's death. She had never taken good care of herself and only last year had had a heart attack that she concealed from everyone except her agent, who was Claire's agent as well, so the secret was shared. Everyone knew everyone's business in L.A. When the item showed up in a gossip column Ada was mortified. But it was ignored, and she understood then that she was old news; no one cared about her health, good or bad. When Dixon shivered and put his hand on his wife's arm, Claire suggested they go inside. The Pacific chill had arrived.

I'm cold, too, she said.

Something walked over my grave, Dixon said.

But Claire appeared not to have heard because she turned suddenly and suggested they eat out, somewhere quiet and out-of-the-way, perhaps the Mexican place off Sepulveda, close by and perfect for a foggy night.

They had not seen much of each other in the past year, Ada often away in San Francisco seeing her businessman. That's what Dixon called him, the Businessman. He owned furniture stores, high-end gear for the wizards in Sausalito. Dixon had an idea he liked her for who she had been rather than who she was, but Ada denied it. Don't be proprietary, Dix. Behave yourself. They had had an affair during the filming of *Anna's Magic*. Claire was off somewhere on location. Was it Toronto? Dixon had cast Ada as the prim younger sister of the randy Anna, whose magic touch with men ran out at the end of the first reel but was restored to her at the end. *Anna's Magic* was a comedy, the only one Dixon made. Ada played a nude scene that was supposed to be chaste but had gotten out of hand thanks to the sinister close-up camerawork of Billy Jeidels. Dixon had no idea what he had until he saw the rushes, Ada's skin deeply tanned and in half-light, her thirty-five-year-old body as taut as a teenager's but definitely not a teenager's. The difference between the moon and the sun, Billy had said enigmatically. What he apparently meant was, No glare, more mystery. She stole the movie, in part because she was no longer a tomboy nor showed any signs of ever having been a tomboy. The audience was charmed, seeing a side of Ada Hart that they had never seen before or even imagined. She became their discovery. She had let her hair grow. She wore half-glasses. She made no wisecracks. She never snarled, instead inventing a soft stutter and a cadence that seemed to work out to about one syllable a second. She played prim when the script called for it but in a series of small gestures made it plain that she was not prim, that prim was the farthest thing from her mind. Prim was a disguise, and she seemed to imply that all her previous roles had been disguises and what the audience saw now was the real Ada Hart, Ada comfortable in her own skin, Ada liberated at last.

They were filming on the Costa Brava. Dixon's screenplays always called for water nearby. Ada was living in a small villa overlooking the Mediterranean. When Dixon saw the dailies of the nude scene he was startled. He watched the sequence three times, the last time in slow motion. It was a forty-five-second scene and as expertly choreographed as a three-hour ballet, and he wondered why he had not recognized it at the time. Under the lights, the set cleared, only Ada, Billy, and himself in attendance, he thought it a fine sequence but nothing more than that. And then he knew that the forty-five seconds was a conspiracy between actress and cameraman, not an improvisation but something well thought out and carefully controlled. Ada did not speak except to hum something at the end; he thought he recognized a phrase from Gustav Mahler.

When he arrived at Ada's villa, she was standing at the deck railing looking out to sea, bulky in a terrycloth robe, drinking a glass of wine. The villa was dark but the deck was washed with light from the moon, huge in the eastern sky. Ada stepped inside to fetch the bottle and another glass. I was swimming, she explained. I swim every night to the float, sit awhile, swim back and return here for a glass. I watch the moonlight in the Med and think about how lucky I am, being here. Being in your wonderful movie. You pick great locations, Dix. It's a side of you I never knew.

I was looking at the dailies, he said.

She smiled broadly but did not reply.

It's quite a scene, he said. When did you and Billy dream it up?

It's improv, she said.

Was that Mahler you were humming at the end?

Liszt, she said.

And was that improv, too?

Of course, she said.

He said, Liar.

She laughed. Well, maybe not all of it. How pissed are you?

Not very, he said. He thought, No more pissed than any general who rose from his afternoon siesta to find his troops occupying the capital. Presenting it to him as a kind of surprise.

He wanted me to do it and I felt like getting it done, she said in her trademark snarl, laughing and kissing him on the cheek as she led him inside where they would be more comfortable. What do you say to another glass of wine?

He stayed that night and the next, and the night after that. When Ada was finished filming she remained in the villa, and a week later Dixon moved in. When they had been together a while they began to talk about life on the set, *Anna's Magic* and other sets. So much hurly-burly, she said. So many, many complications. So many, many needy people in one small closet, and in that way the set resembled a theater of war or a political campaign, where the rules were fixed to suit the mighty objective ahead. Those were the analogies everyone liked because wars and political campaigns were momentous and consequential, whereas a movie was only a movie, unless it was an extraordinary movie, a classic movie, whereupon anything went. Anything at all. That was why there was more hurly-burly on the sets of good directors than mediocre ones. That's a compliment, Dix. The other thing is, on the good sets people are likely to be serious as opposed to delusional, so there's less of the no-one-understands-me-at-home, boo-hoo. We all have this focus and elation because we're doing good work and want to share it, and what could be more natural? The best times I've ever had were with men who were very happy at home, except they weren't at home and had this itch and the missus wasn't around to scratch it. What about you and Claire?

Dixon assembled a taco and handed it to Claire. They had not spoken much. Ada Hart was the first of his old girls to die, a thought that came to him when he sat down and the pretty waitress handed them menus, greeted them by name, and discouraged them from the special. Anytime someone you loved died, the world was suddenly smaller and less interesting and you, too, were diminished. They said that these events gave you perspective but that was sentimental. Perspective was what you had before the death, and after it you were so heavy-hearted and blurred of mind that you could not decide the simplest things, such as what to order after the special was declared off limits. Of course, if you were in the movies, your friends and family could watch your work onscreen; but that was work, not life, and bore about the same oblique relation to personality as a composer to his music. Each time Dix reran *Anna's Magic,* he was aroused by Ada's nude scene, the scene surrounded by his memories of directing the shooting, and his surprise at what had been shot, and his visit later to Ada's villa, Ada in a white terrycloth robe, drinking a glass of wine in the moonlight and then moving inside for another glass. What a time they had had, and it didn't end on the Costa Brava. It ended a year later in New York. Ada found an actor she liked, and Dixon continued to be happy at home.

Claire brought up Ada's funeral. Probably the Businessman would be in charge, but God help him if he ignored Hollywood convention, specifically the selection of speakers and the order of appearance. The Industry always claimed you at the hour of your passing, but took its own sweet time in working out the arrangements. Claire was to begin a film in December. And he had the Berlin business to consider. He had promised to give Henry Belknap a decision soon, and Claire was in the dark about it.

She said, Do you want to speak?

If I'm asked, he said.

You will be, she said.

Then I'll speak.

Do be kind, Dix.

It's a eulogy, he said.

That's what I mean, she said, smiling fractionally.

Let's talk about something else, he said.

Bye-bye, Ada, Claire said in Ada Hart's voice.

He said, Do you remember Henry Belknap? UCLA. A German scholar, he gave me some help on *Summer, 1921*. About my age, a porker. Looks like Sydney Greenstreet. A wiseguy, talks out of the side of his mouth. Very, very smart.

Vaguely, she said.

Dix said, He wants me to come to Berlin.

And do what?

Nothing much.

So go, Claire said. What is it, a weekend? I'll come with you.

It's a residency, Dix said. He wants me for three months.

Three *months?*

Henry gave up UCLA and became a Rektor. He runs a think tank in Berlin. He wants me to come and think. You'll be off on location. You'll be locating while I'm thinking.

First I've heard of Berlin, she said. How long —

He called me last month, Dix said.

She said, Whoa.

He explained that Henry Belknap was insistent, offering a semester's residency, go anywhere, do anything, no obligations except to give them an oral history on moviemaking. The oral history was intended to be his personal settling of accounts. They were eager to have him as one of the eight Fellows; the others were historians and economists. The German film industry was especially enthusiastic, since Dixon Greenwood was a cult figure among the younger directors and actors, who saw him as the unenviable victim of fin-de-siècle American capitalism, a casualty no less martyred than the heroic Hollywood Ten. Henry Belknap's Mommsen Institute proposed to provide him with money for expenses and an apartment in its villa at Wannsee. Learn about Berlin, let the Berliners learn about you. Three months, January through March. He had nothing better to do and he thought he might learn something from the change of scene, winter on the North German Plain, where the wind originated in Finland via the Arctic. Dix knew no German but Henry was reassuring. No problem, my man. Everyone you meet will speak English.

You don't know anybody in Berlin, Claire said after a moment. You'll be bored.

Berlin is never boring, he said.

So what's it about really? she asked.

It's about loose ends.

Oh, *Dix,* she said.

Loose ends for a decade or more, he went on. I can't work. At any event, I don't work. My audience has vanished, gone away, emigrated somewhere. Something happened, I don't know what it was. But I looked around one day and discovered that I was the only one in the room. Everyone else had gone away.

All you need is a decent script, she said.

I write my own scripts, remember?

You know what I mean, she said.

I'll tell you a story, true story, not a script for a movie. Andy Richardson was one of my father's closest friends. Andy manufactured greeting cards, birthdays, anniversaries, but his specialty was Christmas. He had a team of artists at his plant outside of Chicago. Nineteen sixty-two was his banner year. In some locations he even outsold Hallmark. The next year, he borrowed every dollar he could and hired more artists — artists who could draw distinctive Santy Clauses, the Virgin Mary, elves, wreaths, and the Three Kings. Nineteen sixty-three was going to be his breakout year. He shipped more than two million Christmas cards, and then catastrophe. A month before Christmas, Oswald shot Kennedy. Andy was a great Democrat. He was inconsolable, and when he came to work a week or so later he realized that his business was ruined. No one sent Christmas cards that year. Merry Christmas, Happy New Year, we wish you and yours the very best for 1964? Little elves dancing around a snowman? The Three Kings gazing at the star in the east? America was in mourning, or anyway that part of it that bought cards for the holidays. Andy's business never recovered. So he sold it, and spent the rest of his life playing golf. He and Harry were great golfing partners. Everyone liked Andy. But when Oswald shot Kennedy, the bullet hit Andy also.

Claire shook her head. So instead of golf, you're going to Berlin.

When John F. Kennedy was killed, Andy Richardson was the age I am now.

Don't start that, she said.

I like to work, he continued. Always have. I like the set, for me it's a kind of lair. I saw the world from the set, the lights, the camera, the actors with the script I had written myself. Then something happened, damned if I know what it was. Something. The weather changed, drizzle all day long.

He looked up suddenly and said, America doesn't interest me anymore.

That's what you said then, she said. What I'm thinking is, Germany's old news. Germany is the place you went to when you were young and made a bull's-eye, and you know perfectly well that life isn't lived backwards, it's lived forwards. Claire paused a moment, unsure of her thought. Her husband did seem to have a reverse gear, his life's objective a series of successful returns. She said brusquely, So side-of-the-mouth Henry Belknap calls up one day, and the next day you've decided to spend three months in Germany.

It isn't the same Germany, Dix said.

It's the same Germany, Claire said. Despite itself. You're looking for inspiration, go to Paris. Everyone else does.

Germany's been a captive nation, Dix said. The First War, Weimar, the Third Reich, the Cold War. But the Wall's down, Kohl's gone. Question is, What about the corpse in the corner?

She looked at him strangely, then laughed. The corpse in the corner?

Henry Belknap and I spent a month in Germany, summer of 'fifty-six. Henry had introductions to people, academics here and there, and a banker in Hamburg. It was Henry's trip, I was along for the ride. We stayed with the Hamburg banker for a weekend. Evidence of the war was everywhere, though the war did not concern us because it had ended years before, half our lifetime. The banker was hospitable, he and Henry discussed the Hanseatic League, with detours to poets and novelists. The banker was a cultivated man, a widower. In his den he had a wall full of Emil Nolde's prints of Hamburg's harbor, and photograph after photograph of his wife and children. He told us that his children were dead, and so he lived alone. He remarked casually that he had no one to leave his bank to.

He was the sole survivor of his family. He looked directly at us then and spoke with the utmost gravity. You boys cannot know the catastrophe of the war. You will never know it. You can only have it secondhand, appalling — and then he stopped, flustered, as anyone is when he realizes he has said too much, opening a door to an unspeakable room. He returned the conversation at once to some obscure diplomatic crisis of the Hanseatic League in the fifteenth century, a pregnant century, and that was how we spent the remainder of the evening, talking pleasantly, surrounded by photographs of his wife and children. I have never been in an atmosphere where so much was left unsaid. We were discussing the nap of the carpet and ignoring the corpse in the corner. At the end he looked at us, smiling, or it seemed like a smile, perhaps it was something else, and said, We are at the beginning of a great prosperity. Prosperity will save us and we will never again be the nation we were. You're nice American boys. Your parents must be proud. I wish you were my boys because, if you were, I could leave you my bank. He wished us good night, and went upstairs to bed.

Henry and I went on to Lübeck and some other place I've forgotten, but the weekend at the banker's house in Hamburg stayed with me, and has to this day. When I returned to the United States, I mentioned it to my father. I described the banker, the look of his house, the photographs, the carpet and the corpse, and the prosperity. Harry did not interrupt me once. When I finished, he reminded me of the remark of the French general following the loss of Alsace in 1871: "Think of it always, speak of it never."

Listen always for the unspoken thing, Harry said.

Then he asked me the banker's name, and when I gave it he was silent for some seconds.

Hard to know, he said.

Hard to know what?

His religion, Harry said. Whether his boys died in the Wehrmacht or the camps.

I'd guess Wehrmacht, I said.

Perhaps, Harry said thoughtfully. Perhaps not. You'll never know.

The boys are dead either way, I said.

Yes, he said. Where would matter only to their father.

Coffee arrived. Dixon listened to the restaurant's piped-in music, some Beach Boys ballad. Retrograde, he thought. The Beach Boys were as retrograde as he was. He wondered if aspiring composers sent songs to the Beach Boys, hoping they would sing one. Hoping that new music would snap Brian Wilson out of his trance. For himself, scripts continued to arrive but he did not understand them, complaining that they seemed written in a foreign syntax, familiar words and phrases spliced and rewired to resemble the nonsense speech of a dream. Who were these stories written for? At the same time, he had no ideas of his own. The world had moved on, but he had not moved on with it. He believed his audience had vanished, and without an audience he had lost his most valuable collaborator. Like Andy Richardson, he was out of business, adrift on a feature-less sea without chart or compass. The other changes were predictable. The Industry's revolving door had swept away all his old friends and replaced them with aliens young enough to be his own children.

Claire rolled her eyes. You don't know what you're talking about, Dix. Some of them are very talented and well educated. You'd like them if you took the trouble to get to know them. And they'd like you, too. They're smart and they know what they want. They're successful, Dix, and success has its own specific rewards. You work, for one thing. You're back on the set. We both have a craft, and if you're a craftsman it's obvious that it's better to work than not to work, always keeping in mind that it's movies we're talking about here, not world peace or a cure for cancer.

He was looking at his wife with a sideways smile because she was in demand again. The saloon door swung both ways.

You're looking forward to the new one, aren't you?

It's a good part, she said defensively.

I know it is. I read the script, remember? And Howard Goodman is a capable director.

Howard Goodman always shows me to good advantage. He's relaxed on the set, so the atmosphere's good. It's fun, Dix. Everyone has a good time on a Goodman set. The script is solid and the cast is professional, except for that ass. You can't have everything.

What ass?

*That* ass. What's his name, the short one? The one who insists on doing his own stunt work, and if a stunt isn't there he'll demand one. But it'll be fine.

"At a certain level"? he asked, grinning. "At a certain level" was old-fashioned Industry jargon for material that was not junk. It was plausible material that was professionally written, directed, and acted. Well-made entertainment, box-office entertainment that did not embarrass anyone.

Definitely, she said.

Howard's your man, then. Howard's been at a certain level his whole life.

Sarcasm does not become you, Dixon.

He looked at the bill and put money on it.

So what about Berlin? she asked.

I'll decide after Ada's funeral, he said.

They stood for a moment under the restaurant awning watching the fog collect and swirl away. Nearby a family was crowding into a high-rise Mitsubishi SUV, the parents, two teenage children, and a youngster, a boy perhaps seven. The teenagers were complaining loudly. Their mother went around to the driver's door and unlocked it while the father stood behind the children, his arms spread, attempting to herd them into the rear seat. The fog came and went so that Claire and Dix could not see them clearly. The mother was young and the father was Dix's age, but very tall and bent, and wearing a Dodgers baseball hat. The doors were open but the teenage children refused to enter, continuing their complaints, something about a rotten deal in a soccer game, obsolete computer equipment, and an underdone hamburger. The father was nodding but something in his posture — he was stooped, his arms too long for his body, and his eyes turned away — suggested he was not listening. He gazed off in the direction of the steak house across the street. The mother was talking now, gesticulating at the children. The young boy was leaning against the rear fender in an attitude of absolute boredom, and when his father moved to muss his hair — it was a gesture of the most tender affection — he jerked his head away and said loudly, Don't!

Let's go, Claire said.

Stay a minute. I want to watch the end of it.

Claire sighed. You and your third reels. What do you care? What's it to you?

Because I know who they are, Dix said.

Claire gave him her infinite-patience look, then peered through the fog to the Mitsubishi. My goodness, she said. It's Billy Jeidels.

And family, Dix said. They had not seen each other in months. Billy was in the same professional cabinet as Dix, different shelf. He had married ten years ago, a young screenwriter with two children. And they had one of their own, the boy. Dix had heard or read somewhere that Billy was filming commercials for television and that he had won some award, an important honor in the advertising industry. He had been away from feature films since collaborating on Dix's last, a critical and financial failure. Billy shared the blame, unjustly, and his new wife, Gretchen, complained that his long association with Dix had made him unemployable. Dixon Greenwood was radioactive, worse even than Chernobyl. Billy did not take his wife's part but the friendship suffered. They got together now and again for lunch, talking always about the old days and the five films they had made together. It was a men-only lunch because of Gretchen's animosity.

Beautiful cameraman, Dix said.

Yes, he was.

I think he's in a fix now.

That girl is why he's in a fix, Claire said.

The family was still in midargument. Gretchen's voice carried across the asphalt, something about shutting up right now, that money didn't grow on trees, and getting into the car, and this time I mean it. The teenage girl was furious and stamped her foot. Why are you being such a shit, *Gretch?* Arms wide apart, Billy Jeidels continued to press against his children, urging them into the car. Dix heard him say mildly, All right, all right now, and that seemed to be the signal that whatever demands were being made, they were now acceded to. The children safely in the rear seat and buckled in, Billy slowly opened the front passenger door and leaned gently against it. The car was taller than he was. He swayed for a moment, almost losing his balance, still looking into the far distance as if he were making up his mind about something. He drummed his fingers on the car's roof. His wife banged her hands on the dashboard and they heard, most clearly, her next words.

Get the fuck in the car.

Billy came back from wherever he had been and with infinite weariness, left foot, then left leg, right foot, then right leg, he complied. He lowered the window and sat perfectly erect, his elbow resting on the metal sill. The children were quarreling again and his wife continued to scream at him. But he said nothing and did not look at her. It was as if he were deaf and alone in the world. At last Gretchen was silent and the car began to move, gathering speed out of the parking lot and into the traffic on Sepulveda, where it ran a red light and hurtled away, soon lost to view.

He was drunk, Dix said.

Billy was never a drinker, Claire replied.

Perfectly drunk. He had probably heard about Ada.

Was Billy involved with Ada, too?

Off and on, Dix said.

Let's go now, Dix.

They walked to the car arm in arm. Claire drove. After a moment, Dix began to think out loud, recollecting his move from New York to Los Angeles more than thirty years before. He liked California at once, the glitter and the sun, the endless freeways, the disorder and ambition, the blue Pacific, the girls as restless as the tides. Everyone in Los Angeles was from somewhere else and always on the hustle, and the style of things the reverse of Hamburg in 1956: nothing was ever left unsaid. Remember the party where we met, the socialite's house in deepest Pasadena? The English butler? The butler wanted to be a very big star, so he spent his mornings bodybuilding and his evenings passing canapés on a heavy silver tray that he balanced on three fingers of his left hand. He was always winking at the guests, men, women, it didn't matter so long as they had something to do with the Industry. A producer stole him away from the socialite and he was happy to be stolen because he figured the producer was going to make him a star. That was the promise. Instead he got a bigger tray in a smaller house. He got his revenge, remember? He ran off with the producer's wife. He butled his way to the top of the tree, with the help of Mrs. Producer. They're still around, probably retired and living near the golf course at Palm Springs.

Claire began to laugh.

And that's where we met, at one of those famous Sunday night suppers.

Billy Jeidels was there, she said. Ada Hart, too.

I don't remember Ada, Dix said.

She was there. She was with you.

Not with me, Dix said. I was alone, worried about the girl with the black eye. Adorable girl, except for the black eye. She knew every man in the room, and I was wondering which one of them had slugged her, except she was laughing a storm. She didn't behave like someone who'd gotten manhandled. Those shades you wore, they only called attention to the mouse. And when someone finally introduced us and I asked what happened, you said you'd walked into a door. And I said, Yeah, try the veal, it's the best in the city, and you called me a wiseguy and took off the shades and blinked twice. Lenses as thick as von Stroheim's monocle. Myopia, you said, and I kissed the mouse because you seemed so happy to have it, wearing it like a badge. And I knew L.A. girls who wept when they got a bad perm. I knew you were different and I fell in love with the difference.

She turned into their street, sudden darkness after the bright lights of Sepulveda. The air was scented, the fog beginning to disperse. She pulled into their driveway and stopped under the branches of the huge beech. She turned off the engine but made no move to leave the car. From an open window nearby they heard a fanfare of trumpets, the bellicose signature of the late-night news.

He said, L.A. is a bad town when you're not working. It's like being a stowaway on shipboard, but everyone knows you're there, hiding in the lifeboat. They don't mind as long as you stay out of sight.

Is that what it's like?

Pretty much. You don't know where the ship's going, either.

Lost the compass, is that it?

*They* know, or they say they do, and once upon a time I knew. I was able to read the time, see things before they came around the corner. I had second sight. I knew how things worked. That means, how people saw themselves. What they wanted and what they would do to get it. And then I couldn't do it anymore. The clock stopped. I can't tell you the time right now, never mind tomorrow or next month or next year. America has overwhelmed me, and no wonder, it's a big country. Country's big, L.A.'s small. And I'm sixty-four. I need another country.

Dix, she began.

I loved L.A. in the early days. We were so young.

Me too. Loved it to death.

You still do, he said.

It's good to be working, she said. That's true. But I'd be happier if you were working.

I will be, he said. That's a promise.

In Germany, she said.

He did not reply to that. Instead he said, Did you hear what that woman said to him, and the way she said it? *Get the fuck in the car.*

I heard it, she said. Poor Billy.

Yes, he agreed, but said nothing more. He turned to her in the darkness and kissed her. In the moonlight he saw their two worn

Adirondack chairs, side by side under the beech. The chairs were as old as their marriage. They kissed again and after a while he said in his slow voice that for the longest time he could not forget her black eye, livid against her fair skin, swollen, angry, yet her expression was of the purest amusement, and so the black eye was nothing more than a sudden squall on a beautiful summer day. So alarming, and then you adjusted and learned to live with it, and in a heartbeat it was gone, healed like any other wound.

You thought my black eye was sexy, she said.

Yes, I did.

She thought a moment, her head resting on his shoulder. She said she knew he was going to Berlin and that it was all right. He did need a change of scene, a different plot and a different cast of characters, something new. A change of country, she said. A different time and different weather, another narrative. A place to quicken the heart, like L.A. in the old days.

PART ONE

# Berlin, January

# 1

MAX SCHREK weather, the chef explained. He meant that the German winter had the grainy texture and somber mood of a prewar black-and-white, the sort of weather bat-faced Max Schrek was always walking in at the end of the third reel, the atmosphere so gray and indistinct you recognized him only by his defeated slouch and his black overcoat. In this weather, northern Europe generally had a prewar look of listless discord and unemployment. People on the streets were withdrawn, private and silent. The raw wind was part of every day.

You know Max Schrek, Herr Greenwood?

Of course, Greenwood said.

A great actor. Incompatible with the sun.

Every afternoon Werner complained about the weather because he was looking forward to his holiday in Majorca, senoritas and magaritas under a hot yellow sun, an ur-sun, not the pale Berlin button that declined even to cast a shadow upon the earth. In January it was dark by four and cold, too, the Baltic wind driving snow two hundred kilometers across the North German Plain, that featureless tableland two feet above sea level so beloved of Prussian aristocrats and military historians — and Chef Werner also, who had grown up on a farm near Peenemunde in old Pomerania. His eyes glowed when he spoke of the region's agriculture, potatoes, rye, oats, and, in former times, tobacco. Werner cooked all the

Prussian specialties, but Monday nights were reserved for Königs-
berger Klopse, meatballs nearly the size of cannonballs and almost
as heavy. The recipe was his dear grandmother's. Like so many others, she had been butchered by the pig Russians in the frightful
winter of 1944–45. Thank God for the Americans.

They were standing in the dining room of Mommsen House
waiting for the teakettle to come to a boil. The dining room and
kitchen were at the rear of the villa. French doors overlooked a
stone terrace and the wide frozen lawn that sloped to the lake beyond. The big round table was already set for dinner, ten places
for the residents and the Rektor and his wife. Six bottles of wine
were gathered on the sideboard next to the kitchen door. Dusk
was coming on, so Werner reached behind him and threw the
switch that illuminated the huge mural on the wall behind them. It
described a bacchanal, or perhaps the artist's version of a merry
Götterdämmerung. The women residents were infuriated because
the central figure was a spread-eagled woman with a two-foot
vulva, the vulva yawning in what appeared to be a scream of de-
light. The vulva contained teeth, and above the teeth a ragged lip
with a little toothbrush mustache. She was surrounded by men
whose body parts resembled carpenters' tools, handsaws, hammers,
screwdrivers, and awls. Supervising the fun was an army officer in a
brown shirt and leather jodhpurs, brandishing a whip.

I like it, Werner said with a smile.

It's junk, Greenwood said.

An artist has an obligation to his material.

It's still junk, Greenwood said.

I am opposed to censorship, Werner said briskly. My country has
suffered because of the censorship, burning books and destroying
artworks. We are on guard against it wherever it appears. This is the
foundation of our modern democracy. It is important to us, absolute freedom of expression, except where the Nazis are concerned.
That is the only exception. And it means no swastikas. No torch-
light rallies nor hate speech. The women should be open-minded
toward artworks.

You tell them that, Werner.

They refuse to listen, Werner said. He peeked at the teakettle, almost aboil.

Tell them about censorship. I'm sure they'll listen.

The artist is very famous in Germany, Werner said. His work is in all the museums and galleries. He is often on television.

I'm sure they'll take his fame into account, Greenwood said.

They shouldn't come here unless they have an open mind. I think it is that they are opposed to us.

The Germans, Greenwood said.

Yes, they have preconceived us.

Speak to Ms. Kessel and Ms. Ryan about it, and I'd like to be there when you do.

I have spoken to Herr Belknap, Werner said.

And what did he say?

Herr Belknap was most sympathetic. He said he appreciated plain speaking.

Dix began to laugh. I'll bet he did.

He said he would attend to it when he returned from the fundraising. He has gone to Hamburg and then he is on to Düsseldorf. Herr Belknap is a superior type. Did you know his mother was born in Germany? Werner looked at Greenwood sideways and then he said, You should get away.

I am away, Greenwood said.

I mean a warmer climate. A spa or beach somewhere in the south, where the atmosphere is not strenuous. You should take care of yourself with that leg.

My leg is the same, winter or summer.

Still —

And I have work to do.

Work cannot be completed in the German winter, Werner said firmly. This is well known. Winter is the time for hibernation. In the winter we Germans hibernate like bears. We burrow in until it's over. At least your wife should be with you. In this climate, it's unhealthy to live alone.

My wife is in America, Greenwood said.

In a warm climate, I hope.

Los Angeles, Greenwood said.

It is unhealthy, Los Angeles. The smog.

It's strenuous, too, Greenwood said.

I wish you liked the mural, Werner said.

It doesn't remind me of home, if that's what you mean.

The chef smiled broadly, handing Greenwood his cup of tea, no sugar, no milk, lemon wedge in the saucer. Greenwood thanked him and moved to leave the dining room and return to his apartment upstairs, to drink his tea and nap for an hour. Hard little snowflakes beat against the windows, and the lake had become obscured. The chef wished Greenwood a pleasant nap. He said that Greenwood should listen to the wind. The wind had a message. The vengeful howling of the wind was the voice of souls lost over the millennia, when Germans made the mistake of leaving their places of hibernation. Frostbite, pestilence, spear, gunshot. The great German retreats always took place in the winter.

# 2

GREENWOOD sat with his tea in the sitting room of his apartment reading a letter from his daughter, one that began with a rambling account of her plans for her garden, three new varieties of roses and a blue hydrangea. She and Mike had dinner the night before and Mike cooked. The hydrangea was his idea. Greenwood looked up into the oval mirror opposite — there were three mirrors in the small room, each at a different height — and wondered who Mike was. Mike had not been introduced, had arrived abruptly in the middle of her letter, unknown Mike. This was bad screenwriting: you either began with the red-headed stranger or prepared the ground for his arrival. But Mike vanished in the next sentence, replaced by Ernie the cat, who had gone missing but had returned that morning, *très content* after his prowl. And wasn't it fine news about Mom, who seemed at last to have a really good part in Howard's movie and star billing, too. She herself had an idea she would fly to Florida for a week, just to lie in the sun and fish a little. Brother Jerry might join her if he could get away. Of her own work she said not a word, but she rarely did. She and two partners practiced law on the Eastern Shore of Maryland, a location, Dix noted, about as far from Los Angeles as she could get. She ended with the usual request that he buy a computer so she could e-mail him, so much easier for her, and for him, too, once he learned to use it. Tell me everything about Berlin. Love, Nancy. The institute had supplied him with a computer that Henry Belknap promised was idiot-proof and a cinch to use, but Greenwood kept delaying the lesson. The computer sat in its box in the corner next to a space-age digital answering machine that recorded messages up to one hour.

He put Nancy's letter aside and stood, favoring his bad leg, looking into the oval mirror. He wondered if the decorator had a family in mind, one mirror for Dad, the two square ones for Mom and Junior. If you stood at a certain point in the room and looked into the high oval mirror, you could see different aspects of yourself in the other two. From the rear, broad-shouldered Dix, even in late middle age with the build of a tightly packed middleweight boxer, no neck to speak of, narrow hips and a game left leg, but in balance all the same. He gave the impression of a man who could take care of himself, though it would be a while before he got around to it. When Dix looked at himself in the high mirror, he saw a nondescript face, not in any way remarkable, more handsome than not, gray eyes with laugh lines at the corners, a nose turned up at the end, gray hair cut very short, another face in the crowd. But that was not what a stranger saw. The stranger noticed a man of medium height, a largish Roman head on a compact body, too casually dressed for a business executive, perhaps he was an academic or someone connected to the entertainment field — then he looked twice, startled, believing that Dix was someone, a figure from the movies or the evening news. The stranger would turn to whomever he (or more likely she) was with and say, Who is that man? I know I've seen him before, and then name a popular film, identifying Dix as the tough priest or the lieutenant colonel who goes down in flames in the second reel or, snapping fingers, declaring that he had it now. That's the character who took the Fifth again and again at that Senate hearing last week, the witness who never cracked a smile or spoke beyond, I respectfully decline to answer . . . He looked like a standup guy. What do you suppose he's doing in Los Angeles?

Dix turned on the radio and returned to his chair. German radio was playing American music, Ella Fitzgerald's Cole Porter album, the "songbook" that everyone was buying in 1956, two long-playing disks in a sky-blue and brown jacket. Cole Porter was still alive, living here and there in Europe and America. Everyone was alive then, Adlai Stevenson, Gary Cooper, Ernest Hemingway. Harry Greenwood was very much alive, entertaining friends from coast to coast. When Ella began to sing "All Through the Night" Dix smiled, drawn back to his freehanded youth on the North Shore of Chicago, summer dances under high-topped tents in Lake Forest and Winnetka, the moon rising hugely over the vast somnolent lake, the lights of the city visible to the south. They stood on the lawn in their dancing shoes and praised the moon for showing up.

The music went on and on. He was dancing with a wild girl, looking over his shoulder at the other dancers and at the older men gathered around the bar. His father was telling some story, people laughing, leaning forward to hear the punch lines. His father held a highball against his stomach, telling the story deadpan, drawing it out, always with impeccable timing. People gravitated to him, and now he looked over at Dixon, nodded and winked. Greenwood yawned, trying to remember the name of the girl. She was that summer's scandal because she refused to wear a bra. She said she would wear pearls but not a bra. She was red-haired, beautifully built and light on her feet, and spoke in a sarcastic staccato with a back-of-the-throat boarding school accent. He remembered her laughing when he held her close, dancing a tango, the violins soaring. Her fingers were in his hair, tugging. She was humming to the music, dancing barefoot.

It was warm in the apartment and Greenwood yawned again, his eyes closing. All the best parties had orchestras imported from the East, Meyer Davis or Lester Lanin. But this girl chose a supper dance with the violin section of the Chicago Symphony Orchestra and everyone agreed it was an outstanding idea, simply superb, the concertmaster leading with the panache of a Viennese Joe Venuti. She insisted on a jazz pianist from one of the North Side clubs to play during the breaks. The party went on until well after midnight. The strings departed but the piano remained, and they danced and danced. The scandalous girl was puzzled why Dix was going to

UCLA while all the other boys went east to Yale or Princeton. California was practically a continent away. He told her he intended to live on the West Coast and make movies, stories about the way people lived actually, not only in America but abroad, too. Infidelity was his subject.

Adultery, you mean.

Adultery would be included, he said.

I have stories, she said. I have more stories than you can imagine, and I will tell them all to *you* if you promise to make movies about them. Promise you'll listen? And later that summer she told him her stories, one lurid story after another about her parents' lives, tales of disorder behind the usual suburban greenery. See, she said, they turn out to be normal people after all. But at that time, Greenwood was not interested in the appetites of people like himself. After visiting Germany with Henry Belknap, he was drawn to delusions that bordered on rapture and the catastrophes that followed. The Hamburg banker's stony face stayed with him, and in his last year at UCLA he wrote two theses, one on symbolism in the films of John Ford, the other on the despised minorities of Europe. He had forgotten the scandalous girl's stories, but he remembered that she had a marvelous eye for *things* and what they represented. The mink coat, the photograph in the wallet, the bronze Buddha in the library, and the codicil to the will. Greenwood closed his eyes, trying to remember her name, she was so flirtatious in the moonlight.

Her name was Donna something. She had beautiful red hair. Everyone called her D.

He dozed, remembering that she had married, divorced, and married again. She had moved somewhere east and dropped out of sight. He had not thought of her in years, and would not be thinking of her now were it not for Ella Fitzgerald's Cole Porter songbook, and then he was completely asleep and dreaming.

Dixon Greenwood's afternoon dream in Germany:

His right arm was riddled with needle marks, so they detached it from his shoulder in order to present it intact to Herr Doktor Freud. Somewhere in the course of the meandering journey from his house in Libertyville to the Victorian comfort of the doctor's suite at 19 Berggasse, Greenwood was reunited with his arm, but now it was twisted painfully behind his back. The Viennese refused to notice him, looking through him as if he were invisible. They were retired people, flâneurs out for a stroll with their animals, small dogs and, in the case of the dwarf in the derby hat, a turtle on a long leather leash. The good friends escorting Greenwood raced ahead and one by one disappeared into the Mexican church at the intersection, leaving him alone in the narrow street, the pale winter sun just rising. The sun's rays advanced as the minutes passed and still he had no clue as to context. The time appeared to be early morning of a long-ago year. He was a broad-shouldered man conservatively dressed in a dark suit and bright yellow tie, a Borsalino on his head. He was deeply tanned from an expensive vacation. He wore a red rose in his lapel, yet his shoes were badly scuffed and in need of repair. He felt out of place in this milieu, standing in a one-way street in an anonymous Viennese district where houses lined the curb like books on a shelf, all the houses painted milky white and of uniform height and fenestration. The streets were empty of cars and the sidewalks deserted, the flâneurs having vanished, even the dwarf. At the same time, Greenwood believed he was under observation, the scrutiny unseen but profound. He heard the breathless laughter of young girls and then, from somewhere in the vicinity of the Mexican church, he heard the unmistakable whir of a camera's gears. This was comforting and stood to reason; he had spent his life looking through cameras, measuring distances, calculating angles and the available light, studying the perimeter of the frame. He stood a little taller now that he was on familiar ground. No one was ever alone, least of all when they were occupied with their own private thoughts; and in a camera's lens, nothing was straightforward. That was the point. He knew this as a certainty.

The shelf of houses presented a blank façade but the interiors teemed with life. When he heard violins, the rustle of evening clothes, and the thud of a champagne cork, Greenwood knew at once that this was not Doktor Freud's neighborhood and that his visit was misconceived, one more beautiful opportunity lost, and how many opportunities were there in a single lifetime? His spirits fell as the ground shifted. Things had looked so promising, so near a breakthrough. A promise had been made after all, and was now broken without explanation, a disappointment all around. Without question, the great analyst would have been delighted to consult on such a curious affair, an American's arm mysteriously detached and reunited as if by magic. Naturally Doktor Freud would have a European intellectual's condescending view of things, American neurosis corrupted by money and the compulsory pursuit of happiness, the symptoms garnished with crude symbolism. Nevertheless, Freud would insist on hypnosis, and following hypnosis would commence an intimate inquiry, his patient's childhood and early manhood, his parents' marriage, their attitudes toward each other and him, their sexual life together, and his sexual life as well and any fantasies that attended it. And then to the dream itself, salient in these circumstances. Describe for me the book-houses and the narrow street and the shape of the steeple of the Mexican church. Who were these friends, Herr Greenwood, and what was their business with your arm? Describe your earliest memory of the "detachment," as you call it, and the circumstances of its reunification. Come, speak plainly! Speak without fear. You are a man of your word and you have something important to tell me. You have come across the ocean from America in order to know yourself in Vienna. Quickly, please, my time is valuable.

But with no one to guide him, Greenwood was unable to locate 19 Berggasse. The book-houses were shuttered. The breathless laughter and violin music drifted away on the breeze of a soft summer evening, and now he smelled the rich aroma of freshly baked bread. Nothing about this street was familiar. He was hopelessly lost and did not have an appointment in any case. He knew no one in this district. He had no idea how he had come to be in Vienna. The street seemed to reach to the limit of the known world, disappearing at its terminus. He removed his Borsalino and waited. His good friends had disappeared into the Mexican church, the windowless building with the heavy door and the bell silent in the alcove just above. He did not believe he would be welcome in that sanctuary, no matter his distress. His distress was not a matter of concern to whoever was supervising his quest in Vienna. He had no letter of introduction, no appointment. The unseen camera continued to film the empty street; and so, his riddled arm limp at his side, Greenwood was bereft.

# 3

REENWOOD DRIFTED between his dream and the present moment, late afternoon in the villa at Wannsee. Wind rattled the windows of the apartment and a chill had settled in. He heard one door slam and then another, women's voices loud in the corridor, and he was aware also of the aroma of freshly baked bread in a deserted street in an unfamiliar capital city. He had been somewhere in Vienna and now he was in Berlin, a traveler without vocation or fixed itinerary. The dream was present but no longer visible. Something dada about it, the dwarf in the derby hat and a Mexican church. He sat with his eyes closed, struggling with this in-between world. He told himself that he was in Berlin because he had nothing better to do and no place better to do it in, and if a dwarf was part of the bargain, so be it. Alone in Berlin, he dreamed extravagant narratives, often conjuring a high-strung carnival world, one that existed on the dividing line between memory and imagination. He was at loose ends, and everyone knew the cockeyed results of loose ends. You drifted into the past because the present was uncomposed. He took a long sip of Werner's tea, sour on the tongue.

Dix looked up into the high mirror and saw his father's face, the sardonic stare, the thin smile, eyebrows raised in amusement, the look he had when beginning a story. He heard Harry's voice from years ago, back sometime in the fifties. Dix had come home late and heard his father and mother talking in the den. Or Harry was talking and his mother was listening, a story about an evening that had gotten out of hand, three men and the girls they had picked up, everyone disheveled, moving from the jazz club on Fifty-second Street to Ed's apartment in the Village. Ed offered to sketch the girls. Life studies, he called it. Dix stood in the hallway listening to Harry's story, trying to gather the threads. Harry was in midnarrative, drawing it out, his voice somber. His mother said nothing at all and Dix could feel the chill in the room. The girls were footloose, Harry was saying. They were game all the way, and then suddenly they weren't game. Ed took one of them into his bedroom and the other two became alarmed at the noise. One thing led to another. Everyone had had too much to drink, and when I tried to put an end to it . . . Harry paused there without explaining what he had tried to do or what "it" was. Dix heard his mother move to the sideboard; ice rattled in her glass. That was how she got hurt, Harry said. Ed was an animal, out of control, yelling something about Japs. He was in the Pacific, you know, the marines, and I think the war came back to him. He had a kind of breakdown. His mother said something Dix couldn't hear and Harry replied, They were very young. I don't know how young. Old enough to know better, young enough not to care; and here Harry gave a rueful little laugh, a lonely laugh in a room that was silent except for the sharp click of ice cubes. Harry added, They were not innocent girls, no. But we were very stupid and Ed was out of control.

Yes, his mother said. You already said that.

Did I? That was what he was.

And you, Harry? Were you out of control too?

I took her to the emergency room, Harry said, and sat with her two friends while the doctor patched her up. Her wounds weren't serious. They were exchange students, looking for a little fun on the town in New York. Their English wasn't good so we spoke French.

And how did the police become involved, Harry?

The medical staff made a report. The story we gave them was

that she had been mugged. That was the truth, too. That was what Ed did, mugged her. The girls were happy enough to see it all go away. They were nice enough girls but way out of their depth. Country girls unused to a metropolis.

And I suppose you gave them a little money.

Of course, Harry said. They were far from home.

That was the genesis of *Summer, 1921*. Dix worked on the screenplay for a decade, trying it first one way, then another, and in the writing the story broke free from Harry's moorings and took on a silhouette and direction of its own. All that remained of the original were three men, three young girls, life sketches, and the war — not Ed's war but the First World War. The apartment in Greenwich Village became a lake in southern Germany, and the jazz club on Fifty-second Street became a café in Heidelberg. No one was beaten up, no one broke down, and none of the men bore the slightest resemblance to Harry Greenwood. Harry's story was appropriated by his son in the way that any story is remembered fully, then retold in a fashion that suits the teller.

When at last Dix had development money, he and Claire went to Europe to scout locations. The screenplay proposed three artists and the girls who spent a summer with them, and the tragic events at the end of the summer. Dix had the words on the page but he did not have the characters securely in hand. He needed to know things that would never appear onscreen but were essential all the same. He needed to know the music they liked, and what they thought about when they went to bed at night, and their dreams. Who were these artists, and how did they get to the lake? Where precisely was the lake? And who were the girls? They were young and adrift for the summer. They were attractive girls without obvious ambition. But how did they see themselves in the world? Dix believed that the locations would answer these questions.

En route from Paris to the German border, he and Claire stopped at an auberge in the Champagne country near Verdun, a pretty stone farmhouse set in rolling vineyards, a part of the world that already seemed more German than French. The auberge had a spacious dining room furnished in the horizontal Bauhaus style, square chrome tables set wide apart, a low ceiling with indirect lighting. Huge posters featuring various champagnes crowded the wall, all in all a cheerful ambiance. The sommelier suggested Bollinger, vintage 1962, and Dix agreed at once. Bollinger was the champagne they had served at their wedding and everyone had agreed that it drank very well. Claire was delighted, insisting that the sommelier was clairvoyant. Otherwise, he was just another boring European coincidence. In his green vest and silver chain and pointed beard, Claire thought he had the mischievous look of Merlin.

And we've been under the supervision of magicians generally, she said, ever since that character flew in from wherever offering to finance *Summer, 1921,* no questions asked. No changes in your treatment. No girlfriend in the cast. No brother-in-law cooking the books. Merely a soft-spoken middle-aged man in a Brooks Brothers suit with the air of Wall Street about him, wanting to supply a bagful of money to invest in a film about artists and their summer models living on a lake in Germany fifty years ago, unknown actors directed by the all-but-unknown Dixon Greenwood. None of this precisely box-office magic. In fact, box-office poison. That was why three studios in Hollywood turned it down.

Who gave him a copy of the script? Not you. Not me.

Knew your father in the old days, he'd said.

Fond of him. Harry and I were colleagues in Germany at the end of the war. Probably he's told you the story. Or maybe he hasn't. Anyway, there is one. And it's a beaut.

Most affable gentleman, Claire said. Looked you in the eye, said your script was terrific, gave you the name of his accountant, and went away. We never saw him again, though the accountant was meticulous with the books. Your benefactor made a nice profit and so did you. And when you asked Harry about it, he laughed and said he remembered Whit. He'd done old Whit Reade a favor once, that rascal. He had some trouble and I got him out of it and he was a good friend to me, too. Helped you out, did he? Good for him. Whit never forgot his German experience at the end of the war. He believed the myths Germans told themselves were exceeded only by the myths that were told about them.

So given the history of this project, it's logical that the sommelier would suggest Bollinger, Claire said.

They remained at the table until nearly midnight. Greenwood explained to her in detail the next day's business, its importance in the general scheme of things. The date was 1921. Germany had not merely lost a war, it had been traduced, stabbed in the back by — and here the analyst's voice rose in shame and indignation, offering a choir of devils, fifth columnists, intellectuals, industrialists, Bolsheviks, union bosses, bankers, and journalists, and surely no accident that so many were Jews. But the artists, fleeing the city for a summer in the Franconian countryside, would have scant interest in the analyst's choir. The artists were possessed by the thing itself, its misery and collapse, its grief, as Picasso later would draw Guernica and not the aircraft of the Condor Legion. The Condor Legion was present in the pentimento. One world had broken down and another was being assembled before their eyes, and it was this new world that the artists sought to master. They were young. They were reckless. In some sense they were uncivilized. They were encumbered by the recent past — they had lived through it after all, each from a different vantage point, simultaneously remembering and forgetting and remembering again — and desired to account for it, collect and sift the essence of the time, as a prospector patiently pans for gold, confident of a find but mindful always of the bandits in the hills, witnesses to the discovery.

Meaning, Dix said, the audience, the ones sharing a box of popcorn in the theater, startled when the curtain parted and they saw the clearing framed by the blue water of the secluded lake. The artists were accompanied by three Sorb girls, runaways from their village in Lusatia, members of the most recent generation of the great migration from the Caucasus begun four thousand years before, an insistent central European minority known by different names

) 48 (

depending on the region of origin, Sorbs here, Kashubians there, Wends somewhere else — but the tactful outsider would know that "Wend" carried an unfortunate connotation in German. The girls had high Asian cheekbones and were as slender and tanned as breadsticks, cheerful girls with a taste for roughhouse. Among themselves they spoke the Sorb dialect, neither Czech nor Polish nor Danish but a combination of them and others besides. They were an underground people of independent temperament and a keen sense of injustice along with a fierce will to survive. Wonderful-looking people, according to Henry Belknap, who had written about them. Inclined to fatalism, Henry said, but of course Dix knew that, owing to a cryptic footnote in one of the scholarly books he had read preparing for his thesis on European minorities. And the girls had to be discovered in situ, on location in West Germany, no small task since Lusatia was deep in the East, nestled in the Spreewald close to Czechoslovakia. No Sorbs or Kashubians or Wends loitering at the soda fountain in the drugstore at Hollywood and Vine, and no makeup artist could create one from a cheerleader at Beverly Hills High.

Why must the girls be Sorbs? Claire asked.

Because I saw a portrait of one once, Dix said. And she'll be someone never before seen onscreen.

In the morning they drove east, through Metz and Strasbourg to Heidelberg, where after an afternoon's reconnaissance they followed the supposed route of the wandering artists and their Sorb girls, south to the lake in the Franconian hills and the famous dirty weekend that lasted for a summer, not a coming-of-age summer because the artists had already come of age on the Western Front, and the Sorb girls — but the girls were already experienced refugees. There were sights to be seen along the way, sights the artists themselves saw as they wound their way south in the Citroën van, painted by Hans Rosing a shocking pink. In Heidelberg the Greenwoods reconnoitered the city, looking into cafés, absorbing the medieval flavor of the old university town. Then they drove to the military cemetery a few miles distant, row on row of heavy concrete crosses furred with lichen. The sky was overcast. There were no flowers or other memento mori. It appeared to Greenwood that the cemetery was seldom visited, though it was very well tended, the grass freshly cut and the hedges trimmed. Here and there were animal tracks. The surrounding forest had been cleared of deadwood. All the graves dated from the First World War. Officers were in a special section, their men arrayed around them, a sentry line even in death. After an hour's stroll among the gravestones, Claire announced the place was haunted. Yes, she sensed ghosts. She stood in the brittle cold, her breath coming in short gasps. She was unnerved by the winter silence, the leafless trees, the hard ground underfoot, and the evidence of ghosts. I want to leave now, she said loudly. I believe we're disturbing the souls that inhabit this ground. We have no business here. Please, Dix. We're trespassing. Can't you listen to me this once?

Greenwood was not listening. He was standing by himself trying to think the way the young artists thought. When they looked, what did they *see?* What was their responsibility in this military cemetery? He put the three artists in his mind's camera. He observed them lark along the paths, bending to look at a name on a stone, and the rank below the name, and the date of death below the rank. The war would be fresh in their memories. Two of them were veterans themselves, and one, Jan Wendt, had served in the line for five years. Five years on the Western Front, First Marne, Second Marne, the bugles of the new century. His comrades in the trenches wanted to be near Wendt; they believed God was on his side, and at the decisive moment, theirs as well. The stubborn God of Martin Luther agreed to extend his personal protection to Wendt, an unlikely recipient of heavenly grace. Wendt told the story often, so often he came to believe it himself.

Greenwood was assembling biographies, first of Wendt, then of Rosing and Fischer. At the armistice, Jan Wendt was the sole surviving member of his battalion, and naturally once the shooting stopped he was shunned by all. Wendt was thought to be unwholesome. So he would be looking at the graves in the Militärfriedhof from an intimate angle of vision, one that had to do with his own recollections and stupendous good fortune. Bernd Fischer and Hans Rosing would see things differently. Rosing had missed the war altogether, a dubious medical deferment that allowed him to spend the duration in a sanitarium in the Black Forest. Rosing would be unable to imagine the broken bones beneath the surface of the earth. Then — were the girls with them, or waiting in the Citroën? The girls would have no interest in the interments of the cemetery. Sorbs lost no matter who won. Wendt, the irreverent one, would probably light a match on the concrete and then pose for a photograph, a cigarette in his mouth and his boot on the Gothic cross, thinking no doubt of — the girls in the Citroën, a pebble in his shoe, the high whistle of a French .75, the pure arc of a Matisse brushstroke, or the beer and sausage in the rear of the van. The photograph was in Wendt's wallet. Bernd Fischer had taken it with the military-issue Leica he had used in the last years of the war, when he was assigned to the general staff as a portrait photographer. His was the famous candid of General Erich von Falkenhayn when he announced the unconditional objective of the siege of Verdun: "to bleed France white." It was one of the only photographs of the haughty Prussian to capture what was unmistakably a smile, the corners of his mouth ascending slightly, his pale eyes radiating something close to warmth.

On their way out, Greenwood asked Claire to stop the car and shut off the engine. He alighted with his notebook.

She said, What are you doing?

Shhh, he said. I'm listening.

Listening to what?

He said, I'm wondering what they heard, the three of them, as they strolled around the cemetery. What was audible to them as they moved? It's important to understand the circumstances of the visit. Who suggested it? Wendt? What did they notice as they walked among the tombstones? And what were they thinking? Artists listen as well as see. And some of what they hear finds its way into their work, the hiss of water on keel in Homer, the racket of the locomotive in Hopper, the thud of dancing shoes on parquet in Degas. And would they have heard different things, these three, the wind in the trees, the rustle of birds, each other's breathing? Perhaps the girls were roughhousing in the car. Did Jan Wendt decide right then to draw his Marne series? Did the wind in the trees beside the gravestones remind him of the spring wind in Flanders, when the earth turned to mud and the birds returned in flocks? He hadn't drawn anything in two years and then, suddenly, a frenzy of activity. Fifty-two drawings in June alone, sheet after sheet of life in the German trenches, a series that was later compared with Goya's Horrors of War, except they were far more graphic, so graphic many galleries refused to display them. Times had changed, meaning the audience had changed. Wendt was denounced for insulting the memory of the gallant German infantry. He replied that he *was* the German infantry, and it pleased him to insult himself.

Fischer had his vivid landscapes, and Rosing the girls. Rosing drew them alone and together, nude and clothed, indoors and out, with an erotic intensity that is nothing like what he had done before or would do later. Rosing and Wendt fell in love with the Sorb girls, so natural and playful, so ready for anything. Only Fischer was immune, faithful to his young wife back in Lübeck. This is what I have to know. What were they seeing? Did the Militärfriedhof set in motion a string of events, or was it only the first stop of their journey to the cabin on the lake? Of course it was the trigger — do you see how beautifully it will film? The light failing, the Gothic crosses surrounded by the forest, the artists moving slowly among the graves, the scrape of Wendt's fingernail across the stones. And underground, a city of the dead, restless and inconsolable. Wendt would know this in his heart. In any life there's much that's unknown and unfathomable, remote from explanation. But a narrative can bring things a little closer.

This was in 1921, she said.

Yes, 1921.

The war just over.

They have money. The summer is free.

A summer holiday, she said.

Working holiday, Claire, but they don't see it as work.

With the girls along for comfort.

Where do you suppose they found them?

Does it matter?

Of course it matters! Everything matters.

Wendt found them, she said. Wendt found them — and she pointed beyond the gravestones to the spires of Heidelberg, the Schloss and the River Neckar beyond — in that café in the square near the Schloss. Winked at them from across the room. Chatted them up. Made them laugh. Asked if they wanted to come along on an adventure. Asked if they wanted to spend a long weekend at the lake in the hills to the south, not far. They giggled. Flirted some. But they were at loose ends, so they said, Why not? They saw three attractive boys, a little forward perhaps, but spirited, and they had a pink van and money to spend. They were going to the lake and the weather was fine.

Rosing brought the van, Greenwood said. He borrowed the money from his mother.

They came here, Claire said, to the military cemetery before going on. Everyone complained, the girls, too.

But Wendt insisted, Greenwood said.

The girls were impatient.

They call out, Let's go. What are we doing here?

In a minute, Wendt says. Keep your shirts on. All in good time. He's listening hard. He's listening with all his might to the present moment, not the moment before or the moment due to arrive. He's giving his full attention to the clutter in his ears. He's separating sounds, the rasp of his fingernail across the stone, the voices of the girls, and somewhere far away the oompah-oompah of a German band. He is composing a picture. In his mind are fantastic shapes and vivid colors. The present moment has become the Marne.

What are you hearing? Claire asked in a soft voice.

Shhhh, he said. Be still.

She hadn't believed her husband when he began, or hadn't believed that he meant what he said, about the significance of the military cemetery or much else. He said things all the time to judge their effect on whoever was listening; he adjusted his speed to the condition of the highway, a practical trait, often endearing. Dixon Greenwood regarded the spoken word the way musicians regarded notes on the score. Tempo was everything. But she found herself listening attentively as he filled out his screenplay, an impromptu performance spurred in part by her. She believed now that he had something valuable, if he didn't carry things too far, as he often did, an unfortunate inheritance from his reckless father. She and Dix had been married only one year and she was still learning about his emotions, meaning what enchanted him. Now she sat silently watching as he stood by the side of the road, writing something in his notebook. He was smiling, and in his cap and boots and concentrated manner he looked like a patrolman writing a ticket.

What are you hearing? she asked again.

A chainsaw, Dix said.

# 4

NOW DIX WAS AWAKE. The time was just four, early for a drink. He stared out the window at the balcony, melting snow on its iron surface. The apartment was damp and chilly, and outside the wind was rising, yet he was perspiring, his skin humid to the touch. In the western sky he saw a southbound jet's fleecy contrail; wherever it was going, he wished he were on it. He had been working on an idea, something he was unable to put into words. The idea was present but out of reach, a melody that he felt rather than heard. And the harder he sought it, the more indistinct it became. Maybe Werner had a point about the south, a spa or a beach somewhere, some soft climate.

Dix rarely slept during the day when he was home, but in Berlin he took a nap every afternoon. Something about the city encouraged repose. So he had turned on the radio and stretched out on the long couch and closed his eyes, thinking of the girl who danced barefoot on a lawn in Winnetka and the North Shore dissolving into a street in Vienna and the dream that hovered over him. Why Vienna? He had never visited Vienna. He had no particular affection for Austria. He had an idea that his father was somehow involved, his father gone now many, many years and an infrequent visitor to his dreams. He could not remember the last time. He remembered reading somewhere that the Greeks believed that dreams had the power to heal, including the restoration of sight to the blind.

Now he recalled with a shudder that they had unscrewed his arm as you would unscrew a lightbulb from its socket, and that the process had been painless. He was en route to an expert to seek relief in the form of an explanation. Hypnosis was recommended. He was in a hurry, but in his haste he had lost his way. He was certain that his father was implicated; perhaps Harry was one of the friends who raced away up the narrow one-way street to disappear into the sinister Mexican church. So perhaps the dream had been based on actual events after all, a sort of grisly afternoon docudrama, locations altered, personalities altered, names changed to protect the guilty — and behind the scenes a pig of a producer who demanded that he speak plainly, without fear. A producer whose time was valuable. Wasn't it an accepted fact that each character in a dream was some idealized version of the dreamer? It stood to reason. No dreamer went very far beyond himself. How could he?

Dix poured a drink, Polish vodka over ice, lemon peel on top. He heard a door slam somewhere in the corridor, then the sigh of the elevator. He stood stiffly looking beyond the iron balcony to the water. The snow had ended and the light was failing. A two-man scull ghosted along a hundred yards out. A patch of mallards rose and skittered away, settling on the far side of the scull. Weather approached from the northeast as predicted on the morning network news, the blithe American woman with the long legs and leisurely diction, all the time in the world to connect the Warsaw Low to the Bermuda High, and look what's happening right here in Atlanta. It would be dark in a quarter of an hour, the sun too feeble to pierce the dark vein of cloud. Across the lake the lights came on in the villas back of the yacht basin, the yellow glow nervous on the waffling surface of the water. The wind rose. The masts of the yachts disappeared as the light failed, and as he completed this suburban audit, Dix took a heavy step backward, stumbling, closing his eyes because now he knew exactly where his dream came from. A part of every day was reserved for recognition of the unbearable, and to endure its visit for a half-second or a quarter-hour, however long it chose to remain. Its approach was neither visible nor avoidable. You felt a raindrop on your shoulder and looked up, startled to discover a thunderhead above. And in an instant it overtook the sun.

He had driven up to Tahoe to discuss *Anna's Magic* with Lou Kniffe. The producer owned a chalet the size of a hotel. Lou Kniffe — everyone called him Knife — was theoretically on vacation but his people were present, lawyers, accountants, his driver, and a masseuse. Dix arrived late on an October Wednesday and they spent that night and the following day discussing the script, the casting, and the budget. His people and their wives and girlfriends played backgammon while Dix and Knife talked. Knife's people were never consulted at the first meeting, in the event Knife changed his mind or was only fooling to begin with. He enjoyed toying with directors, and listening to his to-and-fro was part of the cost of doing business. When Knife decided he wanted no part of whatever it was the director was proposing, he could simply report that his people had advised against it. His accountants were against it. His lawyers had reservations. Sorry, Dix, I wish you luck. Try me again. Or, if you were low enough on the food chain, one of his people would make the call and say pleasantly, Forget it, Greenwood. *Anna's Magic* is a piece of shit. Knife won't touch it.

Dix thought the meeting went well. The numbers were in line, and Knife liked Ada Hart. The subject appealed to him. Of course he had thoughts about the screenplay. The middle section's slack, don't you think? And the husband sounds like a pansy. Ada should have more to do, and the end is too damned talky. Also, wouldn't Long Island do as well as Spain? I have a place on the South Fork and I'd like to drop in from time to time, see the shooting. But he didn't demand a rewrite of the screenplay, something he usually required as a matter of course. He was surprised that Dix wanted to direct a comedy. Laughs aren't your usual line of country, are they, Dix? He wasn't convinced when Dix explained that that was the point. After *Summer, 1921* he wanted something different. Something a little closer to home . . . Then why are you filming in Spain? And Dix had replied, The material, Knife. The material's closer to home. American layabouts practicing sexual sorcery and feeling not the least bit guilty about it. It's present time, Knife.

Knife turned to his people but they had nothing to add.

What's the real reason, Dix?

Breakthrough, Dix said.

But it's only a comedy. Lotta people waiting for you to fall on your ass, Dix. Lotta people think *Summer, 1921* was a fluke. You picked some numbers at random and won the fucking lottery and now you think you're Alfred Hitchcock.

Truffaut, Knife. They think I'm Truffaut.

Maybe you have a point, he said. Something closer to home. You want to begin thinking about your future, Dix.

When can you let me know?

I'll call you next week, Knife said.

Dix started back to Los Angeles at dusk. He enjoyed driving at night, wrapped inside his old green Karmann Ghia, listening to the radio while he thought about the meeting with Lou Kniffe. The sun was setting over the mountains, brilliant shafts of yellow light glittering on the surface of the lake, sailboats here and there. The road wound around the lake in long sweeping curves, the foliage gaudy in late autumn. He lit a cigarette and opened the window a crack. He was listening to Dr. John, wishing he knew more about the world of popular music, life on the road, the jam sessions and the groupies, the drugs, how it was to play before a lit-up crowd of fifty thousand people, the sweat and frenzy, the sexual charge. Dix drove into the dying sun, nodding his head in time with Dr. John's music, when the car slipped from the pavement, sliding on gravel. He heard one bang and then another and the car seemed to break apart. He had never heard such noise, and when he tried to turn the wheel he found it was frozen. Back of the noise was Dr. John's hot piano and then his cigarette was crushed in his palm. His head struck the windshield and bounced to the roof as the car continued to roll, window glass flying. His palm hurt where the cigarette burned it. He yelled something but could not hear himself above the noise, a terrible drumroll that went on and on. The car was in free fall, striking trees and rocks, settling, then beginning again. Branches flew into the car and out again. The grinding did not cease and Dix wondered if it would go on forever. The steering wheel was broken. The windshield was gone and suddenly it was quiet and he saw stars overhead.

He was outside the car. His legs were beside him but they seemed far away. They were unfamiliar, as if they belonged to someone else, his feet without shoes, his trousers torn. His legs were so far away, his hips and torso also, that he knew with cold certainty that he had been decapitated in the accident. His head was in one place and his body in another. He lay on the downslope looking up, his vision unnaturally acute. He saw each hair on his leg. His mind was clear. It was only that his head was separated from his body and this was evident from the quantity of blood leaking and pooling where he lay. Blood was on his hands and legs, on the ragged glass of the windshield and the leaves stuck beneath his fingernails. Now that his mind was severed from his body he experienced an inhuman tranquillity, the surroundings in sharp focus. A chalet, its windows dark, broke the treeline in the distance, and that was the only sign of civilization. He listened to the tick-tick of the car's engine and knew that he had but a few moments to live. How long could a human being exist in such a state? Not long, certainly, though in numerous cases observed during the French Terror, heads had spoken for some seconds after the guillotine fell. Time moved in close formation, a second had the weight of an hour. In Place Concorde there were tears also, and in at least one recorded instance, a smile. So he did not have long to contemplate his separated body, distraught as it was, his legs in such an awkward attitude, at right angles to each other. In the reflected glare of the headlights, he saw his shinbone, white as the shell of an egg. His body was gone, and now he knew his spirit was following. His head moved then, lolling, unattached. His body receded until all he could see were his feet and his shinbone. To this he was indifferent, though he regretted the loneliness of the mountainside, nature spoiled by the acrid smell of gasoline. Dix vividly remembered the moments before his blackout, the separation of mind and heart, his head in one place and, as he now conceived it, his soul in another, desperately hoarding the seconds that remained to him.

Days later, in the hospital bed, his left leg entombed in plaster and elevated eighteen inches by a pulley device, he believed his life was provisional. He was not entirely certain that he was not in some heavenly infirmary, and when he mentioned this to the surgeon, the surgeon laughed and said he would send an expert to discuss the matter but that he should have no fear; he was in the county hospital and well cared for and would recover fully except for a limp. You're lucky, luckier than you know; by rights you should be dead. Back on location before you know it, Mr. Greenwood. When the priest arrived, Dix commenced a rambling account of his thoughts and emotions during the accident, and the appalling moment when he realized that he had been bisected, with only seconds to make himself — the word he used was "understood." He had visions of the guillotine and the heads of the dead talking to one another. He was alone in the world, the last survivor of a calamity. The phrase he used was "the last member of the audience." The priest assured him that these were normal fantasies that would disappear in time. Do you believe in God, Mr. Greenwood? And in order to cut short the interview, Dix replied, Of course. That very afternoon, the hospital psychiatrist arrived with a list of ambiguous questions and a Rorschach test. Dix fell silent then, refusing to speak to anyone except Claire. He believed she was the only one with the ability to listen, as if they shared a code unintelligible to others, and in that he was surely correct. Never had he spoken to anyone as he spoke to her, and she listened with all her heart.

He told her he was one person before the accident and another person now, and that the two did not agree. He was an equation out of balance. He was divided and would remain forever divided. The long hours on the mountain had taken something from him that could never be returned — refunded, as he said. Was this something he himself had willed? The car had drifted off the road of its own accord. The image of his severed head — he thought of it as a fragment of film rolling in slow motion, the frames vivid and formal in composition — was before him at all times. He assured her that he had remained calm, almost nonchalant as he scrutinized his body, so far away, so — untouchable. He could feel his heart beating and the throbbing pain in his legs, and when he lost consciousness he was certain he was gone. He had erected a fortification, a whole-souled wall against the terror that was just out of sight, and it had crumbled like sand. He searched her face. She was silent, and he believed that he had frightened her. She murmured something about getting home, she had promised the babysitter.

He said, I'm not myself.

She said, No, you're not. But you will be.

Not so sure about that, Claire.

She said, Go back to work.

He said, Work isn't the solution to everything.

It is for you, she said. Me too. It's the way we're built.

He started to say something, then began to laugh. He had to close his eyes.

Dix remained in the hospital for four weeks, emerging on crutches, gaunt and unsteady, convinced that he had had an experience so intense it could not be described. Perhaps that was the case with any experience of enduring value. The moment was not meant to be shared, except with Claire at specific times, and never in its entirety. Then she flew off to Toronto to make a film. Normal life, she said. When you have a contract, you honor the contract. Tell the truth, Dix. Aren't you itching to get back to work? But the truth was: not really. He wondered then if they were built in the same way after all.

He flew to Spain with Billy Jeidels to scout locations for *Anna's Magic*. Lou Kniffe had agreed to finance the film, so long as Dix was pronounced fit by his insurance company's doctors. In two months they had started filming but Dix believed he was only half present; his other half was somewhere on a Tahoe mountainside. Each evening he would rewrite the next day's lines, and explain that he wanted more spontaneity but on no account were the actors to ad-lib. Divided as he was, he felt the movie slipping away from him but was powerless to do anything about it. Ada complained that his set was no fun, too much tension and not enough uproar. You were so cool, Dix, and now you're not. At times the pain in his leg was excruciating, and in an instant the pain would vanish. He brought the film in on time and on budget, but that did not make it a good film. It did well at the box office, but that didn't make it a good film either. What he remembered of its making were nights with Ada and the days with his leg. For the rest of his life the circumstances of the accident would arrive in his mind, an old, though not especially welcome, friend who wanted only to stop and visit for a while, as if they shared a fond remembrance.

Dix leaned against the window glass, watching the shadows darken the water of the lake. The vodka was cold in his hand and he took a short sip, returning at once to the present. The two-man scull changed course and headed for home, the boat sliding serenely on the water. He had met the scullers, two retired accountants in their fifties, fit as mountaineers, taciturn as owls. They always drank a beer in the tavern on the corner when they finished with the boat, and Dix was often there at the same time. The accountants were slick with sweat and exhilarated from their hour's rowing, drinking their beer straight down and then waiting patiently for Charlotte to draw them another, a formal, deliberative process that consumed five minutes. The accountants had no interest in discussing their sculling, their families, or their accounting, and were incurious as to what drew Greenwood to Germany. They were happiest lecturing on the superior security arrangements of Europe, plans that allowed a faithful employee to work until he was fifty-five and then retire with enough money to live on, and time to scull whenever he wished and take vacations in Spain during the worst of the winter weather, and set aside money for the children as well. Wasn't it prudent for the old to make way for the young? And the state provided, as it had every right to do. That was why there was such dissatisfaction and violence in America, too many old people working and the young idle, restless as cats, resentful at injustice. There was trouble of that kind among the young Ossies, people of the former East district, who were unable to find work owing to the fuckups of the older generation and its refusal to give way. Life was not easy in Germany. The Cold War was won and won bloodlessly, but who paid the bill for reconstruction? And continued to pay? We Germans. Greenwood complimented them on their English, fluent with an excellent command of idiom. It seemed pointless to inquire whether they missed their accounting. When eventually they asked Greenwood what he did before he retired — he was older than they were and surely drew a pension of some kind for his years of faithful labor — and he replied that he was a filmmaker engaged in accounting of a personal nature, they lost all interest.

The scull disappeared. The water darkened as the sun set and the clouds lowered, and then Greenwood smiled, watching the little passenger ferry make its slow transit beyond the mallards. Its position meant the time was 4:06 precisely, fourteen minutes to go in the twenty-minute run from Wannsee to Kladow, the charming suburb across the lake, the one with two good restaurants and a wee island just offshore. This was usually the time he set aside his book or his correspondence and made for the tavern down the street from the S-Bahn, careful to swipe the *International Herald Tribune* from the library downstairs in case the scullers were not talkative, or talkative only with each other. Greenwood enjoyed sitting at the end of the long bar with his beer and his newspaper, a leisurely sixty-minute read, the first stirrings of the presidential campaign and the various lurid manifestations of the American empire; and in the air, Irish music, thanks to the beautiful barmaid Charlotte, who had taken her summer holiday in Connemara and had fallen in love with a handsome schoolteacher, six feet tall with hair the color of coal — ach, you should hear him talk, Herr Greenwood, such a comedy! Dix scoured the newspaper for accounts of the entertainment industry but found little worth reading. The reviews were short, the frequent resignations of studio executives not worth mentioning, and the subsequent litigation too complicated for easy summary.

During his first week at the residence, Greenwood invited some of the others in the House to join him at Charlotte's, but they rarely did, fearing distraction from their work and perhaps fearing also that such an occasion might become a habit or, worse, a ritual. Everyone knew that the winter months at Wannsee were disorienting, the sun disappearing for days at a time and the weather raw. A frigid mist arrived, the sullen breath of the Baltic, and at those times the weight of the past was palpable, the atmosphere a refugee gray.

One afternoon he was able to collect three of them to visit the Wannsee Conference Center, the stone villa with its oval conference room and refectory table and high windows overlooking the pretty lake and the swimming club across the water. Not much had changed in the neighborhood then to now, so it was easy to imagine the weather in January 1942, Reinhard Heydrich presiding, Adolf Eichmann inconspicuous in a middle seat. Discussion turned to the unacceptable situation in the East, displaced persons who were a burden on Aryan communities. So they undertook an inventory of facilities, rolling stock and destinations for the rolling stock. The participants were officials responsible for transportation, specifically the railway system, and officials responsible also for food and clothing. A doctor was present to advise on medical matters, should they arise. At the end of the meeting, each participant had his orders. The minutes of the meeting were carefully filed. Framed facsimiles of the minutes were hung on the walls of the conference room so that visitors could inspect the spidery handwriting that methodically noted times of departure and arrival, so many on Mondays, so many more on Tuesdays, and so on, the trains traveling west to east, mostly.

Greenwood, Anya Ryan, and the Kessels spent most of one afternoon at the Wannsee Villa, wandering its rooms upstairs and down, inspecting the many photographs and documents that described the domestic agenda of the Third Reich, returning always to the conference room itself and the ordinary refectory table. On the wall back of the table were official photographs of those present, most of them in business suits; they looked like directors of any industrial concern. Anya was drawn to a photograph in the corridor, Jews standing in the snow, waiting to board railway cars. German soldiers stood casually around them. The Jews carried suitcases, even the small children had bundles under their arms. Snow collected on the roofs of the railway cars and the wooden loading platform. Snow was in the air, soft, fat flakes — fragile, Anya thought, except for those on the platform. For the Jews moving to the railway cars, the snowflakes would seem as heavy as boulders. Unless no one noticed the snow, its whiteness in the gray of the surroundings. The adults would be thinking one thing, the children something else. And then Anya noticed a German soldier, his rifle slung, his palms raised as if in supplication; but he was only catching snowflakes. Anya turned away, thinking that in those times a life had the duration of a snowflake. In her mind she saw the Jews shuffling forward, climbing into the railway cars, men first, the men helping the women, both helping the children, and the snow continuing to fall. Greenwood, the Kessels, and Anya Ryan exited the villa and walked back down the charming suburban street and around the lake, hurrying now to the tavern, chilled to the bone when they arrived.

Charlotte listened to their conversation from her perch at the end of the bar. She did not join in, even when Jackie Kessel said loudly that visiting the Wannsee Villa was like visiting the laboratory where God cooked up hell. Adam agreed, adding a thought of his own. Anya said nothing at all but drank her beer quickly and announced she was going back to the House, she had things to attend to. The Kessels went with her. Greenwood remained. Charlotte said quietly looking at a photograph of her handsome schoolteacher. At last she tucked it away in her purse, giving the purse a familiar pat, as if she were seeing the photograph off to bed. When she spoke at last it was from a distance, and quietly so that no one could overhear. Charlotte recommended that in the German winter one remain within oneself, living circumspectly, resisting temptation. Charlotte called the German winter breakable weather. Things broke easily in the hard northern winter.

Don't fall behind, she said.

Stay warm.

Here, let me fetch you a pilsener.

The staff at Mommsen House told alarming tales of previous residents who disappeared as early as three in the afternoon, returning to dinner befuddled and hilarious, and sometimes not returning until late in the evening, accompanied by new friends trailing the usual noise and disorder. More than once the Polizei had become involved owing to altercations at Charlotte's, a terrible embarrassment for the House. Rektor Henry Belknap was personally embarrassed, though no charges were ever filed.

You Fellows must get hold of yourselves, he said.

You don't want to see the inside of a Berlin jail.

Yes, our winter is difficult. But Germany is a normal country after all, with laws that must be obeyed.

Of course there was no publicity because the House was under the protection of the government, all courtesies extended to the writers, scholars, musicians, and other intellectual authorities from America. But there was no mistaking the police lieutenant's smirk as he laid out the disagreeable facts, witness intimidation, lawyers told to go away, evidence lost or mishandled. Under the influence of drink, American intellectuals were worse even than the Stalinist thugs of Baader-Meinhof and the scuffles in Dahlem in the eighties. Your intellectuals are without discipline, the lieutenant said.

The Rektor promised to punish the offenders, but he never did.

Fuck them, Henry Belknap said, and for a moment Dix did not know if he meant the police or the intellectuals.

Dix returned to his kitchen, broke more ice, cut a lemon, poured two fingers of vodka, and stood glaring at the telephone, willing it to ring. Claire had promised to call from the set, but perhaps her promise was as idle as the Rektor's. And when you were on the set, if things were going well, promises were neglected; they were neglected equally when things were going badly. Dix stood at the window sipping vodka, sorry now that he had not taken a walk in the neighborhood and revisited the villa, if only to end up at Charlotte's, with or without the newspaper.

These afternoons, he said aloud, these afternoons are stretching to eternity.

# 5

THE KESSELS were quarreling. They quarreled every afternoon, regular as teatime. The disputes had to do with Adam's frequent visits to Hamburg and his refusal to accompany Jackie on her excursions around Berlin, a movie in the afternoon, shopping at KaDeWe, a drink at Kempinski's. He was no more enthusiastic about evenings out at the Berliner Ensemble or cabaret in Mitte —

> Truth is tough and hard as nails
> That's why we need fairy tales

— so retrograde and beside the point. Weimar's dead and gone, Jackie. Weimer's a dead letter.

Adam's voice was deep and did not often carry beyond the walls of their apartment but Jackie's soprano was clear enough, so Dix mainly heard her side of the argument. He knew that Hamburg archives were essential to Adam's research, something to do with German emigration in the nineteenth century, all the hopeful boatloads bound for America. Adam taught at the University of Texas and Jackie tutored German. She had been his student once, and reminded him often of the carefree times they had had in the bars and restaurants of Austin, the Longhorns football games on Saturday and the impromptu flights to Cuernavaca or Denver, that year when they were newly together and trying to keep things under the arm. Such fun they had. And you were so cute!

Now they were in Berlin and a life she hadn't counted on, Adam all the time in Hamburg, a city with the charm and vivacity of Brownsville. She should have stayed in Austin, where she had friends and where in winter the temperature was benign, mostly. She missed her friends, and she had three months to go in this this this *place,* where you had to work so hard to have fun and he refused to help out. She said, If you aren't careful you'll have another emigrant to write about. Everyone else was taking French leave, the Whytes to Madrid for a week and the Ellmans to Venice, and they never went anywhere except that snowy Sunday with young Bloom and the Ryan woman to the ghastly Soviet memorial in Treptower Park, thirty feet of marble to commemorate the three hundred thousand Russian dead during the Battle of Berlin, five thousand unknown corpses entombed under the marble, for God's sake, Sunday afternoon at the ossuary. Then a sound like a cello, and Greenwood knew that Adam Kessel was speaking in his reasonable professor's voice, promising — promising something, perhaps a trip to Lübeck or merry Ulm the following week, Frankfurt the week after, and Munich in March if she was good.

The Kessels' door closed. He could hear footsteps and the thud of the elevator door, Adam retreating to his office in the basement for another hour of work before Werner's three-course evening meal, followed by a lecture from an Australian agronomist lately returned from a journey to the farms of Prussia, deteriorating each day because while you could take the boy out of the collective farm you could not take the collective farm out of the boy, and each and every one of those boys (and girls as well) had to be reeducated as to the value of an honest day's work for an honest day's pay, and because of the globalization of the food market, another capitalist scheme to destroy the rural life.

Dix turned up the radio and glanced around the apartment, trying to draw confidence from the things that were familiar, his Olivetti, the Heckel and Kirchner posters on the wall, personal stationery and thesaurus stacked neatly on the shelf under the window, the files scattered willy-nilly, and the photograph of Claire and the children on his writing table, all of it reflected in the mirrors.

There were books also, but he was too unsettled of mind to read them, preferring instead the news of the world on CNN and American music on the radio when he was not collaborating in the afternoon quarrels of the Kessels. He was aware suddenly of fractured Sinatra, static caused by the wintry breath of the Baltic or aircraft interference or conceivably the dying rads of Chernobyl, and then the radio went silent altogether and he was left with Jackie's laughter and the long evening ahead with the Australian who knew everything there was to know about collective farming in Prussia.

Billy Jeidels had given him the name of an actress.

A great admirer, Billy said. She wants to meet you.

She's a wild one. She looks like Romy Schneider.

Call her up, take her out.

You'll go crazy in Wannsee, Dix.

But when Greenwood called, she was out of town. Due back in a week. Can I give her a message?

Tell her Dixon Greenwood called.

No prob, the man said.

Dix was thinking now about his oral history, how much to divulge. Naturally Herr Professor Doktor Blum would want to hear about *Summer, 1921,* how it came to be written and cast. Where did Jana come from? Do you hold with Truffaut that improvisation is the soul of filmmaking? That, and the emotional bonds among the members of the cast. In other words, like life itself. Ensemble or auteur? Spare us no detail, Herr Greenwood.

Dix began to make notes on a white pad. It was difficult enough defending who you were, and exhausting defending who you were not. The critics thought the work led to the personality. They wanted the personality and the defects that went with the personality, as that would give them special insights into how the director made the movies. They did not understand that every creative endeavor was an act of rebellion against that which had gone before. They did not understand that Truffaut's great task in *The Four Hundred Blows* was not to make the boy into himself but to make himself into the boy, not autobiography but anti-autobiography, even the mischievous look-alike Jean-Pierre Léaud, and all the incidents taken from life and acknowledged to have been taken from life but that only meant a faithful recollection of the emotion involved. Not the fact but the emotion from the fact. And while personality was not an innocent bystander, it was not fundamental to understanding, either. God help anyone who tried to deconstruct the magician's art.

Plus, the witnesses did not understand their own part in the scheme of things. The audience liked to believe they were controlled by the artist, it flattered their sensibilities, their connoisseurship and discernment. Any work of art that deeply affected them flattered them also. The artist was pleased to believe that the audience was irrelevant to the undertaking. The artist alone was afire with inspiration — the moment, according to Nietzsche, when something profoundly convulsive becomes visible with magisterial exactitude. The author's aplomb derived from God's will. When Nietzsche discovered that *Thus Spake Zarathustra* was completed during the precise hour of Richard Wagner's death in Venice, he called it the Hallowed Hour.

Dix was smiling to himself, making notes on the pad. If asked, he would not have been able to say whom he was writing to, other than the empty room in which he sat, the one where the lamp cast long shadows on the ceiling and walls.

Often it was necessary to wait for the audience, but unlike an orchestra conductor you could not raise your baton and demand silence. You listened to the restlessness in your own way and took from it what you could. That was what distinguished one artist from another. A story that was incomprehensible in one decade was indispensable the next. The audience demanded the story not knowing they demanded it. They recognized it only when the story was in front of their eyes, and then they praised the prophetic genius of the storyteller. They called you a genius for giving them what they wanted when they did not know they wanted it, and had they been asked would have replied, I don't see the point. Mahler booed off the stage, Matisse banished from the salon. And when you told them they were accomplices, they refused to believe it. They thought you were renouncing your talent. They thought you were hiding something or refusing to take responsibility. They refused to believe that the story would fail utterly if the audience — either the present audience or some future audience — was not prepared to receive it.

Naturally craft was involved, along with the usual deception.

Harry had told him stories of his interrogations in the windowless cubicle in the detention center, a long table, the prisoner at one end and Harry at the other, like old marrieds who had little to say to each other. Harry always began with vital statistics, harmless evidence that tended not to incriminate. And at some point on the second or third day, the witness would begin to fashion a narrative. He would describe his duties, a staff officer filing reports, a logistics major assembling transportation for weapons and ammunition. Q: Were the trains used for other purposes, such as the transfer of prisoners? A: That was not my department; for that information Herr Greenwood must speak to Colonel X in Department Y. The witnesses seemed to want narratives with beginnings, middles, and ends, coherent narratives with a cast of characters and plot twists and a moral, narratives that suggested that they were not anonymous cogs in the mighty Reich machine but figures of consequence, following orders scrupulously, and if the orders seemed irregular, that was not their department, either. They were not storytellers, Harry said, so their accounts proceeded in fits and starts, contradictory and unconvincing. Of course they believed that victory was inevitable except toward the end when nothing was inevitable but collapse. Harry listened as the staff officers went on and on, making the best of things, richly anecdotal, especially when describing the fuckups — hilarious fuckups that all armies experienced since the beginning of warfare. Homer described fuckups. If the apes had had access to pen and ink, they would have described fuckups, too. So we continued day by day, doing what we were told to do, confident that the Reichschancellor knew the score. We trusted, you see. We were too trusting.

With the liars, sadists, blusterers, and amnesiacs, Harry was curt. But he was unfailingly polite with the others, the ideal audience for people trying to tell their own story, adhering now to one line, now to another, always in the vicinity of the truth but never on its mark, trying mainly to account for themselves in a way that seemed — plausible. They seemed grateful for the opportunity to audition, amateurs who apparently were unable to learn their lines. Often when they faltered, Harry suggested a possible turn of events, some incident or motive of which they were unaware. He led them back into their own past, refreshing their memories, discovering new possibilities of imposing order on chaos. Of course they were enthusiastic, and why not? The answer to chaos is repetition.

I wanted to inspire them, Harry said. I wanted to bring them face to face with themselves and their neighbors.

In a roundabout way, that's how you got *Summer, 1921* financed, Harry went on. Whit Reade, the man in the Brooks Brothers suit? He had one of Eichmann's people. Or Whit thought he was. He couldn't prove it. He interrogated this bastard for three days and was about to let him off. Charming German aristocrat, beautifully educated. They spoke English because Whit's German was only so-so. After three days, Whit decided he had the wrong man and the aristo was who he said he was, a functionary in one of the minor ministries. Nothing to do with transport. Nothing to do with the camps. Whatever the Final Solution was, he had nothing to do with it. Whit gave me the transcripts to read and I offered to take his man for a day, try another tack. See if another narrative presented itself, speaking German and only German.

Amazing what happens when you give people openings, Harry said. They can't resist improving their story. Improving it beyond all plausibility. When you catch them out, you make light of it. You convince them they've made only a small mistake, not worth worrying about. They think you're a fool and begin to play games, and before they know it they're in a hole. And that's when you go over their testimony comma by comma. They want to switch to English but you don't allow that. And after a day you've discovered who they are really. What they did actually. This one, he went to prison. Not for long, but he went.

And Whit was grateful and came to me, Dix said.

I signed Whit's name to my interrogation, Harry said. The command would have busted him for letting the bastard get away. He promised to return the favor someday. And he did.

How did he know about *Summer, 1921*?

Whit's the sort of man, knows things. And maybe what he wanted was to get even. *Summer, 1921* evened the score for him. And returned a favor, both at once.

Harry continued his reminiscence for an hour or more. And when Dixon asked him what he made of the experience, and what conclusions he had drawn from the season in Germany in the ruins of the Third Reich, Harry thought for a moment and replied that he was left with a question he was unable to answer. Who is responsible for the demagogue?

Dix said, Were you responsible for Whit Reade?

No, Harry said. Whit acted alone.

Dix wet the pencil lead on the tip of his tongue. He began to write again, then pushed the paper aside and sat with the pencil point resting against his lower lip. His desk lamp cast a soft glow on the yellowish wall at his elbow. He is back in Franconia, the long golden afternoon in June, the last day on location. The boys are in the woods smoking dope, the girls on the ledge overlooking the lake, the water smooth and soft as a bedsheet. The sun is still bright at six, the shadows not so long. Billy Jeidels is setting up for a final shot. This is not planned, it's only that the afternoon is so lovely he wants to shoot film — in case. In case they wanted it later. In case something unexpected occurred. In case Dix had an inspiration. In case the girls did something enchanting.

The girls stir, stretching like cats in the warm shadows. The light falls sweetly through the trees, dappling their skin and the rocks they sit on. One of them says something and the other two laugh, turning to look at the woods where the boys are becalmed, unseen.

Every afternoon they retreat stealthily into the woods, to a clearing nearby where they can smoke undisturbed. Billy begins to film, imagining voices over or voices off. He is thinking of the boys and their drowsy conversation, a complement to the lethargy of the girls; really he is composing an adagio in his head, something to conform to the colors and gestures of the girls. Jana steps to the lip of the ledge and looks down, ten, fifteen feet. The lake is shaped like a clarinet, two miles long and narrow where the girls are sitting. A thin ribbon of smoke rises from the cabin across the water, and some ways down a young boy is maneuvering a red canoe. Jana raises her arms and preens a moment, her face to the dying sun. Billy films all the while, creeping to his right so that he will have her in the frame in the event she decides to dive. Behind her is an easel, and on the easel a half-finished portrait. Jana and Trude embracing on the ledge, Marion drowsing in the foreground; she is asleep now. The brushes rest in a coffee tin, tubes of paint in a wooden cigar box, Rosing's box. Wendt and Fischer wander off into the woods. Rosing likes to paint alone, himself and the models, no witnesses. He requires silence, so he tells them to go away. When he finishes, he joins them in the woods.

Jana takes a final look behind her and launches herself into the void. She touches her toes in midflight and enters the water slim as a sword, her ankles disappearing in a tiny splash that softens at once, the water closing behind her as firmly as a door. Trude claps her hands and moves to the precipice to peer down and then looks back when the boys emerge from the wood, their voices loud, trailing laughter. She puts her fingers to her lips and says, Be still! The boys pay no attention and complete their journey to the makeshift canteen, where they begin to eat ravenously — bread, cheese, chocolate bars, Coca-Cola. When they finish, they sit sulking in canvas director's chairs. They seem not to know what to do with themselves. Wendt — his actual name is Thomas Gwilt and he is their leader, as the artist Wendt was so many years before — pulls a deck of cards from his pocket. Fischer fetches the folding table, and they wait while Wendt shuffles the cards and begins the deal for a hand of Hollywood gin rummy, twenty-five cents a point. Trude comes to stand behind Rosing, gently massaging his neck and shoulders. He indicates she should lower her fingers to touch the muscles in the small of his back. Marion is roused by their voices and awakens, raising her head to discover the source of the commotion. She rests with her head propped in the palm of her hand, looking at the card players, Trude now wandering away, back to the ledge where the easel is.

Billy has stopped filming.

He says, Shall we have a drink?

Dix agrees. Why not?

Billy has a stash of ice. Dix locates the Scotch.

They move away from the others, enjoying the failing light and the drinks in their hands. The boy in the red canoe is slowly paddling to the dock across the water.

Dix says, We're done here.

Billy laughs. And about time. I can't wait to get back to L.A.

Dix says, And cut the film.

It's good, Dix. It's very, very good.

I think so, Dix says. The girls —

Aren't they extraordinary?

The boys did a good job, too.

They finally understood ensemble, Billy says. They smoke an awful lot of dope, though.

They were straight when they needed to be, Dix says. Young Mr. Gwilt will be a star after this. And that's what he wants. I've never seen anyone want it more. Isn't it good to see people get what they want?

He hasn't got it yet, Billy says.

He will, Dix says.

Then Trude is at his side. She is very shy, the shyest of the three girls. It was difficult for her to speak to him. She stood looking over his left shoulder, distressed, her mouth forming an O.

He said, What is it?

It's Jana, she said. She's lost.

We'll find her, Dix said. Which way did she go?

No, Trude said. I mean, she never came up from her dive.

Dix slowly returned from Franconia, his memory dissolving into a helter-skelter of activity, he and Billy running down the path that wound to the lake, the boys following, their game abandoned in midshuffle. Wendt dove in at once, Rosing and Fischer behind him. Dix took a long breath and dove deep, following the underwater ledge. The water was cold and, a few feet down, opaque. They dove again and again but there was no sign of Jana. Billy Jeidels was frantic, diving and swimming far out and diving again. When he surfaced he called her name over and over, and when there was no reply he thrashed about in the water like a man drowning.

And later, when the police arrived and professional divers went to work, there was still no sign. The water was very deep, the divers explained. They searched that night and the next day and the day following but Jana left no trace. The body was not recovered. Wendt was inconsolable and for many months professed to believe that the disappearance was Jana's Sorb deception, a wretched joke. She had gone home, tired of the demands of the film, tired of taking direction and suspicious of his attentions. Wendt said, She doesn't believe in anything. When he told her he wanted her to come back with him to Los Angeles, she said she would never leave Europe. Trude and Marion were the ones who wanted to live in the United States. She was happy where she was, migrating here and there in Europe. They had quarreled, not violently but seriously, and she was angry with him. She had complained for days of boredom, and then late one night she said that what she really wanted was to get off the set, to go on the road for a while, wandering. Sorbs enjoyed wandering, to become flâneurs on the surface of the earth. Often it was necessary not to have an objective, simply to receive what was present for no better reason than the fact that it was present and you were, too. We Sorbs are at home wherever we happen to be, so long as we may speak our own tongue. We like to be let alone, and we seldom are.

She was annoyed that Greenwood had insisted that she use her real name in the film. She believed as a result that she had two personalities, the film Jana and the real Jana. The same was true for Marion and Trude, and yet you are Thomas Gwilt and not Jan Wendt. He thinks it's clever, Jana and Jan. I don't have a last name. Marion and Trude do not have last names. But you boys have last names. It is not respectful.

He laughed at her. You're already behaving like a movie star and the film isn't even released. Remember, you're working with an American director on an important motion picture —

Don't be surprised if one morning I'm not there, Jana said. Wendt told Greenwood later that she was furious, but not so furious that she didn't throw in her newest phrase of American slang.

I'm going to make myself scarce, she said.

Wendt said, But you can't leave the *film.*

It is not my film. It is Herr Greenwood's film.

Wendt believed she was still alive and Greenwood agreed with him. Jana kept her promises.

The formalities were grueling, a hearing before a magistrate and a long wait while the magistrate inquired into the matter of negligence. Greenwood was taken into custody but released after a day. Jana's parents could not be found. The other two girls disappeared when their testimony was concluded. Naturally the story was a sensation in the American press, the occasion for editorials on the historic mistreatment of the Sorb minority, not only in Germany but in all of central Europe and the Soviet Union as well. America would be no different, if America harbored Sorbs. Then the story slipped from the front pages to the pages inside, and then was forgotten. When the magistrate delivered his verdict — "presumed death by misadventure" — there was a final flurry of interest, then oblivion. The Americans packed up and went home.

Greenwood made himself another vodka, a small one. Dinner was in thirty minutes. He stood at the window, looking across the lake to the Wannsee Conference Center. The villas nearby were ablaze with light but the Conference Center was dark, as it always was after visiting hours. Dix noticed none of this, however. He was remembering how much he cared about his film and how disappointed he was that Jana, tired of his demands, tired of taking direction, insulted that her name had been appropriated, did not share his — love was not too strong a word. Back in Los Angeles, working in the cutting room, he saw how unselfconscious her performance was. He began to cut with her in mind. He shifted the focus from Rosing and Trude to Wendt and Jana. Billy Jeidels said his editing was inspired. It would not be accurate to say that Dix made the film as a tribute to Jana — he kept to himself the hope that she was neither dead nor lost but had merely, as she promised, made herself scarce — but that was how it worked out. When he tried to explain what he did, Claire said he was making too much of the accident. That was all it was, an accident. It was sad, tragic even, but it was an accident. Accidents happened all the time on sets. Old men had heart attacks, stuntmen died in cattle drives.

It's a beautiful film, she said.

Leave it at that.

You can direct actors in a film, she said. You cannot direct their *lives.* Their lives are their own.

No, Dix said. Not entirely.

He finished his vodka and stood before the oval mirror pulling on a fresh shirt. He heard the elevator and Kessel's footsteps in the corridor. Silence next door, and with that Dix knotted his tie, winked in the mirror, and put his glass in the sink. He stood at the window looking at the dark water and the lights beyond. The wind had lost strength but he could feel the chill beyond the glass, a presence that seemed to him almost supernatural. He remained deep in his memory.

On such a night in Franconia long ago, unseasonably cold for June, he had spent the evening in his hotel room revising the final week's shooting script for *Summer, 1921.* Everyone was asleep. Satisfied with his work, he had gone to the lobby bar, poured a glass of schnapps, and walked outside toward the empty square. Mist had come up from the river, muffling the glow of the streetlamps, glass moons the size of basketballs. He stepped into the square, the pavement wet under his feet. Dead center a bronze general on horse-back pointed his sword in the direction of Poland. Somewhere a cat screamed and a door banged shut, and he was reminded of the moment in *The Third Man*, Orson Welles revealed in the doorway of the deserted square in Vienna, smiling his cuckoo-clock smile, a cat at his feet, and then vanishing almost at once, leaving hapless Holly Martins dumbstruck.

Dix began to walk, taking his time, sipping schnapps. He was still thinking about the script and the work he had done, not so much a revision of dialogue as a revision of tempo. He was adding pauses and silences. He walked blindly, his head cast down, thinking about the next day's schedule. A car crept by but he barely noticed. He kept to the main street so that he would not lose his way, though the town was very small, hardly more than a village. Past the rebuilt square with its general on horseback, the neighborhoods had the look of the previous century, the houses high and narrow, decorated at the cornices, seeming to lean drunkenly into the street. When he looked up at last he saw that he was at the little park on the bluff high above the river. The iron bridge was below him, skeletal in the mist. Just then he saw Jana standing alone at the railing overlooking the water, utterly still, her hands at her sides. The mist came and went, swirling around her, so that she faded and returned to focus and faded again. She was unmistakable in her red scarf and tan trenchcoat. When she turned and saw him, Dix smiled and gave a casual salute. She was too far away to see the smile but he did not want to alarm her, conspicuously alone in her zone of privacy in the deserted park. He walked slowly toward her, aware of the glass in his hand.

He said, I was working. I decided to go for a walk.

She nodded, looking at him closely.

I often walk late at night to clear my mind after working. And I suppose it's the same with you. But isn't it awfully chilly for June? I hope it's warm tomorrow, for the scenes at the lake.

She shrugged and turned to look at the river, its glassy surface silvery in the light.

I didn't mean to frighten you.

I'm not frightened, Jana said.

You shouldn't be here alone.

It's safe, she said. As you can see, it's quiet. Nothing happens in this town.

Yes, it's very quiet. They roll up the sidewalks.

I beg your pardon?

An American expression, he said. Describing a one-horse town.

She smiled and repeated the words: One-horse town.

Where are Trude and Marion? He paused there, aware that he sounded like a school prefect or a suspicious father. He added, I saw them earlier tonight —

They are out, she said.

— in the dining room with the boys.

She made a little impatient motion, adjusting her scarf. Her manner was formal. She was composed in a way she did not display on the set. In front of the camera or relaxing between takes she seemed a young girl, frequently distracted, self-conscious in her dealings with him and Billy Jeidels. Yet her scenes on film were superb. The camera saw something the eye did not, and from that he concluded she was a natural actress. Now she said something to him in German, and when he did not reply she repeated herself in English.

Are you married, Herr Greenwood?

He thought a moment and said, No.

She said, Not even once?

The men in my family marry late, he said. It's a family trait, like blue eyes or bad teeth.

You were never tempted?

Many times, he said. But then a job would come up and I'd be off to — somewhere.

On location, she said. I suppose on location there would be many unattached persons.

Dix smiled. Yes, you could say that. Definitely unattached persons.

Is that why you wear a wedding ring?

I suppose it is, he said, but saw at once she wasn't listening.

She said, Herr Jeidels is married?

No, he said. Billy is definitely single.

I thought so, she said.

Billy believes marriage is a prison, he said. When she did not reply, Dix said, Are you enjoying yourself, Jana? Working here with me, with Billy, and with the boys? Is this a life you can see for yourself?

Yes, it's all right. I wouldn't want to devote my life to it, acting someone else's story. Who would? You are always caught between the lines, chained up, directed by someone. Do this, do that. You are never yourself. She glanced at her wristwatch.

And he knew then that she was waiting for someone, perhaps Wendt, perhaps another friend. He stepped back and she turned from him to look again at the bridge. Was that a figure in the shadows? Greenwood thought to offer her a sip of his nighttime schnapps but she shook her head, No thank you. No schnapps.

A good actor is always herself, he said.

Actresses are exaggerated, she said.

Yes, they are vivid, he agreed. On the set. Not always in person. Actors have multiple personalities, some more successful than others.

I haven't seen many movies, she said. The last one I hated. Spanish soldiers searching for El Dorado in South America, up one mountain and down another, centuries ago. No maps, only an idea of the destination. They were pursuing a rumor of a rumor, for the greater glory of their king. Running short of food, harassed by Indians. Soldiers die of fever. Misfortunes accumulate. One of the officers has brought his daughter, a lovely young girl. He is bewitched by the quest for gold. Why is she with him? There is no answer to this question, she is simply there, a member of the party, always combing her hair. So they march deeper into the interior of this terrible place. The men begin to quarrel, as they always do. They decide to separate, the officer and his daughter taking to a raft with a detachment of soldiers. They drift slowly downriver, passing first one settlement and then another. Inside the huts are human skulls and bones, dead campfires. The Indians are cannibals who sacrifice their victims. They attack the raft time and again, arrows flying out of the bush. The men begin to die one by one, and still the raft floats on, guided by the officer. His daughter is dying. The raft is overrun by rats. He seems not to notice. At the end he is the only one left alive, entirely unaware that the mission is doomed. He is in a kind of no man's land, starving, without maps, half mad, death everywhere. The raft floats round and round in a whirlpool —

I know the film, Greenwood said. Herzog's film. A great film.

Vainglorious, she said.

Yes, he said. That's what it represents. A study of megalomania.

I hated it, she said.

Allegorical, he said.

I still hated it.

You didn't admire the direction? The performances?

I don't admire madmen, she said.

It's a *performance,* he insisted.

Germans, she said.

Because Herzog is a German?

Because he is cruel, she said.

Below, on the bridge, a solitary figure became visible. Greenwood could not make him out. He walked slowly, then paused, resting his elbows on the walkway railing. He lit a cigarette and stared at the water, the current slack, motionless in the chill and the mist. Greenwood said he had to get back to the hotel. Tomorrow they would return to the lake to begin shooting the final sequence, a complicated shoot. And then they were done. You can go home, he said, and then, teasing, Do you know your lines?

There are not so many of them, Jana said.

Yes, not so many. But those few are *very important.* The summer is ending. You can feel the chill in the air. The boys have their portfolios, Fischer his landscapes, Rosing his portraits, and Wendt — well, it's a mystery what Wendt's been working on. You, Trude, and Marion have sat for Rosing, singly and together, clothed and un-clothed. A summer of tremendous magic, almost sorcery. All summers hence will be lived in reference to this one, when the world was far off, unobtrusive, unobserved. Of course each of you has fallen a bit in love with the others; perhaps, in the case of you and Wendt, more than a bit. And now — what next? You believe that Wendt will take his portfolio and vanish. He is the sort of man who would vanish with no explanation. And he believes the same of you, that one morning he will awaken and find you will no longer be present. So these last days are a kind of dance. The parties have become suspicious. The summer began with a chance meeting in a café, a flirtatious affair among strangers. And now you know each other better than anyone before in your young lives; and, you suspect, will ever know again. Fischer is the first to leave, back to his wife in Lübeck. Marion leaves at midday in the opposite direction. Rosing and Trude leave the next afternoon, but not before giving you and Wendt the choice of his watercolors. His manner, always confident and at times overbearing, is subdued. Marion is talking too much as usual. That leaves you and Wendt, and it is as if a plague or other natural disaster has ruined your civilization. The tents are in place, the coals in the fire still glow, the lake is as it was, but the atmosphere has changed utterly. The silence gathers. Wendt is shirtless despite the chill, and in the dying light the scars on his arms and chest appear waxy. You turn away. Wendt says, We must leave. And you say?

Where?

He says, after a pause that seems to you interminable, Where is your home? I will take you there. And you reply?

Nothing. He knows I have no home.

Wendt raises his head, then lowers it, his eyes narrowing. He is irritated with you. And you say?

I want to see your work, your canvases. I want to know your heart.

So he opens his tin chest and removes the artworks one by one, as if he were unpacking his suitcase. On top are sketches of you, fluent line drawings, unmistakably Jana but Jana without emotion. Jana without soul. An art instructor would call them workmanlike, certainly drawn with facility, charm even, but lifeless. At the bottom of the chest are the canvases, rolled tightly, scores of them, his account of the days and nights in the trenches of the Western Front. Violent, appalling artworks, disgusting to contemplate — and inspired. No part of human anatomy spared. And he looks on them as a father would look at a daughter, the most favored daughter. His expression says, This is my heart. Then he adds, this time in words, I owe these to you, Jana. These are for you.

And you — you believe you have seen the shape of the future. You are witnessing prophecy. The unquiet course of the postwar years is palpable in the contents of the tin box, and Wendt's undisguised pleasure. I owe these to you, Jana. These are for you, Jana, as if he were making a gift of the Sistine Chapel. Tears rise in your eyes but you do not weep. He has laid the canvases at your feet, the corners secured by stones he has gathered. What you are seeing is his fate, the fate of Europe generally. Wendt's heart, the product of his youth on the Western Front. And what do you do next?

I know what to do, Herr Greenwood.

Dix smiled bleakly, wished her a good evening, and walked back across the park to the street. When he turned to look at her, the mist had thickened and she was only a dark shadow under the lamp. The man on the bridge, whoever he was, had vanished.

He thought of the encounter many times, most often when he received letters from film students asking him to explain the Sorb girls, what there was about them that accounted for their extraordinary presence onscreen. The camera seemed to capture Jana's very essence, and that of the other two as well. Was it true that he had borrowed from the German expressionist painters, Nolde, Kirchner, Heckel, and Schmidt-Rottluff, scenes shot in such a way as to make angular bodies alluring and sinister at the same time? Nolde's harsh colors — Rosing's purple shirt, the garish yellow shifts the girls wear — clashing with the forest monochromes and the watery turquoise of the lake. But what they wanted to know couldn't be explained, or not explained in a way that was useful to them. Pointless to inform his correspondents that what he remembered most vividly was Jana in the park overlooking the river, dressed like a middle-class working girl, tan trenchcoat and red scarf, waiting for someone in the night mist; and describing *Aguirre,* Werner Herzog's masterpiece, as she would describe a fatal disease or the wrath of God.

She did not want a drink of schnapps, was not responsive to his questions, and wanted only to know why he was unmarried and what there was about Location that seemed to encourage unsettled behavior. When she asked about his wedding ring, he considered confessing. But he knew it was not important to her. She had smiled cynically when he agreed that he had been tempted many times, but work always interfered. Work was a great interferer. That is to say, he preferred to occupy the rat-infested raft as it drifted toward disaster.

When he told Claire Jana's story, she refused to believe it. Another European fairy tale, that girl is an *actress,* Claire said. She's a pro. So you've been had again, Dix. She doesn't sound to me like some little peasant girl you found in the café-next-to-the-flower-market. If she talked the way you said she talked, she's educated. She's been around. I think you and Billy Jeidels fell for her, two Svengalis from L.A. working their magic on little Trilby from Lusatia. But that's all right because nothing happened, did it?

No, he said.

I did tell her I was single, he added.

Yes, you did. Why?

It seemed like a good idea, he said thoughtfully. Probably I felt like making up a story. It wouldn't be the first time. Probably I thought the lie would bring us closer, director to actress. The encounter was strange, Jana alone in the park, some character walking across the bridge in the evening mist. I had the idea that nothing was as it seemed. You would call it an altered state. So I was entitled to lie a little.

A lot, she said.

It's only data, he said.

Our data, she replied.

He had asked Billy Jeidels if he was meeting Jana and he said he wasn't.

Rosing said he was smoking dope with Wendt and Fischer.

So the identity of the man on the bridge remained a mystery.

Greenwood always refused to answer questions about Jana, her life or her death. He said that all he knew could be seen on the screen, and if they wanted to know about the judicial inquiry, they could read the transcript. Interview the participants, those who could be located. Later on, *Summer, 1921* was seen as an allegory of America's vicious role in the postwar world. It was true that the Sorb girls had a certain Asian cast to their features, and they had been very badly used by — the word was "captors." So the fate of the actress Jana seemed to parallel the fate of the movie Jana, a useful symmetry for those who were attracted to useful symmetries, and many were. Even Claire had a question, and was not entirely convinced when Dix told her that an allegory was the farthest thing from his mind. He had no interest in allegories, then or later.

# 6

ONVERSATION was spirited at dinner, the events of the Balkan war competing with the marital strife of the Clintons. Jackie Kessel had all the latest gossip, downloaded from the Internet. But in this company the Balkans took precedence — except for the Australian agronomist, avid for lacy tidbits he felt were being withheld by a slavishly supine American press, too stupid or lazy to dig deeply into matters well known in Australia, liaisons with stewardesses, starlets, teenage rock stars, women of that nature. Tell me more, Jackie said, so the Balkan war was declared a truce as the company listened to stories of the president and the women of that nature.

The agronomist spoke for forty-five minutes and, as there were no questions, departed ten minutes later. The Whytes had eaten quickly and slipped out a side door, bound for the nine o'clock showing of *Shakespeare in Love* at the theater near the Zoo station. The others vanished on mysterious evening errands. The remaining residents gathered in the library for coffee and cognac. Young Bloom and his Italian girlfriend settled in at the chess table. Chef Werner looked in, poured a cup of coffee, and left. Jackie Kessel announced that at last she had convinced Adam to see cabaret in Mitte and why didn't they all go, an evening out, cabaret that amusingly and scandalously merged the political with the sexual, Reds providing the political and transsexuals the other. It was a very naughty show, all the critics said so. It was the best show in Berlin, even the Rektor had pronounced it vintage Weimar. What about you, Dix?

Greenwood hesitated. He had a headache from listening to the Australian.

Adam will translate the hot parts, she said.

Not tonight, Greenwood said. I'm going to bed early.

The chess players declined.

Anya Ryan shook her head.

Adam Kessel thought that might scuttle the idea, but Jackie was suddenly at the door with her coat on, beckoning. She wore black boots and a black beret with a little blue feather and black gloves. With the look of a man mounting the gallows, Adam followed after her, not without a long, pleading look at Greenwood, who shook his head firmly, no reprieve. No cabaret tonight.

He said, Give my regards to the eternal Footman.

But the Kessels were already out the door.

I'm going for a walk, Greenwood said.

Keep warm, young Bloom murmured from the chess table.

Mind if I join you? Anya Ryan said. I always try to take a walk sometime during the day. She looked at him apologetically and added that she did not like to walk in the neighborhood after dark. Everyone knew that Wannsee was safe, there was never anyone around, but still.

Come along, Dix said.

The street was silent at nine o'clock. Lights within the houses cast short shadows on the lawns and sidewalk. The grounds of the villas on their side of the street, the lake side, were lit by floodlights, a happy coincidence of vanity and security. Robberies were not common but they were not unknown, either. Curtains were drawn but here and there through breaks in the fabric you could observe television's blue nebula. At this hour Wannsee had the solemnity and outer harmony of a fine American neighborhood, Winnetka or Brentwood, lawns tidy, trees pruned, silent as a desert, one side of the street more desirable than the other.

They walked for a block without speaking, companionable in

the winter chill. Anya was a full head shorter than Dix, a nervous bird of a woman who spoke in a guttural voice that contained traces of an accent. She was writing a history of ordinary German life in the nineteenth century, the values people lived by and the importance of the German Idyll, its inwardness and loyalty to rustic norms and its apolitical character. She often said that she was researching the century before, but it might as well have been the thirteenth or the ninth, medieval times.

They walked for a while, the only sound the irregular click-click of Dix's cane. Then Anya cleared her throat and began to speak quietly, as if she were talking to herself. She hooked her arm through his and told him a story. She had been born in the East but had escaped with her family in the early 1950s when she was a small child. They had gone to the island of Rügen on a summer holiday and late on their last night had stowed away on a fishing vessel, a dangerous maneuver. They sailed with the tide, the transfer made at sea, and the next thing she knew she was living in Lübeck, Thomas Mann's gray city. Her father was a doctor, a surgeon often at odds with his colleagues. He had his own way of doing things. It was difficult for him to build a profitable practice in Lübeck, probably because he was brusque. He did not share the complacent attitudes of his burgher patients. Also, he was behind in his training. He had risked his life and the lives of his family to flee the East and now he felt himself a displaced person, neither here nor there. He believed he had nothing to show for his sacrifice, but he was unable to turn back. And so in due course Dr. Witters emigrated to America and settled in Hartford. Anya grew up in Hartford and when she finished her studies moved to the Southwest to teach. Her mother died. Her father retired and moved to the Southwest in order to be close to his daughter and his grandchildren, a mistake. He hated the heat and the enormous sky, the torpor of the day, scorpions underfoot, no herring, no wurst. His grandchildren ignored him. He quarreled with his son-in-law. He concluded that he was not meant to live in a southern climate on an unfamiliar continent so he moved back to Germany, to the island of Rügen, which after unification was under the supervision of the West. He spent his days fishing in the Baltic and on weekends took emergency room duty at the local hospital. Road accidents and tavern brawls. Except for the new hotel and the two expensive restaurants, Rügen seemed no different from former days. Most of the tourists were from the East.

Some men wander because they like it, Dix said. My father did. He was a sort of bumblebee, hopping from bush to bush. He saved passports the way other men save money, and every so often he'd look through them, remembering his journeys. Every few years he'd buy a new wallet. So he had a stack of wallets, wallets bought in Syria, Ireland, at an open-air market in Provence, on the waterfront at Bombay. His wallets and his passports were his diary.

Anya smiled. My father thinks of his passport as a burden. Perhaps a curse.

That's why I'm here, Anya went on after a moment. I thought that if I came to Germany I could see him regularly and that would bring us close. And it has, a little. Not in the way I'd hoped. He's a difficult personality. He believes he has been conspired against. Have you ever believed you were conspired against? It's a bad feeling, it causes you to behave irresponsibly. You neglect your duties. All his life he has been forced to open the wrong door. He took us to Lübeck and that was a mistake, and then to America and that was a mistake also. He did not get along with his colleagues in America any more than he had gotten along with them in Germany. He thought the American doctors were worse even than the Germans. Domineering, he said. Sure of themselves, even the young ones. And the young ones most of all.

Who does he blame?

He blames me, Anya said.

They had paused under a linden tree. Up ahead, a noisy cadre of workmen were gathered around a moving van. They were lit by the fuzzy light of a streetlamp. Beyond them, the road curved down to the lake, and through the trees he could see the dark water, a kind of void. His father never blamed anyone for anything, was patient also in passing around credit. Conspiracies were natural. Harry had a turtle's carapace of an ego, heavy and thick, unbreakable. He was sheltered by it, living within it as the turtle did. And he gave it no more thought than that. His passports and his wallets were all he needed to move from one day to the next, confident that his narratives were welcome, until one day they weren't.

And naturally he blames political conditions, Anya went on. He blames the Russians and the Americans for causing the division of Germany. He believes he lost his future because Germany was divided, forcing him to leave the East for the West and the West for America. Et cetera.

And it's your fault, Dix said.

It seems to be. He says it is. He says I must square the account. When he moved back to Germany he wanted me to come with him, but of course that was impossible. He said I owed it to him, after all he had done. But I refused.

So, she said, a story of a German family.

They walked on, more slowly now in the gathering chill. The wind had come up again. Now and then Anya would point out a particularly grand villa and give its provenance, built by an industrialist, a banker, a merchant, an art dealer. They were three-story villas that suggested the solemnity and ambition of monasteries, and spared only because the Red Army was busy in the East. Between the wars this part of Wannsee was a Jewish neighborhood. Many of the villas had been confiscated by the Nazis during the war and returned afterward, to those owners who could be found. Many had disappeared in the camps or overseas, so the city of Berlin looked after the properties. They were square-built with narrow windows, chimneys left and right, a Mercedes under the porte-cochère, a coat of arms worked into the locked wrought-iron gates. A few houses were dark, their owners in the south somewhere, Italy, Spain, the Greek islands. The great lawns were lit but the dwellings themselves were vacant. They reminded Anya of haunted houses in the stories her mother read to her as a child, ghosts at the windows, ghosts in the air you breathed, always present, never visible. These houses give me the creeps, she said suddenly. I imagine people at the windows, standing in the shadows where you can't see them but they can see you. Anya quickened the pace as they approached the moving van under the streetlamp.

One of the workmen looked up and smiled broadly.

Good evening, Professor.

Good evening, Thomas.

Are you joining us?

No, I am out for a walk with my friend. This is Herr Greenwood.

The workman took off his cap and shook hands.

Herr Greenwood is in the film business. In Los Angeles.

Thomas nodded politely, turning to speak sharply to the other workmen. They were busy manhandling boxes and wardrobe trunks from the van, then stacking them on dollies and walking them down the drive to the villa by the lake. The house was ablaze with light, giving it the aspect of a stage set. A group of young men and women were standing on the porch smoking and drinking beer. An older woman waved at Anya and she waved back. When the woman motioned with her hand, Anya turned to Dix.

That was the director, Frau Baz. Perhaps you would be interested?

He said, What is it?

They film drama for the German television, Anya said. Have you never noticed the bright lights in the windows at night? You of all people should recognize them, lights for filming. They film all day long and often late into the evening, as now. They do this for a living until they can find their way into more serious things. Anya explained that she was a technical consultant. The drama was set at the turn of the century, and she advised them on clothes and what wellborn Germans would say to one another, the forms of politeness and of insult. What operas they would go to and what they would say about the opera. What the women would be reading. What the men would do for recreation and who they would do it with. How they behaved toward their parents. And the servants. How husbands behaved toward wives and vice versa, language they used in public and private. They are trying to be authentic, you see. About the details of daily life. So long as the details don't interfere seriously with the plot. She smiled, raising her eyebrows.

She said, How they arranged liaisons.

Where they would go and when.

Dix laughed, looking at the group gathered together on the porch. How did they arrange liaisons?

Notes passed. Notes on perfumed stationery. The episodes often begin with a note passed from one hand to another. There's always a difficulty, a wife or a husband suspicious. Suspense comes from uncertainty. Will the lovers be discovered? Worse, will they be discovered during the undressing? The unhooking! Corsets and petticoats, garters, stockings. And for the men, cravats and suspenders. Sometimes spats. The studs in the shirt, the cufflinks, the shoes.

Period drama, Dix said.

Turn of the century, Anya said.

And you advise them on authenticity.

I don't have to tell them how to undress, Anya said. They do that naturally, but the boys always have trouble with the studs, the cufflinks, and the spats. When they become frustrated, they are like eight-year-olds. They whine and curse. They throw things. The girls have less trouble, probably because they enjoy it more. When it is cold, as it is now, we shoot them on the terrace at the back of the house with portable heaters to keep them warm, the heaters out of sight. Even so, sometimes they get goosebumps and shiver during the lovemaking. But that, too, is sexy depending on how it is shot.

It is the most popular Sunday program in Germany, Anya said proudly. Everyone watches it. This year it is called *Wannsee 1899*. Next year, *Wannsee 1900*. Each January we advance one year in order to keep history straight. The turn of the century was not such a bad time in Germany. Zeppelin flew his balloon. The nation was prosperous and stable. All Europe was at peace, dancing to Lehár and Strauss. Really, the twentieth century was far away. They called it "the new era" but they did not want it different from the old. Maybe Nietzsche did, but he died in 1900. We have fifteen good years left. God knows what Frau Baz will do after the archduke and Sarajevo. I suppose she'll send everyone off to the front, the girls, too. They can arrange their liaisons in the trenches and field hospitals. But the program will not continue that long. Nothing does.

*Masterpiece Theatre* in German, Dix said.

Not at all, Anya said. Each episode is an original script.

A script-at-a-certain-level, Dix said.

I suppose so. Our best people contribute.

The program announced by a flourish of trumpets?

The adagio from Mahler's unfinished Tenth, Anya said. Critics say it was written to resolve the turbulence Mahler felt in his marriage. But I don't believe it. I think it was Mahler's premonition of the war.

I agree with you, Dix said.

Wasn't one of your movies about the war?

The war and after the war, Dixon said.

But there were scenes —

One scene, Dix said. A flashback, very brief.

Adam Kessel was talking about it at dinner the other night. He called it a classic, his favorite movie. He couldn't say enough about it. I myself have never seen it, but I wanted to after listening to Adam. He fell in love with the girls.

Everyone did, Dix said. They were — unusual. And they never appeared in another movie. They were one-time actors, like those one-time cameras that you use and then throw away. They went back to wherever they came from. Lusatia, they said, but that would have been difficult in 1972. Maybe as Sorbs they had ways and means to fall between the cracks. Wherever they are, they're middle-aged. They're married with children. Probably they have grandchildren. And the grandchildren insist that they tell the story about the strange Americans from Hollywood who came to make a feature film about a summer on a German lake just after the Great War. And then again, maybe they've forgotten all about it, this interlude in their migration.

You never tried to find them?

No, I never did. When we finished shooting, we went home.

One of the girls was lost, he added. A swimming accident. The last day of shooting. Her name was Jana. Her actual name and her name in the film. Let's talk about something else.

Anya said, I'm sorry. Then, after a moment: I love the movies. That's one of the things I love about America. I go by myself in the afternoons when my husband is watching football. I sit in the air-conditioned dark and watch American movies on weekends when the theater is full. I like the tearjerkers and my husband can't stand them. Anya waved to the director and said to Dix, Actors are amusing to be around. They love what they do. I know it's only a television thing, but they try to do serious work, something they can be proud of and make a living from. And along the way they become famous because everyone in Germany watches them on Sundays.

You say the director is good? Dix asked.

Very good, Anya said.

I'd like to watch her work.

Anya asked the workman Thomas for his cell phone. While she spoke to the director, Dix watched the roughhouse on the porch, the boys clowning with one another while the girls looked on. One of the boys was juggling tenpins, the pins spinning furiously in the bright floodlights. He ended with a flourish, catching the last one behind his back and bowing to laughter and applause. They were all wearing jeans and flannel shirts and sneakers. Two of the boys sported wispy goatees, giving them the look of teenagers trying to appear grown up. The girls wore their hair short. When the older woman appeared in the doorway and gestured, they stopped talking and went inside, squaring their shoulders as if bound for a police lineup or final exams. The atmosphere was businesslike and cheerful at the same time, usually a good sign on the set. He could see the troupe through the wide front windows. The girls were donning wigs and necklaces, and suddenly they were turn-of-the-century German girls. The boys were out of sight. The older woman moved among the girls, speaking to each in turn and wagging her forefinger like a conductor with a baton. And then the curtains were drawn and the villa looked as drab and lifeless as its neighbors.

That was Willa, Anya said. The director, Willa Baz. She says we are welcome. She says this will be an amusing shoot, a lovely shoot. Willa wanted me to tell you that Dixon Greenwood is welcome on her set. She is honored.

Anya and Dix stood in a corner back of the cameraman. The atmosphere was tense, the cameraman taking light readings and the soundman muttering into a microphone. The troupe was in formal period dress. The boys were got up in tight trousers, stiff white shirts, and black swallowtail coats, indistinguishable each to the others, except for the blond heavyset one with the gold watch chain and a two-inch ponytail. The actors' faces were heavily made up and they listened attentively as the director explained something in rapid German. Anya translated it for Dix. Willa Baz was telling them where to stand and how to move. She essayed a few gliding steps to waltz music, played by a trio of violinists and a pianist at an upright Bechstein. The boys tried a few steps as the girls giggled. Then ponytail put his arm around the waist of the nearest girl and began to swing in a slow, sliding circle, his arms extended like a bird's wings. In a moment the girl closed her eyes and moved with him, the others stepping tactfully out of the way as Willa watched with approval. When she clapped twice, they stopped dancing and stood at attention, though the music continued.

The director now spoke to each of the actors in turn, raising her voice and gesturing when one or another of them nodded dubiously.

Listen to me, she said in English. *Listen.*

Dix remembered then how difficult it had been with the three Sorb girls, attempting to explain to them the narrative, and how he wanted them to move and react when the men spoke to them or touched them. He wanted them to speak reluctantly, never more than a half-dozen words at a time, because the men were voluble. The girls measured their words with the circumspection of a chemist measuring nitroglycerine. He explained himself in English, then in German through an interpreter. The interpreter was often baffled by the Sorb dialect, and in any case the girls were indifferent to instruction. Each day Dix thought he was making progress and then everything broke down in a clutter of incomprehension, the girls turning away sullenly and threatening to go home.

God damn them, Billy Jeidels said. They're jerking us around.

The girls had walked away to the clearing overlooking the lake and sat in a circle, not speaking, picking up handfuls of gravel and throwing the gravel on the ground, then bending down to inspect the result. After a moment one of them would smile or frown or in extreme cases laugh or burst into tears. Billy shook his head, exasperated, and Dix explained they were practicing geomancy, foretelling the future by means of the patterns the stones made. An occult practice that dated from the Middle Ages, related to the reading of tea leaves. They don't like to be told what to do, Dix said to Billy. They're independent girls, aside from their reliance on geomancy. Never again, Billy told Dix after one tearful argument, never again would he work with foreign actors. Never, no exceptions, because if you couldn't make yourself understood, you were merely a not too innocent bystander. What good were you without control? Truffaut had had the same problem on the set of *Fahrenheit 451*. It drove him crazy because he liked collegiality and he believed at the end of it he had lost authority over his own film. Dix told Billy to get his camera and film sub rosa. He used a long lens to capture the girls as they sat in their enchanted circle scrutinizing the future from the patterns of the stones at their feet, the stones smaller than marbles. The girls were tremendously still, concentrating hard. Billy filmed in natural light, the moment filled with mystery and poignance. He held the frame and held and held as the girls began to rock on their haunches, a kind of torso dance, an adagio; and at that instant Dix knew they were witness to a rare ceremony. The girls continued to rock as a long shaft of sunlight fell through the clouds, a bright white rectangle coloring the stones on the ground and the girls in their yellow shifts. God knows what he would do with the sequence, where he could fit it into the narrative. But it would fit somewhere. The girls rose at last and wandered off in the direction of the lake. They were holding hands and singing softly, and then their voices rose in high harmony, some ancient country melody. Billy stopped filming when they disappeared into the woods, the water of the lake sparkling in the near distance. Dix and the cameraman stood staring at the place where they disappeared. We'll make do with the situation, Dix said. Forget about control, let them do things their own way. Let them be themselves. We'll never find another three who look and move like these three. They're a gift, Billy.

Willa Baz had finished her instructions and filming began. The lights snapped on, the quartet in the alcove played Strauss, and the actors danced. The room was leaden, thick carpets and curtains, heavy furniture, an iron chandelier the size of a washtub. Landscapes in ornate frames decorated the walls, a suit of armor glowed dully in the far corner. In period dress, the young actors seemed at ease in the stifling formality of the room. Glaring lights washed out all texture, giving the furnishings a bright steely look, the ambiance of tomorrow's Bauhaus at odds with Wilhelmine Germany. Something preposterous about it, Dix thought. But everything about commercial television was preposterous. The music commenced, the actors began to sweat. The camera followed first one couple and then another before it focused and held steady. The boy in the ponytail had waltzed his partner to the curtained window, the camera trailing close behind. The others continued to dance but without conviction. He said something to her and she laughed, touching the tiny gold crucifix at her throat. When he put his hand on her breast she pulled away indignantly. She raised her hand to slap him but touched his cheek instead. The camera moved in closer, the music rising up-tempo into a rhythm that was almost swing. The girl seemed to swoon as she spun faster and faster, her skirt billowing. His hands were all over her now. She had ceased to resist, her expression soft and dreamy as she whirled in time to the music. Her body was present but her spirit was absent. She was going through the motions, a swimmer stroking laps, conscious only of maintaining rhythm and when to make the turn. Good actors had ways and means of living inside and outside at the same time, seeking not to mystify the camera but to find a convenient location in its lens, occupying it while yielding only what they wanted to yield. Of course the camera, too, had its own specific assignment, grinding on without reference to the operator behind it or the actor in front of it. Like sailing ships, cameras had a will of their own.

This girl was sharp-featured, more athletic than graceful, and you felt she was not the led but the leader. Her dark hair and tawny skin were shocking against the boy's bulky blondness, and her self-possession seemed to put him at a disadvantage. Yet this was also true: she would not know what was happening to her until it was too late. Now she threw back her head and closed her eyes. She gave a little cry of despair or frustration as the boy with the straw-colored hair struggled with the buttons on her bodice, his thick fingers unable to work the eyelets. He was an oaf, a plumber with wrenches for hands. She gave him no help or encouragement, her eyes staring at a distant point as she continued to turn, her palms rigid on her thighs. Finally the boy tore violently at the cloth, the sound terrible in the closeness of the room. The others stopped dancing and were looking at them both in silent anticipation. There was no sound except for the violins. When her rose-colored breasts were free, he kissed one and then the other, and when at last the girl looked at him, her expression one of surprise and discontent, it was as if she had just then awakened from a troubled sleep. The music ended abruptly, the only sound now the boy's excited breathing. She stepped back, allowing the camera access. She stared expressionless into the lens, and after a long moment the director announced, Cut.

The boy fell back, exhausted.

The girl buttoned up and lit a cigarette.

Good, the director said. The girl raised her eyebrows but did not comment otherwise. Perhaps the smoke ring she blew was a comment.

The boy appeared to have torn a fingernail. Blood was on his hands and now he put his finger in his mouth, sucking on it as if it were a Popsicle. Someone laughed, and then conversation was general.

The girl shook her head and said something rough in German, glaring at her partner, then moving off to join the others, pointing at the ripped cloth of her bodice, shrugging as if to say, What can you do with an oaf? She worked a safety pin to close the tear, then removed her wig and lofted it underhand at the suit of armor in the corner. It caught on the helmet's visor and hung there. Her hair was damp from the wig. She shook her head but still her hair clung to her neck and forehead, tiny curls plastered to her skin. She looked exhausted, watching the smoke from the cigarette in her fingers as if it were a genie about to assume some fantastic shape. In repose, her face lost its edge and acquired instead a youthful tenderness; but she was no longer on camera. Meanwhile, the boy stood stricken, worried about his finger, still leaking blood. A few drops fell to the carpet. He called for a bandage but no one heard him; at any event, no one responded.

So that is how we do soap operas in Berlin, the director said, her voice strident in the chilly silence of the room. We do not have the luxury of do-overs. Do-overs we cannot afford. So I demand excellence the first time. I will now give them ten minutes to collect themselves and we will complete the scene. And in an hour we will have this episode in the can, as you would say.

Greenwood was suddenly lightheaded, sweating under the hot lights, weary and dispirited as if he were climbing at altitude with a distance yet to go. Struggling at cross-purposes, the dancers had used up the oxygen. Everyone had gone slack from the moment the director said, Cut. Now they were sprawled in chairs or on the floor, smoking and drinking mineral water. One of the violinists ran a forlorn phrase, and the pianist struck a single chord on the Bechstein. They were gathering themselves for the last take.

It's been some time since you've been on a set, Herr Greenwood.

A few years, Dix admitted.

And you enjoyed yourself?

The girl did very well, he said.

She's new, she'll learn. Karen has talent.

She has a presence, Dix said. She knows how to use the camera.

She knows where it is. She knows how much to take from it and how much to give it. That's something that can't be taught, usually.

She's a natural, that's true.

Her partner isn't a natural, Dix said.

It's difficult for her, Willa replied. She had lowered her voice but her tone was still hard-edged. Karen hates Karl. She thinks he's stupid and clumsy, and he is. She won't get it through her head that he's supposed to be stupid and clumsy, that's what the part calls for. That's why he has the part, he was born to it. How fortunate for him that he's a dancer because otherwise he's the bull in the china shop. In another week she'll dump Karl for a poet. The poet will die of consumption, but not before they have a glorious romance in his house by the sea. Karl will come looking for them intending to challenge the poet to a duel. He has ancestral dueling pistols and longs to use them, especially against someone who has never handled a firearm. Ach! Willa laughed. She said, These bourgeoisie, they're the ones who introduce we Germans into such trouble. Like clockwork every two generations they decide to have a war or a coup d'état or a reformation in the name of the Reich. They wish to purify the nation. They are the cause of our distress, these careless bourgeoisie. The hereditary ones are the worst. We thought we had gotten rid of them but they're back, like vampires. They will haunt us forever. Isn't she beautiful, our Karen?

Yes, very pretty.

Karen Hupp. She refuses to change her name. Her parents are working people from the former East. Her mother is a seamstress. Her father was a functionary in the government. They are proud of her.

Dix nodded. He would not call Karen Hupp beautiful. She was provocative. She was alluring and moved in interesting ways. She knew how to be still. She behaved as if she knew she was being watched, but that was the case generally with capable actors. He observed her now as she leaned on the Bechstein, talking quietly to the pianist. She drooped, her chin in her hand, a flower deprived of the sun. The cigarette in her fingers looked to be as heavy as a crowbar. He did not know if she had a sense of humor and guessed that she did not. Yet the wig on the helmet's visor was droll.

Karl is old Prussia, the director said dismissively. His family had estates but they were lost after the war, so now Karl's father works at the stock market in Frankfurt. And Karl is satisfied to remain where he is, working on *Wannsee 1899* and whatever else comes along, so that he doesn't have to leave Germany.

I'd say he's made a wise decision, Dix said.

The director muttered something Dix did not catch. Then she said, They all want to go to Hollywood, all our best ones. That is the only way to become an international star, to be known in China and Brazil as well as Europe, and to amass a fortune. But there are no German actors in Hollywood. No one except for character actors and the Austrian Arnold Schwarzenegger and he, too, is a character actor and married to one of the Kennedy girls so he doesn't count. Do you think there is an anti-German bias in Hollywood? Will none of us be accepted unless we can lift Volkswagens and marry a Kennedy girl? No one will speak of this but I know what it is, this bias against us. It's because of the Jews in Hollywood, isn't that so? Willa Baz fluttered her hands and avoided Dix's eyes. Perhaps she had made a mistake. Americans were so touchy. Greenwood. Grunewald? What sort of name was that? A name you could not take a chance on, so Willa smiled warmly and said, Not that you could blame them. Everyone has a bias according to their own history of humiliation and insult. The French don't like the English. The Japanese hate the Koreans. It is in the nature of people to hate. It's the reptile in our brains, this is well known. Yet talent is talent regardless of nationality, isn't that so? Still, the French made their way to Hollywood, the women particularly.

And the English and the Italians, she added.

Dix was watching her as she spoke, her voice rising and falling in frustration and deep anger.

The Nazis ruined everything, Willa said with sudden vehemence. We Germans only wish to be normal again, to live in a normal manner with our neighbors, even the French. What's past is past except with us it's never past, so Germans will continue to be excluded from Hollywood except for the war movies, and when they needed someone to play Mengele they chose Gregory Peck. Is this normal?

In Hollywood it is, Dix said.

Karl is the only one not tempted. He believes his future is here. He believes in a German renaissance, Berlin once again as it was after the Great War, the center of the avant-garde. He thinks that Berlin will be the capital of the twenty-first century as Paris was the capital of the nineteenth and New York the capital of the twentieth. Berlin is the crossroads of Europe. Our continent is sliding east as your continent is sliding west, and for the same reason. That is where the conflict is, where the consequences of the modern world will be worked out, and it is our artists and writers and filmmakers who will set the terms. Tell the stories. Explain to people what is in front of their own eyes. The nations of central Europe were the ones who invented totalitarianism, the ones who saw the contradictions. But it is time Germans created their own future. Dream our own dreams, as Karl says.

Karl has more to him than I thought, Dix said.

Do you think so, Dixon? Do you mind if I call you Dixon? In any case, Karl is supported by his father. Karl has an apartment in Mitte, and downstairs a heated garage for his Audi, and he's still an oaf but an interesting oaf. Did you have a rich father, Dixon?

Dix said, Yes, he owned boats. He owned the *Normandie* once upon a time.

Willa Baz gave a low whistle. Was he Greek?

He didn't say, Dix said.

Surely, Willa began and then stopped, her color rising. She supposed that was Greenwood's answer to her question about Jews and Germans in Hollywood.

One other thing, Dix said. In the heat of the moment, your Karen Hupp seems to have lost her crucifix. He pointed to a spot on the floor near the window, the crucifix glittering, its chain spread in a golden fan. Willa regarded it bleakly, then bent to rearrange the chain in a figure eight, adding a little kink where it met the cross. She called for the lights, then motioned for the cameraman, who began to film, starting at a bare part of the parquet and tracking the crucifix, ending in a mute, static close-up. At the last minute, Willa stepped into the light so that her heavy shadow fell across the crucifix. Three beats, and the camera stopped filming.

Thank you, Willa said.

A scene-ender? Dix asked.

Perhaps, Willa said. Perhaps not.

They'll like it in the cheap seats, Dix said.

Not only the cheap seats, Willa replied, and moved off to have a word with Karen Hupp, who seemed agitated, talking earnestly to Anya Ryan. She looked to be explaining something, glancing now and then at Karl, who continued to nurse his wounded finger. After a final word with Willa, Karen wandered off to see about Karl, and in a moment they could hear her low voice, crooning as she bent to inspect the finger. Dix watched them from a distance.

He's a baby, Willa said.

Yes, Anya said. He wants sympathy.

How did the weekend with your father go?

Anya shrugged. The usual.

All men are babies, Willa said.

Can't stand a man who can't stand the sight of blood, is that it? Dix said.

Dixon, Willa said brightly. Do you notice the similarity?

He said, What similarity?

*Wannsee 1899. Summer, 1921.*

I hadn't thought about it.

The creator of the series admired your film so much he used a similar title. I spoke with him the other day, and he said to tell you, with his compliments.

# 7

ANYA INVITED HIM to her apartment for a nightcap, but he declined and went along to his own apartment, a few doors from hers. His leg hurt. He was wide awake and ill at ease, feeling like an amnesiac who had fetched up in an anonymous hotel in an unfamiliar city with no idea what he was supposed to do there. He watched CNN for a while, then knocked at a pornography channel, robust Scandinavian girls in a desert tent with a sheik who looked like Rudolph Valentino. He moved along to a western, arriving in the middle but knowing at once that he was watching John Ford's *She Wore a Yellow Ribbon*. Ford himself had told him that the movie took only thirty-one days to shoot, the cinematographer drove everyone crazy, insisting that the company stand around in the hot western sun until the light was exactly right, and only then could everyone take their places and filming begin.

Dix waited for the scene he wanted, when the troops of the Seventh Cavalry presented their retiring captain with a pocket watch. He slowly opens the box and hefts the watch, gruffly thanking his men. And after an awkward moment Wayne is gone, though from the manner of his departure it's obvious he'll return. The scene lacks finality, and the audience knows the Indians are not defeated. You had to admire Wayne's great economy of speech and gesture; Gielgud could not have done it better. The trick was to keep your hands still.

Dix switched off the television set and sat in the dark, thinking about *Wannsee 1899* and wondering how similar material would translate for an American audience and calculating that it would translate very well if the actors were appealing. You could set it in Savannah or Washington Square, or even Chicago, the ups and downs of class in America. Even the preposterous dance scene would play. Of course no one would watch it. Such a drama would never find an audience, because Americans were interested in class only as it applied to the British. He thought a moment more, then went to his desk and wrote a few lines to Claire, describing Willa Baz and his evening on the set, and returning to Mommsen House and the network news, Scandinavian pornography, and *She Wore a Yellow Ribbon.* The Indian chief looked like a Nazi.

*Have you ever thought that you were on the threshold of amnesia? Not quite here and not quite there? I'm sure it will pass. I miss you. I hope things are good on your set. Tell Howard hello from me. I had a very strange dream the other afternoon. I'll tell you about it when we talk.*

He poured himself a cognac and went upstairs to his bedroom. When he saw the winking red light on the answering machine, he knew before he touched the button that it was a message from Claire, her first in many days.

The time was noon and she was eating a sandwich in her trailer, keyed up because she had no way of knowing what they were on to with this movie or if they were on to anything. Probably Howard knew, but if he did he wasn't saying. Everything *very* close to the vest with Howard. You were that way, too, Dix. But I always knew when things were going to hell because you'd snarl at me. I knew when the film wasn't fixable, that there was nothing in God's earth that could turn the turkey into a duckling, because you'd snarl at the children as well as me. But I don't know Howard as well as I know you, so I can't say how this movie will play out, but I'm not encouraged.

But the weather's very fine, cool in Los Angeles, sixty degrees with a bright sun and no smog. That's what I like about L.A. in the winter.

She said, Everyone asks about you.

What's he doing in Germany? Is he working on a project?

Who would want to be in Germany in the winter? Working with Germans.

I tell them I'm not sure what you're doing. Dixon's in his close-mouthed mode. I explain about the fellowship. And then I say that everyone needs a change of scene from time to time. Still, I'd like it if you were here with me. How pleasant can Germany be? Right now you could get on a plane, be in Los Angeles in eleven hours. I'd meet you at LAX. We'd drive up the coast for a long weekend together.

She paused then and he could hear her breathing.

So if you're as fed up with Berlin as I am with Los Angeles, maybe you'd think about a visit. Things are tangled up here and you could help me get them straight. You were always good at that. That was one of your strengths. You know the problem, too many egos competing for the same small space, with the usual confusion, hurt feelings, and aggression. And I think Howard's lost a step and doesn't know it.

Can I tell you what I think the problem is here? I think the plot of this film is in actual fact an excuse to get a fifty-year-old man in bed with a seventeen-year-old girl without it seeming exploitative and sleazy. No question about it, the girl's adorable and the man's adorable, too, and when you see them in bed in their underpants it's doubly adorable, the girl especially, and the grisly death at the end makes it a film of trenchant social commentary of which the Industry can be justly proud. And it goes without saying that the action takes place in a suburb somewhere, and everyone knows what soul-destroying joyless places they are. So they're very earnest and committed over at the studio.

But I forgot. You read the script, didn't you?

But you didn't say what you really thought.

Howard's thinking Academy Award, maybe more than one. I'm in line, he says.

So it's junk, she said after a little pause.

And one other thing. I hate the part, the prissy missus, naïve, deceived. She wasn't always that way but they've been rewriting. Some new kid fresh in from Princeton or NYU, supposed to be a wizard with women, better than Oscar Wilde. So now half my scenes are shot in the kitchen, making a pie or browning the roast. Fetching a beer for my fifty-year-old and saying — this is today's contribution from the wizard — "Cold enough for you, honeybunch?" And it won't escape anyone's notice that he looks younger than his age and I look exactly what I am, fifty-five. So he and the babycakes look terrific together and I don't look so terrific except in the last reel, at the wheel of my sporty new convertible, hair flying, tape deck rising in song, heading for glorious Bainbridge Island and a new life. Or that's what the script promises. Maybe Howard will have another idea by then, and the wizard can work it up.

Dix began to laugh.

Maybe I'll die, she said. Maybe he'll have me die of a broken heart.

But no. Howard has lots of ideas. That will not be one of them.

The fifty-year-old will get Valhalla. I'll get Bainbridge Island.

It goes without saying that the wizard is a great admirer of *yours,* darling. So you're far from forgotten, in fact you're a sort of living god he takes time to worship. He seems to have memorized every shot in *Summer, 1921* and your other movies as well. This is the way he looks at the world. The world is the movies, and what he doesn't know about the movies isn't worth knowing. Sometimes I wonder what else they know, the wizard and his friends. They've seen and committed to memory every shot of every film ever made, the bad along with the good, and sometimes the bad in preference to the good. And that's the idea, today's shot winking at yesterday's, parallel worlds so to speak. In that way the incoherent becomes coherent, and signifies. That's how they explain it, the bad shot recalled and reworked into a good shot depending on the context. It's a question of the specific situation, each context bearing on the other, inducing a sense of déjà vu in the viewer. So the overall meaning is situational. Are you following me, Dix? I hope so.

That's what I listen to all day long. Isn't it a riot?

Dix had walked downstairs, still listening to her message. Her voice had grown more sarcastic as she went along. He pulled out the cognac bottle and poured out a finger, sipping it thoughtfully as she continued to speak of life on the set, the parallel worlds of the Industry, the bad shots reformed into good shots, owing to the grammar of the wink and the situational meaning of the overall. She said she had some *mar*-velous gossip about the costar, but that would have to wait for another time. He heard her say something in a muffled voice, and chuckle.

Okay, she said. Gotta go.

Duty calls, he said aloud.

They want me on the set im-*me*diately, she said.

He said, Go well.

I'll call you tomorrow. Try to be in, Dix.

Do my best, he said, raising his glass in a toast to the ceiling.

I wish you were here, she said, and rang off.

That was a private joke. He didn't wish to be in Los Angeles and she didn't wish to be in Berlin. They spent so much of their life apart, and when they were working there was no room for the other. That was the bargain they had struck, work always took precedence, and work was a solo flight. So when they talked they traded stories of an esoteric kind, opening the door a crack to admit the other so that when they reunited things would be less strange. He had his dream, Anya Ryan, Willa Baz, and the *Wannsee 1899* set. She had her careless script and a young wizard who could write women's dialogue as inspired as Oscar Wilde's. He thought somehow that he was more in touch with her world than she was with his, but that was because she had never been to Berlin. It would be a pleasure explaining to her that when he first arrived he had difficulty telling east from west, north from south, because the sky was so overcast he could not fix the position of the sun.

PART TWO

# Berlin, February

# 8

Anya's directions to Munn Café were explicit: take the S-Bahn from Wannsee to Potsdamer Platz, turn east and then south to Kochstrasse. Frau Munn's is around the corner from Checkpoint Charlie in the direction of the ruins of Gestapo headquarters, now a tourist destination called the Topography of Terror. Look for an alley, Munn's is halfway down. It's just a neighborhood place, Anya said, but everyone goes there. The schnitzel is the best in Berlin. Karen is very pleased you are coming, Willa also. She believes she got off on the wrong foot the other evening and wants to put things right. She admires you, Dix. About one o'clock? We'll be in the room back of the bar.

The remains of a demonstration littered the streets converging on Potsdamer Platz. The streets were mostly deserted, dust and bits of paper flying here and there on the wind. Everywhere he looked were construction sites, office buildings and hotels in various stages of completion, and empty lots on which anything could be imagined — a missile silo, Chartres Cathedral, or a Burger King the size of the Reichstag. Dix thought of toys piled under a Christmas tree, the children tearing into one package and discarding it at once for the next, believing in tomorrow's newer, shinier gift. Meanwhile, the wrappings accumulated. Sections of the Wall were visible now and again, a reminder of how things were not so long ago. The wild aspiration of the construction, cranes towering everywhere over the ravaged earth, gave the district a kind of clamorous optimism, a fresh Wagnerian Book of Fate, not the twilight of the gods but the dawn. The city was emptying its treasury in the hope that a new world of steel and glass was at hand, the world bearing a superficial resemblance to Los Angeles. Surely the Rhinegold was in there somewhere.

A lone police car stood sentry on the littered sidewalk, and when Dix passed by he received a sardonic wave. At the intersection a gathering of youths looked at him suspiciously as he approached. Dix believed he was inconspicuous in his Borsalino hat and scarf, his canvas jacket and his cane. He assured himself that his square head and heavy build marked him as a Berliner. He strolled to the intersection, seeing it now as a movie set, all the actors on script and in place. He had done this his entire life when venturing into an unpredictable situation. He thought he could turn himself into anyone he wanted, in this case a native Berliner or even a savvy expatriate, perhaps English, perhaps Russian, though not the sort of expatriate who approved of disorderly demonstrations. Too experienced, he thought, and too prosperous. He would admire passionate protest but would not take part. When he walked past them, one of the girls pushed his elbow and snarled.

American fokker.

He turned to face them, leaning on his cane and glaring at them, each one in turn. They were moving around him in a nervous circle. Damaged goods, he thought, wondering all the while how they knew he was American. Perhaps Americans gave off a high-decibel whistle, a pitch sure to attract the attention of a highly strung European.

American pig, the girl said.

Go home, go back to New York.

He took a step toward them. Of course it would be the environment, natural or political, the disappearance of the forests or the consequences of nuclear waste. It was all one environment, ballistic missiles, land mines, cultural imperialism, the arms race, the slaughter of the whales, and the contagion of AIDS. At one time in his life, these angry children were his audience. They were the ones who came to see *Summer, 1921* five or six times, professing to find in it their own indictment of the modern world, expressed at last in film. And they were not wrong. They had made him rich and famous, and he certainly looked the part, with his Borsalino, his canvas jacket and his game leg, his weary blue eyes and his half-smile. Wasn't image the signature of the modern world? And what would they say if they knew?

He said, Take care.

The police car had moved slowly up the street and paused. The officer did not open the door. Dix saw the flare of a match, and smoke spill from the window. The officer casually draped his arm out the window and watched.

Fokker, the boy said.

Fokker yourself, Dix said and walked away.

He was late. Munn Café was located down the alley some blocks from Checkpoint Charlie and its gimcrack museum. He was not familiar with the district, but the remains of Gestapo headquarters seemed not to be in the vicinity. The alley was filthy with broken bottles and discarded newspapers; a derelict rummaged through an ashcan scattering refuse around him. The faded sign over the narrow steel door read *Munn Café* in Gothic script. When Dix opened the door and pushed aside the weather curtain he found a cavernous room with marble-topped bistro tables and a long hardwood bar at the far end, the room weakly lit by globes overhead and wan winter sun from the windows.

All the tables were occupied, the waiters sweating as they delivered steaming plates of wurst and schnitzel and tall glasses of beer. The walls were dressed with framed graphics of the German expressionists, the glass in the frames so dusty that the subjects were difficult to identify precisely, but they all seemed to concern war, pestilence, disease, famine, and predatory young women. The posters were years old. The room was so large it seemed to absorb conversation, so that the ambiance had the disconsolate quality of a waiting room in a country railway station, a hollow echo of garbled speech and grunts of laughter. Munn's looked as if it were centuries old — centuries of schnitzel and beer, centuries of black tobacco, centuries of whispered confidences and failed conspiracies — but the date over the door read *1945*. From the look of things, the decades since had been hard on Munn Café. The long bar itself was deserted except for two old men and an obese bartender who looked as if she had come with the Cold War. Dix stepped closer and saw that behind the bar were photographs of patrons — from their demeanor he guessed they were officials or entertainers, and two were American army officers, posed with a pretty blond woman in a party dress and necklace. The woman was smiling beautifully, and then, when the obese bartender laughed gaily at something one of the old men said, he knew that she was the pretty woman in the photograph, indisputably Frau Munn herself.

Then Willa Baz was at his side, saying they were worried about him, concerned that he had gotten lost or met with some urban misfortune. Berlin was in the business of transforming itself, all the old landmarks disappearing. Berlin was a labyrinth for those who did not know it well. Perhaps her directions were misunderstood.

I was detained, Dix said. An unavoidable discussion.

Well, she said. You are here now. Take off your coat.

As you can see, Munn's is popular.

See that one over there? Willa pointed to a woman in black and whispered her name.

Musician, she said. The man with her is her manager. He did something in the Honecker regime. Ministry of Justice, Ministry of Foreign Affairs. I forget which. But he was an important functionary in the GDR. He also writes novels of the police type.

She plays beautifully the violin. She played for von Karajan when she was only a schoolgirl. Now she goes everywhere, Vienna, Munich, even New York.

Willa introduced him to Frau Munn, whose smile transformed the discouraged surroundings. When Willa asked if she would show them her scrapbook, she said of course, after lunch, always a pleasure, in a feathery lisp that fluttered like the flame of a candle. In an instant Munn Café went from smoke to mirrors, suddenly glamorous and vivacious, crowded with American army officers, Maestro von Karajan, cabaret entertainers, and the musician in black. Dix said he hoped very much that Frau Munn would return with her photograph album, and she said she would.

He and Willa went around the bar to the small back room, more brightly lit than the front. Karen Hupp and Anya Ryan were waiting at a round table near the window. When they were settled, a slender, strikingly handsome Vietnamese came to take orders. Karen and Anya were drinking beer, Willa wine. Dix ordered beer and everyone chose schnitzel. The Vietnamese pretended not to understand Dix, and when Willa said something to him the Vietnamese said something back and for a moment they glared at each other, the Vietnamese theatrically tapping his pencil on the tabletop. At last he muttered a short comment and went away, gliding across the floor like a dancer.

What did he say? Dix said.

He doesn't like Americans, Willa said. He doesn't like the sound of your language, so he pretends not to understand it. He prefers French, altogether more musical. I think he means subtle. He thinks we Germans should have a quota for Americans. Only so many allowed in.

The Vietnamese are an angry people, Karen said.

No kidding, Dix said.

They feel they are misunderstood, Karen said. So they are indignant.

The Vietnamese returned with the beer and the glass of wine. He slapped the glasses hard on the table, spilling a little from each glass.

Careful, Dix said sharply.

The Vietnamese smiled unpleasantly and went away.

Not so many Americans come here, Willa said. Munn's is not on the tourist route. As you can see, we all know each other here.

Karen went on about the Vietnamese, a talented nationality only now emerging from the shadow of their criminal colonial past. One had an obligation to be sympathetic. Colonialists bore the mark of Cain and the French were the worst, worse even than the Germans. The Germans were only imitating the French and the appalling English, trying to export the German enlightenment to the unfortunate dark races of Africa. The Belgians and the Dutch were very bad. The Portuguese were stinkers. The Spanish were terrible. The Italians were never very good at colonialism, being a dreamy, operatic people. They were no better at colonialism than they were at warfare. Also, they were lazy. The Russians were compromised in other ways, their realm so large, eleven time zones after all, and Slavs were always unpredictable, so ostentatious in their suffering. The Americans imitated the English in their Indochinese adventures, opposing the Russians as the English had opposed the French. This was the consequence of ignorance, paranoia, and male hysteria. Karen went on in that vein a little, adding the degraded experience of the Pacific peoples generally, the Tamils, the noble Tibetans, the Malay, and the unlucky Khmer. There were indignant former colonials in the Middle East and North Africa, and South America as well. These resentments would not be overcome in our lifetime on earth. The need for reparations was obvious, but would never be satisfied. Live with it, she concluded.

What are you working on now, Dix? Willa asked politely.

Dix was still beset by Portuguese, Tamils, North Africans, Italians, and the unlucky Khmer, but he managed to reply, Nothing.

Willa nodded, taking a swallow of wine.

Dix is always working, Anya murmured. No matter what he says.

The Americans are not as bad as the Belgians or the Dutch, except for Indochina and Haiti, Karen said.

I'm enjoying myself in Germany, Dix said. I enjoyed myself the other night on your set. Something will turn up.

A German story?

Perhaps a German story, Dix said.

Americans have the superiority complex, Karen threw in.

That's a very pretty scarf you're wearing, Anya said.

It's an ordinary scarf, Karen said. The oaf Karl bought it for me at KaDeWe, thinking it would change things. He wants me to be nicer to him on the set.

Willa waved her hand, enough of Karl and the set. Your first film, she began.

That's many years ago, Dix said.

It had an audience —

Yes, but the audience went away.

The American audience?

The American audience most of all, Dix said.

*Summer, 1921* did well in Germany, Willa said. I remember seeing it in Leipzig. The authorities decided that it had a useful message, fascists and their decadent art, the corruption of young girls. Decadent art, decadent artists, virtuous girls. So they permitted a week's run at a small house near the university. Of course the sexy minutes were cut. The girls were seen with their clothes on, so the story was prudent.

Prudish, Dix said.

Yes, prudish. The movie sold out each night and that worried them, so after a week they closed it down.

I'm afraid it didn't do well in Germany, Dix said. Germans don't like Americans telling them about themselves. It's the same with the French and the English, but they don't worry about it because Hollywood doesn't care about them. So much to do so close to home, you see.

And the Americans as well, Willa said.

Americans don't care, Dix said. It would be better if they did.

Willa took another long swallow of wine, gazing now into the middle distance. The tables around them were clearing and the room had become quiet.

And that's what you're doing at Mommsen House?

One of the things, Dix said. Thinking of the vanished audience.

In the silence that followed, Anya cleared her throat. She said, Dix has talked about traveling to the East.

Yes, Willa said. A good idea.

I would introduce you to my father, Karen said. My father is retired now but he knows our country very well. It, too, has been misunderstood. No one wishes us well. The Wessies hope that one day we will disappear, poof! We will vanish like your audience. She moved her hands in a gesture that seemed to include all the eastern provinces from Pomerania to Saxony, and Greenwood had a sudden vision of the population disappearing into swamps, the dark forest fastness, ravines, and hidden places beneath the earth's surface. She said, My father would be happy to give you a tour. I know it.

You should do this, Dix, Anya said.

I am from the East also, Willa put in. I grew up in old Prussia, in a small town near the Oder. Later, I worked in Dresden for the radio. I was the news announcer at noon and hourly until eight in the evening. I read the news for fifteen years, and when the Wall came down the station was purchased by others, a group from Hamburg. It had been a government station and then one day it was private, as if someone had purchased a state highway or an army battalion. They bought it for next to nothing, and I was out of a job at once, although I had always been faithful. No one ever complained about my work. There were no demerits in my file. I never missed a broadcast!

The Vietnamese waiter was now between them, balancing his tray with one hand while he passed the plates of schnitzel with the other. The tray listed alarmingly, then righted itself. He served Anya and Karen smoothly but paused before selecting Willa's plate. He gave Willa the large portion, Greenwood the small, handling the heavy plates as though they were feathers, setting them down delicately at each place. They landed without a sound, and then Greenwood noticed Frau Munn at the door, watching each move without expression. He imagined her as a character from one of the German legends, standing in the door of her cottage, trolls peeking from behind her skirts.

Willa thanked the Vietnamese, who made a little exaggerated bow before he danced away, pointedly ignoring Frau Munn. A complicated relationship, Greenwood thought, a Vietnamese émigré and a German who had survived the war. The Vietnamese was old enough to have survived his war also. In both cases, the Americans rolled the dice. He guessed that Frau Munn was some years older than he, the Vietnamese much younger.

Greenwood said, The schnitzel is good.

It's the specialty of the house, Anya said.

So, Greenwood said after a moment, you were fired.

Like that, Willa said, snapping her fingers.

Any explanation?

She laughed through a mouthful of schnitzel. She said, They did not want Ossies in charge. They think we are unsound. They want their own people to manage the accounts and the news also. So one of their song-and-dance men arrived from Hamburg. He was very young. He had never been in Dresden or anywhere in the East. His German was of the guttural Schleswig type. No one could understand him. Some of the technical staff remained, and when one of them tried to sabotage him — a clever prankster, he manipulated the sound levels — he, too, was let go along with the other oldtimers. They said we lacked flexibility. We refused to accept the changing nature of things, by which they meant we refused to accept their authority. They said we lived in the past, and of course that was true. Things were different when our government was running things, I can tell you. There was spirit. There was confidence and pride of craft. There was security —

Yet here you are, the director of television films. Surely a step up.

Yes, Willa said. I was fortunate.

Willa was a director in one of the Dresden theater companies, Anya said.

It was my passion, Willa said. But I liked the news also.

What did you like about it? Greenwood asked.

Willa's eyes glazed a little and her expression softened, as if she were remembering a tender moment from her youth long ago. Its order, she said at last. Its tidiness. Its resolve, I should say.

Coherence, Greenwood said.

Yes, coherence. And predictability. I knew, and my listeners knew, that what I told them was a version of events. The facts were not always in order, and much was deemed beneath notice. But the arrangement did adhere to a certain scheme of things and everyone knew enough to read between the lines. Our citizens did not live in a vacuum after all. They had eyes to see and ears to hear and while not everything was known, nothing was forgotten, either. We believed an editor's responsibility was to edit, to give the news shape and familiarity. People knew where they were because the news was familiar.

Consoling, Greenwood said.

That is correct. The news was consolation.

Because it was censored, Greenwood said.

Wrong word, Willa replied. What is news but a description of action after the fact? The actors and the acted upon. And who is to say which one sits at the head of the table. So the teller of tales has a place of honor also. I would say that the news was shaped, as a piece of clay or a block of granite is shaped to make a sculpture, a mermaid or a heroic general or a bird in flight or, in the event this was news from abroad, from America or Western Europe or the famished nations of the Third World, something like — that! She pointed to the poster above them, a drawing of a grieving woman.

Käthe Kollwitz, Karen said. A very great artist.

She lived in Berlin, Anya said.

Her great subject was the grief of the proletariat, Karen explained.

So we brought order to things, Willa said.

And the Wessies had different ideas for our block of granite, she went on. The Wessies had one view of things and I had another. So I was fired because they wanted a Hummel doll. They didn't want Käthe Kollwitz. Käthe Kollwitz was not in their plans. I took my severance and went back to my theater and in due course I was hired for the Berlin television — and here Willa looked up, her eyes narrowing, as the slender Vietnamese approached with three glasses of beer and a glass of wine, courtesy of Frau Munn, who appreciated their patronage, as usual, such distinguished foreign guests in her humble café —

Danke, Willa said.

No problem, the Vietnamese replied in English, adding a thin smile before he glided off in the direction of the bar.

Where was I? Willa asked.

Fired by the pigs, Karen said.

Hired by Berlin television, Greenwood said.

Yes, the head of production and his assistant came down to Dresden to see my direction of *Mother Courage*. We had an interview, and they hired me that night. You have a name for it in your country. I was the affirmative-action woman. They wanted to demonstrate their Wessie open-mindedness, their open arms. They wanted an Ossie. For the diversity, and also because it would be good for them, too, knowing one. So they chose me. She took a swallow of wine, smiling over the rim of the glass.

Willa had a friend at the station, Anya said.

Yes, that's true, Willa acknowledged. He, too, was born in my little town near the Oder. But his family moved to Berlin when he was a boy. He didn't like the life there, the East Zone. He wanted to be part of the economic miracle. He was a boy who believed in miracles. And one day he went west and found himself in television work, though he never forgot his hometown. We stayed in touch, the way friends do. And when he had an opening, he called and offered a job. The Wall was down, he could do what he liked. By then he was a higher-up and able to make his own decisions. That was when his head of production came to Dresden and we had our interview, a sort of show trial. He pretended to ask me serious questions and I pretended to give him serious answers. That is, I agreed to everything he said. I was grateful for the opportunity to explain myself. We ate very well. We got drunk and went dancing later, the assistant, too. They told me how much I would like Berlin, its worldliness and confidence, how robust it was, how unlike other cities of the West. A strange sensation for me, listening to them. They truly believed that we were one nation again.

One nation, still two peoples, Karen said.

So you can see how fortunate I was to be born in the East. It was only this accident of birth that allowed me to contribute to their diversity.

Tell him about the trouble, Karen said. They are such bastards. No wonder we hated them and their puppet state.

Willa took another sip of wine. She said, They didn't like it that I was a member of the Party. But they brushed it aside. The Party wasn't a serious thing at all to them. It was old news. The Party didn't exist anymore except in the minds of a few sentimentalists, bitter-enders who didn't know or hadn't the imagination to see that the world had turned. When the Wall came down, our state came down with it, and the Party also. Good riddance, now we were free. We were free to be like them.

Schwein, Karen said.

They didn't have anything specific on me, Willa said. I wasn't in the secret police, and if I had informed, they couldn't prove it. They weren't interested anyway. What would you say to an American who had declared allegiance to the Confederacy? You would call him retrograde. You would call him out-of-date. Perhaps you would call him a racist, but you wouldn't take him seriously. What's the word for him? Crank. This was the finding with me. I was the victim of youthful indiscretion, like a case of the clap when you're a schoolgirl. They were very good about it, very understanding, sympathetic even, that we had been manipulated by rascals. But that was over, and now we had the opportunity to be good Germans.

Willa raised her eyes to gaze at the Kollwitz drawing.

So that's what we have, she said, legends and a flag we can't wave and a few hard old men and a few more skinhead romantics who drink too much beer and assault Scandinavian tourists. We did have something of value in our state but it's vanished now. Our leaders they are putting on trial. Our people they patronize. They falsify our history as we falsified their history, but the difference is, we knew we were doing it. And when there's an inconvenient question, a question they want to pretend doesn't exist because they want you for their diversity, they call it youthful indiscretion. We wink at each other during the interview but there is no doubt who is in charge. No doubt whatever. Willa paused, considering something.

She said, I suppose there was some virtue in your Confederacy also.

Southerners thought so, Greenwood said.

Only southerners?

And their northern sympathizers, not very many.

They are bastards, Karen said again. They are brainwashing us.

Some sympathy also in the western states, Greenwood said.

They tell us to leave it behind, our inconveniences. We are supposed to say goodbye to our fifty years, like a friend who has grown too difficult. But you can't erase your memory. You can't forget the place you grew up in; it's your conscience after all. Listen to me, Dixon. You can't forget the hopes you had, that when the system matured . . . Willa shrugged and tried to smile but failed at the attempt.

And even today there are admiring accounts of prewar southern society, Greenwood went on, speaking directly to Willa. Some revision of attitude toward the pastoral life on the plantations, its chivalry, the wholesomeness of the agrarian existence, its leisurely pace and abundance. Its neighborliness. On many plantations the slaves were looked after like members of the family. The family was the center of things, along with Christianity.

Anya looked sharply at him.

As opposed to the haste, aggression, disorder, and injustice of the crowded northern cities, Greenwood concluded.

Lost in thought, Willa was silent.

We had nothing in common with the American South, Karen said indignantly. We were an advanced industrial nation!

That's what the CIA thought, Greenwood said.

I wish I had my news program back, Willa said glumly.

Someday you will, Greenwood said.

But I'm bringing the news to them in my own way with *Wannsee 1899.*

We are all trying, Karen said. And we don't need the approval of your CIA.

Greenwood smiled. In the 1980s, he said, the CIA thought East Germany had a gross national product only slightly less than Great Britain's.

They wanted to destabilize us, Karen said.

The Vietnamese arrived to clear the plates, humming a tune that sounded suspiciously like "The Battle Hymn of the Republic." The table was silent while he went about his business. Everyone ordered coffee, except Karen, who took schnapps.

My husband stayed behind in Dresden, Willa said when the Vietnamese had gone. He refused to move to Berlin, even the East part. He believed that the fascists had infected the city. He thought Kohl and his people were a kind of plague. Move to Berlin, catch the fascist disease. Dresden was his home and he was loyal to it. We lived in his family's cottage in the country. His father lived with us. My husband was adamant. If I wanted to sell my soul, that was my business. Cowardly business, he said. So he stayed put.

Also, she went on, he had his own interests. Football. Dominoes.

He is an enigma, she concluded.

There was a sympathetic murmur around the table. Karen turned her head impatiently, waiting for the Vietnamese to return with her schnapps. Anya was staring thoughtfully at the Kollwitz poster. Again Greenwood thought he had been caught in a time warp, and he had to remind himself that the year was 1999, the millennium almost done, the new era around the corner. He thought that these Germans did not live in the past, the past lived in them.

Dix said, Are your children with him?

Willa replied, We had no children.

I'm sorry, Greenwood began, and then caught himself. Many people were happy without children, Germans especially. He smiled an apology but Willa appeared not to have heard him or, if she had, was indifferent.

I have not seen him in years, she said. I know he was involved with someone and I suppose he still is. Why not? It's logical. Living alone is unnatural. He worked for the post office. He delivered letters. The woman he became involved with delivered letters also. I suppose they're still delivering letters. The fascists did not interfere with the postal service.

Coffee and schnapps arrived. Greenwood noticed that Munn Café was almost empty, with only a murmur of conversation in the outer room. He looked at his watch and saw that the time was past three. The windows were gray with fading afternoon light.

You were never happy with that man, Karen said.

We were together twenty years, Willa said. We were together almost as long as you have been alive, so you are not qualified to say. You should keep your mouth shut. He was an enigma.

He didn't want to leave home, Anya said. That's understandable.

Your marriage was a misalliance, Karen said.

Willa made a dismissive gesture and drank her coffee.

The time had come. Greenwood turned in his chair to call for the bill but the Vietnamese was already at his side, the reckoning in hand. He placed the bill carefully on the table and declared loudly that the service was not included. When Greenwood made no move to examine it, merely put his thumb over the total, the Vietnamese turned his back and walked away.

The schnitzel was good, Greenwood said.

Schnitzel is the specialty, Anya agreed.

Are you serious about traveling in the East? Willa asked.

I'd like to meet your family, yes. The enigma, too.

Forget him. He does not like Americans.

This is normal, Karen said. You should not be offended, Herr Greenwood.

Takes more than that, Greenwood said.

You're interested, Willa said. I can tell.

We can go tomorrow, Karen said.

I will direct you along the Oder, Willa said. There are many fine villages where I have friends and some relatives also. A good inn is nearby. The countryside is very beautiful. I will show you Seelow, the site of the last battle of the war. The Russians won it, of course, but they paid a terrible price. Our army fought like crazy men. One of my uncles was killed there. And my aunt was lost, no one knows how, at the end of the war she was unaccounted for. It's only a plain on the west side of the Oder, the soil is poor but some things can grow. In the spring and summer the Adonis rose blooms, a white rose that grows only there and someplace in Siberia. There are storks' nests also. An unusual place, as you shall see.

Good, Greenwood said. We'll do it.

It's only a few hours' drive, Willa said. It's a very poor region now. There are only a few small farms. And some very large landholdings. When the Wall came down, the Junkers came back into Prussia to reclaim their estates.

We'll need a car, Karen said.

I know one of them, Willa said. I'll introduce you.

I'll rent one, Greenwood said.

He has a wife and six children, all boys, Willa said. They all look alike.

We'll need an early start, Anya said.

He was too young for the war, but his father was involved. Hers too.

Yes, Greenwood said.

He and his wife are helping to rebuild some of the churches of the region.

The peasants are happy about it, Willa added. They miss their churches, the old ones anyhow. The young ones don't care. The young ones want blue jeans and modern music. What does Martin Luther have to say to them?

They will deliver the car to Mommsen House, Karen said.

Willa looked around warily, then lowered her voice as if she were afraid of being overheard. She said, Your film meant so much to us. Some of us went three, four times. We had never seen our country filmed in this way, artists going about their work normally, creating the future. Of course the circumstances were strange. They were unfamiliar to us. We knew nothing of the outside world and how others saw us. So we were naturally defensive. We wrote critical articles but after the articles had been written and the arguments made and debated, the film stayed with us. *Summer, 1921* became part of our lives. I think it became a myth, truth and falsehood woven together in such a way that we could not separate them. So we lived with contradictions. This was a difficult time for us, our socialism did not seem to be working properly. So much was forbidden. The future was so difficult to see that after a while we ceased to think about it. When we saw your film we were excited, believing we were watching something fresh even though the action was taking place in 1921. The Sorb girls were exquisite. Where did you find them? The authorities said that the girls were underage, an example of the decadence of Western capitalism, child prostitution. But we decided you meant to display the vigor and resilience of the proletariat, girls choosing their own path in life. Which is true?

Willa did not wait for an answer but rushed on, deconstructing *Summer, 1921* scene by scene and frames within scenes. She thought that on the whole the boys were less successful than the girls, except Wendt. She thought at first she was seeing a younger brother of Steve McQueen, he had the same spirit and coiled quality. A to-hell-with-you look, even when he was loving Jana. And when he painted he was coiled then, too, and we had the feeling that if anyone had interrupted him, he would have shot them dead and without remorse. They seemed to live outside of time, those six, and that was another thing forbidden to us. We were not permitted to live outside of time. Can you tell me where you found the boys, Wendt specifically? And what happened to him later?

When Greenwood said he didn't know where Wendt was, that Wendt had never made another movie, that he had disappeared somewhere inside North America, Willa shook her head sadly.

His name was Thomas Gwilt, Greenwood said.

Yes, Willa said. I remember. He was a wunderkind.

I suppose he was. He thought so. And the critics did.

Greenwood was accustomed to insincere enthusiasm. In Los Angeles, insincerity was a sacrament, the bread and wine of Industry communions. That was the way people went about things, the intensity varying according to what they wanted and how badly they wanted it. Greenwood listened for the false notes but did not hear them; he wondered if he was tone-deaf to the language of German women. But there was no mistaking Willa's distress. She sat with her face turned away, staring out the dusty window at the gathering darkness.

Then Frau Munn was hovering over them, smiling at each client, her cheeks dimpling, asking if they had enjoyed their meal, what a pleasure it was to have them at her table, and if they would like to see her pictures, she would be honored to fetch the albums, her photographic record of life in Berlin before and during the war, the look of this very district in the spring of 1939 and the fall of 1940 and all the years thereafter until the Red Army arrived —

Yes, of course, Greenwood said.

Please, Anya said.

I must go, Karen said abruptly. I have a fitting.

I will get my albums, Frau Munn said.

Karen gathered her things and thanked Greenwood for lunch. The Vietnamese was attentive, she said. You must leave him a good tip.

In dollars, Greenwood said, but Karen was already striding out the door.

Willa watched her go. When Frau Munn appeared again, bearing three thick leather-bound albums, stacking them on the table, opening the first for their inspection, they leaned in close. Frau Munn began to describe the war years, the difficulty of maintaining the café while Allied bombs were falling. The regulars were loyal but there were fewer each night. All of us were frightened and trying so hard not to show it. Each night we pulled on masks to hide our fears. We wore clowns' faces and the more we drank the crazier we became, singing and dancing as if each night was our last. You never heard such laughter. My café was a favorite of musicians — she turned a page, a girlish Frau Munn with a slender black-haired woman in a tuxedo holding a clarinet — and often after hours we would play swing music, Kurt Weill's songs, "Bilbao Song" and the others. And if someone from the Gestapo came in, the band would switch to a march. But if you listened carefully you could hear syncopation, and the melody just off key. She slowly turned page after page, the musicians yielding to American army officers, officers to civilians, and always in the background attractive, threadbare young women smiling with an irony beyond words, the smiles plastered on their faces like masks.

So we survived, Frau Munn said.

So many nights, she went on, I thought we wouldn't.

The date above your door, Dix said. It reads 1945.

You noticed, Frau Munn said softly, her lisp suddenly pronounced. A new time for Germany, a new time for the café also.

She went away, the albums in her arms appearing as heavy as anvils.

Dix looked at Willa, who put more money on the bill.

I know where the audience has gone, Dixon, she said.

# 9

WILLA DROVE, Dix sat beside her. Anya and Karen were in the rear seat, Karen dozing. Willa was enumerating the name changes of the great boulevard as it ran due east from Berlin to the Oder, and Poland beyond the Oder. The names went by so quickly that Dix could not acquire them except for the last two, Stalin Allee and Karl-Marx-Allee, the last decreed by the authorities after Khrushchev declared Dzugashvili persona non grata in the Soviet experiment. When the Wall came down and East Germany ceased to exist, Karl-Marx-Allee remained; Marx was German after all, long dead and harmless. Dix was watching the street, straight as a ruler and wide as an airplane runway, no coincidence, concrete apartment buildings on either side with an esplanade in the middle, an appalling public space with the aspect of the exercise yard of a penitentiary. Now and then he would find a face at a window, an elderly inhabitant standing motionless, staring into the street watching the traffic and loose paper flying above the gutters and sidewalks. Dix wondered if the apathetic faces at the windows were Willa's audience, the dispossessed and left behind, the ones waiting for the next tick of the clock. The rented black Mercedes was conspicuous among the Trabants and Opels and heavy Man trucks. Willa talked on and on, identifying this building and that, her voice sardonic when she pointed out an installation important to Soviet state security, now derelict behind rusting iron gates. Dix's attention began to wander, then lapse altogether.

Willa was a fast driver. They were quit of Berlin now, hurtling past towns that got smaller each mile, dour clusters of buildings frozen under a dim prewar sun. This Germany was a different nation from the Germany to the west. This one was agrarian, and in its rundown simplicity seemed from another era. Dix had the sense of leaving one Europe for another. This one had more in common with Poland and Russia, the land flat and stubborn, life guided by the heavy hands of the Church or the Party. But he saw no churches nor any evidence of commerce. A nation without offices or factories, and in the towns no markets. They passed a Gypsy caravan by the side of the road and a little farther on an abandoned, looted military barracks behind a thicket of barbed wire. The towns had the look of small towns in the Dakotas, a few old people carrying cloth satchels, and no children at all. The taverns that marked each town square were dark. The squares were very different from those in Britain and France and Dix did not know why, until he noticed the absence of war memorials — a stalwart infantryman or a general on horseback or a simple obelisk with its row of names. Died for King and Country. Mort pour la France. Probably there were memorials to the Soviet dead but they were out of sight. Here and there were barns and houses in disrepair, rusted bits of machinery in the fields. The houses looked inhabited but it was hard to know for sure; there were no specific signs of life. He felt he was watching the opening frames of a film from the 1930s, some German cousin of *The Grapes of Wrath*. What was visible had no obvious narrative and Dix concluded that in this region life flourished behind closed doors or underground or deep in a collective subconscious, at any event out of sight of the casual traveler. The linden trees by the side of the road were stunted but robust against the horizon. The raw fallow fields rolled off the horizon and ended, as if the horizon line marked the limits of the known world.

Welcome to Prussia, Willa said.

Where are the people?

They're around, Willa said.

No children, either.

Children go to school, even in Germany.

Touché, Dix murmured.

You're not seeing the real Prussia, Willa said. The real Prussia is farther north, in old Pomerania and east into Poland. In the north during the winter it's so cold you can hear the trees snap. Look beyond the manmade wreckage to the land itself. It's consoling in its contours, don't you think? It's dramatic in its simplicity. Before the war there were huge forests and game everywhere, boar, bear even. My uncle has wonderful stories of hunting in the forests. People had what they needed despite the feudalism. Our socialism got rid of the feudalism, but something was lost, too.

Ignorance, mostly, Karen snarled from the rear seat.

Anya stirred and rested her chin on the front seatback between Willa and Dix.

Willa said, We are transitional people now.

Provisional, Dix amended, suppressing a smile, wishing that Claire were in the car, listening to Willa's German voice, mesmerizing as it turned, now forward, now back, orbiting like a satellite that would never know rest, each thought undermining the one before. But still the satellite spun. *You are not seeing the real Prussia.* To an inhabitant, the visitor was never seeing the real thing. The real Libertyville lay to the west of Milwaukee Avenue. The real Chicago was Bridgeport or Streeterville. The real New York was either downtown or uptown. The real America was always the heartland, though why Illinois was any more real than Massachusetts was a mystery. In Washington they always spoke of "the country" as if it were apart from themselves, as indeed it was, mostly.

We were only doing our duty, she added.

Anya said, East German socialism harmed the men. The men lost vitality. The state was vital, the men weren't vital. They were bullied. They served the state, not their wives or children, not even themselves. They lost themselves to the state. The more brutal they

) 134 (

became, the weaker. And in due course, the women followed the men. They felt they had no other choice, such was the way of the world. The East German state coarsened everything it touched, and in the end it collapsed in a day.

Willa said grimly, That's the way it seemed in America?

Not only America, Anya said. I knew East German men. My German Idyll research took me to many libraries in the East, various conferences and discussions.

Academics, Willa muttered.

Academics, yes. And writers, lawyers, even Stasi thugs. They liked to keep tabs on me, where I went and who I talked to. From time to time they interrogated me. An interview, they called it. They wanted to know everything I heard. They weren't allowed to travel outside their own country, so you would think they would be interested in the outside world. One is always interested in what is forbidden, isn't that so? But they had no interest, none at all. I began to think of them as narcissists. They were concerned only with themselves, and the security of the regime.

Americans have always hated us, Willa said. Americans are obsessed with what the fascists did to the Jews. Yet when the war ended, the Americans befriended the West and rejected the East, along the usual capitalist lines.

Anya said something in German and Willa said something back, also in German.

The Americans are hypocrites, Karen said. And now I am going to sleep.

Sweet dreams, Anya said.

Tell me more about the men, Dix said.

Foreigners cannot understand, Willa said. Then, in the awkward silence, she cleared her throat. You understand, Dixon. I was not saying an anti-Semitic thing. Anti-Semitism is far from my own mind. I was only pointing out the contradictions in the American position. And not only the American, but the British and French also.

The Americans are the worst, Karen said.

Go back to sleep, Willa said.

The men, Dix prompted.

They're abnormal, Anya said.

They're normal men, Willa said.

They are obsessed with pornography, Anya said loudly.

Normal men, Willa repeated.

Bewitched by sex shops, Anya said.

That is an American obsession, Willa said.

They are incapable of normal sex.

You have been in America too long, Anya. You have been brainwashed.

I was in Berlin when the Wall came down, Anya said. I stayed a week, sharing the enthusiasm. Remember the lines around the block? East German boys come to visit the sex shops near the Zoo station. Boys old enough to be grandfathers, Willa. Busloads of them, and they all stopped at Zoo station because of the sex shops. That was what the West meant to them.

The women were silent a moment as Willa accelerated to pass an overloaded hay wagon, a teenage boy at the reins of two exhausted horses. He covered his face with his arm as they passed, road grit rising in their wake.

Not that I am against pornography myself, Anya put in. In its place it is wholesome.

So, Dix said, searching for a neutral phrase. It sounds like East Germany missed the sexual revolution.

There was no need for the sexual revolution in the Democratic Republic, Willa said.

Anya laughed. The 1917 revolution took care of that.

Men and women got on as they have always gotten on.

Yes, that is true, Anya said. Without sex shops.

The sexual revolution was an American invention, Willa went on. And it was a male thing. It was what the men wanted. Isn't that so, Dixon?

Not in Los Angeles, Dix said.

Anya said, Here is one theory. In the East they looked on the state as their Teutonic father, to be obeyed without question. According to Freud, they would have a subconscious desire to murder the tyrant. But it seems that Freud was misinformed because they didn't want to murder him. They wanted to serve him as a loyal son. The better they served, the more privileges they gained. When I put this thought to one of my academic friends, she said that the East German state reminded her of an American corporation and its destructive paternalism. Fit in or ship out. But there was no place to go, no "out," except jail or a labor camp or degrading rehabilitation, "reeducation" under the supervision of the authorities. In any case, the men gladly accommodated. Could it be that they did not love their mothers?

Freud was a charlatan, Willa said. The Viennese, they were all corrupt. They lived in a pornographic dream world. Hitler was Austrian.

Certainly Freud did not have a place in East Germany, Anya said.

Willa replied in German, sarcastic agreement from the sound of it.

It's my opinion, Anya said.

Academics are unreliable, Willa said.

This one was an honored member of the Party, Anya said smoothly. Speaking off the record, of course.

Poor Germany, Willa said. So misunderstood.

Dix felt himself surrounded by the scent of women so he cracked the window an inch, causing a rush of frigid air, and a complaint from Anya.

Dixon? Willa said. You understand what I meant about the anti-Semitism?

I heard you, Dix said.

It's always uncomfortable, isn't it? It's not a good conversation. One is always misunderstood, these intimate things, events of so many years ago. It is hard to find a language to express our thoughts, our ordinary words and phrases won't do. In every language there are words untranslatable into other languages, "heimat" in German, "añoranza" in Spanish. Buchenwald is a suburb of Weimar, as

Dachau is a suburb of Munich, and Sachsenhausen of Berlin. "Suburb" seems not the word, yet that is what they are, suburban villages that contained concentration camps. We did not cause the events, but we take responsibility for them, and the responsibility includes the chore of finding the language to express the responsibility. Perhaps it is somewhat true, what Anya said, that we have not taken account of the outside world, not that it was forbidden to us, but . . . She sighed heavily, foundering, tapping the steering wheel with her knuckles. She said, I always tried to take account of it in my work, stage business, a remark or gesture, to let them know that we *knew* —

You did? Dix said.

Allegory, Willa said.

Allegories related to the Third Reich?

Certainly, she said.

The West was trying to destroy us, she went on. So naturally there were resentments, surely you can see that.

They motored on. Dix scrutinized the monotonous winter landscape through half-lidded eyes. And still in a corner of his mind he saw the faces at the windows that lined Karl-Marx-Allee, the ones waiting for a clock's tick or a visitor, an audience waiting for the show to begin. When the road entered a copse, the car was suddenly deep shadow. Willa murmured something and Anya laughed softly. Her mouth was only inches from his ear, and he felt her moist breath. They continued back and forth and at length Karen joined in, contributing a rambling anecdote in a sleepy voice. He had the idea they were telling stories of romantic encounters, love gone wrong, love in the afternoon, love lost and found. They were speaking companionably in German, giggling, running into each other's sentences, breathless with amusement. Dix rested his head against the window, closed his eyes, and fell asleep, their voices feathering away into a kind of hum.

He was in a forest, the Mercedes parked somewhere behind him. The light was weak. The women had vanished but he knew they were not far away. He was on a path following hunters into the interior, the only sound the crunch of new snow underfoot. It was bitter cold. Dix was in city clothes and the hunters in loden coats and Tyrolean hats with bright feathers spilling from the band. The hunters were familiar to him but he could not identify them in their heavy clothes through the filtered light.

One of them motioned to him.

Come along, the hunter said. It's only a little farther.

He had been designated an Observer and therefore took careful account of the hunters' tactics, their deliberate approach, the gestures they used, and the weapons they carried, beautifully tooled twelve-gauge shotguns with walnut stocks and leather slings, heirlooms from the look of them. When the lead hunter raised his hand, the others went into a military crouch, cradling their shotguns in their arms. Small birds darted among the trees, and then he heard rustling nearby, the sound reminding him of polite applause. The lead hunter fired unexpectedly and they all got off shots, wildly it seemed to Dix. Faced with unexpected challenge, they were undisciplined. When they rushed forward, he stayed behind to take stock of things. He heard them blundering along the path, their shouts growing fainter, the explosions ceasing. And then he was standing in silence as the light failed and dusk came on. He took a small notebook from his jacket pocket and began making notes, a detailed account of the lapse of discipline, random fire in the distance, men rushing forward without caution. They lacked circumspection. They did not inspire confidence. The leader was hopeless, and then Dix realized he had no idea where he was. He believed he was somewhere beyond the horizon, in the everlasting region with no name or verified history, a place where legends began. There were many such forbidden places in the world, places in books and places in the imagination. He felt himself within a zone of tremendous privacy, and of privilege also to be present where so few had been. He remained a moment longer in a state of enchantment, a city man out of place in a wilderness, but untroubled. He put the notebook away, remembering his responsibilities, the work he had to complete. He heard a noise behind him but ignored it. He believed he was sovereign in this place.

Come along, the voice said.

It's only a little way.

The voice was unpleasant, harsh in the silence of the wood. Still, he was not afraid, owing to his sovereignty and his assignment: Observer. When he turned to search for his car, he was thrown off balance, seized roughly by the shoulder and thrust ahead into the dense underbrush and abandoned once again. In the distance he thought he saw a cabin, a thin ribbon of smoke rising from its chimney. He could smell the woodsmoke but there were no lights inside the dwelling. Round and about he heard the bursts of shotgun fire and then in a clearing near the cabin he observed the quarry, a small black bear, appearing and vanishing almost at once. Dix followed on, shivering, slipping on the hard ground. He wondered if the bear was real or only a phantom, a kind of spirit-bear that would be native to a region where legends began. The bear was so small he believed it harmless, a circus animal or a pet you would give a child. He was alarmed when it arrived at his side, attempting to stand on its hind legs, a leash hanging from its neck. The cabin receded as the hunters returned, stationing themselves in a semicircle facing him and the bear, the animal defiant now and baring its muzzle in a low growl as the hunters unslung their weapons. He thought if he reached the safety of the cabin he and the bear would find protection. He took a step forward and realized then that the hunters were known to him, the stout one, the thin one, the one in the Tyrolean hat, the bald one and the woman who was with him; but his memory would not work and he could not put names to the faces. The bald hunter gestured dismissively, and the woman with him opened her mouth in a soundless laugh. Dix knew then that he was on location; a film was being shot, and as Observer he had no cause for alarm. He and the bear ambled on in the direction of the cabin. The hunters moved aside into the shadows, disappearing, talking among themselves. Their voices were familiar, and still he could not put names to them. He listened to their voices and soft laughter, the ambiance festive again. He wondered if they were having a party. Whatever they were doing, he was not invited to participate. When he opened his mouth to speak, he could not find his voice. The bear waddled off, the cabin vanished into the darkness. He whirled blindly, searching for the path to safety. But there was no path. What he heard was the sound of birds' wings beating furiously.

Almost there, Dixon.

He awoke slowly, stretching his stiff left leg. He placed his palm under his knee, massaging, trying to ease the pain.

You have been asleep one hour.

You must have had a wonderful dream, Willa said. You were smiling.

# 10

WILLA'S AUNT and uncle lived in the stone gatehouse of an estate. A rutted road wound back from the gatehouse to a high barn and up a rise to the main house. The land was heavily forested except around the main house, where it was bare, sloping east to the unseen Oder. The house was plain-faced, a three-story center section with two-story wings on either side and a chapel connected to the west wing. The chapel's rose window was visible from the gatehouse, along with an empty paddock. Willa pointed all this out, adding that the main house and the chapel had been restored from rubble caused by Russian guns in the final offensive, March 1945. Then she turned to greet her aunt and uncle.

Their house was small but comfortable, the walls washed white, a floor of magenta tile, the windows narrow with thick glass to keep out the wind. Even so, the panes rattled against the windy gusts. There was a chess table in one corner, the game in progress, and a schnapps bottle on the windowsill. They had put out the tea things, a china pot and flowered cups, a plate heaped with pastry. Greenwood felt self-conscious entering a strange house in the company of three women, as if he required an entourage to move from place to place. Willa made the introductions in English. Reinhold and Sophie Lenord, these are the friends from Berlin that I spoke about, Dixon Greenwood, Anya Ryan, and Karen Hupp. Karen you know from the show. She's the naughty one. Anya and Dixon are visitors from America, living also at Wannsee. She turned to Dix and said that Reinhold and Sophie were her favorite aunt and uncle. Sophie was her mother's sister, though sadly enough they had not spoken in many years, a family situation.

Everyone shook hands and Reinhold indicated that Dix should sit in the overstuffed armchair next to his own heavy rocker. He was a big man, well over six feet, with a thick cloud of white hair and pale gray eyes behind wire-rimmed spectacles that looked too small for his face. But it was not the hair or eyes that commanded Dix's attention but the steady tremor in his heavy hands. When he bent to stir the fire, the iron poker rattled against the grate. Dix guessed that he was in his early seventies, though he might have been ten years older or younger. He had the vitality of a much younger man except for the tremor. He and his wife appeared very fit, athletic in ski sweaters and corduroy trousers.

Are you comfortable, Herr Greenwood?

Ja. Herr Greenwood was comfortable.

Willa was talking to her aunt, Karen to Reinhold, confidential German business from the sound of it. Dix gazed at the schnapps bottle, so near and yet so far. All his life he had avoided meals with strangers, an invitation to small talk and insincerity unless a raconteur took charge. He remembered visiting Ireland as a young man, the summer following his graduation from college, one of the first journeys he made with his father. They fetched up somewhere in the west of Ireland, visiting Harry's Anglo-Irish friends. The house in Ireland was much larger than this one but equally dark, everyone suspicious. The food came in small portions and the wine was poured into tiny glasses, to the obvious distress of Harry Greenwood, who complained about it later and then blamed himself for not bringing a house present, two magnums minimum. These were friends who had fallen on hard times, struggling to maintain their estate in the socialist era of confiscatory taxes and reduced incomes. They were nine at table. Dix remembered the worn carpets and forty-watt bulbs in the lamps and the bare places on the walls where the pictures had been taken down for auction. Even the English setter looked malnourished. Yet the landscape was lovely, the gardens well tended and the lawns mowed; perhaps there was a little less lawn each year. A gray sliver of the River Shannon was visible through the flowering rhododendron. Everyone made an effort. One of the women wore a long velvet dress, the velvet worn at the sleeves and seat. But she had an emerald at her throat and diamonds on her fingers. The men wore well-cut tweed jackets from their auspicious youth. He remembered the general air of pinched embarrassment, people making do with too little (or less than they thought they were owed), leading to resentment of Americans, people who had too much for their own good and certainly much, much more than they deserved; and there had been a recent Washington indignity, he had forgotten which one, and they had gone after Harry, demanding explanations. Harry remained good-humored, then began to tell stories of Europe before the war, the time they walked from Montmartre to Montparnasse and greeted the dawn in the Luxembourg Gardens and that movie actress happened by and joined them — it was Hedy Lamarr, wasn't it, Nigel? And Nigel's look of perfect bafflement as his wife laughed and laughed. Yes, it was Hedy Lamarr wearing a mink coat and we all walked over to Le Sélect for a corrected coffee, and a day later we left for Scotland and the final round of the British Open — when was that, Nige? 'Thirty-seven? 'Thirty-eight? — and other stories of those years, remembered in retrospect as brilliant though at the time there were shadows in every doorway, and all the late-night conversations ended with speculations concerning the coming war. Harry Greenwood was superb that night, leaving the company loose, disheveled, laughing; for those few hours they all looked twenty years younger. And when he began to tell the story of F. Scott Fitzgerald on the *Normandie,* Nigel sighed and left the table for the cellar, returning with a dusty bottle of claret, avoiding the look in his wife's eyes. Dix remembered that it was still light when they rose from table, everyone hilarious. The lawn was painted a luminous brilliant orange by the setting sun, and they all stood at the window admiring it. Harry recalled other dawns in other countries, making each dawn a kind of fiesta.

Then one of the tweed jackets turned to Harry and said, In Berlin at the end of the war, weren't you, Greenwood?

Briefly, Harry said.

You were an interrogator, I believe. We never met. I was in another department. We did the evaluations in my department and I must say you were a bit of a puzzle to us. You let them off pretty easy, is what we thought.

I had the mechanics. So I talked to them about the machine.

And got damn-all.

Got plenty, Harry said evenly. You weren't reading carefully.

They were war criminals.

Some were, some weren't. Most of mine weren't. My mechanics were — mechanics.

Yes, we could see that from your reports. What did you call them? Your "auditions."

That's what I called them because that's what they were.

Filthy Nazis, "auditioning."

Not all were Nazis, either.

We thought you had — rather a soft spot.

Come along now, Nigel said, herding everyone onto the porch to look at the sunset. He began to describe the various landmarks, an ancient oak here, a stone wall there, and the Shannon glittering in the distance.

Harry said, The soft spots were in your department.

No need to take offense, old boy.

But I do, Harry said. And if you'd read the dossiers closely, you would understand why. Now apologize.

But the man didn't apologize. He turned to Nigel's wife and thanked her for a pleasant evening and went away, Harry watching him all the while. Dix noticed his father's fists clenched at his side. The others were talking skittishly, and at length his father joined in, but after a few moments made his goodbyes, and he and Dix returned to their car. When Dix asked Harry what *that* had been about, Harry shook his head in irritation. People refuse to recognize complexity, he said. What's shame in one man is grief in another, and they are not the same thing. What's pig-stupidity in one man is cowardice in another and blind evil in a third, and they are not the same thing, either. You'd think that would be simple enough to understand but it's not, not at all simple.

Dix came back from his reverie. The voices around him were gruff, Willa describing the murderous traffic leaving Berlin and when will you visit us next, Reinhold? Sophie, you must insist, it's been months now and the city changes each day, the construction you cannot imagine, our Potsdamer Platz a thing of skyscrapers and streets without traffic, shops, restaurants, and all the architects are foreigners . . .

Berlin has always been a city of riffraff, Reinhold said.

We must be tolerant, Sophie said.

Riffraff and bankers, Reinhold said.

Shall we have our tea? Sophie offered.

When the tea business was concluded, everyone balancing cups and pastry on their knees and laps, grumbling about conditions in Berlin, Willa explained that her aunt and uncle were retired. They were pensioners but stayed active and involved, managing the estate for the absentee landlords. They were great hunters. They were hikers also, getting about everywhere on foot.

They had a lively interest in the outside world, Willa went on. They were particularly eager to talk to Americans. They had never met one, yet Americans seemed to be part of their lives, the air they breathed, present everywhere and visible nowhere, like the Christian God of Martin Luther, ha-ha-ha. They see more of Texas and California than they do of Austria or even Poland. It's a big change for them, America in their living room at night. England, too, sometimes.

We have a dish, Reinhold said.

Willa got it for us in Berlin, Sophie said.

Before, we lived apart, she added. We occupied this little space at the bend of the Oder. We had few visitors. Who would visit this little village? And we were content ourselves, living apart. And then Willa gave us *that*. She pointed at the television in the corner and everyone dutifully looked at it. All of this was going on under our noses, Sophie said. We didn't know a thing about it.

Entertainment, Reinhold explained.

From everywhere, Sophie said.

Mostly from America, Reinhold put in.

We traded one propaganda for another, Sophie said with a smile. We traded governments. We traded armies. We traded cars also, our Trabant for a Volkswagen. Filthy car, the Trabant. Is it true that in the West they are buying them as souvenirs? Kitsch? Never mind, I know it's true. I heard about it on the evening news, they showed a Trabant in Paris! Reinhold, I told you we should have gotten a better price for our Trabant. But how were we to know? On the whole, she said after a moment's pause, we prefer your propaganda. It's much more . . . She sought the word.

Entertaining, Reinhold said. He rose to stir the fire once again, the poker rattling against the grate. When he finished, the embers were glowing with a fine orange flame. He stood looking at the fire, the poker nervous in his right hand. He said, Do you watch television much, Herr Greenwood?

A little, Greenwood said.

We don't watch too much, he said. Sophie and I, we play cards after dinner, drink a little beer, sometimes read a book aloud or play chess. But when it's there, you turn it on and find yourself watching whether you want to or not. He gave a little mirthless laugh. Much of what we see on television seems to us a capitalist fantasy, a world we know nothing about. As Sophie said, we live apart. I don't have a way to judge a world where people buy cars for souvenirs. But we looked up one day and there we were, a part of the audience, no different than if we lived in Rome or Cleveland. The first day we turned it on we saw blond girls on a sandy beach in southern California, can you imagine? I tried very hard to feel part of the audience, to think of myself as one of millions of Europeans watching the girls on the beach, a community after all, but it was difficult, and for Sophie, too. We have never been outside Germany. We have only been one time to Berlin!

Sophie said, We went to see Willa last year, to watch the filming of an episode of *Wannsee*. You were not present, Karen. But your lover Karl was there.

He is not my lover, Karen said.

He isn't?

In the script, Karen said. In the script only.

He is very handsome, Sophie said.

He is an oaf, Karen replied.

What a shame, Sophie said.

It's an interesting program, Reinhold said loyally.

Yes, authentic, Sophie said. Everyone in Germany watches it.

Greenwood felt a movement behind him and turned to see a slender girl standing in the kitchen doorway. Her orange hair was spiked and she glittered with colored glass, rings on her fingers and sewn on her blouse, hanging from her earlobes and screwed into her nostrils, and one also pressed into her cheek, a glass dimple. She stood swaying from side to side as if she were listening to music, and then Greenwood saw the headphones and cord that ran from her left ear to a device on her hip. She wore a perfectly blank expression, her eyelids half shut. She was barefoot. Her clothes — a white blouse and a knee-length skirt — looked as fallible as a lace handkerchief.

This is Ingeborg, Reinhold said.

Greenwood nodded and rose from his chair but the girl did not move or make any sign of recognition.

Our granddaughter, Sophie said. She lives with us.

Hello, Ingeborg, Willa said without enthusiasm.

She is tired, Sophie said. She was late last night, out with friends.

Our son and his wife, Reinhold began, but did not finish the sentence.

Young people, Sophie said by way of explanation.

In the strained silence that followed, Ingeborg turned her back and glided from the room. A minute later it seemed that she had never existed. Sophie poured more tea and passed the pastry plate.

Things were as they had been, the atmosphere normal. Dix cleared his throat and said, So you feel part of the audience, watching *Wannsee 1899*?

I suppose we do, Reinhold said. He thought a moment, then shook his head, neither yes nor no; perhaps yes and no. Greenwood, watching him carefully, believed Reinhold's idea of community extended to the boundaries of the former GDR. It evidently did not extend to the remarkable girl in the kitchen doorway. Reinhold said at last, Do they watch it in America?

It's not available in America, Greenwood said. Maybe one day, from the satellite. I'm not sure *Wannsee 1899* will travel. It's very German.

The blond girls in southern California travel, Reinhold said indignantly. They are traveling everywhere, to India and Belgium, Belarus, I suppose. The difference is, they are American, isn't that correct?

Call it *Wannsee 1999* and put Karen in a bikini, Dix said. It might work.

That is foolish, Karen said.

Is it because it is German that it cannot attract the worldwide audience? Reinhold asked. Beethoven was German, Bach was German. Cranach, Dürer, Kant, Heisenberg, Steffi Graf is German. I suppose you will tell me now that the world is an American suburb and southern California the world's sandy beach. All right, America is the world's culture —

Low culture, Karen put in.

— and everyone is interested in America, how things work, how people behave, and so on. What they wear, I suppose. What they eat and how they eat it. There is no thing in America too small to be beneath notice. The underwear, the activities of leisure, even the erotic adventures of your president. The other night I saw a hockey game, and still I cannot quite believe. I do not think the American programs are genuine.

They're not, Greenwood said. It's only television. It's entertainment.

Dreck, Karen said. Escapism.

No kidding, Greenwood said.

America owns television, Reinhold said glumly. Television is the world's culture.

We make an effort to keep *Wannsee 1899* authentic, Willa said. Within limits, she added slyly, grinning, her mouth full of pastry. Our customs, the furnishings, the music and the dancing, the way people talk to each other. Anya is our adviser on these matters. Do the American programs have advisers? Historians, social scientists, people familiar with the period?

I have no idea, Greenwood said.

Doubtful, Anya said.

Mafia programs have wiseguys on the payroll, Greenwood said, suddenly beginning to enjoy himself.

Is this so, Anya? Sophie asked. You come all the way from America?

Arizona, Anya said.

Wouldn't a German do just as well? Reinhold leaned forward, staring at Willa.

Anya was born in Germany, Willa said. She was born in the DDR and went west with her family. She is an expert of the period.

The German Idyll, Anya said.

Reinhold shook his head and grumbled, Retrograde.

Conservative in nature, Anya said.

Submissive, Reinhold said. Women submissive to men, the proletariat submissive to the capitalists. Paupers ruled by princes, a politics supervised by the lackey Martin Luther, who supported the class structure and thought it unwise to challenge the natural order whereby the poor supported the rich and were honored to do so. And they call it the German Idyll. That's where the fascists came from.

Thomas Mann also, Anya murmured.

But Reinhold did not hear. He rose heavily from his chair and went to the window that afforded the view of the Oder and unfortunate Poland beyond. The sky lightened and now flurries appeared, hard little flakes that swirled in the gray air. He said slowly, My grandfather was part of that world as it was coming to an end, dying of exhaustion, so many internal contradictions. He was a cavalry officer who went on to manage an estate in Pomerania. The owners spent most of their time in Berlin, and in Italy on holidays. When in Berlin they lived in an apartment in Charlottenburg. They were friendly with the king. They returned to Pomerania in the summer and stayed on for the fall harvest, working the fields alongside the farmhands. There was a death and a divorce and one thing and another, the war, the Depression, the second war, illness. In the second war the estate was lost behind the lines and the Red Army destroyed it, down to the last brick. As a child I remember my grandfather talking about the parties they had, everyone on horseback during the day and in evening dress at night. They were great sportsmen. The aristos were a hard bunch, played hard, worked less hard. And not one of the family survived the war. Not one. Naturally they fought with the fascists. What would you expect? The Reich was their life, it didn't matter which one, First, Second, or Third. The family dated from the Teutonic Knights, always at least one son an army officer. For eight hundred years they had one son in the army, and then the family was extinguished and their land donated to the people. The authorities turned it into a collective farm, and last I heard it had been carved up and the land redistributed. The soil is poor. The farm was not a success.

There was corruption, Sophie said.

No more than in other states, Karen observed.

My grandfather was a casualty, too, Reinhold went on. When they burned the house, they burned him, thinking he was one of the family. A natural mistake. He had the bearing of a cavalry officer, even as an old man in his eighties, handlebar mustache, six feet tall, not an ounce of fat on him. He was a marksman. In the evenings he smoked a clay pipe, just like the cavalry officers in Fontane's novels. They burned him at the *stake*, Herr Greenwood. Reinhold turned from the window, opening his mouth to say something more, then decided against it.

How did you hear of his last days? Greenwood asked.

A friend, Reinhold said.

One of the farmhands, Sophie explained.

A witness, Reinhold said.

The last year of the war was terrible, you can't imagine it, Sophie said. The worst winter in a hundred years, no food, no heat, burning and bloodshed, rape, and not only in Pomerania. Here in our small village also. No one knew of us, no one cared. Who were we? The winter went on forever. The last battle of our war was fought just over that ridge. She pointed out the window to the low lines of hills and the river just visible beyond. They fought for days and days as if the future hung in the balance, but the future was already decided. I can't imagine what they were thinking. No one retreated, but when the lines finally broke they came right through the village, first our army, then the Red Army.

They weren't thinking anything, Reinhold said.

They were animals, Sophie said.

Enough of that, Reinhold said. Our guests have heard enough.

He gave the fire a last nudge and walked to the hall closet, bringing out heavy coats and scarves, laying them in a bundle on the chair near the door. He added a pile of woolen mittens and ski caps.

He said, The sun is out. We will take a walk now.

# 11

GREENWOOD walked with Reinhold down the path to the road, where they waited for the women. Reinhold had slung a twelve-gauge shotgun over his shoulder. They stood facing the gatehouse, the barn and the main house high in the distance. Reinhold was saying something about the village, its population and agriculture, its history and economy. Greenwood was half listening, and when his eye strayed to an upstairs window he saw Ingeborg glittering in the sun, her glass ornaments dancing with light; she looked like a princess in a fairy tale. She leaned against the windowpane and stared into the middle distance, swaying to some mysterious rhythm. When the sun's rays flooded the window she seemed to burst into fire, and then a cloud intervened and she became only a troubled girl staring into the desolate landscape, her grandfather and a stranger in her line of sight. She slowly lifted her fingers to her mouth and drew deeply on a cigarette, smoke spilling from her mouth like steam from a cauldron.

There is no work for her, Reinhold said.

Does she want to work?

No, Reinhold admitted.

Isn't it difficult? So much unemployment —

She doesn't know how, Reinhold said. None of them do.

She's waiting for us to leave, he added bitterly. Then she may leave also, without making false explanations to me as to where she is going and who she is going with. What her plans are, and when she will be home.

Teenagers, Dixon said.

Ingeborg is twenty-four, Reinhold answered. He turned abruptly and set off down the road at a brisk pace, the women strolling far behind, Willa and Anya in heavy coats, Karen and Sophie in sweaters. They all wore bright scarves and ski hats. In short order, Reinhold turned off the road and onto a cart path. He increased the pace until Dix, leaning heavily on his cane, began to lag. The land fell away from the path in a gentle slope. Here and there were the buildings of working farms, small holdings from the look of them, the fields carelessly cultivated. To love this terrain would take a stubborn pride, along with the knowledge of the bones of your ancestors underfoot. Dix looked for some variation in the landscape, and began then to wonder about the effect of terrain on human personality. Did vast distances, brutal sun, and the monotonous contours of sand account for the sublime hospitality of the desert Arabs? This land would induce stoicism, a steely patience and resolve. Perhaps also a feeling of undeserved inferiority. Dix thought of his own upbringing in the country north of Chicago, the rambling house on three acres of land, the lake nearby, huge oak trees flanking the driveway, some of them two hundred years old and more. They were flourishing when Lincoln was a boy. Of course he found the physical surroundings consoling; it was the people who were monotonous, so as soon as he could flee, he fled. He believed the North Shore simple arithmetic when he craved higher mathematics, and only later did he understand that much was concealed behind the closed doors and complacent conversations. The abundance of material things seemed to make nature dispassionate, but that was before he learned to listen carefully, especially to girls who danced barefoot under a summer moon. So much for believing what was in front of your own eyes, and that held true for this wasteland in eastern Germany, frozen under its prewar sun, remarkable only as the scene of the last battle of the Third Reich. What he saw now was anonymous farmland reputed to conceal the bones of a hundred thousand infantrymen, Germans here, Russians there, all far from home. Eyesight yielded only so much. All the rest was imagination if you were a stranger, and memory if you were not.

This was beautiful country for filming, though. You would be able to suggest the ghosts rising from the earth, beginning with Attila and later the Teutonic Knights and shuffling forward to the last months of the Second World War. A director would be tempted to film in black and white but that would be a mistake. Film in color, but mute the colors so that the audience would be unable to identify them exactly. A film of straight lines including the human forms, women especially. Dix watched a farmer emerge from his barn, look at the sky, and walk back inside again. He seemed to move with a suspicious lightness of step and Dix wondered what was going on inside the barn. He had come to a rise in the path and now could see the Oder, old and slow-moving, circling the hills as a belt circles a belly. The color of the river was gray and the fields beyond were light brown, with drifts of gray snow in the shady spots. The washed-out sky was empty except for a lid of clouds to the east, Poland under cover once again.

So, what do you think? Reinhold was sitting on a bench at the base of a tree stump smoking a briar pipe. The women were behind them, gathered around Sophie, who was pointing at something on the horizon.

Greenwood said, I was wondering how it would film. The shape of the land, the colors, the aura of it.

You are thinking of filming here?

No, Greenwood said. But it's my business. It's what I do. I look at things and wonder how they would film.

An unusual landscape, Reinhold said. And it has a soul.

That's what makes it interesting.

It has a history, Reinhold said.

I know it does.

The Russians were just there, he said, pointing vaguely in the direction of the river. One million men in Zhukov's army and another million under Konev, and as many more on the way. We could not kill them fast enough. They came on and on from everywhere in the Soviet Union. Some of them looked like animals, mixed Slav and Asian blood. Probably some of them had Genghis Khan's blood, Tamerlane's blood, even Attila and the murderer Alexander. Millions swarming from the steppes of Russia and beyond, well equipped, well fed, brutal men nourished by centuries of resentment and blood lust. Against them we had old men and boys too young to have hair on their nuts. And their casualties were twice ours. In the official version we were the ones who took casualties. In the official version the Wehrmacht was outfought and outgeneraled. They taught us the official version for fifty years. The Red Army liberated us from the fascists and millions died. Even so, the Americans arranged a sanctuary in the West, and in due course the Americans had both an atomic bomb and a spy network, thanks to the fascists. And I should know. That was the history I taught. Seelow, it was called. The Battle of Seelow.

Reinhold's voice had risen but now he looked off into the woods, gesturing wearily.

Our boys fought like tigers. They knew the war was lost and still they fought. They fought until they ran out of ammunition or were overwhelmed. They were overwhelmed by the Dark Ages. They looked up from their trenches and saw the tenth century come to life once again.

My wife is out there somewhere.

She went off one morning and never returned. She was searching for food. A neighbor saw her on the road and next she entered the forest and that was the last anyone saw of her. After the war, I met Sophie and we married.

My brother, too, out there somewhere. You can replace a wife but not a brother.

My brother was just fifteen. They came for him one afternoon, boys barely older than he was. They had a sergeant with them but the sergeant was useless, shell-shocked and incoherent. They gave my brother a uniform that was too small for him and a choice of weapons. He chose a SIG 710. That's a machine gun with a barley-corn sight and a tripod. It weighed more than ten kilos. My brother could barely lift it but he accepted the responsibility. They gave him instruction in our back yard while the sergeant looked on, talking nonsense. They were a dozen or more deciding that they could halt the Red Army. You know boys, they wanted to do what their fathers and brothers had done. Now it was their turn to save the Reich. We could hear the explosions and see the smoke in the east. When they were satisfied that my brother knew how to aim and fire, they marched away. But not before shooting the useless sergeant. We never saw my brother again, and in the horror and confusion of those last days, we knew we would never discover what happened, where he died and in what circumstances. I am sure he fought well.

But they did not take you, Dix said.

I was not at home.

And that was the history you taught, Dix said.

I taught what followed the war, Reinhold said. That was what high school students needed to know. I taught for twenty years, and then I was able to join the administration, where Sophie was. We in the administration took care of one another.

Reinhold continued to gaze east as he talked, and it was hard for Dix to know how much Reinhold believed of what he had said. He seemed to be speaking with irony. He was silent for a moment and then he laughed. I taught school during the day and listened to Willa in the evening. Willa and her news. She spoke softly over the air and the effect was like a German lullaby, carrying us off into Traumland, nothing to fear in the night, Comrade Honecker was in charge, defeating the enemy within. Why are you here really, Herr Greenwood?

Walking with you, Dix said.

I mean, in our Germany.

I know what you mean. I'm visiting. I'm a tourist.

No one tours East Germany.

I was asked, so I came.

You should go where the other Americans go, Munich, the Black Forest, Heidelberg.

I have an interest in difficult regions, Dix said. And if I had not come with you today, I would know nothing of the last days of the war, and your brother's death, and your wife's.

Stand still, Reinhold said suddenly. He unslung the shotgun from his shoulder and stood holding it in both hands like an ax, peering down the hedgerow to the forest. The light was so pale it was hard to tell where the ragged hedgerow ended and the forest began; an unmarked borderland, Dix thought. Reinhold raised his chin and narrowed his eyes, his rabbit nose beginning to twitch. He moved off lightly down the hedgerow, motioning for Greenwood to follow, and follow quietly. The ground was hard underfoot as they stepped over roots and broken branches, here and there small holes that the night animals made. The slope was steeper than it looked and Greenwood stepped clumsily, leaning on his cane, trying to avoid the roots and the animal holes. On both sides of the hedgerow the field looked to be indifferently tended, the furrows uneven and filled with small white rocks so soft they disintegrated when Greenwood stepped on them. Ragged pieces of iron had leached to the surface among the rocks. In one place the furrows ended, as if the farmer had become exhausted or bored by the chore and had simply abandoned it for another day or not at all. Dix could hear Reinhold's breathing, and then the German halted, his head cocked to one side, listening, kneeling with his hand at his ear.

Can you smell him?

No, Greenwood said. Who?

Animal, Reinhold said. Boar, I think. Listen.

A heavy rustle in the treeline thirty yards ahead caused Greenwood to start, then freeze where he stood.

Strange, Reinhold said. His voice was hoarse, barely a whisper. They do not usually show themselves. He sighted along his shotgun, then lowered it, and when next he spoke his words sounded memorized, as if he had last uttered them at a lectern or in front of a blackboard. He said, They are discreet as politicians, our boar. They believe in mystery and power concealed. They make noise but they do not move unless forced. They live in the deep forest and have no cause to leave, everything they need is within range. Because they are seldom seen, they have become the matter of myth, like wood spirits. Old, old beasts, you can find their forms on the walls of European caves thousands of years old, the snout and the tusks unmistakable. They have not evolved, you see. Instinct and form, unchanged. They are fast, fast as a horse, and strong as a bull. An excellent sense of smell. They guide themselves by smell. And they are irascible and impatient. The meat of the boar's head is a delicacy, tremendously succulent. This one is close by. He is disturbed, watching us with his bad eyesight and smelling us also, our stink. We have invaded his domain, and that he cannot allow. So he is making up his mind. What is to be done?

Let's leave him to it, Greenwood said.

No, Reinhold said. What we start, we finish.

I can *smell* him, Reinhold added.

And Greenwood could, too, a rich scent of musk and dirt, a kind of wormy breath from the grave; if corruption had an odor, this would be it. The rustling ceased and what they heard now was the thin breeze riffling the brittle branches of the oaks and lindens of the forest. The birds returned, fat black crows common to woodlands everywhere. Reinhold moved his shoulders and began to advance one step at a time, angling away from the hedgerow and into the uneven furrows of the field. He seemed to want a clear line of fire and now snapped the shotgun off safe and waited, his briar pipe — cold these many minutes — clicking between his teeth, wagging up and down like a semaphore flag. The boar's odor thickened but the beast himself remained invisible. The crows were settled in the tops of the trees and now began to call each to each, spectators signaling that intruders were near.

Show yourself, Reinhold said.

We should let him be, Greenwood said.

One of the legends, Reinhold said. Earth had been taken prisoner by a demon at the bottom of the sea. One of the gods took the form of a boar forty miles wide and four thousand miles long. He dove to the seabed and rescued Earth and brought her to the surface cradled in his left arm. He was venerated thereafter.

Boars have always been associated with the otherworld, Reinhold added.

He appeared indecisive, moving his head this way and that as if determining the direction of the wind. Then he was suddenly at the edge of the forest and sliding between the trees, moving with the agility of an infantry scout. In seconds he was lost to view, swallowed up without a backward glance or a word of explanation. Greenwood looked back up the hill and saw the women gathered in a little cluster. Something in their postures — they were standing close together, their heads drawn forward as they watched the drama below — reminded Greenwood of wives awaiting the return of their men from the front, and then something else that suggested widows, because they were standing on ground that had been soaked with blood. Bones and iron had leached to the surface, residue of the great spring offensive of 1945. This field was a giant ossuary disguised as a simple farm. No wonder the plowman had given it up, stopped where he was and returned to wherever he had come from. Greenwood moved his foot and dislodged a twisted piece of brass and what looked like the remains of a leather belt. Willa gave a desultory wave, then turned to say something to the others. Greenwood could hear Karen Hupp's mocking laughter drift down the hillside, mixed with the cries of birds, now scattering in ragged flight. When he heard a low whistle, he knew that Reinhold had found his prey.

Greenwood trudged down the slope and entered the forest, feeling the damp at once. The interior was dark and the boar's stench overpowering. He stepped cautiously, deeply uneasy. He was conscious of his foreign status; he was unaware of the boar's mythic stature. He had no business in this forest. The closeness suggested the claustrophobia of the ancient caves with the drawings of bison and boar and naked hunters with spears, some otherworld concealed from outsiders. Then he noticed the remains of a fire in a shallow trench, and next to the embers, a rusted bayonet.

The German was standing under a fat linden, his shotgun resting against his thigh. He was trying unsuccessfully to light his pipe, all the while keeping his eyes on the thornbushes directly ahead of him.

He's in there, Reinhold said.

I don't see him, Greenwood said.

He's there. He's hurt.

I still don't see him, Greenwood said, and as he said it the thornbush moved, parted like the curtain on a stage. The boar's snout appeared, twitching, then settled almost delicately to the ground. He observed the arched tusks, ragged with long use, and the dull eyes and pointed ears, the great hump rising back of his head. The beast seemed spent and incurious; a bored audience, Greenwood thought. An unpredictable audience, preoccupied with its own wounds and fevers, its long day of combat, its many enemies, its need for food. But when he stirred, the bristles of his pelt flared in irritation. The pelt was matted and the bristles looked as tough as bone. A bad audience.

Hundred fifty kilos, Reinhold said. More maybe.

Greenwood nodded. The boar was breathing heavily, glaring at them, trying to gather himself and failing.

Too old, Reinhold said.

For what?

For anything. No good for eating. Too old to be of use. Diseased, probably, or a wound that has not healed. Someone got to him first, there are good hunters in this district. We enjoy the chase. Not so many boar now, though. Not like before the war when there were herds of them, sporting men arriving from all over for a beat through the forest. Army generals, capitalists from Frankfurt and Munich. The head was the prize. Look here, Reinhold said, pointing. Blood spoor. Gut shot, I suppose. Herr Boar is done for, his days in the forest are ended. God knows how long he has lived here, perhaps forty, fifty years. Perhaps he was here the day the Russians invaded. Possibly he watched from his lair, a young boar full of fight and cunning. But his speed and strength did not count against artillery and mortars and bombs from the air. He was terrified, no doubt. So he took care, concealing himself. Retreating farther into the hills and ravines, waiting for the combat to end, then feasting on what remained. The war would be a puzzle to him, would it not? Invading his domain, the place where he ruled. And you would say this is logical; primitive animals can never defeat advanced arms and modern infantry and aircraft. Nevertheless he is alive and all the others who fought him are dead. It's very droll, no?

Reinhold backed away from the linden and picked up the rusted bayonet, hefting it in his palm. He spun it underhand at the boar. It bit the ground and stuck, quivering, a few inches from the beast's snout. Reinhold laughed loudly, watching the bayonet sway like a metronome, then come to rest.

A souvenir, he said. A souvenir of the war he avoided so successfully. And living to a fine old age, roaming the forests of the Fatherland.

So, Reinhold concluded, now we can go.

And leave him?

Why not? Reinhold said.

Greenwood said, I thought you finished what you started.

Reinhold smiled unpleasantly. I didn't start it. He started it.

It's his forest, Greenwood said.

He's dying, Reinhold said.

But not dead.

A sentimental approach, Reinhold said. I did not judge you a sentimentalist.

What are you afraid of?

Afraid?

It's only an animal.

You finish him, then. Reinhold handed him the shotgun.

You're the hunter, Greenwood said, handing it back.

You feel sorry for our boar, Reinhold said.

As you say, he's dying.

So we kill him. That's what you want?

He's in pain, Greenwood said. And as if to confirm that, the boar grunted, raising his huge head, continuing to glare. The light was going now and it was difficult to make out the shape of the body in the bush. The hump had disappeared into the thornbush, and it was easy to imagine a mighty animal, an ur-boar, survivor of the murderous century, and dying now as the century ended.

Look at him, Reinhold said. What sort of nervous system do you think he has? Our boar feels no pain, only anger. Revenge. If he could attack, he would. He has lived by his wits for a very long time. Let him die in his own time.

And how long will that be?

How would I know? Two hours? Two days?

And still dangerous, Greenwood said.

Not anymore.

And still in pain.

Reinhold made a dismissive motion with the barrel of his shotgun.

The boar moved his head again. His haunches trembled, then lay still. Reinhold was busy filling and lighting his pipe, the flame dancing from the tremor in Reinhold's fingers; and suddenly Dix knew that Reinhold was one of the infantry holding the line at Seelow, his frenzied retreat from the Oder earning the usual reward, shell shock. The cloying odor of tobacco mingled with the boar's rancid scent. The beast appeared benign, as harmless as a cave drawing. Reinhold was the dangerous one, cradling the shotgun, breaking it and removing the cartridges, fumbling them, muttering all the while. When he snapped the breech shut and stood with it at port arms, Dix was reminded of the eerie photograph of Lee Harvey Oswald in the back yard of the apartment house on Neely Street in Dallas. Reinhold's expression was as unreadable as Oswald's but the weapons were equally lethal. Dix took a step backward.

I allow them to live, Reinhold said.

Even wounded?

Wounded most of all, Reinhold said.

Give me the gun.

With pleasure, Reinhold said. I doubt if you can do it.

Dix accepted the shotgun along with the two cartridges. He broke the gun, inserted the cartridges, and moved toward the thornbush.

Aim for the heart, Reinhold said. The shoulder. A head shot doesn't work so well because our boar's brains aren't so well developed. For Herr Boar, the brain is a numb muscle. So you want to avoid the brain and aim for the heart. The heart is the engine. Our boar is the one the poet had in mind when he said, Fate determines character.

Dix looked at him.

So you see, Herr Greenwood, our beast is not so easy to kill. No doubt he can smell your fear. Mine, too. It gives him confidence, the smell of fear. So get close, you don't want to have to take a second shot.

He heard Reinhold walking away and in a moment he was gone and the tobacco smoke with him. The forest was silent, the birds vanished, the beast quiet, though continuing to settle. Close up, Dix was able to observe the animal's great bulk, its yellow tusks and scarred pelt. He had never seen an animal so large, with such — he supposed the word was "potential." The last time he had fired a shotgun he and his father had gone with friends to the Chesapeake. They had waited from daybreak for a duck but had seen nothing; and, at last ready to quit, his father had taken a passing shot at a mallard and crippled it. The bird flew away in a stutter, falling, then rising, finally settling in the middle of the cove. With a discouraged sigh, Harry had launched the dory and rowed to the place he thought the bird was. But the mallard had disappeared, scauped or swam away or flew into the rising sun. The old man paddled about for fifteen minutes, returning to the blind in a foul humor. He hated to leave anything crippled. Against the rules, he said. Against the *code*. So he unscrewed the thermos and they sat for another half-hour, drinking vodka and hot bouillon and admiring the sunrise, waiting for the crippled duck to return for the coup de grâce.

Dix turned the gun this way and that, looking for the safety catch. When he found it, he eased it back. He had never enjoyed using firearms. He liked the aesthetics of the hunt, rising always before dawn, the feel of rough clothes, the walnut stock against his jaw, the first faint glow of the sun on the horizon. Missing one bird after another, he waited for his father's sigh, Oh, *Dixon*. But this execution did not require marksmanship, only a desire to get it over with.

Cradling the shotgun, he hung his cane from the thick branch of a fir and limped the few feet to the thornbush. He pointed the shotgun at what he thought was the boar's shoulder. It was hard to tell in the half-light of dusk, the shoulder dissolved into the hump and the belly, the head out of sight now, hidden by the thornbush. The animal made no sound and he wondered if it knew what was in store; or perhaps it had merely withdrawn into itself. He imagined it forty miles wide and four thousand miles long, reaching through Poland to the vast interior of Russia, beyond the Urals to the steppes and farther, to the marshes of central Asia, governing the region in a lavish, indolent embrace. He heard the boar grunt and heave, the thornbush breaking apart. He slid forward, unsteady, feeling his way with the barrel of the shotgun. Darkness closed in and the air was full of drizzle, the forest pristine and sweet-smelling. Something touched his foot. When he fired, the noise was appalling in the deep forest silence. Dix stepped forward, gunpowder in his nostrils. When he pushed aside the branches of the thornbush, he heard movement far away. The animal had vanished.

# 12

WILLA WANTED to visit friends, so the next day they
drove south to the vicinity of Tannenberg. Dix tried to
sleep but was peppered with questions about the hunt.
What happened in the forest? Nothing happened in the forest.
Reinhold said something happened in the forest and that you were
responsible. That's right, I was. No harm done. That wasn't what
Reinhold said. Reinhold said you insisted on killing a wounded
boar. He said there was an argument and he gave you the shotgun,
and you refused to tell him what happened —

Your uncle Reinhold spent too many years in the war, Dix said.

He was never in the war, Willa said.

Then where did he get the shakes?

Schnapps, Willa said. He got the shakes from schnapps.

Did you really kill a boar? Anya asked.

No, Dix said. I didn't.

Reinhold was so upset —

I don't know why you think Reinhold was in the war, Willa said.

Hunch, Dix said.

You must understand that we are not all Nazis, Karen said.

They were late for lunch. Willa's friends spoke no English so the
meal was an agony of translation and mistranslation until Willa
finally gave it up, leaving Dix happily silent, eating sausages and

reading the *Herald Tribune,* the artillery rumble of the German language in the background. Later, when Willa apologized for the inconvenience, he told her about the actress who traveled to Oslo at her own expense to attend productions of Ibsen's plays, two dozen of them in a single fortnight. She spoke no Norwegian but she knew the plays so well — her portrayal of Rebecca in *Rosmersholm* was considered definitive in English — she followed them with little difficulty. That is foolish, Willa said, what was the point? Sound, Dix said. The sound of the Norwegian language, the way the syllables fell, and the pace of the long lines as opposed to the short, and the gestures that went with them. She wanted to hear the sound of Norwegian laughter, though there was little enough of that in Ibsen. When the cycle was complete, she booked passage on a boat that visited the fjords, and by the time she returned she had a passing knowledge of Norwegian, and Ibsen's achievement seemed all the greater. She had visited him at home.

Why are you telling me this? Willa asked.

I like the sound of German, Dix answered.

After lunch, they turned north for Berlin and it was not until late in the evening that he deposited Willa and Karen at the Zoo station, then motored through Grunewald to Wannsee, the streets there deserted, the suburb quiet at midnight. Charlotte's was open but when Dix suggested a nightcap, Anya said, No thanks. She had to call her father in Rügen.

Papa has been ominously silent, she said.

Anya said good night and hurried inside Mommsen House but Dix lingered. A light snow was falling and the big house and its floodlit lawn looked like any North Shore stockbroker's million-dollar white elephant. He had begun to think of the villa as home; in any case, it was where he returned to. Dix remained in the cold for a while, watching the snow fall on the fountain and the iron sundial nearby, thinking of snowflakes as a procession of seconds, time advancing in the silent German night, accumulating on the fountain and the blank sundial, anonymous and without premonition, merely a snowy evening in a glass paperweight. Time was never lost, only reserved. And it did not advance, it retreated. This was the winter retreat. The boar came to his mind and went away. He scanned the floodlit lawn and realized that only yesterday the actual streets were crowded with retreating infantry, their disorganization, their shouts and the clump of their boots the announcement of the chaos to come. Snow continued to fall, heavier now, dry flakes that flew like dust, whirling around the fountain and the sundial. He thought of Reinhold's brother and his comrades, the brother fifteen years old with a SIG 710 on his shoulder, grateful to be asked to serve, without remorse. There were hundreds of them at the end of the war, roaming the German countryside. The Allies called them wolfpacks, teenage boys armed to the teeth with nothing to lose and a nation's honor to avenge. How delicious it was to be so outnumbered yet so feared by the armies of occupation. American soldiers were terrified of them, the war almost over and the Wehrmacht defeated, except these boys hadn't heard that news. They lived outside of time. They were in love with night. They were without fear and determined to kill any enemy soldier they saw. They lived in the wild like animals, emerging in the dark to kill someone, anyone — a sentry or a careless truck driver, an infantryman asleep in his tent or the sympathetic lieutenant who rummaged in his pack for a Hershey bar or a stick of gum. Cigarettes were what they craved. The war ended but the wolfpacks remained, disbanding eventually and returning to wherever they chose to return, inventing some story or not bothering to invent any story. Reinhold had not mentioned his brother's name, nor whether he was older or younger. No doubt he died as Reinhold said he did. Reinhold did speak with a certain pride along with sadness. Dix supposed it was sadness. As he said, you could replace a wife but not a brother.

This was the vision he had conjured from the snow. Now Dix took a deep breath and walked toward the bright cone of light on the porch. His head was down and he was otherwise preoccupied but he did not fail to notice that on the second floor the curtains of Anya's bedroom window parted, Anya on the telephone. He watched her hand rise and fall, a gesture of frustration or despair. She stared from the window into the courtyard, and when Dix made a gesture of encouragement, she gave no sign of recognition.

Claire's message was on the answering machine. Her voice had the breathless timbre of a golf announcer describing the doomsday putt on eighteen, the undulations of the green, the spike marks around the cup, the weather at dusk, the odds against. Claire was describing betrayal, betrayals everywhere, producers' betrayals, betrayals of agents, publicists, the costar and her wretched husband, the cinematographer, others too numerous to mention. What was there about the set that brought out the worst in everyone, when rumor piled upon rumor, and all rumors were believed. Things collapsed in a wreckage of incompetence. The commissary was incapable of supplying a hot lunch. The hairdresser was drinking before breakfast. The company was more conspired against than Hamlet, with the result that "they" — and here she paused, and when she resumed her voice had acquired a sudden excitement, putt made — had decided to take well-deserved French leave, destination Maui, to give the producers a little something to think about, and half the crew is down with a virus anyhow. Howard's triple pissed, Dix.

So. Someone had an airplane.

They were meant to leave yesterday, but when the pilot checked the weather he discovered an El Niño–related storm — actually, the word he used was "hurricane" — and so they decided to fly much farther west, she didn't know exactly where. But they intended to refuel at Guam and check the weather in the South Pacific. Java, Borneo, the Celebes, one of those sultry destinations. And they'd take their sweet time and not be in any hurry to let Los Angeles know where they were, what they were up to, and for how long.

She said, You have no idea how awful they're being, the demands they're making and the interference. Howard calls them baby-faced hoods. Howard's fed up and so am I. We're not being allowed to do our work as professionals. Howard's lost confidence, and he's not the only one. Everyone's in a bad temper. We're in a coal mine and the canaries are dying. Soooo. That's the story so far. We've decided to play hooky in the South Pacific.

Tell me this, Dix.

Are things more serious in Berlin?

He rolled his eyes at that.

So, she said, things are on hold until the creative issues are worked out.

Money, Dix said aloud. When they said "creative issues," what they meant was money. He broke ice cubes into a glass and quickly filled the glass with vodka and drank half of it. Now her voice had lost its lilt, the words coming between long pauses. Her voice was false, leaking around the edges, unfamiliar to him. In the background he heard an electrical hiss.

That's where I am now, she said. High above the Pacific. The sun is shining but I can see yellow clouds below. Do you know how I feel? I feel marooned. We're three hours out and it's a smooth ride and everyone is playing cards in the salon. Except me. I'm talking to you in nasty Berlin and feeling marooned on an airplane. Did you have a nice day? A good dinner? How's the weather? You're never there when I call. Why are you always out? Your message is so impersonal. *Dixon Greenwood, leave your number.* So inhospitable. So gruff. So — not wanting to hear from anyone. Leave your number, I dare you.

Oh, honey, she said, things have gone to pieces.

*Claire,* he said aloud, wheeling to face the machine, hearing only the electrical hiss. She had never called him honey in her life. Honey was the word she used for colleagues, or the children. He was suddenly at a loss, alone in a foreign apartment on the other side of the world, his drink frigid in his hand.

Marooned, she said again.

It isn't good anymore, she said. She didn't want to continue. She used to love acting, now she hated it. She used to love the set, indoors or out, soft clothes, rough clothes, barefoot or slippered, dressed up or dressed down. She loved learning her lines, pulling on a new face, any face they wanted, cruel, naïve, haughty, naughty. She loved the tension and the rivalries, the tricks, the scene-stealing, the unexpected gesture or bit of business, even of drudgery, the stuff that in its mindlessness resembled calisthenics. And she always loved the crew, so sarcastic in their comments, and the takes, one take after another.

Try it this way, Claire.

Try it that way.

Try it slowly.

Claire, try lowering your voice when you call him darling.

She loved making something new, even the unsuccessful film had one thing to admire, a line of dialogue or an unexpected glance. She loved the paraphernalia, the microphones and cameras, the heavy lights overhead. She loved making out, certainly loving it more with some men than with others, the sticky makeup and whispers in his ear, the times when the director said Cut! but said it softly, too softly for her to hear, and she and her screen lover ground on and on, as if they were teenagers at a drive-in. Now she loathed all of it. Her heart turned hard overnight. She was like a gardener who had fallen out of love with flowers. One fine morning she walked into her garden and destroyed the rose bushes branch by branch. She could not stand the sight of them, so shapely, blood red or pink or cowardly yellow or shroud white, the feeding, the pruning, the weeding, the *caring*. Young roses turned into old roses, the vines as thick as your wrist, gnarled arthritic vines, tough as crowbars. And then the blight set in. They are beyond me, she said. I am in one place and they are in another, so I can no longer tend my garden. I have lost my desire. I have lost my will. I can't pull on the new face or try it this way or lower my voice when I call him darling. I am sitting in an airplane six miles above the earth, thinking of the years I loved the camera, and the years when it loved me back. It happened overnight.

And now — I can't do it anymore.

I abandoned the set, she said.

I have never done that. You know I haven't. It's against the rules, and not only the rules that are written down. A professional owes something to the product. That's what you always said. Loyalty to the material, you lived by that rule. And I agreed. We always agreed about professional things. We agreed that even among whores there was a code of conduct, some one thing that was inviolable.

Something personal, she said after a moment's pause.

Then I lost my desire. I'm afraid I have turned from the world. I lost my desire. And we are not together.

Greenwood had moved up close to the machine, looking at it as if it were a human being showing the first signs of breakdown. Claire was remorseless. Her voice was not her own. Now he closed his eyes and tried to picture her marooned in her airplane in the clouds, the slap of playing cards in the salon, wild laughter, someone crying Gin! and the rattle of ice cubes in a glass. She would be sitting with her feet pulled up, compact as a cat, staring out the window at the gathering storm below, the leading edge of the hurricane, talking into the telephone in her distressed stream of consciousness, holding on six miles above the Pacific Ocean. He waited for her to continue, staring blindly at the wretched machine, willing it back to life. The electrical hiss seemed to grow, then a scratch of static and he knew the connection was broken.

First he called Howard Goodman in Palm Springs but the telephone rang and rang, no one at home, no servants, no "people." Then he called his lawyer, whose secretary said he was in Vegas, unreachable until the morning. The lawyer's partner was fishing, due back the following day, weather permitting. Claire's agent was located on the seventeenth green at Bel-Air. Between putts, Herb Risser expressed dismay that Claire had left the film and was in an airplane bound for Asia. And you say Howard's with her? And who else? All this was news to him. He had no idea. She had told him nothing, not a hint, honest injun. He knew there was trouble on the set but hadn't taken the news seriously because there was always trouble on Howard Goodman's sets. He couldn't work without trouble. Trouble was Howard's oxygen. Some sexual anarchy, he had heard, nothing out of the ordinary; nothing involving Claire, he added quickly. And perhaps the stimulants had gotten out of hand. That girl with the green eyes? She's been vacationing in Cambodia. The producers were pricks but Howard knew that going in. So did Claire. They weren't born yesterday, so they knew they were in bed with pricks. Howard thought he could handle them. He assured me when I asked him on Claire's behalf. Due diligence, Dix. He said the young one had trained on Wall Street and was brilliant, just brilliant, the sort of boy you'd be proud to have as a son-in-law or even a son. He was a sweetheart, Howard said. Can you hold on just a sec, Dix?

Jesus Christ, Herb Risser said a moment later. Three putts. I took three putts from nine feet. He said, I don't think you've cause for worry. You know how things are, the Hollywood pissing match.

Dix said, What do you know that I don't know, Herb?

Nothing. Honest injun.

The agent agreed to check around, learn what he could, and call back. Berlin, isn't it, Dix? Are you getting on all right? I worry about you over there, Germans aren't your type of people. Something's wrong with them. God, they're cold. They're the coldest people I know.

Dix replaced the receiver, trying to identify the lie. Maybe it was all lies, even the three putts from nine feet. He picked up the telephone to call Billy Jeidels, then decided not to. Billy wasn't in Claire's loop. And a blizzard of telephone calls would indicate panic, and with panic came the rumors, and after the rumors the newspapers, and after the newspapers the lawyers. There would be no end to it. But Claire sounded terrible.

He prepared another drink, his third, and sat in the chair by the window overlooking the lake. The time was now well past midnight, no lights anywhere. He heard the rumble of the train to Potsdam, then silence. He tried to recollect the starlet with the green eyes, she had a name like Gwladys or Fiona, but everyone called her Madcap. Her father was an MP. Her mother was French. She was a high-spirited girl, gorgeous to look at. Everyone liked to have her around because of her looks and good humor, and now suddenly she wasn't so good-humored. He and Claire had talked many times of the atmosphere on sets, a complex chemistry, a mirror image of life as it was actually, perhaps life as one wished it to be. All unhappy sets were alike. The main element was the director, his confidence, his sense of himself, his concentration, his enthusiasm for the picture. No one knew beforehand how the personalities would mesh, so many egos, so little oxygen. So the director had to have some actor in him. He had to know how to play his own scenes, and this was as true for a cast of veterans as it was for youngsters. Howard Goodman was an overactor, never one word where three would do. And he misread people, although Claire was one of his favorites.

You're too hard on him, Dix. Cut the man some slack.

Really, she went on, he's a professional. It's only that he likes to make mischief. He's a mischief maker, and that's what keeps him going. And he loves the bedroom scenes, particularly when the lovers don't like each other. When they detest each other, in fact, and desire only to make the other look bad. The scenes when hatred governed but the audience was in the dark. The acid test of direction, according to Howard Goodman.

Dix remembered laughing and referring to Howard Goodman as the Tolstoy of the Higher Hackery, and watching as Claire's smile turned into something very like a smirk, though she denied it when he accused her. He only rarely heard her talk about her own lovemaking scenes in that way, a rush so headlong that she did not hear the word "cut." She talked about it when she had had drinks and somewhere in her mind was remembering her bohemian parents, who had made a life for themselves in the ski country of Vermont, long before it was fashionable. They were as voluble and indiscreet as Harry Greenwood, but voluble and indiscreet about their private lives; they retailed their own adventures, not the adventures of others. Other people's adventures were tedious while their own were hilarious, filled as they were with late-night après-ski anarchy, drinks before the fire, a lively wine-drenched dinner, and sauna mischief later. Dix heard her mother's voice in Claire's, something sly and insinuating along with apprehension. Claire was a long way from Mad River Glen, but she remembered her family's ski lodge as vividly as Dix remembered summer dances at the country club overlooking the lake. Lucky childhoods, uninhibited by the standards of the time; if you wanted something badly enough, you were entitled to take it. You were limited only by the reach of your ambition, and equally by the ambition of your adversary.

They had both become bewitched on movie sets, it was part of the fun. You lost yourself in the role and before you knew it, you were cheating. You wore so many faces it was hard to remember which was the home face and which the away face, which the smile and which the smirk. Usually the affair wrapped when the movie did. Everyone went home or across town or across the country to make another movie. These affairs rarely flourished after the lights went out because the lights were part of it, as the new-car smell signaled the new car. The lights, the camera, the makeup, the action, and always the potential for something inspired. The affair was as natural as the clothes you wore and the directions you gave. If you didn't have an affair it meant you were missing out, with no specific regrets except the glum thought that an awful lot of genuine affection was wasted. Or not wasted. Misplaced.

Dix went to the sink and threw away the dregs of the vodka.

Those days were in the past.

Claire may have had a thing at one time with Howard Goodman. Howard definitely had a thing for her.

But wouldn't that be unlikely now?

Not necessarily, he said aloud.

Claire loved high-stress atmospheres, and the truth was this: a set romance was like a romance in wartime, sharing the danger and the uncertainty. Falling in love on the set or on the battlefield was a great dose of good luck, and good luck meant staying alive. Luck was an essential ingredient of the set and the battlefield. You believed you were invulnerable because people were watching, and the work was so fine. Some of the wartime romances succeeded wonderfully, so long as neither party went to another war. Another war meant another romance because each war created its own high-stress atmosphere, different objectives, different combatants. But he had rarely heard her details and he did not like hearing them now. He did not like hearing them over a cell phone in someone's airplane bound for Java, Borneo, or the Celebes, destinations that promised bad news. Something would break that would be hard to fix.

Years ago she told him that her father always offered a reward for the first girl to undress in front of the fire, and another reward for any girl who wanted to follow up. Claire watched from her room on the second floor, leaning over the inside balcony that looked down on the rec room with its stone fireplace. She laughed and laughed at the antics, then when she was older did not laugh so much. Still, everyone was having such a good time, pleasantly relaxed after a day on the slopes. She could not fail to notice that they were not having such a good time the next morning, the breakfast table silent and everyone getting an early start home or to the slopes. Her father and mother were always laughing when the room was empty at last. They would sit across the breakfast table from each other and have coffee together, trading stories from the night before and deciding themselves to take a run off-piste on Super Paradise, a little later in the day when the chores were done.

Dix washed the glass and put it away. He turned out the lights and climbed the stairs to his bedroom. What had she said? She said she was in a coal mine and the canaries were dying. The children were rampaging in the sandbox and — Are things more serious in Berlin, Dix? He felt like the infantryman rummaging in his pack for a Hershey bar or a stick of gum. But there was nothing for him to do but wait for the next telephone call, and hope that she was not as troubled as she sounded.

# 13

WILLA ASKED HIM to lunch at Munn Café. She had an idea she wanted to explore, and also she wanted to apologize for the behavior of her uncle Reinhold. They met in the back room as before, and when Willa started in on Reinhold as a throwback, a peasant pig without manners, Greenwood waved her silent. It was an interesting afternoon for him, Reinhold's search for the ur-boar. A mysterious encounter all the way around. Even the conclusion was mysterious, and perhaps the conclusion most of all. Willa seemed grateful for the reassurance. The Vietnamese served them beer and she asked question after question about him and Claire, the life they had together, and the Hollywood of the sixties and seventies. She believed those two decades were the golden age of the Industry, *Bonnie and Clyde, Midnight Cowboy, Butch Cassidy, MASH, Cabaret,* both *Godfathers, Chinatown,* and of course your own, Dix. *Summer, 1921* and *Anna's Magic.* Almost as an afterthought she asked him about their children. How did children grow up in such an atmosphere, so feverish and extravagant, everyone always so busy. Didn't the children get in the way?

He told her the story of a down-on-his-luck poet who arrived in Los Angeles from Greenwich Village in the early seventies, staying with a cousin who worked for one of the studios. The poet had had some unspecified trouble in New York and was asked to leave.

Greenwood owed the cousin a favor so he hired the poet to write additional dialogue for a film then in production. We called it a mercy fuck, Greenwood said to Willa. Every film had one, usually more than one. The poet was amusing and reasonably hard-working and did what he was told to do, and was not bad at what he did. He loved Los Angeles. He loved the beaches, the girls, and the freeways. He said he would never leave. He said the Industry, in its maliciousness, spite, insecurity, and flashes of brilliance, reminded him of the *Partisan Review* in the thirties and forties. What Delmore said to Mary and what Mary said to Bunny and what Bunny said to Philip, and what Philip did. At *Partisan* it was the romance of politics and the integrity of the intellectual, and in Hollywood it was the romance of celebrity and the integrity of the accountant. For Trotsky, substitute Darryl Zanuck. So it was not surprising that a tremendous amount of work got done, and now and then something superb. Not often. Often enough, when you considered the odds against.

Later on, the poet wrote some not-half-bad celebrity biographies and ended with a starlet in his bed at the beach house in Malibu. But every now and then he'd return to New York to see how everyone was getting on; and they were not getting on very well, at least compared with him. And so many were dead. So he stopped going.

The children weren't a nuisance, Greenwood said.

Willa looked at him strangely.

So many narcissists, she began.

The children fit right in, Greenwood said. He signaled for more beer and started to reminisce about Jerry's birth, a difficult cesarean. They were filming in Baja and he gave the crew the day off so he could be with his wife. The doctor had asked if he wanted to be present at the birth, and Claire looked up in alarm and said, No, it's impossible. It's the modern way, the doctor said, and Claire replied that they were modern people but not *that* modern. Greenwood held her hand while they wheeled her down the long hall to the delivery room, and then he went back to her room in Maternity and opened the window and lit a cigarette. The day was fine. He smoked and watched the cars in the parking lot, making bets with himself whether his first child would be a boy or a girl. When a Porsche scooted into the lot with a young blonde at the helm, he guessed girl; he thought probably the blonde was one of his fans, a member of the audience. She wore a linen miniskirt and carried a thick paperback book under her arm. He remembered standing at the window, thinking about the particularly demanding scene he would shoot the next day. Billy Jeidels had one idea and he had another. Probably he would do it Billy's way but the scene was salient; the back half of the movie depended on it. He imagined the blond girl in the theater, it would be Brentwood or the Palisades or Santa Monica, her eyes narrowing at the scene bleached white by the sun. Two lovers were on the run and she would be pulling for them, except the man was a sonofabitch.

Cars came and went. The white Porsche baked in the sun. Greenwood pitched the cigarette out the window, watching it tumble end over end and bounce on the asphalt in a little shower of sparks. That gave him an idea so he stayed at the window for another thirty minutes, thinking the way people on the run thought, thinking about camera angles and the bright splash of light on the surface of the water at Baja. He was back in Baja, thinking about the next day's shoot, the preparations for it and the consequences of it. The runaways meet an ingratiating stranger, and their lives unravel from that moment of carelessness. He began to make notes, losing himself inside the idea and the technical details surrounding it. Did the scene begin from the point of view of the lovers or from the point of view of the stranger? He was searching for more paper when Dr. Andaman arrived to tell him that the birth had been difficult, more difficult than expected. He described the complications in language Greenwood did not understand. When he repeated himself in plain English, Greenwood was still at sea. Then the doctor explained that Claire had lost blood and had not yet regained consciousness.

No, you can't see her yet.

Another hour, maybe.

Stay here, Dr. Andaman said. Where I can find you when there's news. He was looking into the mirror, holding his own steady gaze. Morris Andaman was blandly handsome, with curly hair and a button nose, a stethoscope around his neck and a Rolex on his wrist. He was a great favorite of the Industry. Everyone went to Morris Andaman for their children and every so often someone would cast him as a walk-on when they needed a sympathetic doctor to deliver bad news. His looks were safe and the audience would know without being told that he had done everything he could, everything humanly possible. He would be well paid for his morning's work on the set. That was the point, putting a bonus in the doctor's pocket.

Now Andaman frowned and, almost as an afterthought, added that the baby was healthy. A fine seven-pound boy, he said, with a crown of silky blond hair and the lungs of a stevedore. Greenwood smiled wanly. A boy, not a girl, and his father had been fair. Both he and Claire were dark.

Who does he look like?

Not you, Andaman said.

Well, then —

For Christ's sake, Dix. The baby's less than an hour old.

He said, How serious is it?

It's serious.

When Andaman went away, Dix turned from the window and sat heavily on the high hospital bed. The room was flooded with afternoon light. He wished he were practiced in prayer. He did not want to think of Claire in pain or distress of any kind and hoped that if God existed, he was on her side. Dix was thinking in the abstract. You could not put yourself into the mind or body of another and to think otherwise was sentimental, the sort of thing they did in movies. When he had been so crazy after his accident, Claire listened patiently and at length, but she was on the outside looking in. She was an observer looking at the cracked glass and wondering how the pieces fit together. The inside was his alone, and the same would be true for her now, in seclusion in her bed in the recovery room. Even their sense of time would be at odds, she unconscious of it and he praying that it would be slow-footed, dilatory, sluggish in its retreat. What he could do now was think about her and pull for her, all the while wishing that the clock would stop.

Yet there was responsibility. The baby was not her idea, she wanted to wait another year, perhaps two. What's the rush, Dix? If we wait a year, it'll be the Year of the Owl and she'll be a genius, so smart and good-natured, a painter maybe, or a musician. Claire had gained thirty pounds during her pregnancy and hated each pound. She waddled about the house like a duck and took to calling Andaman Dr. Quack. She was often dizzy and her back hurt. She missed her evening martini. She could not concentrate enough to read and at night was plagued with sleeplessness. She thought she had lost her youth for keeps and was angry at him for wanting the baby and for his frequent absences, shooting film in Baja where the light was bleached, everyone hot. At least Ada Hart was not on the set. There were the usual rumors concerning the young French actress but Claire chose to ignore them, except when she was sleepless at two in the morning, prowling her house like an overweight cat, self-conscious, surly, always hungry, wondering who had caught her husband's attention on the set in sunny, sandy, romantic Baja. At that time they were citizens of hostile nations, each with its borders, each with its own language and laws. Hers was a nation of one, his teeming — usually with intrigue, occasionally as sedate as Switzerland, everyone retired by ten, no heavy drinking or all-night poker, no drugs, no sexual turbulence. There was no sense complaining because their nations were stronger than they were, and they loved them equally. She remembered the rough judgment of the Miami gangster in the second *Godfather:* "This is the business we have chosen." Strasberg had added a little metallic click to his voice, so it went, "This click is the business we have chosen click." And then something later to the effect that some sudden execution wasn't personal, it was business: "I didn't inquire." Sometimes that was the way adults got on, not inquiring too closely.

When she was pregnant they talked for an hour each night on the telephone, Greenwood exhilarated at the end of the day, Claire exhausted and peevish, too, because it seemed to her that everyone she knew was on location and unreachable. She hated being out of touch, ignorant of the news of the day, meaning the latest gossip, who was screwing whom literally and figuratively, and which productions were in trouble and which not. During her early morning prowling she wondered if the business they had chosen was one that would admit children or whether the children were walk-ons, grace-and-favor cameos like the roles Andaman played. Dix always called each evening to ask how her day had gone and she described the garden, the fifteen varieties of roses and the twenty-year-old rhododendron; and just think, when you call me this time next year I'll be able to tell you about our child, the cute words and phrases, et cetera, et cetera. She had half a dozen scripts to read but so far hadn't gotten to them. Not in the mood, Dix. When she asked how things were in Baja, he replied with a merry story filled with innuendo; he made her laugh and she thought that was better than the usual you-can't-believe-how-hot-it-is-on-the-beach. He always said, Don't worry, meaning it, assuring her that the set was turbulent, as usual, but nothing that would interfere with them. The French actress had all she could handle with Billy Jeidels.

Interfere? she asked, laughing in a strangled sort of way.

Interfere, he repeated, laughing also. Interference was general in the movie business, was that not so? Quack quack, she said, wishing him a good night and sweet dreams. She knew she had many hours before sleep came, if it did. She knew, and he knew, that she was dispirited, her voice disappointed. And he always replied, after a moment's pause, "I love you, Claire," meaning that, too. By day they lived in the Industry's make-believe world. They did not have to live in it at night as well.

The Vietnamese arrived with schnitzel and tall glasses of dark German beer, Frau Munn in his wake, supervising the placement of the food and beer, squaring the flatware next to the plates. She had a word to say about the weather, filthy, and the forecast, encouraging. She left them with the photographs she had neglected to show them the last time, Gestapo headquarters brilliant with flags and eager young officers in uniform gathered in Anhalterstrasse to greet the Führer, Adolf Hitler languid in the rear seat of a giant open Mercedes. The other photograph showed a street full of rubble, children and old people picking through it, date 1945.

Bon appétit, Frau Munn said, and went away chortling.

Dix took a long swallow of beer and a forkful of schnitzel, still remembering the hospital. He was restless, pacing Claire's room, filled with energy thinking about Baja and the shoot in the morning, and foreboding thinking about Claire, recalling his own time in the hospital near Tahoe, how dispirited and unstable he was, and how superb Claire had been. He stared out the window at the parking lot baking in the heat, and then walked into the corridor looking for a drinking fountain but hoping Andaman had returned with news, whatever it was. Two elderly men attached to metal trees were having a walkabout in the corridor. The trees were festooned with bottles, IV spaghetti wires running from the bottles. They were discussing the afternoon races at Santa Anita. The girl in the Porsche was standing with her back to the corridor wall, her bare arms limp at her side. She still held the book, her finger marking the place. Up close she was a different girl, not the Apache who had loped across the asphalt, gaily it seemed, as if she had been summoned from the country club pool for a date with a doctor. She was out of place in her miniskirt and polo shirt and tanned arms, a thin gold chain around her throat, all but the worried expression on her face. The two old men were arguing about a longshot in the sixth race. She noticed Dix, then resumed her contemplation of the floor. She was tracing the bold chevron pattern with the toe of her sandal. She looked up then and smiled nervously.

She said, My brother.

My wife, Greenwood answered.

Is it serious?

He paused, glancing down the corridor at the nurses' station. It was empty and there was no sign of Andaman. He said, I'm sure she'll be fine.

Motorcycle, she said. My brother and his Harleys.

They called me at school, she went on. I'm a teacher. The principal walked into my class and said my brother was hurt, they didn't know how badly, and fifteen minutes later I was here. I think I broke all the speed records. They said he was lucky he was wearing a helmet and leather pads. He's always been in shape, strong. He's a horse. Has the brains of one, too. Eddie, she said.

Greenwood smiled at that.

She said, Do I know you?

He said, I don't think so.

You're in the movies, she said.

Dixon Greenwood, he said. And you?

Sharon Hamel, she said. What's wrong with your leg?

Accident, he said.

Like Eddie, she said.

Not like Eddie, he said. I drove a car off a mountain.

Ouch, she said. She peered at his bent leg, then broke into a grin. Nice cane, she said. It's a sort of Astaire cane, the cane he used in *Top Hat*. Did he give it to you?

The cane was an ordinary birch cane, curved at the top. It was about as Astaire as a pair of Wellington boots. Dix said, My wife bought it for me.

It's very handsome, she said. Then, after a pause, You probably know my father, Shay Hamel. Everyone seems to.

The critic, he said.

I don't like him either, she said.

I don't know him, Dix said.

That's strange, she said. He's everywhere, my father. No gathering too large or too small. He likes being seen. He likes the bright lights. He likes meeting people whose work he's trashed. He thinks it's cool. He likes to see how they react to him, whether they turn their back or give that Hollywood shit-eating grin. He particularly likes it when they claim to have forgotten his review, or never to have seen it at all. He most particularly likes it when they say they never read reviews, because then he can tell them what he said and how much pleasure it gave him to say it. He offers to send them a copy, so they'll know what they missed. He hated *Summer, 1921*. Too much indirection. Too many Germans. He didn't care for your politics, either. Marxist impressionism, he called it. And the girls couldn't act. He coined a word for them, pornolitarians. And your last film, too, was a failure in his eyes. And I think I can promise that he'll hate your next one.

Poor sap, Dix said.

That's what he's good at, hating.

When she put her hand to her mouth and grinned, he noticed that her fingernails were ragged, bitten haphazardly. Eddie doesn't like him either, she added in a confidential tone that indicated approval that Eddie was in the majority, for once.

Good for Eddie, Dix said.

I loved *Summer, 1921*. I loved it to death.

What did you love about it?

The boys, she said. I loved the boys, the way they stood up for themselves. The way they didn't give a shit about anything except their work and the girls. And I loved the girls, too, how they looked out for each other and refused to be taken advantage of. All of them were outsiders, exiles trying to make their way in the world, and the world wasn't making it easy for them. The movie made me wish I was one of them, lost for a summer in a place I had never been and would probably never get back to. But I wouldn't think about that. I'd live in the present, as they did. If you had a summer like that one, the future would take care of itself, wouldn't it?

I suppose it would sometimes, Dix said. Not always.

And I wouldn't have this stupid job, teaching English to jerks. I suppose you're working on a new one.

We're filming in Baja now.

I can't wait, she said. Is it like *Summer, 1921*?

Not much, he said.

I'll like it anyway.

You can come to the opening. Bring your father.

He has to retire one of these days, Sharon said. But he's like Eddie, strong as a horse. He works out every day with weights. She paused, evidently trying to make up her mind about something. You're his bête noire, she said finally. Lots of directors he hates, but you have a special place in his black book. And one more thing about him. He never forgets. He never gives up because he loves hating, just loves it to death. So you've got that to look forward to, Dixon Greenwood.

She had moved close to him, talking so rapidly her words ran into themselves. Then she wheeled toward the nurses' station, squeezed his hand, and hurried down the corridor where she was met by a serious-looking intern in a white coat, a clipboard in his hand. They spoke a few moments and at last she laughed, putting her palm on his chest. He continued to talk earnestly but she did not seem to be listening, her head turned away as she pushed at his chest. When he broke away to take a telephone call, Sharon sauntered back to Dix, smiling happily. Eddie would be all right, cuts and bruises and a sprained ankle and something nasty to his knees, maybe surgery later. Nothing that couldn't be fixed. Eddie dodged the bullet, she said. Lucky boy. The Harley was totaled. He wants me to call our father and give him the good news but I don't see why I should do that. Let's leave old dad in the dark a little longer. He wasn't around when it counted. She raised herself on tiptoe and kissed Dix full on the lips, her arms around his neck, hanging there. She smelled like peaches.

I'm in the book, she said. Call anytime.

My boyfriend wouldn't mind, she added after a moment.

Can I come down to see you in Baja? I won't cause any trouble. I'll be helpful.

We can go in there right now if you want. She spoke into his ear, indicating the door behind them. That's my brother's room but he won't be up for at least another hour. You want to, I can tell. I can *feel* it, Dixon. You want to fool around just like I do. What's the harm? You're not going anywhere, and anything I have to do, I can put off. We have the whole day ahead of us and tomorrow, too, if we want. I'll call in sick. I'll tell them Eddie's near death and he needs me. She stepped back and smiled. The day that had begun so routinely in her classroom now showed promise in a hospital. Hospitals were sexy, so long as you were not sick yourself, and everything happened for a reason. She said, We've both had lousy days and now we're owed. Injuries are hard on the survivors, too, because we're the ones who *care*. We're the ones pacing the floor, waiting for the doctor to give us bad news. Saying our prayers. God, it's a beautiful day. So what do you think?

Dix said, Go home, Sharon.

That's no fun, she said. That's no fun at all. Fun's *now*. You remember what the girl said in *Summer, 1921*. I've remembered it my whole life, it's what I live by. I fell in love with the writer of that line. They're at the lake. The girl has taken her clothes off to go swimming. He's taken up his brush and begins to sketch. His eyes go to her, and then to the canvas. You, he says. Don't move, ever. You will never be more alive than right now, at this moment, living through my brush on the canvas. She laughs and says she's living whether she's on his canvas or not. *He's* living on the canvas. She's living in her own skin. They go back and forth, he's irritated with her. He tells her she has no imagination. She doesn't understand that she can be in two places at once, and one of them is on his canvas. Then there's something else, I've forgotten. Sharon impatiently slapped the book against her thigh and he saw it was de Beauvoir's *The Second Sex*.

He tells her to stop breathing, Greenwood said.

And she refuses!

She does not. She holds her breath, posing. And then she laughs, not pleasantly.

She goes for a swim, Sharon said.

And she raises her arms over her head, does a little turn, and sails off the cliff in a perfect swan dive.

She never holds her breath, never. She would never do that. That would violate her code of conduct.

Nevertheless, Dix said.

Sharon turned away with a little irritated shrug.

And that's what you live by?

Being in two places at once, Sharon said.

What does that give you?

She smiled and said, Perfect pitch.

He said, Give my regards to your father.

The moment was lost, and she knew it. She said, What fun we could've had in Baja.

Baja's work, he said.

And that's the trouble with Baja, she replied.

Greenwood turned when he heard movement close by.

If you have a minute, Dix, Andaman said.

Bye, then, Sharon said. She disengaged herself and strolled off down the corridor, waving at the intern, performing a little above-the-waist shimmy before she turned the corner and disappeared.

He said, How's Claire?

Who was that? Andaman asked.

A fan, Dix replied.

# 14

T HEY WERE SILENT while they ate, Willa watching him over
the rim of her half-glasses. In the outer room, Frau Munn
was telling some story, not anything amusing because no
one was laughing. The Vietnamese arrived with more beer and
then went away. They were at the same table as before, the Kollwitz
graphic on the wall behind Willa, a chipped glass ashtray resting in
a puddle of beer. He was becoming a regular. A week ago he had
never heard of Munn Café. He had not known that Gestapo headquarters was down the street, and now all these places had become
familiar. Potsdamer Platz, Anhalterstrasse, and the imaginary beast
the length of South America. Dix realized suddenly that he could
live in Berlin.

Nothing wrong with leading a two-way life, dividing your time
between America and Germany, the transatlantic life of a rootless
cosmopolitan. There were ways to go about it. He could set himself
up in an apartment in Savignyplatz or in Mitte or Alexanderplatz
or a three-story villa in Wannsee. Buy a Mercedes and a scull, take
up golf, get a subscription to the Philharmonie, bet on football,
even make a movie — and the city would welcome him. That is, it
would remain indifferent — a vast, restless audience seated in the
dark with its own desires. What was one more foreigner in a city of
nearly four million souls? So you could go about your business, living between the lines, reading the time in your own way, and soon

enough joining the audience in the dark. You would never understand the city but you inhabited it all the same, and after a while its ghosts would become yours also. Like the boar in the thornbush, the city would be felt but not seen. You would observe certain features. You would smell it, you would hear its growl, you would feel its grit, but it would remain mysterious, possessed by its history, at once owned and disowned. Living in such a way, you would fashion an alternative personal history.

Never learn the language, though.

Allow the Germans their privacy.

Dix finished his schnitzel, pushed the plate back, and lit a cigarette.

Willa said, You have a bad look on your face. When he shrugged and did not reply, she changed the subject.

Did you ever make a film with your wife?

No. Why do you ask?

It would be the logical thing. Then you both could be in the same place at the same time.

He shook his head. Logical, perhaps. Not advisable.

Why not advisable?

We have different styles, he said.

And you, she said after a moment's pause. You haven't worked in years.

Many years, he said.

Your last two weren't successful.

Duds, he said.

Commercially, she said.

That, too, he agreed.

The material was no good?

It was the usual material, material that had been successful in the past. Who said there are only two plots in fiction? A stranger comes to town. Someone goes on a trip. I made two of one, three of the other. It's remarkable how far craft can take you, and craft's not to be despised. It'll get you around town but it won't get you to the moon, and maybe after a while you forget where the moon is or what it looks like. Then one of the studios got the idea of a remake of *Summer, 1921.* A remake or a sequel, they didn't care which. They wanted to make a buddy movie, the buddies more in love with themselves than they were with the girls. You can guess who they had in mind for the buddies.

Oh, dear, Willa said.

They wanted to do it, too. I went to the meetings because I didn't have anything better to do. Then almost anything was better and I stopped going to the meetings and they lost interest.

You gave it up, she said.

I gave it up, it gave me up, I can't remember which. I remember thinking it was a colossal waste of time, and I had plenty of time to waste. But not with them.

Yes, she said.

I can't go through the motions anymore.

Well, she began.

I won't work just to work.

You have money, she said.

I have enough.

Willa began to rock her beer glass back and forth on the tabletop. She picked up Frau Munn's cherished photographs, the before and after of the soul of the Third Reich, her eyes moving left and right like a spectator's at a tennis match. She looked at the photographs as she rocked her beer glass, then put them carefully aside, propped against the saltcellar where they could see them.

You could if you wanted to, she said.

Work again? Of course.

It would have to be the right project, she said. And it's hard to know what that would be.

I haven't seen one in years, he said. I don't know the world they're filming, and they have no interest in mine.

So here you are in Berlin, she said. Everyone says we will be the capital of the twenty-first century.

Have you asked Beijing about that?

We all know it is coming, the German renaissance. Germany itself again, its destiny in our own hands. We will be the magnet for European culture. I imagine something will turn up for you. Still, you must feel rusty. So many years since you've been on location, telling people, do this, do that. Studying angles. Worrying about point of view. Worrying about language, worrying about score, lighting, sound, worrying about *pace*. Worried that the end will fail to guarantee the beginning. And so much has changed. The equipment's improved, you know, new machinery. Stuff you wouldn't believe.

He said, It's still what's on the page and where you point the lens.

And the cast, she said. Don't you miss it?

Of course I miss it.

He looked for the waiter, wanting another glass of beer.

She went on to describe the gear she's seen at Studio Babelsberg, state-of-the-art film, cameras, microphones, lights. Sound studios wired for everything but weapons of mass destruction. She continued to talk but she did not have his attention. He'd turned away to look at Frau Munn's trove of photographs. The before photographs were more interesting than the after, young officers standing smartly at attention, their right arms crowbar straight and at a raised angle to the ground, palms down, eager, each officer, to sacrifice life itself for Führer and Fatherland. In the near ranks, Dix noticed an overweight major whose interest seemed to be elsewhere, his salute drooping. He was the one you would write the film about, a Nazi too stupid or nearsighted to grasp the grandeur of the occasion, perhaps some modern Schweik or even a thug too hung over to know where he was; or, less likely, a combat veteran who disapproved of the war strategy of the regime; or, less likely still, a dissident. The rest of them were elated to be there in the presence of the Führer, dressed down in a gray suit with a swastika armband, no hat, a bored expression on his face. Five decades later, no wonder so many Germans wanted to be like Americans, enjoying the blessings of the free market in which to pursue happiness without the inconvenience of memory. They believed Americans forgot things, history mostly; they put unpleasantness behind them, got on with their lives, threw up a memorial, achieved the envied but elusive closure. Americans didn't have time for revenge! They refused to take responsibility themselves, refused even to assign it elsewhere. What a marvelous state of affairs, stepping cheerfully from one year to the next with scarcely a stumble or a look backward. Who wouldn't envy such people? Of course there were disadvantages, not one volk but many. Not even a common language that could be spoken with confidence and privacy. One would miss the thickness of the German language and culture, and perhaps the burden also, its weight and originality.

Dix continued to contemplate the overweight officer — too young for a captain, too thick-witted for a colonel, major would be his rank — his tiny eyes and full jaw, his sideways glance. He didn't look like the sort of man who would volunteer for line duty, the Eastern Front or North Africa or manning the Atlantic Wall. The major would have made a decent staff officer, good with maps and logistics, an order taker, good with follow-through. He had the look of a survivor, and if that were the case it was conceivable that he was still alive and in good health, a grateful pensioner living out his retirement in some picturesque village in the southern mountains, hiking for exercise, perhaps sculling on the nearby lake, a fond grandfather, proud of his exemplary postwar life, proud of the industry and discipline of his fellow citizens, Germany a prosperous member of the family of nations. If Frau Munn showed the major this photograph, he probably wouldn't recognize himself; or if he did, he would look away and smile, take another sip of beer, trying to remember the occasion of the visit of the Führer and his suite. It was an awards ceremony, six officers recognized for services to the Fatherland, everyone so proud, though the services were unspecified. All in all, things hadn't turned out so badly. When mischievous Frau Munn showed him the after picture, the one from 1945, the old man would glance at it without apparent interest and return to his beer. He remembered those days, the hunger and the filth, the disorder under the heel of the enemy's boot. What a long way the nation had come!

Dixon?

Yes.

You must come with me sometime.

Where?

To Babelsberg and the movie museum at Potsdam, wonderful stills and artifacts, old posters of Murnau's films, Schreck as Nosferatu, von Stroheim, even Dietrich. All the materials from the great period of German cinema, Weimar and a few years after Weimar. Before everyone went to Hollywood.

One of these days, Dix said. He looked at his watch, wondering if Claire had called. Wondering also where she was and with whom and what her plans were. Wondering if the airplane had landed at last at Pago Pago or some flyblown thousand-dollar-a-night resort in Malaysia, perhaps someone's sloop anchored off Panang or Surabaya, far from home, far from the set, under Asian skies.

I have an idea, Willa said, putting her hand on the check as Dix reached for his wallet. He said, Let me. She shook her head firmly, No, this one is mine. It's business, isn't it? I have a business account.

Dix pointed to the before picture. What do you think of this? What comes to mind?

Nothing much, she said. Gestapo hoods.

Look at the officer toward the rear, under the window. The overweight one.

What about him?

Look at him. What does he suggest to you?

Willa thought a moment. He eats too much wurst, she said.

He's the story, Dix said.

Why is he the story?

He stands out. Look at his eyes, his posture. His uniform's too big, his hair's unkempt. He doesn't fit in.

He fits in, Dixon. They all do.

What do you suppose he did before the war?

She gave him a sidelong glance and answered, Actor. Not very successful. He felt conspired against. The Jews conspired against him, so he never got the good parts. He got the small parts in bad pictures, all because the Jews saved the good parts for themselves. So he did the logical thing for an actor without much talent or presence. He became a Nazi, broke a few shop windows, kicked people around, and in due course — he had friends in high places — got himself promoted to major and joined the Gestapo, the unit that harassed the entertainment industry, theater and films. Goebbels liked him. He became a censor. And dabbled in pornography on the side, definitely. How's that?

Not bad, Dix said.

I said this was a business lunch, Willa said.

Yes, you did.

I have an idea. A good idea. An idea you should think about.

I'm thinking about the overweight major.

You could work if you wanted to, Willa said.

I know that, he said.

I mean *now.* You could work now.

Dix looked at her and nodded.

Yes, she said. She fished in her purse and came up with a sheaf of banknotes, counting them out and placing them next to the check. Next week, she said. You could begin work next week. You could discover in a day whether you still have the desire. You'd know at once whether you want to do it as opposed to thinking about doing it, which you do all the time, whether it's a boar in a forest or an overweight major in a Gestapo lineup, Frau Munn with her smile or the Vietnamese waiter with his bad manners. Everything you see and hear you convert into film and don't bother to deny it, I know I'm right.

It's my life, he said.

I know that. It's transparent. I don't think you have any other life, much as you might think you do. You look at what's in front of your eyes and convert it to film. The world is one great screenplay as far as you're concerned, and it doesn't matter where you are or who you're with. Berlin excites you, doesn't it?

Berlin appalls me.

It's the same thing, Willa said. So, this has possibilities, no?

No, Dix said.

Liar, Willa said.

He finished off his beer and reached for his coat.

Besides, she said, you'd be doing me a favor. Promise me you'll think about it. That you won't say no just because that's what you've been doing for years and years and it's comfortable. No rolls nicely off your tongue, no no no no no. This is what I have in mind. I want you to direct an episode of *Wannsee 1899*.

What restrictions? he said after a moment.

The usual, she said.

Forget it, he said.

There are no restrictions, Dixon.

# 15

THE S-BAHN was uncrowded in midafternoon, the commuters silent except for the shabby old party in the seat across the aisle. He was unshaven. He wore a leather cap and a canvas jacket and muttered to himself between swallows from the can of beer in his jacket pocket. Greenwood sat listlessly looking out the window, Willa's script in his lap. Pockets of snow lingered here and there in the streets and on the station platforms. The city slowly gave way to suburbs, Lichterfelde, Zehlendorf, Schlachtensee, a thin skin of ice on the pond. The houses grew higher and the lawns wider as the train retreated from the city center, the iron logic of the metropolis; Evanston, Wilmette, Winnetka. The sidewalks were vacant, circular Mexikoplatz all but deserted. Suburban life did not flourish in the daylight. The beer can clattered to the floor, the old party dozed. At Nikolassee he roused himself and stood, swaying. He tipped his hat and said something unintelligible to Greenwood, then stepped off the train and settled on a bench in the cold. He began to speak again, louder now; no one on the platform paid attention. Greenwood watched him as the train moved off. He guessed the old party's age at seventy-five, perhaps a little less. In Germany, with men of a certain age, you always tried to calculate the year of birth.

There was no telephone message from Claire when he returned to Mommsen House, and nothing in the mail, either. He put Willa's script on his desk and went back downstairs to see if Werner would brew him a cup of tea. The chef was cutting up rabbit, legs in one greasy bundle, thighs in another, viscera in the sink. His hands were bloody so he wiped them on his apron before putting the kettle on. They would be but four at dinner, the Kessels and Anya Ryan besides Greenwood. The others were sightseeing, the concentration camp at Sachsenhausen. They had hired a van for the journey, Sachsenhausen being at the northern limits of the city, in Oranienburg. At least two hours were required for the complete tour, the barracks, the ovens, the brick pit where the firing squads assembled, the hospital where the experiments were conducted.

They hired a guide, Werner said.

They intended to dine out somewhere in Mitte, probably the overpriced restaurant down the street from the Adlon. If they wanted to spend their money in that way, who was he to stop them? Werner continued to work as he talked, separating the limbs of rabbits, blood dripping from his fingers. He was not in the mood to discuss tourism at Lager Sachsenhausen, preoccupied as he was with Majorca.

Did you have a pleasant day, Herr Greenwood?

I had lunch at Munn Café.

That dreadful woman, Werner said.

She's very nice, Greenwood said. She has a trove of photographs. She shows them to her customers, the before and after of Berlin. She has one of Hitler reviewing the troops at Gestapo headquarters.

She lives in the past, that one. She doesn't know that Germany and the world have moved on and no one cares about the war. And there are some questions of the authenticity of the photographs. Munn Café survived the war, God knows how. Frau Munn is a mystery.

Food's good, Greenwood said. We had schnitzel.

It's ordinary schnitzel, Werner said. Everyone knows that she uses a microwave. The food is prepared beforehand and she uses a microwave to stimulate the meat before it's served. She uses Chinese waiters also.

Vietnamese, Greenwood said.

Asiatics, Werner agreed, dealing a vicious blow to a rabbit's joint and adding the leg to the greasy bundle. I don't know what it is about my country that attracts Asiatics, perhaps the Russians told them about our schnitzel and beer. The Russians ruined this country. Don't you find it a puzzle, Herr Greenwood? We only wish to be ourselves, and that is difficult when we are diluted by the Asiatics.

Greenwood stood in the doorway watching Werner work. When the kettle began to steam, he fetched it and poured two cups of tea, putting pots of sugar and milk and a lemon wedge next to the tea.

He said, Werner? Have you ever watched a television program called *Wannsee 1899*?

Of course, Werner said. Everyone watches *Wannsee 1899*. They film it here, only down the street a little ways.

So you like it?

It's authentic, Werner said. Absolutely. He paused then and turned away, spooning sugar into his tea, adding milk, stirring rapidly. It's excellent, he said after a moment. It's the story of old Prussia. It's our story told by ourselves. As we would wish it told, Herr Greenwood. It's the curse of the twentieth century that outsiders come and tell us not only what to believe now but what we believed then. They are trying to tell us how to think! These strangers that come into our country and think they understand our history better than we do and that we are so lamebrained we cannot be trusted with our own facts. They believe that we will accept them as our doppelgängers, what shit. You yourself would wonder — and here he paused, searching for the most contemptible nationality — if some *Frenchman* came to your country and told you how to interpret your revolution. You would say, Who is this schwein? I tell you, Herr Greenwood, this is the worst thing that can happen to a nation. You lose control of history. You lose control of your memory, no less. And it is not only the lectures in books. It is happening now in our Potsdamer Platz, which daily comes to resemble your city, Los Angeles. And who are the architects? Italians, Americans, and English. It's insulting. It's a terrible situation.

I can see, Greenwood said.

And it gets worse, Werner said.

And that's why everyone watches *Wannsee 1899*.

Of course, Werner said. It's us talking to ourselves.

Well, Greenwood said doubtfully. I'm not sure —

Of course you wouldn't understand! How could you understand, your country is so large and — self-possessed. Everyone believes they are a little bit American, whether they want to be or not. You are in charge of your own myths. Why was Marx hated so? Why did the world have fifty years of Cold War? Because you felt insulted. Marx challenged your *history,* your view of yourself. Marx looked at your history and said it was bunk. Bunk, propaganda, and illusion. So you did with him what you do to anyone who takes the contrary view. You tell him to bugger off. You deport him. You assemble a Senate committee and hold him in contempt, and if he doesn't cooperate, you blacklist him. He doesn't have a place at your table!

Red-faced with anger, Werner took a vicious swipe at a rabbit's thigh, sending it slithering across the cutting board and into the sink. He fetched the thigh and rinsed it in cold water.

He said, I have been reading.

I can see that, Werner.

I have been reading about the blacklist. Other things.

Dreadful, the blacklist.

I did not mean to offend you, Herr Greenwood.

You haven't, Werner.

There are many who believe as I do, he said.

Who want to be in charge of their own history?

Yes. And who admire *Wannsee 1899*.

A quiet period in your history, Greenwood said.

Mostly, it was quiet, yes.

Greenwood poured more tea, adding lemon, and made as if to go. He wanted to write down what Werner had said so he could repeat it to Claire word for word.

I wish you luck with your history, Werner.

There is something I meant to tell you.

Save it, Greenwood said. We can talk tomorrow.

Werner said, Someone called for you this afternoon. Whoever it was stopped at the front desk but left no message, I think.

There was nothing in my mailbox, Greenwood said.

A woman. I got only a glimpse of her.

Young? Old?

You must ask Marlene. She spoke to Marlene. I heard her say something about seeing your picture in the newspaper.

I didn't know my picture was in the newspaper.

Oh, yes, Werner said. It was there. It was a few weeks ago. An announcement of your presence at Mommsen House.

Greenwood nodded. That would be the explanation. One more middle-aged American tourist having breakfast in her suite at Kempinski's thinking it would be exciting to meet Dixon Greenwood, so why not hire a car and drive to Wannsee, see if he's available for a drink or dinner and a chat about the motion picture business. Probably they had a friend in common, a college classmate or a mutual friend in the Industry. He sipped his tea and watched the light struggle in the western sky, wondering what the chef had against Frau Munn other than her microwave, the disputed photographs of a time long past, and the Asiatic waiters, the ones who were diluting the Teutonic gene pool. And then a fantastic idea came to him, and he looked up.

Short or tall, Werner?

I did not see her clearly.

Brunette, about fifty-five though she looks younger?

I don't know, honestly.

Probably wearing a black beret?

Werner said, She was trim.

Beautifully built. A husky American voice.

No, Werner said.

A mink coat —

Perhaps, Werner said.

Walking with her head forward because she's nearsighted? He

was certain he had it now. Claire on the flight from Singapore to Paris or Rome and then on to Berlin. That would be like her, she enjoyed surprises, the more improbable the better. It would be like her to sashay into Mommsen House and ask for the American director, what was his name? Oldwood? Greenwood? She needed to speak to him urgently, so she would go away for a while and then return. No, no name. Claire had shown up once in Chicago while he was filming, walking into his suite at midnight, talking a kind of pidgin English and declaring that she was lonely on the coast and — Are you happy to see me, darling?

She spoke German, Werner said.

Greenwood turned away, dispirited, his hand so unsteady the teacup danced in its saucer. Another false spring come and gone. In that brief moment he had imagined them together in Berlin, introducing her to Willa and Frau Munn, Anya Ryan and the Kessels. The thought elated him and would not go away. He had imagined a week together, showing her the city, with special attention paid to the Topography of Terror and Sachsenhausen, with a side trip to Hitler's bunker and Treptower Park later on to visit the Soviet dead, dinner at Munn Café so she could inspect Frau Munn's trove of photographs, the before and after. Mahler at the Philharmonie, George Grosz at the Alte Nationalgalerie, not forgetting Libeskind's Jewish Museum, the building that was so overpowering they could not decide what to put in it; so for the time being it was vacant, including the thirty-foot-high dungeon that tapered to the ceiling where a single small window indicated the world outside, false hope for the imprisoned. All this would be new to her, and then a long journey by car through Poland and the Baltic states to St. Petersburg. Neither of them had visited Russia. She had always wanted to go to Petersburg and walk along the boulevards and dine at a restaurant overlooking the frozen Neva, imagining Russian life of the nineteenth century, horse-drawn carriages moving through snowflakes the size of marbles, Nevsky Prospekt, the Admiralty buildings, pink granite, and bridges.

But Claire was not in Europe after all. She was somewhere near an open Asian sea. The possibility of seeing her made him realize how much he missed her. He was tired of talking to himself. Berlin seemed to demand solitude but it did not reward solitude. He wondered if Asia was the same for her, but of course it wouldn't be because she was in an airplane filled with friends. Dix closed his eyes and leaned against the doorjamb, sipping Werner's tea.

I'm sorry, Herr Greenwood.

I had an idea it might be my wife.

From America, he said.

A surprise visit, Dix said.

Your wife should be here with you, Werner said.

Yes, you mentioned that before.

A wife or a warmer climate, Werner said.

I was going to take her to St. Petersburg.

Petersburg is worse than Berlin! And it is filled with Russians.

So they say, Dix said.

And dangerous. Gangsters everywhere.

We've never been, Dix said.

There's something else, Werner said. Something I've forgotten.

It doesn't matter, Dix said.

Your visitor. I thought I recognized her.

Who was she, then?

I have no idea, Werner said. I had only a glimpse. But she looked familiar to me. Why, I cannot say.

# 16

GREENWOOD SAT in the chair by the window with his tea, cold now and bitter. He watched the scullers heading for home, bending like jockeys in the saddle. The *Wannsee 1899* script was open in his lap but he did not look at it, preferring instead to admire the sculls' wavy chevrons on the surface of the water. He remained without moving for several minutes, beguiled by the stillness of the gathering darkness, wondering all the while who had come looking for him at Mommsen House. When he went to the kitchen to prepare a vodka, he remembered that the last time he had done so, he was listening to Claire's voice with the hiss in the background. He returned to his chair and picked up the script, thumbing the pages, weighing it with both hands. Heavy product, he thought. Willa had translated it herself; a free translation, she explained with a laugh. The writer was from the former East, a professor of philosophy who moonlighted as a screenwriter and quite successfully. He was much in demand. A better screenwriter than philosopher, she said. He taught at Weimar, the city of Goethe. He hoped for the open hand of Goethe but instead he got the smirk of the commissars, so his philosophical works were — pinched, she said with a wide smile.

It's a pretty good script, she went on. He's a professional, never uses two words where one will do. Never uses any words at all when he can help it. Understands the camera, where it can go and where it can't. Sometimes his politics get in the way, but isn't that often the case with talented individuals with axes to grind? Narrative makes a convenient whetstone, does it not? He's homosexual and despises blood sport so all his scripts begin with a hunt. And pay attention to the music, please.

The directions were explicit: in the opening moments the soundtrack was silent, then filling gradually with the violins of the adagio from the first movement of Mahler's unfinished Tenth Symphony, the one that moves so deliberately that a listener could believe it represented the beat of a sleeping heart. The scene began with two hawks wheeling in a brilliant sky, the hawks turning and falling, then rising as full of emotion as young dancers, their eyes patrolling the woodland below, the birches and maples afire with autumn color. They were watching a hunting party track stag in the forest of the estate in East Prussia, the one in the vicinity of the Masurian Lakes, south of Königsberg near the Polish border. They were the old baron, his three sons, and their weekend guests, robust men in traditional hunting kit, brown trousers and green jackets with suede patches at the elbows, leather boots and wide-brimmed felt hats, each carrying a side-by-side shotgun armed with a double load. The women followed on horseback, single file on a bridle path. There was something sinister about the atmosphere, though the day was sunny and summerlike, unseasonably warm, the sky a Prussian blue. The underbrush was thick, giving way here and there into a clearing, then closing again. Heavy storks' nests crowned the alders and maples, and now and then the party heard the hoot of an owl. And all this time the disconsolate melody of Mahler's adagio.

The baron, his sons, and the weekend guests were moving in a line through the forest, the beaters and the dogs in the wetlands ahead, heard rather than seen. The beaters wore heavy boots, struggling through the marsh. They approached the hunters shouting Hut! Hut! and striking the marsh trees with their canes. The dogs' jaws moved continuously, the beaters cupping their hands to their mouths as they called out. The afternoon was warm enough so that the men were sweating. They had ordered the women to be quiet but from time to time brittle laughter intruded, feminine vivacity in counterpoint to the seriousness of the hunt. The men instinctively raised their shotguns when a fox showed itself, then sped away into the undergrowth. There was something remorseless about the manner in which the men forced their way through the forest with the women trailing companionably behind in their bright clothes and conversational attitude. The camera focused on each man in turn, beginning with the red-faced baron with his fleshy nose and bristling mustache, an irascible expression on his face as he pushed through the underbrush. My property, his demeanor seemed to say, get out of my way when I'm on it. A hunting horn hung from his neck on a lanyard, and his shotgun was cradled in his arms. His oldest son walked with his youngest son; they were laughing soundlessly over some joke, careful not to be overheard by their father. The middle son walked alone, deep in thought, apparently oblivious of the task at hand. Rolf was unmistakably a city boy, with his two-inch ponytail and soft face, uncomfortable in rough clothes. He picked at the seat of his trousers, ambling negligently, as he would have done on a city street or park path. He carried his shotgun carelessly by the barrel, the stock on his shoulder like a student's book bag. Every few moments he glanced behind him, searching for the women, reassuring himself that they were in the vicinity. Watching Rolf, his older brother, Christian, muttered that he had the look of a condemned man reviewing the misfortune that had brought him to this place, a woodland penitentiary with no reprieve in sight.

The camera paused briefly at each of the weekend guests, hearty middle-aged men, all but indistinguishable in their hunting uniforms, at ease in the surroundings, eyes moving left and right, as alert as scouts on reconnaissance, watching for stag and listening hard for the bleat of the old baron's hunting horn. By degrees the film slowed so that the hunters were advancing in time to the music, and physically overwhelmed by the towering birches and conifers of the forest, watched all the while by the two circling hawks and the owl, permanent residents of this unquiet, unpeaceable kingdom.

Then the camera drew back, rising, until the hawks were only commas in the sky. Away to the north and east were the Masurian Lakes and settlements connected by pathways. Not quite a wilderness but not civilization, either. The camera lingered, then returned to the hunting party, focusing now on the women, beginning with the baroness — younger than the baron by two decades, she handled her mount roughly, her expression one of haughty boredom — and moving on to the three young women, two blond and lovely, the third brunette and not lovely. The plain one rode superbly, leading the way on the path, handling her horse as if she had been born on it. Her two friends were mocking her, imitating the way she sat and gripped the reins, her straight spine, the mannish swing to her shoulders. If she heard the laughter behind her, she made no sign. She was trying to keep the men in view, her head turtling forward as she attempted to penetrate the underbrush and the thick-waisted trees, and when her horse balked, she dug her spurs into its flesh. Now and then she caught sight of the lagging middle son, the barrels of his shotgun dully reflecting the occasional shafts of sunlight that fell through the crowns of the trees. His hat was off white and he wore a red scarf, unnecessary on such a warm day, and a mighty irritant to his father, a stickler for the traditions of the hunt. But the boy had never understood these rituals, forms as rigid as a sonnet. He had always been a dreamy boy, slow to anger, quick to retreat, a sly boy, his mother thought, with an unwholesome personality.

The camera rose then to display the panorama, the women behind, the hunters in the middle, the beaters and the dogs ahead, advancing toward them — and between the beaters and the hunters, shivering in a swale, a stag with a fine rack. Mahler's adagio faded and the sounds of the hunt arrived, the hysterical baying of the dogs, the shouts of the beaters, the crash of the underbrush, and back of it all the playful laughter of the young women on horseback. There were fragments of conversation, too, the beaters complaining of the heat, the brothers planning a midwinter escapade in merry Munich, the weekend guests speculating on the size of the old baron's landholdings, not a centimeter less than one thousand hectares and probably much, much more, prime Prussian soil, fields and woodlands with small lakes to break the monotony, every species of wildlife and the necessary woodsmen to maintain them, although the manor house did seem rundown, not at all comme il faut, even considering the plain style of Prussian aristocrats, any show of wealth seen as a sign of weakness.

The young women continued to gossip, concentrating now on the attractive shyness of the middle son, so out of place in his rough clothes and firearm, a young man more at home in a classroom or drawing room, or lying in some lover's arms on the grassy banks of an urban river, reciting poetry and making love. He was the sort of boy who needed a woman's protection against the brutalities of the world. His brothers were devils, so they fit right in — and here the girls began to whisper, describing the latest carousal, this one in Berlin, or was it Hamburg — dancers from a cabaret, women of the lowest type . . . The conversations were sporadic and confusing and then they subsided to a stony silence, replaced gradually by the strings and woodwinds of Mahler's tender adagio, all movement now in slow motion as the advance continued.

When the old baron raised the hunting horn to his mouth and blew a single note, the hunters surged forward. The women urged their horses into a trot. The beaters froze where they stood, knowing that the dogs had the stag cornered, and wondered which dog would feel the puncture of the antler's points. They listened for the anguished whine. The camera did not leave the baron's broad German face, the veins in his forehead rising to resemble heavy twine pulled taut. The single note seemed to last forever. The old man's enormous hands squeezed the horn and his cheeks billowed like a sail caught in a sudden gust, his cheeks coarse and red and streaked with sweat, milky droplets hanging from the wiry gray hairs of his mustache. His eyes grew wide and frightened, as if he had seen something terrible, and all the more terrible for being utterly unexpected. He seemed to struggle as the single note soared on and on, and then the horn fell from his mouth, his cheeks contracting as his eyes continued to stare at the unexpected thing somewhere beyond on the horizon.

Now his head jerked from side to side in spasms, a thin string of blood running from his nose and collecting in his mustache. His arms were raised high to the sky, the horn still held in his vise grip. He muttered something unintelligible and began to stagger, heaving this way and that. His hand went to his heart and he sagged to his knees, drooling, blood rushing from his nose and mouth. On all fours, he raised his head and toppled, crashing to the ground, rolling once and then lying still, his blood beginning to pool, his blue eyes wide open and staring at the shafts of sunlight that fell through the trees. The camera focused on the shotgun, its oiled stock and blue-black barrel, delicate chasing along the silver panel above the trigger, the baron's crest and initials in Gothic script. The horn remained in his fist. The single note receded to silence and the natural sounds began once again, the dogs first, followed by the hunters pushing through the forest's undergrowth. The baron lay in a small depression, the greens and browns of his hunting clothes joining with the branches and leaves of the forest floor, his pulmonary blood equally inconspicuous. One of the weekend guests passed within ten feet of him and saw nothing, so intent was he on stalking the stag. His three sons were well ahead and the beaters farther ahead still. The women were picking their way along the bridle path, twisting and ducking to avoid the heavy branches of the firs and beeches that lined the way.

At last they heard a single shot followed by a faint cheer. The dogs were howling and the women knew without being told that the stag was dead and that flasks of schnapps were being passed around and toasts drunk, the old baron pronouncing the traditional words. The blond girls rolled their eyes and snickered at the faraway shots and laughter, a celebration such as would follow a great battle against eastern barbarians, not a single truculent stag, an animal beautiful to look at, a noble carriage and bearing. A celebration of the strong bullying the weak, a kind of violent lovemaking, re-morseless certainly, but there would be primitive animal ecstasy, too, blood and bruises, loathing, pain, exhaustion, deep sleep. The women continued to maneuver their horses down the bridle path, eager to join the celebration and learn who had fired the fatal shot, and then to watch the expert gutting of the stag. But ahead the baroness had halted and was slowly dismounting, kneeling, her hand to her mouth. And then she was screaming, high thin notes that rose ever higher, beyond the woodlands to the lakes and streams, rising and spreading to the very limits of the vast estate, and then dimin-ishing to silence, while the hawks continued to circle in lazy arcs and the beaters, the hunters, and the weekend guests turned to seek the source of the wailing.

Greenwood rose to refill his glass, switching on the overhead light and the standing lamp in the kitchen. The room had been dark except for the single reading light next to his chair. He absently dropped ice cubes and covered them with vodka, deep in thought, thinking that the screenwriter had done a creditable job. The setting was provocative, everything shown, not told, leaving the viewer with the slightest suspicion, surely false, that someone had killed the old man, shot him dead where he stood, the killer his wife or middle son, Rolf, or one of the weekend guests, nothing so prosaic as a stroke. And that, too, had been well prepared for, the old baron corpulent, irascible, an unquiet temperament. Such a man in-vited distress, stroke or heart attack or apoplexy. There was nothing about him that invited sympathy, either — only the look of terror in his eyes when he knew something dreadful had happened to him. But you would need a very good cameraman, someone with experience, a cameraman with lyric gifts, intimate with shadows. And the soundman would have to know his business, recording each conversation, and separately the ambient sound; the mix was the director's responsibility. The blond girls, avid with excitement, urging their horses forward in order to witness the celebration was a sequence of tremendous potential, concluding the moment they came around the turn in the bridle path and saw the baron down, blood on his face and hands, his widow kneeling beside him, her fists raised to the sky. So they would look at one another, appalled, and rein their horses and wait for the others, the sons, the weekend guests, and the beaters. Of course the music was an inspiration, though Dix remembered Mahler's adagio as sinister, not tender.

Well, any adagio could be made tender.

You could bend an adagio to any wind.

Dix began reading again, able now to put faces to the characters. Karen Hupp would play the plain brunette girl, the most forceful of the three. And it was always interesting to make a graceful girl awkward, a suggestion of asymmetry; she would still be Karen but not the same Karen. Karl would be the middle brother, Rolf, so ill at ease in the feral shadows of the forest; and if it worked, a triumph of casting against type. Dix placed himself again in East Prussia in 1899, the look of the estate, the weather, the rituals of the hunt, the weapons and the customary horn, times past though not lost, a vivid and unforgiving country capable of inspiring fierce devotion. He recollected his experience with Reinhold and the lure of blood sport, its danger and lust and competition, and always a mystery at the heart. He was seeing all this through the camera in his head, filming as he was reading, seeing Karen's face and Karl's, and the undefined features of the baroness.

The script cut abruptly from the forest to the funeral, the interior of an ancient village church, the flickering candles emphasizing the darkness within. The scene opened with the casket being borne down the center aisle, the woodsmen of the estate acting as pall-bearers. The casket was heavy and without decoration. The church windows were narrow and undistinguished, except the one where the camera lingered, a death dance, twenty-one brightly colored panels, skeletons clad and unclad, with scythes and without, grinning and lifeless; the word in German was Totentanzfenster. The nave was narrow and high, rising to a four-sided bell tower tapering at the summit and crowned by a small weathered cross. The church was constructed of darkwood, the wood glowing dully with the sheen of five centuries of palmsweat. The camera patrolled the interior, concentrating on the faces of the mourners as they sang the opening hymn.

Rain began to fall when the doors opened and the procession spilled into the road and began to march in the direction of the family cemetery. The scene would be filmed as if it were happening in any century back to the Reformation, with no suggestion of the modern world except for the occasional sparkle of jewelry. And silence from the mourners, the only sounds the rustling of their garments and the thud of their footfalls on the wet cart path, the cemetery in the distance, graves in uneven rows and a small mausoleum on the rise back of the stand of white birches. The widow led, her three sons a step behind. The pallbearers struggled with the heavy coffin, watched closely by the villagers gathered at the iron gates of the cemetery. Other landowners were present along with the weekend guests, including the blond girls, who were heavily veiled. Karen stood apart from her sisters, watching the middle son follow the coffin to the gravesite. In close-up, the camera detected smiles and mischief behind the smiles. When the coffin reached the cemetery gates, from somewhere amid the birches came the low notes of the hunting horn, the notes rising and deepening into the familiar moan of an oboe. Taps at reveille, Dix thought, and just as suddenly recalled the look of the land in northern Illinois, the lakes, rivers, swamps, and forests of his youth, sodden with autumn rain, the uneven rows of headstones, the birches, and here and there an oak so large that two men could not embrace it. No one used hunting horns, though. The hymn that Harry had requested was "Ain't Misbehavin'," Fats Waller's score, and Dix remembered the smiles on the faces of all the well-groomed men and women in the pews. Even his mother smiled. And in place of the carriages assembled in front of the baron's church, Ford station wagons.

Then the pastor was reading from the Bible and the pallbearers strained to lower the coffin into the ground, and then to fill the pit, shoveling the clotted earth until it covered the coffin, and tamping it down until the surface was smooth, finally covering the grave with fir branches.

Greenwood rose and dropped more ice cubes into his glass and poured vodka. He was trying to get the sense of things settled in his mind. He sought a neutral place from which he could eavesdrop on the Germans talking to each other, explaining themselves, as Werner wanted them to do; but not by words, by gestures. They seemed to be unraveling knots.

He picked up the script and continued reading. The time was later that afternoon, the camera approaching the grounds of the manor house, the gardens, the ragged hedges, the corroded sundial next to the arched gazebo, and finally the heavy façade of the building itself. The rain had turned to drizzle. Inside, the family was gathered in the vast hall, the sons standing in front of the fireplace, where a few logs smoldered. The room was dominated by a huge portrait of the original baron, one of the sixteenth-century barons, and a good likeness of the dead man as well, the wide forehead and the mustache, the severe cast to the eyes and mouth, and a long scar running from his nose to his ear. The widow remained veiled, so that when she spoke her voice was muffled and seemed to be coming from somewhere else. She was motionless in her chair, describing in a firm voice the business of running the estate, the care of the fields and the livestock, the work the woodsmen did, and what they earned. Many souls depended on the estate, the managers, the woodsmen, the servants, the stablehands, the families that cared for the livestock. The entire village, really, was dependent in one way or another on the estate. It was like a small nation and the baron's family was the government, responsible for order and the general well-being. Like most families of the Prussian aristocracy, they were not rich. Instead, they had land, the same land in the same family for generations, and that would not change. She would not permit change, for she understood the particular virtues of their way of life, singular in the world. They asked nothing of anyone. Still, their situation was not enviable. There were debts, and someone had to provide.

She said, Your father was not a provident man.

And in that way he was weak.

He refused to recognize the position he was in, and take steps to correct it. So someone had to clean up his mess. Christian — she nodded at the oldest son — had his army commission, so he was not a candidate. Ernst — she looked at her youngest son — was not yet mature, and was unsuitable in other ways. Someone in this family had to take up a trade or, equally useful and altogether more practical, marry someone rich — an Englishwoman, some woman, some suitable woman who had an appreciation for the spiritual side of the life they led and the land they led it on. These were things the better English families understood. The family was indistinguishable from the land they occupied and owned, owned fundamentally no less than you owned a wedding ring, a pair of shoes, or a horse. Someone would have to do his duty. Someone had to make it his life's work to restore the fortunes of the estate, otherwise they would all be lost. They would be adrift. They would cease to be a serious family.

The camera moved from face to face, the boredom of the oldest son, the grief of the youngest, the wry expression of the middle son, Rolf, who anticipated correctly that he would be nominated to marry the debutante and bring her and her bank account back to Prussia, where they would ride horseback all day long while his mother managed things, because nothing could dislodge her from her manor house amid the Masurian Lakes; and that would be the end of his life at the university, his friends and his poems, his philosophical discussions in smoke-filled cafés, his travels to Italy and Greece. His mother seemed to be looking directly at him, though it was hard to tell, her veil was opaque. He looked down, studying the figure in the carpet. It seemed to him that he had been studying the figure in the carpet for the length of his lifetime, his mind directed elsewhere as one parent or another lectured him on his responsibilities, and how he was neglecting them in favor of his life in the soft, sunny cities far to the south, cities remote indeed from the family estate in rigorous East Prussia. Someone coughed. When he looked up, he saw his mother staring at him. She had removed her veil and joined Christian at the fireplace, a general and her aide-de-camp inspecting the troops. The sixteenth-century baron stared down at Rolf with hooded eyes. Ernst was staring also, with a demure smile on his thin lips. A servant arrived with a spray of flowers and was waved away.

Rolf, she said.

He said nothing, merely stood with his hands behind his back, his fingers locked.

I want you to visit our cousins —

Distant cousins, he said, knowing exactly whom she meant. I have never met them.

— in Gloucestershire, explain to them about your father.

His debts?

No. How gallantly he accepted his death. The English admire gallantry.

He turned again to the figure in the carpet.

You will go during the English "season." You will meet someone, your cousins will see to it. You are a charming boy, and I know you will find something agreeable. They are not hot-blooded, these English girls. But they have other qualities. They are domestic. They are good with horses.

And rich, he said. She must be rich.

All of them are rich, his mother said.

He did not reply. His mother the baroness had never been out of East Prussia except to go to Berlin twice a year, to buy shoes and for a physical examination by a doctor who had been a friend of the family's. She distrusted country medicine, a farrago of superstition, folktales, and useless herbal remedies. Her Berlin doctor was an internist with a special competence in metalism and phrenology. Of course she distrusted Berlin generally, finding it decadent and moneygrubbing, the natural milieu of an industrial metropolis financed by Jews, a race that avoided the strenuous outdoor life. Jews were indoor people, sallow from lack of sun and wind. The baroness always returned to the estate with a sense of relief at having escaped the claustrophobic capital, its sarcasm, its license, its noxious swamp gases, and its indoor people bent over ledgers, and now the Communist proletariat agitating for revolution. The first thing she did on arriving home was to take her horse for a bracing gallop through the forest.

Tell them he died on his horse, she said.

But he didn't, Rolf said.

Don't be insolent, the baroness said.

They appreciate horses, she added. The English do. They would have sympathy, a healthy man struck down while riding his horse, directing the hunt. Tell them the horse was not destroyed. Tell them he was put out to stud.

Rolf nodded.

I will write to our cousins tomorrow, she said.

I must collect my things at Heidelberg, he said, speaking deliberately, having given the matter careful consideration. I have my books, friends I must see. I have consultations with my professors, and a paper that is overdue. I have examinations, he added, the end-of-term examinations that determine the ranking.

Never mind them, she said.

And I must collect my clothes.

Later, she said. Collect them later.

Things I will need for the journey, he continued, to Gloucestershire. Rolf was already calculating his assets, wondering if he had enough money to get to Italy. He had good friends in Venice and Rome. He was fluent in Italian and could earn a living tutoring foreign students or translating novels.

We will go to Berlin together. I will buy you shoes.

I have shoes, Rolf said firmly. And that gave him the thought that he could walk to Italy if need be.

I can get his things for him, Lieutenant-aspirant Christian said smoothly, laying a massive arm on his brother's shoulder. That way he need not trouble himself. He can concentrate on what must be done, learning the manners of the English, familiarizing himself with the English manner of doing things. They are very particular about form, you see.

I must insist —

You leave at the end of the month, his mother said.

And he needs to study his English, Christian said, his thick fingers massaging his brother's shoulder muscles.

My English is fluent, Rolf said.

Yes, it is, the baroness said. You have always been an exemplary student, perhaps too exemplary for your own good. Book knowledge is not the only knowledge, and in the end perhaps not important knowledge. In any case, you speak well. What is the name of that poet the English admire so?

Wordsworth, Rolf said.

Study your Wordsworth, the baroness instructed.

Droll, Greenwood thought. Another side of the character Rolf, so clumsy at life, so graceful at music. Within his own family, he was a sacrifice. Everyone make way for Christian, future field marshal of the Reich. The baroness was less successful. There was no hint of her antecedents, no hint of what animated her beyond her estate and her horses. Vast ignorance was uninteresting unless it led to unexpected insights; ignorance combined with power had dramatic possibilities, but this baroness was a cartoon. Would she be more interesting if she were an arriviste, as cold-blooded as the baron but tough because of who she was and where she came from? Dix put the script aside and lit a cigarette, wondering if Willa's translation was faithful. He thought he could guess the rest of it: Rolf and the empty-headed debutante returning to Prussia with a trunk full of clothes, a brace of geldings, and a letter of credit. The deb would be experienced, perhaps somewhat older, and middle son Rolf would continue to yearn for soft, sunny, southern climates for the remainder of his days or until 1914, whichever came first. The English girls would be viscountesses, or conceivably — touring the salons of Mayfair and beyond — Rolf would find an American, a southern belle who knew about the importance of land, horseflesh, lost causes, and Christianity. She would fit into the East Prussian estate as she had fitted into the plantation near Richmond. Difference was, the peasants would have white skin. No doubt there would be some tension between the belle and the baroness while the unfortunate husband dreamed of the sensual life in the hill towns of Italy.

Responsibility would weigh heavily on Rolf's shoulders, unless it developed that his empty-headed debutante was as fierce as the baroness. So perhaps he would find a way. And then Dix remembered the judgment of middle children: geniuses surrounded by morons.

The telephone was on its third ring before he heard it, so absorbed was he in the philosopher's script. Rising to answer, he decided he would not anticipate what was to come. The writer had tricks up his Marxist sleeve. Best to let him disclose them in his own time, in his own way.

Herr Greenwood?

The voice was hesitant.

I am Jana, she said.

Yes, he said impatiently. He was still in the manor house with the baroness and her sons. He had no idea who Jana was.

Jana, she said again. I saw your picture in the newspaper.

How can I help you, Jana?

I am living in Berlin now.

Yes, he said.

When I saw your picture, I decided to call on you in Wannsee. They said you were out, but they gave me your telephone number. Your voice is strange, Herr Greenwood.

Do we know each other, Jana?

She gave a little dry laugh, the laugh muffled at the end as if she had placed her hand over the receiver. After a moment, she said, Oh, yes, I think you do. Didn't we spend a summer together? It's very clear in my mind. I am the one who didn't want to devote myself to films. Acting in someone else's story.

He heard her voice but her words eluded him. He stared into the oval mirror and it seemed to him many seconds before he spoke, in a voice not his own, *Jana?*

Yes, I am Jana. You thought I was dead.

Where are you? He shifted the telephone from one ear to the other, as if that would improve the connection, though he heard her clearly.

I told you, she said sharply. Here in Berlin.

Berlin, he said.

Yes, Berlin. You are surprised?

I'm sorry, he said. I'm very sorry. I didn't recognize your voice. It's been so many years and I never expected —

I thought you would remember me, she said.

I've never forgotten you, Jana.

And I have thought about you often, Herr Greenwood. You remember the evening by the river, we talked of the future, and I said no more films. I kept my word.

You did indeed, he said, and not knowing what else to say, added, Congratulations.

Herr Greenwood —

Call me Dix, he said.

I liked working with you.

We made a wonderful film, he said.

We did, she said. And Herr Jeidels?

He's fine, living in Los Angeles.

Good, she said.

He's no longer in films, Dix added.

That is a pity.

They talked on for a few minutes. She asked about the boys, Tommy Gwilt and the other two, but Dix had to admit that he'd lost touch with them because he, too, was on the sidelines of the movie business. After an awkward pause, he said, Jana, I'm involved in something now, it's out of the ordinary but perhaps you'd be interested. I'd like to explain it to you, then you can decide for yourself. Perhaps lunch. Can I take you to lunch?

She thought a moment. I wouldn't mind, she said.

Tomorrow?

Of course, Jana said.

I'm very happy you called, Dix said.

I thought you would be, Jana replied.

PART THREE

# Berlin, March

# 17

THE DAY was sunny so Dix waited for Jana on the steps of Mommsen House. When she came up the driveway he recognized her at once by her walk, a determined duck-footed shuffle. She was wearing a tan trenchcoat and a seaman's watch cap, and when she removed the cap, shaking her hair loose, he saw that she had hardly changed in the many years since he had seen her. Evidently the same could not be said of him, for she avoided his eyes as she strolled up the driveway, pausing to inspect the sundial, checking the time against her watch; and then, when they were within a few yards of each other, she broke into a startled smile and said, Dix. He embraced her, shaking his head, saying that she was exactly as he remembered her, even the trenchcoat.

No, no, Jana said. Look at the gray in my hair and the wrinkles. And I am five pounds heavier, five pounds at least.

But thank you, she said.

And you, too, are the same.

You didn't recognize me, he said.

I have never seen you in an overcoat. An overcoat changes the look, wouldn't you say? She stepped back and appraised him as if she were a tailor estimating his height and weight. She said, The last time we talked it was summer, late at night. The fog coming from the river, no one about. I was waiting for someone, you were out for a stroll with a glass of schnapps in your hand. I couldn't imagine what you were doing there. We talked about Herzog's films, which you loved and I detested.

And you disappeared the next day.

Was it the next day?

Yes, Dix said.

I had had enough, she said. So I went away.

We were worried, all of us were worried. We didn't know what happened, we thought you had drowned. There was a police inquiry, an inquest —

A person has the right to go away if she chooses, Jana said.

"Presumed dead by misadventure" was the verdict.

Yes, I heard.

And you didn't care?

I had had enough. So I went away.

Dix turned away, too relieved to be angry. Jana seemed to have no grasp of what she had done. He said, You should have told someone. You should have told the one you were meeting on the bridge.

She looked at him strangely.

He said, Who was it?

You don't know?

No, Dix said.

I thought you knew, it wasn't a secret. I was meeting Billy Jeidels. He liked to take long walks at night and we often met in the park by the bridge. He said he was interested in the Sorb people so I told him all about us, our language, where we came from, and the things we believed, including the right to go away when we chose to.

They walked up Glienekestrasse, Jana bringing him up to date. No, she was not married. She had been married but it hadn't worked out so her husband left her for another woman, not a Sorb. One Sorb in a lifetime was enough for him, he said. They lived now in Stuttgart with their child. Jana remained in Berlin after the divorce because she found it exciting and because she had a job she liked, security guard at the Brücke Museum in Grunewald, with its expressionist canvases and limited visiting hours. She had a small apartment in Kreuzberg near the Landwehrkanal. A health club was nearby, and there were many galleries and avant-garde theater groups in the district. Often in the evening she would go to plays. Recently she had been involved with someone but now that had ended and she was living alone and finding it pleasant. On the whole, she preferred living alone, for the privacy it afforded. She had her solitude at night and her security work during the day, and she could do as she liked. Dix waited for her to continue, but that was all she said. He wondered where the excitement came in.

On an impulse he suggested they take the ferry to Kladow and lunch at the Italian restaurant on the quay. Had she ever taken the ferry across Wannsee Lake? No, never. This was her first visit to Wannsee. They stood at the rail for the twenty-minute journey, watching the single sculls slice through the water. He told her the story of the retired accountants but she did not seem interested. He stood with his back to the bow, shielding his face from the wind.

After they ordered lunch he told her about Claire, now adrift in Asia on someone's airplane. He said he had frequent messages from her but nothing for the past few days. He was never in when she called. He was worried about her because she did not sound like herself, yet there was nothing specific to cause alarm. There was trouble on the set of the film she was making. He and Claire were often apart and they both knew that the set was a dangerous place, easy to lose your bearings. Still, her messages on the machine were — perhaps erratic was the word. She seemed to be in another zone of time. Dix spoke to Jana as if she were an old friend. Perhaps it was only that she figured in his distant past and he was grateful that she was alive.

I worry, he said.

Haven't you always been independent?

Yes, Dix said.

She is exercising her independence.

In Asia, Dix said.

Why not? Jana said.

After a moment, she said, So you finally found a wife. You said you had been tempted many times. I am glad you gave in. And I notice you are wearing the same wedding band.

Very observant, Jana.

Why did you lie to me?

Not for the obvious reason, he said.

That's true. So there was a reason not so obvious.

I wanted you to trust me.

An unmarried man is more trustworthy than a married one?

In some circles, yes. But it was a mistake.

I knew you were lying. Billy told me.

Helpful Billy, Dix said.

Jana smiled. As you said, the set is a dangerous place.

Did you find it dangerous?

Not dangerous, not really.

Alluring?

Yes, I would say alluring. I was so young, barely fifteen. Trude and Marion were a little older. We stole money from our families and left home to have an adventure, to see what the world was like without answering to anyone. I suppose to learn about the people who lived elsewhere. We had never been out of our village in Lusatia and we knew there were many things that were different outside. Another time zone, as you would say. Of course we had no idea what we were looking for and what we would find. We had no idea, really, where we were going. We were only girls looking for an adventure, and boys were part of the adventure. So we made our way to Görlitz and across the Czech border and back into East Germany in order to find our way west. No one paid much attention to us. We had only the vaguest idea that the West was closed to us, and I imagine if we had known the difficulty beforehand we never would have tried. But we crossed from East to West, never mind how. And one day in that little café in Franconia you found us, and the next thing we knew we were acting in a movie. At first I liked it, I never knew where working left off and playing began. I didn't see any difference between the two, and my friends didn't either. There were no movie houses in our village so we didn't know what to expect, do you see? So we went along with everything, why not?

She laughed then, covering her mouth with her hands. The things we said to each other when we were alone, speaking our own language. We knew we were involved in a scandal. We were forward with the boys. Jana looked across the table and smiled apologetically.

You seemed much older than fifteen, Dix said.

Everybody thought that, Jana said. They thought I was twenty then. And sometimes they think I am twenty today.

I can hardly believe it even now.

I lived in a village, she said. But I was never an innocent.

You said you were twenty, Dix plowed on.

Of course, she said. What else would I say? You were offering me a role in a movie. What did you expect? Can you imagine what that meant to me and to Trude and Marion? Coming from where we came from, with the life we had led? I would have said anything you wanted me to say, and if what you wanted was something impossible, I would have said I didn't understand the question. I understood little enough as it was. But I didn't mind, it's fair to say. When I was that age I believed that the moment you understood something was the moment that it became boring. When Dix smiled, she said, Why do you suppose I left home?

He looked out the restaurant window at the single sculls. There appeared to be no wind but the men were working hard in their jockey motions. In the distance the passenger ferry approached. The scullers eased up and allowed their craft to drift, and in a moment they were rocking in the ferry's wake. One of the passengers waved and the scullers waved back, resting on their oars. Dix glanced at Jana and remembered the encounter in the café so many years ago, the girls whispering, their heads together, he and Billy approaching their table with an interpreter, offering to buy them a Coke or a glass of beer, the interpreter introducing them, Mr. Greenwood and Mr. Jeidels from Los Angeles, America, in Franconia to scout locations for a film; and the doubtful expression on the girls' faces but accepting Cokes all the same, trusting the formal manner of the interpreter, beginning to giggle as the Americans explained what they were doing and the time they would need. Trude and Marion asked for cigarettes, Jana declined. They sat around the café table, asking the girls where they came from and whether their summer was free — and would they mind reading a few lines into the camera — and their eyes widening as they realized the Americans were serious. He remembered Billy's playful nudge; deal closed. And Billy saying later, My God, Dix, aren't they the most ravishing girls? That one especially, meaning Jana. They don't have to act. They only have to *be*.

I think I was frightened, Jana went on. Nothing was familiar. My English was poor so I had to guess what was wanted of me. This was difficult in the beginning but not later on, I thought the set was an atmosphere you could become addicted to, and that was exciting. I saw nothing wrong with addiction. Addiction meant thrills, and wasn't that what the world promised? Wasn't that why we had taken money and left home? To meet you in the café was a dream beyond imagining. That day, we opened the door to a room we hadn't known existed. And it must have been wonderful for you and Billy. Everyone wanting to please you. All of us trying so hard to do what you wanted us to do, smile on cue, take our clothes off, stand here, stand there, blush, speak louder, speak softer, be silent. Even me, though I pretended not to care. To receive a nod or a smile, a pat on the back, a word of encouragement, to be welcomed into the society. Three girls from a village near Görlitz, a village that isn't even on the map. Whoever heard of Lusatia? Sorbs, always in the minority, always second-class citizens, barely better than Gypsies. To be on the set. You and Billy, so in charge of things. I wondered where you found the confidence, though of course you were Americans, and Americans always had confidence. Born with it.

We weren't as confident as we looked, Dix said.

We didn't know that, Jana said.

We knew we had something, we didn't know what.

Be serious. You knew more than that.

We hoped it was good. We thought we had something newborn, something never before seen.

And so you did, Jana said. Everyone said so.

Yet you went away. You had had enough.

I had enough, true. And I was free to go.

Enough of what? Dix said, dreading the answer.

Taking my clothes off, she said. Tired of sleeping with Billy.

Billy?

Yes, Billy. What's become of him?

He makes television commercials. You were sleeping with Billy?

Billy was sleeping with me, Jana said. I assumed you knew.

Dix moved his shoulders, yes and no.

Which is it? she asked sharply.

I suspected, he said. I didn't think about it. I didn't know you were fifteen and needed a chaperone. I was focused on the film, concerned with the set, only that. Billy, he began, but did not finish the thought. Billy Jeidels was sovereign in his realm, never a second thought, no regrets. The world was made up of jesters assembled to amuse him.

So I decided to disappear, she said.

And you succeeded. You succeeded very well.

How long did you look for me?

I don't remember. A week, ten days. The police came with professional divers. Tommy Gwilt never believed you were lost, but he was heartbroken all the same. She's gone away somewhere, Tommy said.

He wanted me to run away with him, Jana said after a moment. He had it all worked out. I would disappear and in a week we would rendezvous somewhere. I forget where. Some city in the West, Freiburg or Cologne. Remember, shooting was almost finished, and all my scenes were completed. So that was the plan. I would disappear and we would meet again in Freiburg or Cologne and we would be together forever. He had an idea that after a while we would go to the United States, and I would have a film career like his. But when there was an inquiry, he became frightened and did not make the rendezvous. Somehow I neglected to think there would be an inquiry. I thought I would be a simple missing person, a Sorb girl no one cared about. We have been disappearing for years and no one ever thought to look for us. Why would they now? So my life turned out to be different from what I expected because Wendt lost his nerve.

Wendt was his film name, Dix said. His real name was Thomas Gwilt.

I know. But I always called him Wendt.

What did he call you?

Jana, she said. But the difference is, Jana is also my real name.

So many identities in the film business, Dix said. Hard to keep them straight sometimes. He looked out the window to see the ferry nosing up to the dock. They were the last customers in the restaurant. No waiters were in sight. He finished the last of his coffee, paid the bill, helped Jana with her coat, and soon they were on the landing. A wind had come up and with it a winter chill. They stood silently watching passengers disembark, mostly women carrying grocery bags. He turned to Jana but she was in her private world, staring out over the water. She pulled the watch cap over her ears. The breeze brought color to her cheeks, making her appear even younger. Perhaps she could give an evening lecture at Mommsen House, how a young woman got her start in American film, had enough, disappeared, and decades later saw the director's picture in a German newspaper and decided to get in touch; and what she had made of her experience in the movies, and her situation now, the apartment in Kreuzberg, security guard at a museum, divorced. Then Dix remembered the last time he saw Billy Jeidels, in a Los Angeles parking lot with his family, Billy touching his son's hair and the boy's fierce rebuke, *Don't*. He would not be surprised if Billy thought of Jana for a moment or two every day of his life, and he would not be surprised if he didn't.

Jana said, I suppose it is not true that my life turned out to be different than I expected. I didn't expect anything. I didn't know what to expect. I didn't know you were supposed to expect. I was not brought up with the idea of expecting. Do you think most people expect a certain life? When they are fifteen years old, do they think out what lies ahead? And where they want to be?

It's a long time since I was fifteen, Dix said.

Well, I didn't.

It isn't absolutely necessary, he said.

Did you? Did growing up in America guarantee that you had a right to expect things?

I wanted to be a film director, Dix said. It's an outlaw business and I wanted to be one of the gunfighters. It never occurred to me to do anything else. And that's what I did until the audience went away and the ideas ran out. I don't remember which came first.

You were fortunate, then.

I made *Summer, 1921* and the two others that I liked, and two that I didn't like, though they play better now than they did then.

I saw *Summer, 1921* six times and then I stopped going because people would look at me strangely and once, when a man approached and asked if I was Jana, I had to invent a story. He didn't believe me and I don't blame him. I haven't seen it now for ten years, maybe more. Each time I saw it, I found something new. All these years later, it still has something scandalous about it. I always hoped that I would see Trude or Marion on the street or in a café somewhere and we three would go, and when the picture ended we would rise and take a bow before disappearing.

Have you been unhappy in your life, Jana?

Not really, she said. It was difficult for me the first few years. I had no money. I did not want to go back home. I was a nomad in the West. For a while I worked in a carnival as a clown, and that was what I enjoyed the most, because carnival people are kind. Everyone in a carnival is running away from something. I worked in a bookstore in Bochum, a jewelry store in Düsseldorf. I had offers all the time to be an artist's model, but I knew where that would lead and I didn't want it. I worked in one place or another and found myself at last in Berlin. Berlin is like a carnival, you can disappear in it. I have a job I like. I have my apartment. Did I tell you I have a cat? I enjoy Berlin, my evenings at the avant-garde theater. Perhaps sometime we could go to the theater.

Alas, I have no German.

I could translate.

All right, then. We'll go to the Berliner Ensemble.

Jana wrinkled her nose. There are more progressive theaters, she said. Places you never heard of. Places in basements, churches even.

Dix handed their tickets to the ferry's mate and they stepped aboard. The scullers had gone and the sun had dipped below the shoreline. The breeze had raised a chop on the lake and to the north high clouds were building. Jana preferred the open air so they stood in the stern, watching the mate cast off. The vessel swung, gathering speed, and Kladow receded.

She said, Thank you for lunch.

He said, Would you ever do it again?

Act? Perhaps. I don't know. I doubt it.

You have it in your bones, he said.

Do you think so?

You never lost it, he said.

Hard to know, she said. All those years.

You're a natural, he said.

It's hard for me to believe that about myself.

You knew it then, he said.

Of course. But I didn't know anything else.

I may direct a film here, Dix said.

Jana looked at him with a slow smile, then out across the water. Lights were visible in the villas along the shore. She said slyly, Would I have to take my clothes off?

Only if you wanted to, he said. The part doesn't call for it. But I could write it in.

No, thanks, she said.

It's a baroness, he said.

She began to giggle, her hands over her mouth.

A baroness with a past, he went on. A baroness whose husband has just died. A baroness who must now take charge of things.

When she looked at him sideways, he said, Do you know *Wannsee 1899*?

No. What's that?

It's the most popular television program in Germany, an ensemble cast. It has to do with German life at the turn of the century.

I have no television set, she said.

I'll give you one.

I have no desire for a television set.

You wouldn't have to watch it. It could just — be there.

That is foolish, she said.

Dusk fell like a curtain. He began to describe the episode, the hunt, the death of the old baron, the funeral, the graveside service, the family conference later. As he talked he focused on the baroness. The baroness led the narrative but she was not the philosopher's baroness but Dixon Greenwood's baroness, a woman with her own history, her own secrets, one who was interested neither in revenge nor in riches, but who desired only safety.

Might you be interested in that?

I might be, Jana said.

The pay would be good, Dix said. So long as you don't disappear.

I won't disappear, she said.

Did you receive anything for *Summer, 1921*?

The allowance you gave us. That was all.

I'll look up the books, he said. I'll see that you get what's coming to you.

What happened to it, my money?

It's called producer's net, Dix said. It disappeared.

# 18

T HEY HAD LISTENED to a German management consultant describe the transformation of the economy in the 1950s, the economic miracle of Herr Erhard. The phenomenal success of German industry had made possible the remarkable political stability of the nation. Certainly there were problems then, and problems remained. The central bank had not always used its power wisely, and perhaps Herr Kohl had stayed beyond his time. But if you can imagine the condition of the nation at the end of the war, then surely "miracle" was not too strong a word. And now the East was at risk. Despite the billions poured — and here he used a German word that had a double meaning, the second being "flushed" — into the East, the situation there continued grave. The Wall's fall had unforeseen consequences. In short, the government needed time.

Everyone had benefited from the collapse of the Soviet Union. Perhaps it was time for those beneficiaries to aid in the reconstruction of our East, so that the burden might be shared.

When the management consultant left, Henry Belknap and Dix stayed behind in the drawing room for coffee. Henry said the new-minted East German capitalists reminded him of medieval Christians. They confused devotion with sorcery. The medievals knew nothing of the teachings of Christ. They could not read, so the Bible was a mystery. The Mass was incomprehensible. So they relied on superstitions, incantations, magic wands, exotic potions, dances around a totem pole, or the various nights of the living dead. They relied on priests, whose words they only dimly understood — but the priests could read, so the Bible became a kind of amulet.

That's where they are, Henry said.

Somewhere between Transylvania and the economics department of Harvard, Dix said.

On the whole, I think they prefer Transylvania.

Dix heard a noise and when he turned he saw Anya Ryan in the doorway with an older man in a beret. She said, I want you to meet my father, Otto Farber. They both wore overcoats and Anya's father carried a satchel. He removed his beret at once. Henry fetched them coffee while Anya explained that her father had arrived unexpectedly from Rugen. They had dined at Munn Café and — would it be all right for my father to stay the night?

Henry said, Of course. The guest room was vacant.

Dix went to the sideboard to pour cognacs. Herr Farber was not at all what he imagined. He was not much taller than Anya and very slight. His black hair was plastered to his scalp and he seemed the opposite of brusque. His manner was shy, almost apologetic. He looked around the drawing room as if he had never seen such a place, the bookshelves floor to ceiling and a television set the size of the fireplace next to it. Anya helped her father with his overcoat and when he looked at her gratefully, Dix reflected that every parent was seen one way by their children and another way by the world and these ways did not intersect; and everyone was a product of his own time and place, described one way by those who had lived through it and quite differently by those who looked back on it.

Henry played affable host, offering Herr Farber a cigar, describing the evening lecture, the roots of the German economic miracle and the consequences of it. Otto Farber listened attentively but did not comment.

And how is the situation in Rugen, Herr Farber?

Our weather is improving, he said.

And here also, Henry agreed.

It's difficult. But we survive. I enjoy it because the island is lively in summer and tranquil in winter. And because my daughter is nearby.

We are glad Anya is here, Henry said.

We are all fond of Anya, Dix put in.

And I, too. I am her father.

I'm tired now, Anya said. I want to go to bed.

This is a fine house, Herr Farber said.

Do you like it? Henry asked.

Papa, Anya said.

Herr Farber quickly gathered up his coat and beret and thanked Henry and Dix for their hospitality. He and Anya stood at the door and at that moment Dix saw no resemblance between them. Herr Farber's hair shined in the light and when he bent to lift his satchel he bore a fleeting resemblance to the little tramp, Charlie Chaplin in person; and then he and his daughter were gone.

He didn't say if he liked the house, Henry said.

Anya and her father do not get along, Dix said.

Is that so? I didn't notice.

I'm sure he liked the house, Henry.

I didn't like the way he said "fine." When he said "fine," he meant something else. He meant ostentatious, and this is just a villa like any other.

They sat a moment, finishing their coffee and cognac. Something moved in Dix's memory but he could not capture it. Henry was complaining about a lunch he had been asked to give for sponsors of Mommsen House, more time away from his translation, the guests an American industrialist, the head of one of the Frankfurt insurance companies, some supremo from steel, and a Hamburg shipper, and if you'd join us it would help me out —

Henry, Dix said. Remember Hamburg, 1956? Our weekend with the banker? His wife dead, his children dead, no one to leave his bank to? He called us nice American boys and said that if we belonged to him, we could have his bank. What was his name?

I can't remember, Henry said.

I can't either, Dix said. We liked him. He was a gentleman.

I had a letter of introduction, Henry said.

Was he Jewish?

Henry thought a moment but did not reply.

I'm asking this. Did his family die in the camps or at the front?

I have no idea, Henry said.

Anything in the house give you a clue? Anything he said?

Nothing he said. I didn't think about it.

I didn't either, Dix said.

Henry said, I assumed he had fought in the war or otherwise supported the effort. Maybe a Nazi, maybe not. But there were many Jewish banks in Hamburg. Expropriated by the government. Some of them survived the war and I assume their owners returned, those who were still alive, living in America or England. So we have no way of knowing. He's surely dead by now, and as he told us, he was the last of the line. Why are you asking?

Something my father said, Dix said vaguely.

Strange we never thought about it, Henry said.

Harry did. The first question he asked.

The Holocaust was a subterranean subject in 1956. Not on our minds.

It was on Harry's, apparently.

Shall I try to find out? The family provenance.

Yes, do, Dix said.

So will you come to lunch with my supremos?

I'm out of town next week, Dix said.

Well, Henry said quietly, some other time, then. He had drunk too much wine at dinner, causing his words to thicken. He explained that he was months behind in his translation of Babel's Red Cavalry stories. Such wonderfully succinct stories, each word in them had the weight and aspiration of a cathedral. His would be an entirely fresh translation, with an introduction as well. But instead he was lunching with industrialists, something Babel would have appreciated, God knows, once the laughter stopped. Henry went on in that vein for a while but Dix had ceased to listen. He was thinking about the Hamburg banker, his formal manners and precise diction, and his confusion when he'd opened the door to his past, not wide enough to see inside, just enough to know it was crowded. The banker and Jana were two sides of a coin. *Summer, 1921* had been her last film because she had no desire to play someone's life; and so she had disappeared, gone on the run, lived anonymously, true to her word. That was the faith she had in film, that the characters were real and that when you played them you became them. But what if she were offered her own life, a Sorb's story at the end of the last century, when borders had meaning, and that when you strayed beyond them something was forfeit. He reckoned Jana's age as in the vicinity of forty-five, about the age of the baroness. So the climactic episode of *Wannsee 1899* would be seen through the baroness's eyes. Jana's eyes, if she'd allow him to borrow them.

Dix looked up at something Henry said.

Do you miss Los Angeles? I think you do.

Not now, Dix said.

When Dix returned to his apartment, the answering machine's red light was blinking. He poured a nightcap and listened to Claire.

Where are you now? she began. How is it that we miss each other every time? You always told me you were the sort of man who could ignore a ringing telephone if what you were doing was more interesting. I've seen you do it a hundred times, and when I complained that someone may be in distress, one of the children or a dear friend, you always said, Perhaps, but it's never happened, has it?

After a long pause, she went on: I have no idea what the time difference is, hours and hours I suppose, and I have no idea whether you're ahead or behind. The International Date Line has always been a mystery to me and to you, too. You're a mystery to me, Dix, living as you are on the other side of the world. I have no idea what your life is like, what you do and who you see, how you spend your days. Whatever you do with them, I suppose there's always a drink at the end. Maybe two.

Just so you know. I always thought of you as a man of honor.

So here's the news.

Howard's been in touch with Los Angeles but he won't tell them where we are. Everything's gone to the lawyers, Howard's lawyer and the studio's lawyers. Fuck them, Howard says. Until he has a satisfactory piece of paper we're staying out of sight. I don't know what he's doing, really. I'm only along for the ride. I have nothing better to do. I'm confused because of the time changes and the hours I've spent looking at the blue Pacific. All this distance and I haven't seen a single boat, just hours and hours of blue water. The weather was so clear west of Hawaii. But still I couldn't find a boat.

Dix heard a scratch and imagined her lighting a cigarette, perhaps blowing a fat smoke ring. Her voice was controlled, and she was using her actor's tempo. He recognized the voice as her own but it was different, too, as if she were continuing a conversation begun with someone else. She was silent again and he noticed that the electrical hum was gone. She might have been next door.

So I suppose you want to know where we are.

We put in at Guam, refueled, and flew to Hong Kong. Lou Kniffe met us in Hong Kong. He came in from Brunei. Where's Brunei? What mischief is there in Brunei? I always worry when Knife's in range, Knife and his people, his starlets, his plans that are always a little over the top. But there's nothing I can do about it. It's his airplane.

I know you liked him.

And he liked you.

So we're in Mandalay, she said. And the dawn didn't come up like thunder this morning because it's pissing down rain, the southwest monsoon. Knife has business with the generals who run things here. Not movie business but other business, dirty business, I'm thinking, so we have an army escort wherever we go, courtesy of the generals. Don't laugh, they're very helpful, scattering cyclos on the road and pushing peasants out of the way whenever we want to stop to look at a stupa. There's us in the van, and an army jeep in front and another behind, armed to the teeth. They look hardly older than boys but they surely do understand crowd control. You probably didn't know that Knife has apprenticed himself to a monk, Burmese by birth. He met the monk at a retreat in Malibu and they've become inseparable, studying texts. Knife is taking instruction in Buddhism so the monk is with us at all times, explaining things. He has a beautiful shaved head and the smallest feet I've ever seen, and beautifully manicured nails. Hands, too. Wee fists. His skin glows and he wears a saffron-colored robe, silk from the feel of it.

Maybe he got it at Saks.

Or Armani, she amended, giving a gruff little laugh.

Knife is gaining merit, she went on. Not earning merit, *gaining* merit. This is important. He explained it at breakfast this morning — only rice and cold tea for him and the monk, bacon and eggs for the rest of us, and a bloody mary to get through the day. Knife's planning for his next life, and while you'd think he'd want to come back as Spielberg or Clinton, he doesn't at all. It's a white elephant he has in mind, because that's the afterlife of choice for the Buddhist elect. It's a kind of sacred elephant. The monk confirmed it. So in order to enhance your possibilities for the next life it's necessary to gain merit in this life, and that's where the white owl comes in.

So many different Buddhas, she went on after a moment's pause. And so much to aspire to, charity, compassion, sympathy, balance — those four and others besides. The Buddha that Knife seems most attracted to is the one with the smile on his face, fat as a sow, jowls the size and shape of wine bags. He's the representation of "enoughness," contentment with things as they are. And why not? This Buddha has eaten and drunk everything within reach, enjoying himself as only Buddha can, hence the smile. This fine Buddha stands in for Fat Lou himself, Lou with the two Jaguars, the houses in Beverly Hills and London, the dishy girlfriends, the vintage champagne arriving from Madame Taittinger herself, the trophy carp in the oval pond, the pit bull in the cage, the matched Purdeys, the converted DC-10, just about everything a boy could want — except, conceivably, charity, compassion, sympathy, and balance. And those, too, within reach.

But I'm getting ahead of myself.

I was telling you about the white elephant. Or, rather, Knife was speaking of the white elephant and the merits one needed in this life in order to succeed in the next. So this morning we visited a pagoda in the countryside, the Irrawaddy in the distance, the fields and hillsides crowded with pagodas — white and gold pagodas glittering in the afternoon sun. God, it was hot. I thought I would faint.

At the entrance to the pagoda, half a dozen women were tending their birds, the small birds in cages and the large ones tethered, leather leashes around their necks. A great white owl held pride of place. A beautiful creature, Dix. Silky white feathers, huge yellow eyes, and a beak of the shiniest, blackest ebony. The birds were for sale. That is to say, they were for sale-and-release. Knife and the monk were in heavy confab, which bird to buy and for how much. Because at this pagoda, a visitor gained merit by buying a bird and releasing it at once — an act of charity and compassion, an act that set just the right note of humility before facing the judgment of Buddha himself. Obviously, a mogul the size of Lou Kniffe would be satisfied with nothing less than the owl. To purchase and release an owl of that nobility would be to gain much merit. The price was one hundred thousand kyats.

You'll be wondering how much that is in real money.

It's about twenty-five dollars.

But the crone in charge of the owl has sized Lou up, she's scrutinized the bench-made loafers and the alligator belt, the polo shirt the color of butter, and the Girard-Perregaux as thin as a dime. So the price has suddenly risen to two hundred thousand kyats, and it's then that Knife begins to bargain, his wallet in his fist, stuffed with greenbacks. But now the monk takes him aside to have a word, and Knife's face falls. Knife has never paid list for anything in his life. It's not his nature to pay list. List is for chumps. Something always comes off the top for Knife or it's no dice, no sale.

An awful moment, Dix.

The idea is to give the owl its freedom, and to do this as an act of charity and compassion, and thereby gain merit. How would it appear to the great Buddha if the aspirant bargained like a common merchant? Behaved as if he were in a bazaar buying a piece of cloth instead of at the threshold of a pagoda, moved by the sight of a leashed owl? So you could see Knife wrestling, a lifetime's habit renounced — for the sake of an owl. For merit, and for the sake of the elusive white elephant. At last he turned his back on the crone — he could not bear for her to witness his defeat — and fished in his wallet for the fifty dollars, and handed it to the monk to give to the crone. He kept his eyes averted all this time, until finally the monk had the leash off and the owl in his hands. They carried the owl together to the parapet, the vast valley and the river beyond. You could see the monsoon coming from the south, a cloud so dark it seemed to smother the green fields and the huts and pagodas resting on them — and on their count, they released the bird, who seemed to stutter and flail, then spread his great wings and soared off into the valley, dipping once, then nestling into a giant fir; and was shortly lost to view, concealed in the fir's thick branches. The sun was overtaken by cloud, a wind came up, and the downpour began. Knife leaned far out over the parapet, searching for his owl.

We applauded, of course.

The white elephant, ever so much nearer.

Even the monk seemed content.

And the crone. She was very content.

Then — you can wait your whole life long and never find a moment as filled with possibility as this one — Knife extends his left arm and brings his fist to his mouth. He sights along his arm and moves his index finger. He swings left, swings right, searching for his two-hundred-thousand-kyat owl. At that moment he was aiming his Purdey twelve-gauge; and the owl was as good as mounted under the itty-bitty Matisse in his study, stuffed to within an inch of its life, his latest effort, merit gained. And then he realized what he was doing and turned to face us, and with his usual snarl announced we were returning to the hotel.

He left early this morning by army aircraft, bound northeast into the Shan States. He won't say what he's doing there — "scouting locations," which we know is a lie. What do you suppose he's doing, Dix? My guess is, it's ten-year-old virgins or yesterday's opium crop. He says he'll return close of business tomorrow, and then it's back home.

I'm sure it's opium. The monk is with him, so it wouldn't be girls, would it?

I hope not. The thought of it makes me sick.

So that's my news.

We'll be home in a couple of days.

Oh, one last thing. Ada Hart made Knife the executor of her estate. And do you know what? She left everything to charity. Ada hadn't a single living relative, isn't that sad? So Lou Kniffe will supervise the disbursements to the Girl Scouts, the cancer fund, NARAL, and the Audubon Society.

I remember what a good eulogy you gave for Ada. Everyone said so.

You talked about a life as uncompleted action, "however long or short, the arbitrary interval governed by a malicious sovereign." I wasn't sure what you meant by that, but now I think I do. You can never know another's spirit. Isn't that right?

# 19

THE WEATHER had turned warm overnight, a false spring
that brought café tables and chairs onto the sidewalks of
Berlin. Patrons drank beer in the sun in their shirtsleeves. In
the glare of the sun their winter faces appeared waxy and pale as
soap. Willa Baz was in high good humor as she and Dix collected
the Mercedes at the Avis downtown and began the two-hour drive
east, out Karl-Marx-Allee, the streets crowded with bicycles. Dix
knew where he wanted to film, so they were en route to meet
Reinhold and Sophie Lenord. Spring rushed in through the open
windows and Willa talked on, saying again and again how delighted
she and her producer were that Dix had agreed to direct the season's climactic episode of *Wannsee 1899*. He had described to her
some of the changes he wanted to make in the philosopher's script
and she agreed without hesitation. Whatever you want to do, Dix,
it's fine. We only insist that the material be historically accurate.
Within limits.

Within limits, he said.

And Jana has agreed to appear?

I think she will, Dix said.

What a coup, Willa said.

They were stopped at a traffic light, enormous concrete buildings looming over them. The street was choked with diesel fumes.

What limits? Dix asked with a smile.

The usual limits, she said. Sometimes we can't afford what we need.

Understood, he said.

I know the script isn't all it should be. Yet our philosopher has interesting ideas. He believes Germany is the first modern state. Oh, yes. Germany is the cradle of Marxism, after all. Marxism was our great export in the nineteenth century.

Sophie Lenord explained that her owners would rent the big house for one month, reluctantly, and only after conditions stipulated by the estate agent, Herr Erfurr in Potsdam, were agreed to. Of course a substantial deposit would be required. Anything damaged must be replaced in the original, and that included any damage to the fields and outbuildings. Herr Erfurr had a full inventory of fixtures and fittings; there were to be no structural alterations whatever, and no disturbance of the streams and woodlands. Frau Lenord was to be present at all times. Herr Greenwood and Frau Baz would have one morning to look at the house and grounds to see if the location was suitable.

Sophie recited this while standing under the porte-cochère, holding the iron latchkey in both hands, her fingers crossed.

Do they want final cut, too? Dix asked.

I don't understand, Sophie said.

Herr Greenwood's joke, Willa said.

Dix smiled. It's fine, Sophie.

Willa said, Where's Reinhold?

Hunting, Sophie said. She paused a moment and added, Reinhold does not approve.

Why not?

Sophie shrugged and looked away down the gravel road to the Lenord gatehouse. A thin line of smoke rose from the chimney but nothing else moved. Reinhold advised against it, she said.

Dix said, Shall we go inside.

Why not? Willa said again.

Reinhold does not think Americans should be in charge of

*Wannsee 1899.* He does not like Americans on the property, Sophie said, unlocking the door and standing aside so Willa and Dix could enter.

The downstairs — large foyer with its iron chandelier, large rectangular dining room, larger living room, narrow staircase leading to the upper floors — was unsuitable, the furniture of an indefinite contemporary style, appearing almost weightless in the torpor of the room, its dark walls, high ceilings, and narrow windows, an exact space of suffocating formality and rectitude. The furniture made it ludicrous, Bismarck in Capezios — low-slung glass cocktail tables, Eames chairs, white-bordered mirrors, and a scythe-shaped sofa, an ensemble suited to a condominium in South Florida. The art on the walls was Titian-sized and aggressively abstract. Of course substitute furniture could be rented, but even so, a country baroness — even a turn-of-the-century country baroness — would never put up with a fireplace so shallow, with a mantel of beige marble, the Chinese yin-yang ideograph chiseled into its veined face. The darkwood floors and paneled walls seemed set in the frown of a profoundly disappointed German governess.

Dix said, What do they do, the owners?

I don't know, Sophie replied. They never said. For them it is a weekend house. They come down on weekends with their young children, sometimes with friends. We pick them up at the airport. They keep to themselves. On Sunday mornings they take long walks, the children, too. Sometimes they ride their horses. They have a big lunch and then we take them back to the airport. They own a small plane and he flies it.

Where do they live? Greenwood was looking at a portrait on the wall above the sofa, a young girl in blue jeans and a jersey sitting on a bench, her dog beside her.

Düsseldorf, Sophie said.

That explains it, Willa said.

Not very promising, Greenwood said. The furniture, the *look* of the room. It's all wrong. The fireplace . . . And then he realized that the house he had in mind was the manor of the Anglo-Irish, the one near the River Shannon where he had dined so long ago with his father, a house just this side of threadbare, but gallant.

Impossible, Willa agreed.

It's a fine house! Sophie protested.

I want to see the master bedroom, Greenwood said.

He opened the window, admitting a warm breeze with a breath of chill from the dormant fields, a barn in the near distance, various small farm buildings farther out. Hills rose in a low swell, woodlands divided by fields, rail fencing here and there in long thin lines. A twisted shoelace of a stream meandered through the hills. The sun was low on the horizon of the southern sky. In the misty light, patches of gray snow clung to the hollows. All was as it would have been in 1899 at a country estate in Prussia in the fresh morning hours before a hunting party set out, so quiet you could hear ice melt. And then a collie dog wandered out from the barn, the dog in the portrait. Greenwood stood on tiptoe and tried to pick out the woods where he and Reinhold had cornered the boar. But the woods and hills looked identical, as undifferentiated as the trees themselves and the terrain that rolled away to the Oder. The fields were utterly vacant and idle, it was only March after all, and weeks remained before the first signs of spring. He stood with his forehead pressed against the cold glass, trying to imagine things through a camera's lens. He watched the sky for hawks but there were no hawks, no obvious point of reference except for the branches of trees against a pale sky, a sinister aspect.

He heard a noise behind him, Sophie or Willa moving about. The room was large enough to give an echo and small enough so that the aroma of beeswax was sharp in his nostrils. He turned to see Willa sitting on the bed, a handsome four-poster with a lace canopy, indisputably a woman's bed. A comforter was neatly folded at its foot, a book lay open on the bedside table among framed photographs of the children and a reading light with a Tiffany shade. Willa was staring at the ceiling and shaking her head.

She said, Hopeless.

He said, Not entirely.

When he turned back to the window she muttered something and left the room, her footsteps noisy in the corridor. He concentrated hard and imagined that the woman sitting on the bed was Jana, the baroness rising late, stepping barefoot to the window to observe the hunters already gathered in the field beyond the barn. She stood watching until someone called to her and she waved from the window, *We do not begin until noon.* And the baron raising his voice in mock protest, then giving up, tapping the timepiece he kept in his waistcoat. Servants were passing drinks. The dogs were charging in circles, eager to start. Jana stood at the window in her nightdress, watching the men gathered in groups, talking, checking their shotguns.

The baroness's three sons stood off to one side, waiting at a respectful distance; the girls were nowhere to be seen. The baron was not to be disturbed in the moments before the hunt was to begin. He was in conference with his head gamekeeper, who was nodding doubtfully at something the baron was saying, the direction of the wind or the line of march or the location of the stag, the weak shots and the marksmen and the necessity of overseeing them all, especially the women. The gamekeeper, with his Slavic eyes, his wiry build, and his suspicious manner, reminded her of her father. He was quick to anger and quick with his fists, like her father. He was proud of his stamina, able to walk all day long without rest and in the evening eat everything that was put in front of him. When he finished, Jana and her mother were invited to take what was left. While they ate, he told long stories detailing his grievances. Over the years the grievances accumulated, but it never occurred to him to do anything about them. Her father had the imagination of an ox. For many years, Jana had sent money to her mother, hoping she would summon the courage to leave her father. But she never did, so the money had gone for the care and feeding of the ox. She never called the gamekeeper Fritz, always Herr Smit, and never with a smile. She found disagreeable tasks for him to do, and now and then she caught him glaring at her with a sullen expression of

— she supposed it was recognition. And when she glared back, Herr Smit was always the first to shift his gaze. Now, in the field below the window, the gamekeeper touched his forefinger to the bill of his cap — the gesture was just this side of insolence, but the baron was too dim to notice — and ambled off to do whatever it was that the baron wanted done. All these thoughts ran through Jana's mind as she stood at her bedroom window watching the preparations for the hunt.

Yes, Dix thought, this is where the story begins, in the morning as days begin, the baroness in her bedroom thinking about her life, what had been and what was to come. No one ever knew how such a day would end, and if its end was forecast by its beginning; only the audience was in on the secret. He wondered if Mahler's adagio began in the bedroom or later when the hunt was under way. It would be later, he reasoned, because the scenes would roll into one another, starting in the bedroom from the baroness's point of view, and next the panorama of the hunt, the funeral, and the family conference. The adagio would begin with the hunt.

She stood in the shadows and undressed as she watched the men prepare, sighting down their barrels, checking ammunition with the diligence of infantrymen. She listened to the fragments of conversation that drifted up to the window where she stood. Rough laughter, too, for bets were being placed. She paused in her dressing and slowly reached for the carafe on the chest of drawers behind her, her fingers light and smooth on its glass neck, easing the stopper from its mouth as she poured a half-tasse, the wine cold on her teeth and tongue. The room was chilly but she barely noticed; it was always drafty in the big house, and she had grown up in cold. She savored the wine, allowing it to gather in her mouth, swallowing slowly, so cold in her throat and scratchy farther down. Now she watched the girls strolling into view. They walked like Berlin girls, all hips and arms, except for the plain one, who was not flirtatious, at least in this company. City girls had a loose gait, it came from walking on pavement, in groups, always dressed up, a kind of ceremony, their eyes always watchful. A groom held their horses and the girls mounted, arranging themselves in the saddle. When the groom let go, the horses reared briefly, then cantered off, one following the other. The girls seemed unconcerned, but Fritz Smit, returning from the baron's errand, loudly instructed the groom to bring the animals under control. By then the horses had cantered away into the field, where they stood now, shaking their great heads, imperious. The girls were laughing, excited by the ride and the prospect of the hunt and the gay supper later on, the long table in candlelight, roast venison and champagne, and conversation with the baron's handsome and most eligible sons.

Jana watched this without expression, remembering her own tense school days, the shabbiness, the drudgery, the taunts of her classmates, and the ox always somewhere in the wings. She ran her fingers through her hair and muttered something to herself, an oath or a prayer, it was hard to tell which. She was remembering the difficulty she had had, learning to ride when she visited the baron for the first time. It was a weekend party and she was with a new friend, a distant cousin of the baron's, perhaps a bit irresponsible. They had met at the circus, a métier he understood and approved of. He was full of life, that one, and apologetic when he invited her to come with him to his cousin's estate. He promised a boring weekend, except when they were together at night. You'll like Alex, Wil said, somewhat old-fashioned in his ways, not at all worldly. He belongs to old Prussia — often irascible but he has a good heart and a first-rate wine cellar inherited from his father. He is ill at ease with women because his mother was strict, a humorless disciplinarian. Do you know how to ride, Jana? No, she did not. The horses she was familiar with were not horses you rode but horses you walked behind, heavy reins in your hands, stepping carefully to avoid the steaming shit. She had difficulty staying on and twice was almost thrown. The baron found her discomfort amusing but she was mortified; and mortified, too, that her riding costume, her habit, was just the slightest bit off-key. Much was off-key in those days, not that the baron noticed. He likes you, Wil said, and if you work at it you might come to like him and the life he leads. Is that what you want? You have to think of the future, Jana, and where you want to be in ten years' time. How do you see yourself in the world? Alex was a country baron and unconcerned with life in society, as he put it. He enjoyed hunting and managing the farm. Not a socially adept baron at all, and he had no one to advise him. His parents were dead and he had no brothers or sisters, only an elderly uncle who served in the diplomatic corps abroad.

My father, Wil said.

They don't get along. City baron, country baron, Wil added with a laugh.

Alex was attracted to her at once and found it charming that she was awkward on horseback. He taught her to ride and he taught her to shoot, but that was all he had to teach her. Jana was a quick study, and she discovered soon enough that Wil had not exaggerated when he had described the baron as not at all worldly. The world was a mystery to him, and he had no interest in it. She continued now to watch the Berlin girls manage their mounts. They looked as if they had been born to it and their clothes were impeccable, including the hats, gloves, boots, and braided riding crops. Mornings on horseback in Grunewald.

The baroness tied up her corset and a silk blouse over it and a tailored wool coat over the shirt. Then she thought again and removed the coat and the shirt in order to unlace the corset. She liked herself loose, liked the watery feel of silk against her skin. She combed her hair in the reflection of the window glass, one short stroke after another, smiling at the memory of the dissolute Wil, married now to a condessa and living in Estoril. What a time they had had, watching the acrobats and then imitating the acrobats. He asked her often, How do you see yourself in the world, Jana? She always laughed and said she did not see herself poor; and beyond that, who knew? But the truth was, she did not see herself in the world at all. Where did Sorbs belong? Wherever Sorbs lived, they were among strangers. Her mother sang a lament that ended, You are a dead people, you are few, learn to be silent, stretch in your graves. She believed there was no natural place for her. She had always lived by her wits because the world was a cold place, vagrant and untrust-worthy. She had always moved on before the knock on the door. She grasped the baron's country life but did not know if that was what she wanted for herself, for the remainder of her days. In time she grew accustomed to weekends at the estate, and in time became fond of the baron. When he proposed marriage, she found herself agreeing. She knew that on the estate she would be secure, and her privacy maintained. Wil announced he was leaving for Portugal, but as his last act of friendship promised to give her away on her wedding day.

When she heard a soft knock on the door, she did not reply. When the knock came again, louder, she said quietly, Go away. I will be down soon enough. I am dressing. Tell the baron to wait. And then she pulled on her long skirt and buttoned the silk blouse. She finished her half-tasse of wine and drew a wide leather belt around her waist, cinching it tight, and called for the maid to help her with her boots. All this time she was staring out the window at the hunters in the yard, shotguns on their shoulders, impatient for the baron's signal. Her sons were there, too, the loud ones and the shy one. They were fine-looking boys except for the eldest, who had inherited his father's heavy face and body; and in the way of life's perverse comedy, Christian was the one who knew her best. They could read each other's thoughts, announced by a raised eye-brow followed by a sly smile, *I know what you're thinking.* A humor-less boy, always seeking advantage. At times she wished nothing more than to see the last of him, but she thought also that Christian was dangerous outside the borders of the estate. The estate was his realm. Beyond its boundaries were lands to be subjugated or pil-laged because their laws were not his laws, their people not his peo-ple. Christian would bring a world of trouble to himself and others, yet when the baron died he would not be a suitable heir. His stage was the army, and God knew how many German requiems would be sung in his name or on his order. She would do the world a favor by keeping him caged on his thousand hectares, allowing him to kill every beast within range. And perhaps he would kill her, too, in the end.

The maid arrived to help her with her boots, and went away when she was finished.

The baroness was closest in temperament to the middle son, who felt himself a stranger in the family. She and Rolf looked on life from the same wary angle of vision. Anything given could be taken away. Eternal vigilance was the price of happiness; perhaps privacy was the better word. Now she watched Christian dismount and strut restlessly, calling to his father to commence the hunt. They were physically alike, though the baron was two inches shorter and heavier in the chest and belly. Christian weighed nine pounds at birth, born in this bedroom where she stood. Jana was twenty-two. She was alone when labor began. The baron was in Königsberg buying a horse. Her maid summoned the doctor from the village, who arrived with Fritz Smit's wife, childless herself and terrified, appalled by the blood and the screams of the baroness. Useless, a useless woman, unlike Jana's own mother, who had great powers of healing. Her mother was fundamentally sympathetic, perhaps too sympathetic for her own good. Somehow Jana got through that day and the next day. She named him Christian Wilhelm, Wil. Her own joke but the baron was pleased, naming his firstborn after a relation, distant though that relation was.

The baroness poured another half-tasse of wine and stood looking approvingly into her full-length mirror, remembering the births of her sons, each birth more difficult than the last. With the third, she thought she would die. At the end of it she felt her spirit ebb, drain like the tide. When she awakened she was alone in the bright light of early morning. Then she heard something stir, the baron at the window, holding his son, grinning like a half-wit. He rocked the infant in his arms, humming a sentimental German lullaby. She remembered that he rubbed the hunting horn against the infant's cheek and laughed delightedly when the child closed its tiny fist around the mouthpiece. She shut her eyes and turned her face to the wall. She heard the sound of marching feet, and then she gave an involuntary gasp of pain. She fought for breath. Somewhere on the margins of her consciousness she heard the baby cry and her husband hurry from the room calling for Frau Smit.

Come at once, my son is in distress. *My son,* he said again and again, *is crying.*

But the infant continued to bawl, a howling that seemed to fill her sickroom. She heard more marching feet, the clump clump of infantry boots. When she opened her eyes, Christian and Rolf were peeking through the doorway. The doctor was at her side. She heard him mutter something. The baron's whiskers touched her chin. He was holding the baby, and when he moved to give it to her, she shook her head. The doctor said, There, there, and caressed her arm. She felt pressure on her arm and in a moment she was asleep again, but the sound of marching feet would not go away.

Later, the doctor advised against more children; and she remembered his surprise at her too quick assent, and then his sardonic smile. Your hips are too narrow, he said. They are normal hips, she replied. There are other ways, he went on, and she answered that she knew that. She knew what they were. The doctor stepped back, alarmed, appraising her as if seeing her for the first time; at any event, he was listening closely. Jana said nothing more, but did not take her eyes off the doctor, who tried unsuccessfully to avoid her gaze. He coughed and stopped smiling, having blundered into something — the word he said to himself was "unwholesome." He had known the baron for many years, doubting always that he would marry. He seemed content on his estate and rarely traveled from it. He had never spoken of a desire for a wife and children. Then he turned up with Jana-whatever-her-name-was, a companion of wretched cousin Wil, a careless boulevardier. The doctor debated having a word with Alex, but Alex was not the sort of man you "had a word with" on a personal matter, so he remained silent; if Jana was the woman he wanted, Jana was the woman he would have. Of course she was agreeable. Why wouldn't she be agreeable, Miss Nothing from Nowhere. In a stroke she had the big house and horses for riding and whatever other country pleasures she wanted for herself, and all she had to do was agree to live permanently in the country because the baron hated cities, Berlin especially. She took to it and became something of a woman of mystery, aloof, difficult to reach, often abrupt. The men in the village called her the Tatar princess because of her high cheekbones and almond-shaped eyes and strange accent, an accent no one could quite place. But she was no more a princess than he was. She was a Sorb from top to bottom, with the usual Sorb resentments. Of course the doctor had heard rumors about their life together, but rumors were the inevitable small change of rural life, and Prussians ran things to suit themselves. Who knew what she wanted really, besides the big house and horses and a full larder and the rest of it.

Wasn't it always a mistake to mix the races? The Sorbs were a sinister people. Who was this Jana anyhow? Where did she come from? And now that she had done her connubial duty, what would she expect as her reward? Whatever it was, the baron would gladly pay it. No question who was in charge of things at the estate. Just then the doctor wondered if Alex was afraid of her.

Jana remembered the conversation, looking at the doctor and apprehending what he was thinking, but maintaining her level gaze. She said to him, Who is marching outside? Tell them to go away.

He didn't care for her tone of voice, and he had no idea what she was talking about. Then he noticed the rhythmic beats. Smiling broadly, he told her it was the baron's idea. Fritz and the men were building a rail fence around the house.

She said, To keep bandits out, or me in?

It is for the children, Baroness.

He thinks they will run away?

The baron was worried.

Of what?

He did not say, Baroness.

I will have it torn down, she said.

But it is almost finished.

Anything done can be undone, she said, and closed her eyes, turning her back on the doctor.

Jana tied an ascot around her neck and checked the window one last time. Herr Smit had brought her horse around and stood with it now in an attitude of boredom. She caught the baron's eye and waved. She hurried downstairs and emerged into the sunlight and greeted her guests. The baron raised his horn and blew a long note, a rising note in a single breath that seemed to last forever. She smiled blandly at her husband as he marched off, favoring his bad leg. The hunters gathered their gear. The girls reined their horses, waiting for the baroness to lead the way. The beaters moved off to the east, their dogs racing ahead, and suddenly it was silent, the quiet of the graveyard.

Willa cleared her throat and said, Dixon? What are you doing?

I'm imagining a life, Greenwood said.

# 20

S O YOU'RE REUNITED with Jana after all these years, Henry
Belknap said. Isn't it remarkable how people show up years
later, and right away you're plunged back into the time when
you first knew them? And now you have an episode of *Wannsee
1899* and that never would have happened if you hadn't come to
Berlin. Jana either. Who would believe it? Not me. When you arrived in January I gave you three weeks, maximum. Then you were
back to L.A. on some hoked-up errand, bye-bye Dix. Whereupon
Jana arrives and you're back in business. Who's she playing?

The baroness, Dix said.

There isn't any baroness in *Wannsee 1899*.

There is now, Dix said.

Can she do it?

Beautifully, Dix said. If she wants to.

And does she?

I think she does, Dix said.

Tell me this one thing, Henry said. You speak no German. Have
no feel for the language that I can see. How do you work it out
with the actors? How do you know when they're speaking correctly, inflections and so on.

Tempo, Dix said. The timbre of the voice. What they're doing
with their hands and their mouths. The look in their eyes, so that I
can know when they're faking and when the audience will know

they're faking. There's an aura when the gears mesh. And I do have some feel for the language.

They were sitting in Henry's crowded office, books and manuscripts stacked on the long table and piled on the floor. The walls were decorated with photographs of Isaac Babel, Walter Benjamin, Richard Strauss, and Max Beckmann. A bronze bust of Willy Brandt rested on the mantel. Henry's assistant arrived with a bucket of ice and a bottle of Polish vodka, warned Henry that he had a dinner engagement at eight, and went away, returning almost at once to say that New York was on the line, an urgent conference call. Dix poured two glasses while Henry shifted his huge bulk and reached for the telephone. Mostly he listened, and the expression on his face did not convey urgency. Dix examined the photographs, each in turn, and discovered that Babel, Benjamin, Strauss, and Beckmann all bore a mild resemblance to Henry Belknap. Brandt didn't, except for the heavy pouches under his eyes. Dix turned to the window and watched the scullers struggle against the chop until they gave it up and drifted, collapsed over their oars. He decided that when he left Mommsen House he would remember the scullers more than any other thing but the weather. The false spring had ended the week before. Cold weather returned as the days lengthened. Each morning a thin glaze of frost covered the lawn, and the trees were as bare as the day they were born.

Why no women? Dix said when Henry finished on the telephone.

Who do you suggest? Henry asked.

I can imagine Rosa Luxemburg and Madame Blavatsky flanking Benjamin.

Get me one of Jana, Henry said. I'll put her next to Beckmann. But first tell me about her. What's changed?

Her voice has changed, Dix said. It's deeper, rich as an oboe. Willa says her accent is a little hard to understand sometimes but that may be an asset. She's sometimes slurred around the edges, so you have to *listen*. You have to watch her when she talks. She seems to carry the world with her. You have the feeling she'd be difficult to surprise. Everyone's nervous around her, as if she were fragile and might break or throw a tantrum or a bomb. It's as if Garbo came out of retirement, looking as she looked when she was twenty, except for the eyes.

Henry raised his eyebrows and nodded.

Not far-fetched, Dix said. Jana could have been Garbo. She has Garbo's presence and integrity. Of course when she showed up on the set of *Summer, 1921* she had no idea who Garbo was. She had never seen a movie. She knew what they were but she had never seen one, and the idea of being in one was — startling. Everything was new to her, the paraphernalia, the lights, cameras, microphones, a script, lines to read, and a cameraman and a director, all new. For Jana and her friends it was like being asked to be queen for a day, not knowing exactly who a queen was or what she did, only that it was surely desirable. If you had grown up in a village in Lusatia, among people whose fate was to be alone and disregarded, then to suddenly find yourself in a movie was — miraculous.

Sorbs, Henry said. Not much is written about them. Scholars study them, but no one else is interested.

And I was the miracle worker, Dix said.

Henry was sipping his drink, looking uncomfortable.

Jana was fifteen, Dix added.

*Fifteen?* Henry said.

Jeidels was sleeping with her. One of the actors was sleeping with her. I think she was tired of being slept with.

That's monstrous, Dix. She was a child.

Not unusual in Hollywood, Dix thought but did not say. In Hollywood, fifteen would not raise an eyebrow. He said, She played nude scenes in the film, and played them convincingly. No one ever played them better. She played them as if she were born to them. She didn't look fifteen. She didn't act fifteen. When she told me she was twenty, I believed her. Why not? Simple ignorance of the ways of the world is not the property of the young only. I didn't inquire closely because I had a movie to make, and Jana was the centerpiece.

You took her at her word, Henry said.

I didn't ask. She volunteered.

Everyone who saw the movie fell a little in love with Jana.

That's true, Dix said. But she didn't like it.

Is that why she disappeared?

Partly. But mostly, she said, because she was tired of being told what to do. She said she was tired of acting someone else's life.

Probably she was tired of taking off her clothes for the camera.

Yes, she mentioned that.

And now she's back.

She said she changed her mind.

About taking her clothes off?

Not about that, Dix said. As far as I know.

Baronesses are famous for taking their clothes off, Henry said.

I told her I could write it in. She said not to bother.

Henry looked at the clock on the wall, then rose to refill their glasses with ice and vodka, shaking his huge head in amusement. He poured slowly and handed Dix his glass, murmuring, Prost.

After being alone all these years, maybe she wants to be a celebrity. She's tired of being unknown and wants to be known.

A star once again, Henry said.

She's tried one, now she'll try the other. Maybe the idea of celebrity appeals to her, a foreign country, one she's seen but briefly. Maybe she thinks she didn't give celebrity a fair chance. And she's thinking now of her picture in fan magazines, being interviewed on television. Asked her opinion of the events of the day. She'll be the most famous Sorb in Germany. Joschka Fischer will invite her to lunch. Boris Becker will offer tennis lessons. But the main thing is the foreign country, celebrity a remote and exotic land, like Burma or Uruguay. Except once you arrive, you're there for keeps. No exit visas from Celebrity.

Do you believe that?

No, Dix said. I'm glad she's back.

You never believed she was dead, did you?

Never did, Dix said.

A few of us thought that was wishful thinking, you avoiding responsibility for the accident. Looking on the unlikely sunny side of things. The sunny side was not your side, Dix. It was out of character.

Claire agreed with you, Dix said. Billy Jeidels, too. And I'm sure they were right. But I had no doubt in my mind that she was alive somewhere, living anonymously. I thought she had heard some summons, an appeal, and felt obliged to disappear back into the Sorb world, wherever that was. I had no idea. I thought she went away as if she were in a dream. I thought she was tired of living among foreigners. Tired of looking at a camera's lens. Tired of Jeidels and tired of me. Tired of the script and tired of being ordered around, reading lines that had been written for a character in a story. One of the things she did when she went away was to join a carnival troupe. She put on makeup and a false face and played clown for a while, and when she tired of that she worked in shops. She told me everyone had the right to go away when they wanted. And we had no right to interfere.

She was clever about it, Henry said.

She never thought there would be an inquiry. She couldn't imagine anyone caring about what happened to a Sorb girl, certainly not the authorities. The authorities thought Sorbs were garbage and she was part of the garbage.

And you begin tomorrow.

Can't wait, Dix said.

What is it, then? You haven't found anything you liked in fifteen years. Scripts arrived, you'd throw them away. You said your audience had vanished. So it must be Jana.

Not only Jana, Dix said. It's the script. A good one, and when I get finished with it, it'll be very good.

Here's luck, Henry said, raising his glass. You know what Babel's mother said to Babel? *You must know everything.* Know everything, Dix.

Dix smiled but did not reply. Knowing everything was not in his bag of tricks.

Still, Henry said. I don't understand you. Some half-assed television drama —

Not a half-assed television drama, Henry.

But not a real feature film, either.

For Christ's sake, Henry. *It's Germany.*

And that explains it?

Just keep your mouth shut about Jana, please.

Henry was silent a moment, then moved to extract a sheet of paper from the foot-high pile on his desk. He held it at arm's length with one hand while he sipped vodka with the other. When he spoke, it was with apparent reluctance.

He said, I checked around in Hamburg. Herr Mueller died a few months after we visited him. The firm, Mueller and Sons, was sold to one of the Hamburg banks. A sale of assets only, so the name Mueller and Sons ceased to exist. No one I spoke to seems to remember the old man. His firm was nothing special, just a small private bank with limited — and here Henry looked at Dix with a wry smile — "footings," as the bankers say. I asked Adam Kessel to give me a hand. Adam knows everyone worth knowing in Hamburg but he drew a blank also. When the old man died, his reputation seems to have died with him. It's a pretty closed world, Hamburg banking.

Strange no one remembers, Dix said.

Not so strange, Henry said. It's forty-five years ago. When Adam asked his contacts whether the family was Jewish, they said they had no idea. Mueller was such a small firm. And it was so long ago. One elderly banker, now retired, said he believed that Herr Mueller was "not political."

Dix said, What does that mean?

Could mean he wasn't a Nazi.

Could mean anything, Dix said. Remember, when we visited, he spoke to us about the war. Unimaginable, he said, unspeakable. And then he said no more, but for those few seconds he was a man possessed by demons. But which demons? Tell me this. Did the bank continue operations during the war?

The retired banker thought not, Henry said. He believed that Herr Mueller was absent.

Absent?

The word he used, Henry said. But he admitted he might be wrong.

So he could have been in the army or in the camps.

Or in America or Britain. He might have been lucky and gotten out of Germany.

And returned after the war, Dix said.

You're not convinced. You like uncertainty, Dix.

I like Harry Greenwood's thought. It only matters to Herr Mueller.

But surely, Henry began.

And he's dead. His wife and sons are dead. Even the bank is gone.

Dix returned to his room to await dinner. The Kessels were arguing next door but he paid no attention. The light on the answering machine was winking but he paid no attention to that, either. He made a drink and stood looking into the mirrors, and then he took the script and sat in the chair near the window. Night had come on quickly and the lights across the lake were busy. When the phone rang, he answered it without thinking and was delighted to hear Claire's silky voice. As if by unspoken agreement, they did not speak of work. Claire had news of the children, nothing alarming: Nancy had returned from Florida without mishap, and Jerry had a new girlfriend. Name unknown. Dix described the nightly battles of the Kessels and put the phone next to the wall so she could listen to the one in progress. When he asked her how she was feeling, she said she was tired. He said, Free an owl and gain merit. There were many ways in this life to gain merit; a bequest in a will, for example. But it would have to be done with sincerity.

How long do you intend to stay in that dreadful country? she asked.

Not long, he said. He promised to leave for L.A. before the end of the month, and that was for certain. She heard something in his voice and asked what he was up to actually. Not much, he lied. Liar, she said.

Something may be brewing, he said. I can't talk about it. Bad luck to talk about it. She let that pass and went on to propose a vacation, someplace they had never been to and where they knew no one. An island somewhere, the Caribbean or the Mediterranean, a place where there was uninterrupted sun and the food was good. Cyprus, he said. She countered with Malta. They began to laugh about the disastrous vacations they had had. Aspen when it rained and Scotland when it rained and the time they went to visit her parents in Mad River Glen and it rained there, too, in February. She said she was lonely without him, and he said she did not know what lonely was until she had spent a winter in picturesque Wannsee, but all that would end before the month was out.

So much to tell you, he said.

She said playfully, Have you been faithful to me? He caught his breath and said that he had. Me too, she said. So we don't have to worry about that. They went on in that spirit a moment and then she said she missed him dreadfully. She was snappish and impatient with people. What she wouldn't give for a good night's sleep —

Dix said, Jana was fifteen.

Claire said, Fifteen what?

Fifteen years old when we shot the film.

When you shot *Summer, 1921*?

Yes, he said.

When did you discover that?

Jana showed up the other day. She told me.

Jana showed up in Berlin?

She called me up and I took her to lunch and she said she was fifteen. Fifteen when we were shooting her nude scenes, and she was sleeping with Tommy Gwilt and Billy Jeidels. She ran away because she was tired of living another life onscreen. That's what she said. She ran away believing that no one would care or look for her because she was just another Sorb girl, of no consequence.

I'm sorry you told me. I wish you'd waited.

Waited for what?

When you were back home. I don't know what to say. We're living in two places, and neither place has anything to do with the other.

Dix sat with the script in his lap planning the next day's shoot, beginning at eight A.M. in the baroness's bedroom, Jana at the window, slowly dressing for the hunt. He hoped to God the cameraman knew his business. Willa said that he did and that his English was fluent. Tell him what to do, Dixon, and he will do it. Dix wanted long takes, minutes long, the way Huston filmed *The Dead*. The voice-over would take time, the tone and pitch of Jana's voice had to be exactly right, a lonely voice with the dust of centuries on it, a voice that knew grief and would know it again, because the worst horrors were to come in the new century.

He rose and stepped to the window, tapping his glass on the pane. The Kladow ferry came into view, a tub of a boat but its lights were welcoming. He wanted to film it but no such boat existed on Lake Wannsee or anywhere else in 1899. Somewhere near the Oder he would surely find a small lake, a blue lake that in its peace and simplicity was utterly deceiving. That was where the final scene took place, the baroness and her son at war, everything between the lines. He finished what was left in the glass and watched the lights go out in the villas on the far shore. Across the carpet of water he saw the banker's face, sallow, deeply lined, stricken, a face filled with remorse, a face without a trace of pride.

# 21

THE SCRIPT OPEN in his lap, Dix sat happily in a canvas deck chair on the lawn, bundled in a heavy sweater, muffler, gloves, and his Borsalino hat, surveying a scene of confusion, the cast and technicians milling about, restless as an army before taking the field. Frau Lenord stood to one side, wringing her hands, watching for breakage. He told the cameraman that he wanted one camera inside the bedroom and the other outside on the chair boom. They would film in natural light, one long take. Of course there would be false starts, practice swings before the game was afoot; but once afoot, they would follow wherever Jana led them. Now he began to place the cast, the beaters, the weekend guests, the sisters, the three sons, gamekeeper Smit, and finally the old baron. Gunther was a recruit from the Berliner Ensemble, wide as a barrel, bowlegged and weatherbeaten, with muttonchops and a lower lip as pendulous as a sausage. He had been an actor for forty years. Gunther had played saloonkeepers, artists, industrialists, Nazis, Iago, and Mack the Knife. But this was his first baron.

How do you want him? Gunther asked.

Slow, the way farm machinery is slow. But powerful. Capable of anything.

Intelligent?

After his own fashion, Dix said.

The estate is his life, Gunther said.

Every inch, Dix agreed.

I saw you once in Munn Café, Gunther said. You were having lunch with Frau Baz. I hoped we would meet.

Munn's, Dix said. I like Frau Munn.

The baron would not go there, Gunther said.

Dix sat back in his chair and watched the actors take their places, long minutes of incoherence as dogs raced about and the horses strained against reins held by their grooms. Dix watched them briefly, then made adjustments, the beaters and the dogs farther back, the sisters and their horses up close, the older and younger sons in the middle ground, and the middle son alone under a huge beech. The baron was conspicuous by his very size and bearing and he would be in motion, now talking to his guests, now to his oldest son, now giving instructions to Smit. As he strutted about, he caressed the hunting horn that hung from his neck. This was Jana's scene but the camera would move at intervals to the company on the lawn, seeing what she saw as she saw it. Dix wanted everyone relaxed, in an anticipatory mood before the hunt, a Prussian ceremony centuries old, the outcome never in doubt but always a surprise somewhere along the way. The mood was not festive, for the hunt was serious business. Frivolity came later. The hunters were checking their firearms and ammunition bags, eager to be off. The beaters stood in a submissive cluster, smoking briar pipes and saying very little. The forest teemed with game, not all of it harmless, and the hunters themselves were often impetuous, firing before they knew what they were firing at. Dix waited for the cast to settle and become familiar with the surroundings, who was close by and who was farther out, and the line of march. They were all friends and knew the ritual. Now and then Jana appeared at the window, looking down at the gathering in a kind of weightless trance. Everyone understood that the hunt could not begin until the baroness arrived.

Jana leaned from the window, in profile against the oyster sky. The wind teased her hair but she seemed not to notice. She was still full of sleep in the dressing gown and holding a glass of something.

A daughter of the forest, Dix thought, never comfortable in this great house with its oversized portraits of overfed ancestors, heavy furniture and servants underfoot, its breathless stillness; and the assumption of superiority, that the world always yielded if pushed hard enough, and the family and the land it occupied was primary, and a near-perfect society of its own. She never understood where the sense of superiority came from — it seemed wired into the genes, a physical characteristic like blond hair or a clubfoot — but it was implacable and as natural as the air they breathed. Sorbs took some pride in their minority status and the fact of their survival over the centuries, when every hand seemed taken up against them — the difference between the confidence of the oppressor and the cunning of the oppressed. Each took pride in its own survival, the oppressors that they had not been overthrown, the oppressed that they had not been extinguished. Each believed in its superior will, the force of its collective personality and unique birthright, the one formed by habit of command, the other by a remorseless sense of grievance. The baron assured her that this was a balanced equation, one that would evolve with time but never fundamentally change; a revolution had been tried once, in 1848, and, though exceedingly violent, had not been successful. The Germans were a conservative race, and change never came willingly. We have occupied this land for four centuries and no one can take it from us. Perhaps, the baron said. Perhaps we Germans fear the future just a little, because of the barbarians in the East — and here he fluttered his hand, Asia begins just over there.

This air — she breathed it, too. She had to learn to breathe it, but now it was hers as much as it was theirs. This was the world she had joined, the one she had occupied for twenty-five years. She had borne three sons in the very bedroom where she stood, making them wait while she finished dressing. She never felt wholly a part of this life, and even now the baron would say things to her in phrases she could not comprehend. He spoke a family language dense with allusion, to times past, to family secrets and family lore, to vendettas and alliances, to village gossip and folktales and legends and country superstition. Her sons understood every word, even when very young, causing her to wonder what was latent in them, what they were capable of, and what part of the family history they would claim. And yet she felt her own attachment to the house and its surroundings, the family she had created, and the natural world beyond her windows, the animals and the streams and forests, the lake deep in the woods. She had her own claims, by virtue of occupation. Twenty-five years was more than half her lifetime. She had arrived for a weekend and stayed on for a life. She had surrendered something of herself but she had acquired something also, and that was now who she was. The villagers thought her mysterious and in important ways she was aloof from her own knotty Prussian family. She believed she had acquired the habit of command without losing her sense of grievance, meaning her membership in the minority. Not a day passed that she did not think of Lusatia, the five towns nestled up close to Czechoslovakia, and the Sorb diaspora. And she wondered what might have become of her had she resumed her wandering. But for better or worse she had made her life, had created it no less than a sculptor created a figure from a brute slab of marble, and she would not renounce it. She had worked too hard, given too much, and in some region of her mind she was proud of who she had become. Yet she believed she was capable of stepping outside her dual identities. They were arbitrary in any case; and one was an accident of birth. She believed she was entitled to a laissez-passer, and when flight became necessary — as it surely would at some unknown hour in the new century — she would walk away, find another homeland, pull on a fresh nationality. Europe existed for such migrations.

Dix was watching her carefully all this time, noticing her lips moving ever so slightly as she continued her scrutiny of the set. She was rehearsing her lines, her hands firm on the windowsill, and now he saw that she was focused on the horizon, beyond the barn and the fields to the forest. She believed she was unobserved as she raised her hands in a salute to the hawks wheeling high above the treeline, describing figure eights in the oystery sky.

Herr Greenwood? The cameraman was at his elbow. We are ready.

Cameras placed?

Yes, Herr Greenwood.

Dix called to her. Are you ready, Jana?

She signaled that she was, and moved into the interior of her bedroom so that she was visible only as a shadow.

The warmups took two hours, one mistake after another, equipment failures, mental lapses, failures of composition, cues missed, and then, when a sequence was filming smoothly, an army helicopter appeared from the east, hovered a moment, and flew away, only to return a little later, loitering on the perimeter, the slap-slap-slap of its rotors bouncing sound levels to lively heights and lending a martial air to the proceedings. Through all this, Jana kept her composure, leaning with nonchalance against the window sash, smiling a tight little smile that seemed to say, So this is the glamorous life I've been missing all these years.

It will take a minute, Herr Greenwood, the soundman said.

Hurry it up, Dix said.

He strolled away down the slope, giving the company time to organize itself in private. He scuffed the grass and thought he detected a change of season, a temperate watery odor, the insinuation of spring. The day was cold but the wind was without conviction, an aging prizefighter hanging on against a much younger opponent. The thought cheered Dix, a reminder that April was not far off, and April in L.A. was delicious. He watched the hawks hovering over the treeline and remembered the first day of shooting on *Summer, 1921,* Jana and her friends overwhelmed at what was expected of them, and frightened by the disorganization, the shouted commands in rough language. When Dix told them to take their places, they had forgotten where those places were. Trude and Marion began to snuffle and Jana demanded a ten-minute break in order to warn Dix that unless the crew behaved like gentlemen, she and her friends would "walk." Dix began to laugh, the slang was so incongruous, and then he realized that Tommy Gwilt had put her up to it. He promised a benevolent, obscenity-free set, but in return "you girls" had to follow instructions to the letter, learn your lines and take your places when told to do so. You do not call ten-minute breaks just because you feel like it. Jana listened intently and replied in the Sorb language, something to the effect (he later understood) that she and her friends were not to be treated like farm animals. She was on the edge of tears when she said it, and did not look him in the eye, but she meant what she said.

He did not know what it was to be in charge, the one whose say-so was final. You had to keep everything in your mind because each part in a movie related to every other part. And when, time and again, they came to you for decisions you were unprepared to make — unprepared because your instincts failed or your knowledge lapsed — you made them anyway, with a show of confidence and absolute certainty, having no idea whether your decision was correct. Only Howard Hawks could get away with a casual, How the hell do I know? You decide. So he was first on the set on that first day, feeling like the pope on the balcony of St. Peter's, giving the blessing while laying down a stern dictum — and the day was a bust, everything that could go wrong did go wrong, although he did not admit that to Claire when he called her that night. A beautiful beginning, he said merrily, couldn't've hoped for better, and I'm sure we'll come in on time and on budget.

When he hung up the telephone, he poured a glass of schnapps and called Harry. He had never called his father for advice or sympathy and did not know why he was doing so now, except that he was at sea. He was so discouraged, half believing that his beautiful film was misbegotten and that he was to blame. Harry was watching one of Nixon's press conferences and cackling because the president was on the defensive yet again, fumbling his answers to the usual softball questions. Harry had a theory that Nixon did not have the gift of narrative, and that lack made him appear to be lying even when he was telling the truth. *He does not know how to tell a story.* Dix had to listen while Harry reprised the Q and A. Then

Harry thought to ask what was on his mind, and Dix said he had begun to doubt his own judgment. When he described the day's chaos — I am a general who has lost control of his army, was the way Dix put it — Harry laughed and laughed and observed that first-day jitters were normal, like your wedding night or opening day at the ballpark, all that excitement, all that potential, a clean slate just waiting to be written on.

You must believe you are home, Harry said. The familiarity of home, the ownership of the property, the owner's authority to open a door or close it. Plant a garden or plow it under. So pull up your socks and get on with it. Do what you do best with a light heart and a brave spirit. Huston has a theory that will clear it up for you.

When you film a red wagon, never say, This is a red wagon.

Dix said, Come again?

You heard me, Harry said.

That's very helpful, Dix said. I can take that to the bank, can I?

Harry laughed again and replied, Trust your swing, Dix. That's what John meant. Trust your swing.

Behind him he heard a dog bark and then quiet, except for women's voices. Someone coughed. They were waiting for him but he did not turn around or make any sign that he was paying attention or that they had a schedule to meet. He slowly took off his wristwatch and put it in his pocket. He stood watching the hawks wheel in the open sky, hearing Mahler's adagio as he remembered early days on the set of *Summer, 1921*. The second day was as confused as the first but each day things improved until by the end of the week the set was alive with nervous energy, so febrile that Dix worried he would be unable to contain it. Then he understood that it didn't have to be contained. The film was not scored until the last minute, a long, slow, blues piano, a recording of Jimmy Yancey and a sideman on traps, and only in the final frames. By then they knew they had something fine, and the Yancey fell into place as easily as a period at the end of a successful sentence. The girls were difficult but brilliant and he took care not to treat them like farm animals.

When someone touched his shoulder, he turned around.

We are ready now, Herr Greenwood.

Then let's go, Greenwood said.

Frau Jana would like a word with you, the cameraman said.

Dix found her in the second-floor bedroom, still standing at the window. The hawks had gone. She said she was nervous, more nervous than she had been the first time. Probably that was because back then she didn't know enough to be nervous. Dix reminded her to speak slowly, and not as if she were exchanging confidences with another. She was to speak as she would speak to herself, in the absolute privacy of her own mind. Take all the time you need but I want to make this sequence one long shot, you understand? She said she was worried that she did not look like a baroness. You're every inch a baroness-from-the-wrong-side-of-the-tracks, he said, and explained what he meant. You have grown into it, he said. In spite of yourself, you have grown into it and now you must live with it. This is your home, and you must live with that, too. You have made a great struggle and it has brought a kind of peace. Think of yourself at the Brücke, the Berliner Ensemble on Saturday night, your apartment in Kreuzberg, your cat.

Yes, my cat.

The men you've known.

Those, too, she said.

So you are standing at your window reviewing your life, knowing that this is the last time you will review it in quite this way. Because in a few hours your life will change completely. Later in the day your husband will die. You have an intimation of this. You have always had second sight. Remember your geomancy?

She looked at him strangely. Geomancy was in the other movie. *Summer, 1921.*

Was it? he said. He had gotten lost inside his own words.

Yes, it was. Geomancy has no place here.

I suppose not, he said. But you know that something will happen this day.

All right, she said.

Remember, very still.

Like a mime, she said.

Less than a mime. Much less. An aerialist.

I understand. And you have confidence?

Completely, he said.

They filmed Jana simultaneously from inside and outside the bedroom. She talked to herself, her lips barely moving. Her face and body would carry the scene, the look in her eyes and the tilt of her head, the minimal grace of her gestures. When she moved a lock of hair from her forehead and turned to the interior of the room, the gesture acted as punctuation to her thoughts about her father and her relations with the gamekeeper Smit. She seemed to lose herself inside her memory, more real to her than what was occurring in front of her eyes, so that the hunting party on the lawn below was faded and static, a still photograph. When she recalled her conversation with the doctor she smiled slyly and raised her eyebrows, and when she unlaced her corset her motion was so swift as to be almost sleight of hand. At the end she raised her arms in a luxurious stretch and let them fall, like an orchestra conductor at the end of a movement. The hunting party began to stir, and that was the moment Mahler's adagio commenced.

They shot the hunt in three long days under a cooperative sun, everything successful. Then the weather turned, a cold, heavy downpour from a gravy-colored sky that washed away all color. A three-day blow, Gunther predicted. Dix returned to Mommsen House, planning to shoot Jana's final scene on Monday, when fair weather was predicted to return. He arrived at Wannsee at nine, ate a quick dinner at Charlotte's, and walked into his apartment at ten, dead tired but happy to be on time for the network news. He felt he had been out of touch for too long, the world's disasters unobserved.

He poured a drink and watched a report on Russia, Yeltsin drunk again, Muslims on the march from Chechnya to Dagestan, rumors of a plague of locusts in central Russia, mysterious illnesses farther east, more trouble at Chernobyl, a fresh prime minister in the wings. Dix had the sense of a wounded animal, insulted and un-predictable because goaded beyond endurance, one way of life collapsed and its replacement not yet in sight, a nation alternately an object of scorn and of pity. One more reason for the Germans to feel apprehensive, threatened once again by the irresponsible barbarians to the east.

The rest of the broadcast went by routinely. Dix began to listen again when the news turned to Los Angeles, the Academy Awards. He realized then that the ceremony was on Sunday, two days hence, and he remembered how eagerly he had awaited the event in years past. This year he hadn't even mailed his ballot because he had walked out of two best-picture nominees and had not seen two others. Oscar time was always feverish in Los Angeles, and he could feel that now in the mile-a-minute commentary of the entertainment reporter, her account spiced with the usual self-serving gossip from Industry insiders. He turned away for a moment, and when he turned back he saw his own face, a tanned and rugged thirtyish Dixon Greenwood in black tie, standing at a microphone with an Oscar in his fist. He was so startled he missed the first part of the report, hearing only:

. . . said to be in Germany working on a soap opera for German television *in German* with the star of his first film, the cult classic *Summer, 1921,* the young actress called Jana who has been missing for thirty years, and believed *dead.* The reclusive Greenwood hasn't made a film in many years, and sources were at a loss to explain what he was doing in Germany and why a soap opera. And where did he find Jana? The story was first disclosed by the critic Shay Hamel, who dismissed the project as Greenwood kitsch, and probably pornographic. But all Hollywood is abuzz . . .

Dix groaned when he saw his own photograph followed by a still of Jana with Tommy Gwilt and one of Hamel. That bastard, Dix said aloud, but by then the entertainment reporter had vanished, replaced by the weather woman, the one with the long legs and leisurely diction, the one he watched nearly every night.

Dix threw away the dregs of his vodka and mounted the stairs to his bedroom, glowering at the mirrors and wondering what effect the publicity would have on Jana, or if it would have any effect. He hoped she did not prize her anonymity too highly, for she was about to lose it. He had been a fool not to anticipate this, the result of being away from the game for so long. You forgot the world's rhythms, how things worked, and Germany seemed so remote, governed by a different code of conduct. No sense worrying how the bastard Hamel got hold of the story. It was in the nature of stories to leak, and the better the story, the more scandalous its elements, the faster it spread. And before you knew it, whole populations were feeding off it. This one had everything an inquiring reporter could hope for, including a movie star rising from the dead. Thank God filming was almost complete, only the one last scene on the lake.

He had been ignoring the insistent wink of the answering machine, but now as he looked at it, he decided another nightcap would help things along, so he went down to the kitchen, fixed the drink, and returned to his bedroom.

The first calls were from newspaper and magazine reporters and one of the German networks, requesting interviews and photography sessions. His agent called, asking hesitantly if Hamel's story was true. A soap opera? On German television? Jana starring? Dix, I think you should call me back so we can talk this through. Have you signed anything? Then Lou Kniffe called from Sri Lanka to say that Claire and Howard Goodman and the others had returned commercial because he had urgent business in Colombo with the khedive or whatever the hell he called himself, and was it true about a pornographic film *in German?* Have you lost your mind? Call me at once. Next was Billy Jeidels, drunk from the sound of him, asking about Jana. Had he actually seen Jana? Why haven't you called me? You're a prick, Greenwood. You know what Jana meant to me. I've loved that girl from the moment I saw her, mos' lovely lovely girl . . . And then Dix heard a scuffle and Gretchen's infuriated shriek, and the telephone went dead. Claire followed, disappointed to be getting the answering machine. Disappointed generally, her voice powdery and indistinct. You didn't say anything to me about a soap opera in German, Dix. Pornography, is it? That's what the louse Hamel says it is, and I don't want to believe him, so I've decided not to. And also in his column he says that Jana's the star and he'll have more to say about her in his next column, so everyone's talking about Jana and you, together again. Tommy Gwilt called here and asked for your number but I wasn't in. He wants me to call him. What do you want me to do, Dix? I wonder sometimes if you're living on the same planet I am. On my planet we try to keep each other au courant, on the theory that we're married and have been married for years and years and that's what married people do most of the time, so they're not in the dark.

When it's convenient.

So I suppose it's not convenient for you.

Or you think it's not convenient for me.

Gosh, Dix. I suppose it's Germany that's not convenient.

We're away to Bainbridge tomorrow for the last shoot of this ghastly film. Howard's office will know where we are, telephone numbers and so forth, if you want to call with news. Such as when you're returning to L.A., if you are returning to L.A.

Claire rang off without another word. Dix listened to one message after another. Howard Goodman with a bad joke and Bainbridge telephone numbers, two more reporters, and Willa Baz asking that he call her at once, she had a television crew on the doorstep demanding a press conference.

The last call on the machine was the one he dreaded, but he knew would come. He listened to it, then listened again:

Greenwood, this is Shay Hamel in Los Angeles. I need your explanation — or denial, if you're stupid enough to give one — that your actress Jana was just fifteen when *Summer, 1921* was made. Fifteen years old, my source says, a semiliterate farm girl from someplace no one ever heard of. Naked as the day she was born and having it on with Tommy Gwilt. And that you knew her age, approved it, and did nothing about it. So we need to have words, wouldn't you say? Your version of events. Close of business today, please.

# 22

SLEEPLESS, the House quiet around him, Dix took comfort from a remark of Eric Rohmer's, to the effect that his life was colorless. Rohmer said, We didn't have happy years or happy times. Real life was the movies, making them, discussing them, writing about them.

That was another way of affirming that mere existence yielded before product — love affairs, scandals, quarrels, births, deaths, all incidental and without consequence. Life was present to give context to the films you made. You involved life as you invented a film, and lies were part of it. Lies were fundamental. Attention was paid to the work in progress, and when there was no work in progress, attention lapsed and you looked up one day to discover you were ten years older — and where had the decade gone? The answer was: thinking about the previous decade. He believed he had Germany to thank for that insight. He rolled over, his leg throbbing; and then he was back on the mountainside at Tahoe, occupied with his severed head.

The next morning he was up early. He didn't bother to return Shay Hamel's call. He telephoned Willa Baz and advised her to slip quietly from her house and stay with friends or in a hotel. She should decline to answer questions, no matter how harmless they might seem. Refer everyone to him. If she could get Jana under wraps, that would be a good idea, too, unless Jana didn't want to be under wraps, in which case she would tell her story, any story she wanted. The important thing was to let nothing interfere with the shoot Monday morning, the final scene. Principals only, he added — Jana, Karl, cameraman, soundman, me, you, if you want to be there.

She said, Is it true, Dixon? Jana was fifteen?

Dix said, She says she was.

And you didn't know?

No, he said. I didn't.

But you should have.

Yes, I should have.

It's going to be bad, she said.

It won't matter after Monday.

It *will matter*, Dixon. The police —

It was almost thirty years ago, he said.

There'll be an inquiry.

There was an inquiry then. Presumed death by misadventure.

The publicity will be terrible. They'll have a circus.

I suppose they will, he said.

It's an irresistible story. And not only in Germany but all over the Continent and America also.

Debauching the young, Dix said. So the commissars turned out to be correct.

It's not funny, she said. Who was responsible for the story?

Who leaked it? I have no idea. I thought it might be you.

*Me?* Willa's voice was filled with offense. I would never do such a thing.

You're going to have the most watched program in the history of German television.

It is already the most watched program in the history of German television, she said stiffly. Then she paused, reconsidering. Do you think so? she asked.

I'm sure of it, he said.

It was not me, she said. I would never do that.

Okay, he said.

I had no idea she was fifteen.

It was probably someone in Los Angeles.

Perhaps it will work out, Willa said without conviction.

No, it won't, Dix said. Things tend to work out in the movies. Things tend not to work out in life.

When he hung up, Dix stood for a moment pondering his next move. Then he realized he didn't have a next move. His only move was to stay away from the press and make certain that Jana was on board for the Monday shoot. He did not have her telephone number or her address. He had no idea where she was. Then he wondered if Henry Belknap was free for the weekend. They could take a train to Leipzig or Dresden, perhaps historic Weimar for a day, Goethe's house in the morning and Buchenwald in the afternoon, German opera in the evening. When the phone rang he hesitated before answering but finally picked up.

I've been trying to call you, Anya Ryan said. Have you watched television this morning? Your friend Jana was just on, an interview with one of the German networks.

I don't have time for this, Dix said.

You should, though. You should have heard it. She gave quite a show.

So what did Jana say?

Anya began to laugh and then she said, Jana denied the story. She said it was stupid, the work of someone who wanted to destroy her and you, too. She said she was twenty years old when she made *Summer, 1921* and that everyone connected with the film had been perfect gentlemen, generous in every way. Especially you. She might as well have been in a convent, Jana said, and any suggestion otherwise was slander. She feels she has been discriminated against, as was usually the case with Germans in their relations with Sorbs. First you try to exterminate us, then to Christianize us. Now you slander us, girls simply trying to earn a living. But what could you expect from the nation where Nazism was invented? She went on in that vein for some time. It was a kind of monologue, Dix. She said the slander was unacceptable. They should be ashamed of themselves.

She said that? Dix said.

There was more. I can't remember all of it.

And did she speculate where the story came from?

Your enemies, she said. And her enemies, too.

Unspecified enemies?

She did not name them exactly, Anya said. But she knew they were German.

And what did the interviewer say?

He apologized, Anya said.

For himself alone or for the German nation.

The nation, I think. Collective guilt. But he seemed to want an amnesty.

I'll bet he did, Dix said.

Jana demanded that the network look into the historic mistreatment of the Sorb people and then they'd think about the amnesty.

It sounds like quite a performance, Dix said.

Oscar quality, I'd say, Anya replied.

In early morning the mist had yet to burn off. It hung in folds, rising and drifting over the skin of the lake. The sun was absent but loitering somewhere in the vicinity. They set up on a bluff that rose over the water, one camera there and another in the launch that would follow Jana's skiff. Everyone had congratulated Jana on the interview, so brave and forceful, the television idiot looking as if he had been kicked in the groin and at the end was babbling nonsense; and he was so big, he looked like a giant next to Jana. Who knew how such terrible stories began and circulated, when there was no truth to them at all. Being an entertainer meant you were surrounded by lies and half-lies, living inside a cartoon. Jana accepted the compliments with a forced smile while Dix looked on. Now she sat shivering in a canvas chair, her hands wrapped in a crimson scarf, while Karl, as Rolf, stood a few feet away, skipping stones on the water and mumbling his lines. Dix had gone over the scene with Jana, but he needn't have bothered. She appeared well prepared, and understood that the camera would be on her most of the time. It was her scene. Her voice held it together no less than La

Gioconda's smile. Karl's assignment was to react, until the end when he had words of his own.

You're going to tell him the story of your life, Dix said.

Not all of it, Jana replied.

The important parts, Dix said.

He is my son. There are things mothers never tell their sons.

That's what's between the lines, Jana.

And he is not fond of me.

No, he isn't.

He thinks of me as inferior. An accidental baroness.

His father told him things —

That when we met I did not know how to sit on a horse.

Or set a table.

He believes I am ruining his life.

You are, Dix said.

I am trying to preserve what is best for the family, its traditions and code of conduct, its location amid the remote Masurian Lakes. The baron's reluctance to venture beyond the boundaries of the estate. His mistrust of the world outside. He knows his limitations but he does not see them as limitations. He sees them as virtues. And he is not entirely wrong. The world can bring only grief.

And never forget your place in the family.

I suppose that is also in the baroness's mind, she said, and then, after a moment, she turned to look at Karl, still idly skipping stones while he thought about his lines. She said, He is so lumpish. So without wit. He is indulgent and soft, like an animal bred for the slaughterhouse. I think Rolf is quicker, quick on his feet, quick-witted. Karl is miscast.

Rolf the dreamy aesthete, is that it?

It would be more in character.

It would not, Dix said. Karl's clumsiness is part of the bargain.

I see him as slippery, and brutal as marble.

He is a beautiful dancer, Dix said with a smile.

Yes, he has that. He is the sort of man who should be set to music. Jana raised her shoulders and let them fall, all the while watching

Karl bend and throw, concentrating on achieving the fifth skip. She said, I think he is lazy also, dreaming great dreams without a sense of proportion as to how to attain them. These dreams are related to personal conquest. He is attracted to Italy but doesn't know what it is that attracts him. Is it the weather? He likes the sun and the aqua sky. He likes the conversation and the wine. He likes the churches. But at the same time he's thinking, Poor Italy, so undisciplined and without purpose. So operatic in its sorrows. He retreats to it as he retreats to a warm bed at night. Italy is a woman to be ravished. He is thinking in his heart that Italy is an inferior country, without a sense of destiny and mission. Without a desire to lead the world, living on the larger stage. Italy does not exist for itself but for him. He likes it for the dreams it gives him. Best of all, Italy is not Germany. Rolf values Italy the way certain Americans value France.

Dix looked up when the makeup artist arrived and asked if she could begin to touch up Frau Jana. She arranged the pots and brushes on a little folding table and went to work on Jana's forehead and cheeks.

Dix said, You must use your voice like a musical instrument.

Yes, you told me that. About a thousand times.

So I did.

You like to repeat yourself.

So I do. Dix watched the makeup artist apply a thin coat of powder to the bridge of Jana's nose. Her eyes were closed and the powder caused her nose to twitch like a rabbit's. Dix said, Almost done. Are you ready?

I wish it weren't so cold, she said. I am wearing a sweater under my coat and two pairs of stockings and still I am cold. Has the mist gone away?

Not yet, he said.

I suppose it doesn't matter, does it? We can improvise, no?

You'll forget about the cold when the camera begins to roll.

You've written a beautiful script, Dix.

I wrote it for you, he said.

Only a few word changes, a new line here or there, one line

dropped and another moved, and it's as if the navigator changed course forty-five degrees and you land at one continent instead of the other. I love Karl's line, *You are trying to punish me, you do not have the right.* Trying to dismiss me as you would a servant, and then I slap him hard and his hand flies to his face. Tears are in his eyes. He steps back and he is no longer looking at me in the same way. He did not imagine I could do such a thing. And then he looks away because he can no longer bear to see my face. Jana smiled, turning her head so that the makeup artist could attend to the mole on her left cheek.

Leave the mole, Dix said.

Karl said it was all right if I hit him hard, Jana said. He said he wouldn't mind because he has a strong jaw.

He'll mind when it happens.

But then it won't matter, she said. Can you tell me one thing? Where did you get such an idea?

Weimar, Dix said. I spent the weekend in Weimar, at a hotel just down the street from Goethe's house. Such a warren of a house, passageways everywhere, rooms smaller than you expect. A skull on the mantel. Goethe was productive in Weimar. And so was I.

The idea, she said impatiently.

I saw a woman slap a man on the street. And then he slapped her back, knocked her down.

Jana looked at him doubtfully. And what happened then?

He walked away. I helped her up. When I spoke to her, she was mortified. An American, a foreign tourist, witnessing such a thing. It was as if I had broken into their bedroom. She turned her back and walked off without a word.

The makeup artist finished, wished Jana good luck, and went away.

I thought it was a good idea to leave Wannsee, Dix said. All the commotion in the newspapers. Then someone told me about your interview and I knew the story would die. You took away their oxygen. But I went to Weimar anyhow. I needed a change of scene, to go to a place I had never been.

Why doesn't Rolf slap me? Jana asked suddenly.

Because he is afraid of you, Dix said.

She said, I am not sorry I had no children.

It's only a movie, Jana.

You say that? You of all people.

Actors don't have to believe what directors believe.

Children betray you, Jana said.

Not always, Dix said.

Mine would have, she said softly.

Let's talk about something else, she added.

Dix heard a sound behind him and looked up.

Five minutes, Herr Greenwood, the cameraman said.

Greenwood nodded at him and said to Jana, That was quite an interview.

He was a pig, Jana said. They all are. Full of themselves, television babies.

A spur-of-the-moment idea?

I had it all along, Jana said.

And the story itself —

Who knows? she said.

You were the only one who knew it, Dix said.

People know things, Jana said vaguely.

Not that, Dix said. No one knew about that except you. Then you told me.

There are no secrets in this world, Jana said.

If you say so, Dix said.

Amazing what people will believe sometimes.

Who did the telling, Jana?

Karen Hupp, Jana said. She's fierce, that one. She loved doing it. Confusion to the enemy, she said. Karen has causes and the Sorb cause was new to her, a downtrodden tribe she had barely heard of. She was sympathetic, naturally.

So she called someone she knew, someone at the networks or a newspaper.

Yes, she did, Jana said.

You caused a stir, Dix said. When she did not reply, he said, Answer this. Which is true, fifteen or twenty?

Jana shrugged and turned her head to look at Karl. He was standing at the water's edge, his hands behind his back. In his heavy coat and boots he looked like a mariner. She said, There are things that happen to you in your life that you're tired of keeping to yourself. It's exhausting. And so you try to find a way to bring things to light, and mischief is one of the ways. People should know what men are capable of, given the right conditions. A certain atmosphere, an unfamiliar situation, no rules, and a desire to exercise authority. She drew her scarf tight across her knees. What difference does age make? Men should be held to account. They want to live in a certain way, there's a payment for it. There's an American expression, "Living loud."

I think the expression is "Living large," Dix said.

Is that what it is?

In America, he said.

I thought it was the other, Jana said.

He looked at her as she turned away, her smile brief as a heartbeat. She was made for mischief in the way that other women were made for childbirth or the cello. She lived in a realm of mischief, pranks and escapades, exaggerations and provocations. This was how she kept herself apart. Her world was not anchored. She believed she lived as a guest in someone else's house. So she was elusive, often insincere, waiting for the knock on the door, inhabiting the shadows, and when anyone inquired too closely — well, then, she put them off, turned their heads by making something up, and if in the making-up she was able to settle a score, so much the better. She wasn't malicious, merely guarding what was hers. She believed that once she shared what was important to her, it was no longer hers. Dix remembered Billy Jeidel's dull, drunken voice, mos' lovely lovely girl.

Jana sighed, leaning forward in her chair, shivering slightly.

The mist is burning off the lake, she said at last.

We're ready now, Herr Greenwood, the cameraman said from a distance.

) 286 (

Dix rose, offering his hand to Jana.
He said, Two hours more, that's all.
And what happens to Jana then?
Dix said, Whatever she wants.
And do you have an idea what that will be?
To go away again, Dix said.

# 23

JANA'S SLEEP was troubled. She sat with her fists clenched in her lap, her face taut, her forehead damp. Now and then she muttered *No,* pleading, her fingers fluttering, then returning to her lap, clenched. They were stalled in Karl-Marx-Allee, Berlin rush-hour traffic. Dix watched her and listened to Bach on the car radio. He wondered about her dream, where the *no* came from and what it signified, if it signified anything. He hoped she wasn't disappointed. She had brought off her scene in fine style, her voice a steady oboe, always within the range of one octave. She had summoned tremendous expression in her face by the movement of her eyelids and by the parting of her mouth. Her hands were motionless except when she thought to link her forefinger in the gold bracelet she wore on her wrist. Rolf seemed mesmerised, watching her with his sullen expression, his body unquiet. When he moved his hands on the oars, anyone would think he meant to strike her, swinging the oar like a baseball bat. She wore him down with the remorseless monotone of her voice.

This is the life I have led. This is what it has come to, and I will surrender no part of it. She never pleaded, and indeed what she had to say was, in the strictest sense, impersonal. This is what you must do because you must do it, find a woman of means and return with her here, to this place, and settle all debts — and then she ridiculed his preference for warm weather, for languid afternoons and pretty

Italian gardens. Did he have fear of the vast and unsettled German forests? It is from the mystery and sovereignty of the forest that we acquire our courage and our way of looking at the world, what we expect of it. You may take up your travels at a later date. No doubt you will have ample opportunity to do so, and I shall hate the day when it comes because you are dangerous outside your own realm. You should follow your father's example, but I know that is impossible.

And when he said, *You are trying to punish me, you do not have the right,* the sound of her slap could be heard by the cameraman on the shore fifty yards distant. Rolf recoiled, gathered himself, sat brokenly a moment, then moved the oars, and the boat silently made its way to the long wooden pier at the edge of the water. The baroness alighted, and without a word moved off up the path through the forest to the unseen house beyond. The forest swallowed her up and she was lost to view, all but a sliver of the crimson scarf. And the frame froze.

Jana was awake now but settled low in the seat, her knees resting on the dashboard. When Dix asked if she had had a bad dream, she shook her head, no comment, and he turned his attention to the traffic, flashing lights ahead, a commotion of some kind. The line of cars began to move. Rain fell in Karl-Marx-Allee, darkening the huge apartment buildings on either side of the boulevard. Something caught his eye and he looked up to see a young woman in one of the apartments waving a red bandanna; he thought of a switchman at a railroad crossing. A stationary figure in the window of the apartment below stood impassively watching the traffic in the street. There were other observers in windows above and below. Somebody's audience, Dix thought; not Jana's, perhaps mine, an apathetic balcony crowd looking at their wristwatches and waiting for the play to end. The car was stalled again, and now through the rain he saw a plume of white smoke rising and flowing away almost at once. From a distance came the waa-waa of sirens, and when he lowered the window a crack he could hear angry voices and snatches of a martial melody; and how odd that it sounded like a stately phrase from Bach. When his eyes began to water, he knew the white smoke was tear gas and that he had run into a demonstration — farmers, students, workers, teachers, Nazis, Reds, he had no idea who they were. And then he heard breaking glass and a thin animal roar from the demonstrators, who were now marching between the cars, banging hoods and roofs with clubs. A brick sailed through the air and struck the car next to him. A woman cried out and her children began to scream, but the demonstrators came on, not very many of them, marching in a kind of slow-motion swagger. Their grievances were serious but he did not know what they were. He could not read the placards, which had been discarded in any case.

Lock the doors, Jana cried.

Who are they?

Reds, I think. Mostly.

He locked the doors of the Mercedes and watched a loose-limbed teenager take aim at the hood ornament and send it flying with one swing of his club. The boy rushed past them and beat a tattoo on the rear window, the glass caving but not shattering. When other demonstrators surrounded the car, Dix moved to cover Jana with his body. He pushed her onto the floor and lay over her, and it was then that he could feel her trembling. She said something to him but he could not hear her words. Bits of glass fell on them and the noise was terrible. Then he heard police whistles and more shouts and the pop-pop of tear-gas canisters. The demonstrators still came on, pursued now by the police. His eyes began to water and he raised himself on his elbows to give Jana air. She coughed, her hands to her throat, her face white with — not fear, for just then she mustered a grim smile. He felt glass on his shoulders and in his hair and he could see blood on Jana's coat but he did not know whose blood it was. One contorted face and then another appeared at the window. He could see their teeth and the whites of their eyes as they screamed and pounded on the windows and doors. Jana was quiet under him, her eyes closed. The clamor seemed to decrease, its pitch wavering, and then Dix wondered if this was how Europe would end, grievance washing from nation to nation, remorseless as the tides, marching to Bach's tempo. He turned off the radio and touched Jana's forehead. He felt no life at all. He noticed silence inside and outside the car, and the droning of sirens far away, and then the clump of the boots of green-suited police. When he looked up he saw the girl in the window fold her bandanna and slip back into the interior of the apartment.

He touched Jana's cheek and her eyelids fluttered open. When she turned her head he saw she had a gash on her temple, blood leaking down her neck and clotted in her hair and ears. Her eyes were dull and unfocused and she seemed not to recognize him. He told her to be still and he would find a medic.

Can you talk, Jana?

She drew her mouth down in a clown face but did not reply.

He moved to open the door but it would not budge. Then he remembered he had locked it, but when he threw the switch it still refused to open. Helmeted police were all around them but they were too busy to respond to his signal, even when he banged on the window with his cane. One of them looked at him and said something but he had no idea what it was. Dix sat back then, cradling Jana. She tried to speak but no words came and she gave it up with a long sigh, leaning her head against his shoulder. He held her with a tissue against her wound, feeling the beating of his own heart. She murmured something and nestled into him, her eyes closing. When he looked up again he saw a crowd, a television camera, police, motorists who had freed themselves from their cars. They looked at him incuriously, an older man with a young woman in his arms, apparently at peace with the world. The camera closed in, a foot or so from the shattered side window, and Dix turned his back to shield Jana. When a fireman began to work at the car door with a crowbar, Dix put his mouth next to her ear.

You must not die, he said.

I won't, she whispered.

The police are here.

She recoiled, her eyes wide with fear.

They're here to help, he said. You have a nasty gash.

Yes, I know, she said, and settled in again.

He was still holding her when the door flew open and she was taken from him.

They put Jana into an ambulance and drove her to a private hospital in Dahlem, not far from the Brücke Museum. Dix remained behind to make a report to the police commander, a sympathetic Berliner of about his own age, who cluck-clucked over the condition of the Mercedes and offered to have it towed away. The commander asked a few obvious questions, then ordered one of his men to take Herr Grunewald at once to the hospital where his — and here the policeman looked at him with raised eyebrows until Dix replied, Friend — friend was in surgery. When the police returned his papers, Dix nodded his thanks. He said, Very kind of you. You are at Mommsen House? the policeman asked with a suppressed smile. Dix said, Do you know Mommsen House? Oh, yes, the policeman said. I have had many, many dealings with the intellectuals at Mommsen House. Always trouble, he went on. So it was good to see an intellectual in trouble not of his own making and be able to help. When Dix asked him the identity of the demonstrators, he replied that they were a coalition of the disaffected. Angry disaffected, Dix said. Very angry, the policeman agreed. And likely to remain so.

At the hospital, Dix was told Jana was in fair condition.

Was her life in danger?

They thought not. But there were tests.

What sort of tests?

Tests that the doctors would determine, Herr Grunewald.

And when would they know for certain?

Not long, Herr Grunewald. In due course.

He returned the next day and the day after, but still Jana could receive no visitors. On the third day they said she was better but resting. On the fourth day they agreed to admit him to her room but he must remain only a short time, under the supervision of a nurse. Frau Jana was weak and had lost much blood and the extent of her injuries to her head were as yet not known. But she was resting comfortably.

He had brought her books in English and German, and his Erich Heckel poster, *Drei Madchen,* three Sorb girls exchanging secrets. He taped the poster near the door where she could see it, then turned to look at her closely, her head wound tight with white bandages. But her eyes were clear, and he thought he caught a mocking smile when he showed her the poster. The girls were nude, whispering in a forest clearing.

Do you remember any of it? he asked.

Some, she said. Not all.

You said they were Reds.

I don't know who they were, she said. They weren't Sorbs, I know that.

Nameless rioters, he said. A cop told me it was a coalition of the disaffected.

I'm tired, Dix.

I'll come tomorrow, he said. Her eyes showed great weariness, and her head was set at a strange angle. She did not look herself.

Jana settled into the bed, hooking her finger around the plastic bracelet on her wrist. Tell me about the scene on the lake. Was it good?

Superb, he said.

Karl?

Karl was fine.

I thought so, too. He's a real actor.

The scene upset him.

Why wouldn't it? I hate what she said to him.

You played it wonderfully, Dix said.

I didn't believe a word of it.

That's acting, he said.

Playing someone else's life, she said.

There was some of you in it.

Not enough, she said sharply, and turned her face and closed her eyes. The nurse guided him from the room.

Dix went to work at once editing *Wannsee 1899*, episode 145, astonished at how economical he had been with film — or tape, as they insisted on calling it. Willa came by to see the results and pronounced herself delighted, and he admitted to himself that what he had was good. He believed he had an ear for the German language, at least when it was spoken softly, at slow speeds. He was depending on the patience of the audience.

He returned to the hospital the next day but they said Jana was sleeping. And the day after she was not feeling well and receiving no visitors. Dix missed a day, and when he arrived on Tuesday, eight days after the demonstration, the receptionist looked at him in surprise and said Frau Jana had been discharged. Yes, she has gone home. To her apartment in Kreuzberg? The receptionist looked in her book and said, No, not Kreuzberg. Frau Jana gave her address as Mommsen House, Wannsee.

But I have just come from Mommsen House, Dix said.

Nevertheless, the receptionist said. That is her address.

But I have a film she must see —

Frau Jana said nothing about a film, the receptionist said.

Did she leave a note?

No note, Herr Greenwood.

On the street again, Dix began to walk south toward Wannsee. The distance was only a few miles and the day was mild. The time was near noon and he was thinking of lunch at Charlotte's or the Imbiss on Koenigstrasse. He took his time, strolling listlessly like any flâneur, and when the traffic began to build he feared another demonstration. The line of cars barely moved, and then in the block ahead he saw the cause of the obstruction, a giant McDonald's, its parking lot full and the cars waiting for a space or in line for the drive-through. He suspected a school holiday; many of the cars were filled with children.

Suddenly he did not want lunch at Charlotte's or at the Imbiss, or anywhere in Wannsee. Dix hurried in the direction of Zehlendorf, where he could board the S-Bahn for Potsdamer Platz, and a few blocks away, down the squalid alley, he would find Munn Café, a glass of beer and a schnitzel, and Frau Munn's warm smile to take the edge off things. He did not like to think of Jana alone in the world. Yet that was what she preferred.

The café was not crowded. Frau Munn set him up at the far end of the bar. He drank two pilseners and ordered the schnitzel. While he ate the schnitzel he read the newspaper, a London paper, one of several that hung from well-worn wooden racks. There was news of Russia but little from America and nothing at all of the Industry. Then he remembered the Academy Awards and wondered who won. Certainly at the end Ada Hart was mentioned in the necrology; perhaps one of the presenters had a word also. He read the paper slowly but without interest, then put it aside and ordered another pilsener. When Frau Munn brought it, he asked her about the Vietnamese waiter, nowhere in sight. She said he had gone to visit relatives in Haiphong and was due to return to Berlin at the end of the week.

Dix said, Why did he come to Berlin to live?

She said, I believe he was dodging the draft. He arrived many years ago as part of a cultural exchange. He came to East Berlin to read his poetry and one night he slipped through the Wall; and he came to me.

And stayed on, Dix said.

Yes, but he misses his homeland.

So many do, Dix said.

Frau Munn looked at him sharply. His situation is not amusing, Herr Greenwood. Not at all amusing. At the time of the Vietnamese New Year, Nguyen was often in tears. When you saw him the first time, his New Year had just ended. He was not himself. And you, Herr Greenwood. You do not seem yourself either.

Comes and goes, Dix said.

You have the sad face, she said.

A friend has gone away, he said.

I am sorry, Frau Munn said. Was she a special friend?

We were collaborators, Dix said.

And your film? Completed?

Yes, completed.

Well then, Herr Greenwood. Allow me to buy you a schnapps in celebration.

If you will have one with me, Dix said.

Frau Munn went to the refrigerator and returned with a bottle, pouring icy schnapps into tiny flutes. She raised her glass and said, Prost.

Dix said, Your very good health.

Frau Munn smiled indulgently. You never learned our language, Herr Greenwood. It's just as well. German is a difficult language, often unpleasant in its sound, hard to hear correctly. Few foreigners speak it fluently, yet there are advantages. Our language gives us some privacy. We are able to say things to ourselves that we would never say to outsiders. It is a blunt language, as you know. It's my opinion that our difficult language gives us a measure of exclusivity. Our German exceptionalism, our particular spirit. The French are always complaining that no one speaks their language. They impose it on others as a matter of national pride. They are so busy protecting it from outside influences they neglect to use it creatively. They are taken up with their struggle to preserve it, is this not so? They feel they are humiliated when they are obliged to speak English, as they often are. But isn't it a strange emotion, humiliation? You cannot be humiliated unless you choose to be. Humiliation is a self-inflicted wound. We Germans are intimate with our language, and it is never a source of humiliation. How could it be? Speaking German when others cannot makes us feel superior.

I wouldn't think superiority comes into it, Dix said. It's a language like any other. Perhaps more difficult than some.

It is the language of Goethe, she said.

I don't mind being on the outside of things, Dix replied.

Frau Munn said, There are advantages of course. I wonder if this is a specific American condition. So much missed. So much ignored. If the thought cannot fit into an American sentence, then it could be said not to exist. This, in turn, would make an uncluttered Weltanschauung. Surely that's for the best.

Dix looked at his watch as Frau Munn poured a second schnapps.

Do you know, during the war in the Pacific, the Americans used Cherokees to transmit secret messages en clair. No Japanese understood Cherokee. Cherokee was an enigma to them, no better than animal sounds.

It was Navajo, Dix said.

Was it Navajo?

Navajo, Dix said. Navajo definitely.

So many tribes in America, Frau Munn said.

And now I must leave, Dix said.

Americans are happiest with their language! But they do not value it. They do not take pride in it. They assume everyone speaks it. And in time, everyone will.

Do you suppose everyone will be comfortable in it, Frau Munn?

When they are not talking among themselves, they will, Herr Greenwood.

Dix looked at her over the top of the flute. Some American academics say that English is the language of the oppressor and that peoples everywhere would be better off if it were abolished, like thumbscrews and the iron maiden. They view English as a violation of human rights.

They do?

Yes. They are quite insistent about it.

Academics are dreamers, she said.

Dix finished his schnapps and stepped back from the bar. It was a pleasure meeting you, Frau Munn. I wish you the very best.

And you also, Herr Greenwood. Would you send me your photograph for my wall?

Assuredly, Dix said.

And when do you leave Berlin?

Dix thought a moment and blurted, Tomorrow.

So soon? We will miss you. The spring is beautiful in our city.

And I will miss Berlin. The spring especially.

You have enjoyed yourself, then?

I have found my audience, Frau Munn.

In that case, Berlin has been a success for you. I was afraid that you had become discouraged with us. I know we can become strenuous and demanding in our efforts to make ourselves understood. Not everyone approaches us with an open mind. And we, too, are often lacking in objectivity. We have so many shadows, you see, those of us who lived through that time. We have difficulty expressing ourselves.

Dix said, You are my audience, Frau Munn.

She looked at him, holding his gaze with her clear blue eyes. I am flattered you would think of me in that way, Herr Greenwood. It is the way I have often seen myself. I shall try to be a responsive audience.

Dix paid the bill, correct to the last pfennig, and was almost at the door when he heard Frau Munn's lisp once again.

A friend of yours came by yesterday.

He turned, grinning wildly. He knew who it was.

Herr Blum, the archivist. He said he had a most interesting interview with you.

Oh, yes, Dix said. Blum.

He was looking forward to another.

I'm sure he is, Dix said.

But if you are leaving Berlin —

It will have to be another time, Dix said.

Frau Munn hesitated, and then she said, I want you to have something from me, Herr Greenwood. She motioned him closer while she rummaged in one of the bar drawers. She handed him a photograph, a near duplicate of the one on the wall, Fräulein Munn with two American army officers, circa 1945. In this one she was standing about where Dix stood at that moment, her arms linked through the arms of two civilians, her smile brilliant, a pretty young girl out for the evening. Dix noticed her earrings and nylon stockings, a necklace at her throat, and the wide-brimmed hats and long coats of the men. They were unremarkable men, one with a mustache, the other without, but something in their postures and the disdain of their expressions reminded him of tabloid photographs of Chicago gangsters. He stared at the photograph, more than half a century distant — the date in the margin said 1943 — trying to connect that time to this time. He looked at the photograph and thought of the nebula of a long-dead star, a cloud of dust that would diminish but never vanish, an enduring feature of the night sky in Berlin. What seemed to connect Frau Munn then to now was her smile, the same soft smile in both photographs — indeed she wore the same face in both, as if they were trick pictures of the sort found at carnivals, Frau Munn with Jimmy Stewart, Frau Munn with Al Capone. But smiles were superficial. What was not superficial were her eyes, the saddest eyes he had ever seen, eyes that seemed to him filled with unwelcome knowledge.

She said brightly, Look this way, Herr Greenwood — and she took his picture with a one-time Kodak, its flash blinding him for an instant.

Now I have one of my own, she said, and gestured at the wall, her rogues' gallery, photographs of musicians, comedians, impresarios, politicians, army officers, Nazis, poets, grifters, athletes and actors, bankers and thieves, her regulars.

Auf Wiedersehen, Frau Munn.

Until we meet again, Herr Greenwood.

Dix saluted her, a sloppy hand-to-forehead such as one of the American officers might have given. He stood unsteadily at the door, his hand on the weather curtain, his head spinning from the pilsener and the icy schnapps. In the dusty silence he heard Frau Munn's radio, dance music, German swing, Kurt Weill's "September Song," sung by a sinister prewar voice that was just this side of a growl.

Oh, es ist eine lange, lange Zeit

Dix recollected Sinatra's three-in-the-morning baritone and Lester Lanin's society two-step, regret in the first, promise in the second.

But this was not that. This was not in the vicinity of that. He looked back to nod at Frau Munn. She had poured a third glass and was snapping her fingers in time to the music, standing behind her long bar as sovereign as the skipper of a great vessel. She nodded back, smiling, her head cast to one side — and then Dix stepped through the door into the late Berlin afternoon.

# 24

THE CABDRIVER was friendly and talkative, and when he learned that Dix had been three months in Berlin, surprised. You were wise to spend some time among us. Americans were so restless, they arrived one day and left the next, always in a rush. A great city was like a human being, revealing itself slowly, and some of its contradictions would never be resolved. A hospitable city, would you not agree? Not a city of repose, and therefore not a city for the faint of heart. And amusing also, if you had a taste for sarcasm. He asked if Dix agreed that music was the soul of Berlin. Music was to Berlin what skyscrapers were to New York. Had he heard the Philharmonie? The Israeli Barenboim was a genius. Only the other night Barenboim conducted the full orchestra and the baritone dwarf Quasthoff in Brahms's German Requiem. Sublime, sublime. Five curtain calls and still the audience would not leave. Many wept. A beautiful performance, sir.

No, Dix had not been to the Philharmonie.

Not once?

Not once, Dix said.

You do not appreciate music?

The opportunity did not arise.

The cabdriver was silent a moment, evidently disappointed. He said that he and his wife and their son and his girlfriend often went to the Philharmonie and then to the cellar in Kreuzberg for cabaret. Of course Berlin cabaret was not what it once was. Some of the spirit had gone out of it, and many of the great musicians were dead. Greta Keller, she is dead now, but when she was in the prime of her life she was the best. She could sing in seventeen languages! She was to us what Piaf was to the French. That one, she could break your heart with a lyric and then, in an instant, you would be laughing. That is the essence of cabaret, entertainment that is at once ambiguous and perverse. One moment your heart is full, and the next you see that she has cut it with a razor blade.

If I may ask, sir. What is your profession?

The movies, Dix said.

You are an actor?

Director, Dix said.

You were working in Berlin?

On *Wannsee 1899*. You know it?

I know it. I do not watch it.

Dix smiled and turned his attention to the traffic, slowing as they approached the airport. An early morning fog obscured the lights but every few minutes he heard the roar of jet engines. The cabdriver eased his Mercedes close to the curb and stopped.

Maybe an American can make sense of it. It makes no sense now.

I hope so, Dix said.

Prussian nostalgia, the cabdriver said.

Dix laughed. Is that the worst kind?

Not the worst. Almost the worst. But I was born a Rhinelander. I have no patience with Prussians. They are very sure of themselves, always.

Dix paid the fare and laid a fat tip on top.

Thank you, sir. Have a pleasant trip.

I intend to, Dix said.

Next time, see Barenboim.

I have seen Barenboim in Chicago, Dix said.

But Chicago is not Berlin, the cabdriver said.

It is closer than you think, Dix said.

·   ·   ·

There were no direct flights from Tempelhof to North America, Berlin not yet a magnet for either tourism or commerce, the capital of the nation merely another midsized, landlocked German city. The way out was via Frankfurt, Geneva, or Paris. Dix had flown in from Paris and was going out the same way, connecting with the midday run to Los Angeles. Now he was stalled on the tarmac in the fog, aboard one of the scores of aircraft standing nose to tail, awaiting clearance. The intermittent rush of engines told him the wait would not be long, an hour at most. The pilot thought less but admitted he might be mistaken.

The cabin was warm. A steward came by with a tray of drinks. On offer was orange juice, coffee, and champagne. Claire on his mind, Dix took coffee with sugar and said no to breakfast. He heard a rustle of newsprint and gruff laughter following a whispered conversation from the businessmen in the seats ahead, normal cabin sounds, somehow muted owing to the enveloping fog. Nothing was visible in it. He could not see the terminal but he knew it was receding and believed then that he had come full circle, leaving Berlin at about the same time of day that he had arrived. Claire was on his mind then, too. But things never came full circle. Perfect circles did not exist, in nature or in life. Three months was not duration enough for a circle, perfect or otherwise. He believed he had described an arc, a fragment beginning at one point on the circle and ending at another, with much that had gone before and something still to come.

Herr Greenwood?

The steward offered the tray, and this time Dix took champagne.

A rush from the engines, and the jet motored forward. The pilot said something unintelligible; progress, apparently. Dix did not know what he would find when he returned to his wife. For these months they had lived inside different narratives. His had nothing to do with hers and she, too, was in the dark. Each had slept without the other. He had found an audience and she was not a part of it — but that was how they had always lived, never with the whole story but with the scenario. Not the fact, but the shadow of the fact. In any case, he had nothing left to do in Berlin. Shaking hands on the front stoop of Mommsen House that morning, Henry Belknap had smiled and said, You've closed all your accounts, congratulations.

And what happens now, Dix?

I have no idea. Go home. Make it up to Claire.

You'll be back, Henry said.

Maybe so, Dix said.

You've found a home in Berlin. I can tell.

It suits my temperament, that's true.

You think Berlin's an audience.

You don't get away with a lot, Dix said.

You don't get away with anything in Berlin, Henry replied.

Dix massaged his knee, Claire still in his thoughts. He reminded himself again that they were in the movie business, shadow puppets, a bright flickering light, and a happy ending. When you didn't like the line, you rewrote it. When you didn't like the shot, you did it over. Could you lower your voice when you call him darling? He looked forward to describing Berlin to Claire, the people he had met and the stories they told him, Chef Werner and Willa and Karen Hupp and the others, Henry and Frau Munn, and Jana most of all. Harry Greenwood was there somewhere, too, with his tales of wartime interrogations and John Huston's red wagon. The story belonged to whoever could tell it best, and Berlin was a narrator's utopia, the story of the world, ruin and rebirth. No question, the weather caught you off guard. The wind came from all directions and never let up. A prewar wind was replaced in an instant by a freshening breeze from just yesterday. But the old wind lingered, never absent, a part of every day, and in that way you were reminded of the dawn of the modern world. He believed that German weather was motion picture weather, you could make of it whatever you wished. The audience was there, too.

He did believe that sooner or later she would be in touch, a visit or a telephone call as unexpected as the afternoon in Wannsee when he did not recognize her voice or her name. She would never return to a normal life, and in time she would make another film, either with him or with someone else. Certainly she would recover from her injuries, otherwise they never would have released her from the hospital. Still, he was worried about her lopsided look, her face asymmetrical and at odds. They seemed sympathetic toward her. The doctor was very sympathetic. It was hard not to be. She was full of life, that one. She would never surrender. And when Jana found herself boxed in, she said goodbye. A person had the right to go away when she chose to, and the absolute right to accept the consequences, and return at a time of her own choosing.

She cherished privacy, and surely there was something to be said for possessing the identity of an inconspicuous people, a people ever on the margins of an environment organized and supervised by — another breed of cat, as Harry used to say. Of course there were disadvantages. It was hard to climb other people's stairs. You had to keep your nerve and maintain a conscious equilibrium so that you could never be overthrown. Mischief was in there some-where, too, an appreciation of life's sinister aspects and an urge to get even, if only for an hour, to let them know that you were still among them. Dix lifted his glass and wished her well on her jour-ney, hoping she would return soon. He seemed to need her, not as a lover but as a provocateur. He admired her conscience, and the in-subordination that went with it. Almost always, when you were at-tracted to someone, you saw the person you were not.